Torn Asunder

Renny deGroot

Also by Renny deGroot

<u>Fiction:</u>
Family Business
After Paris

<u>Non-Fiction:</u>
32 Signal Regiment, Royal Canadian Signal Corps
– A History

Dedication

For Jimmy Carton

Your songs and stories over the past several decades
provided the inspiration for this book

"All true men, like you men, Remember them with
pride."
John Kells Ingram "*The Memory of the Dead*"

Key Historical Figures (mentioned in the story)

Ashe, Thomas: As Commandant of the 5th Battalion of the Dublin Brigade during the Easter Rising in 1916, he led his battalion through the Battle of Ashbourne. Sentenced to death for his part in the Rising, his sentence was commuted to penal servitude for life. He was interned in Frongoch Internment camp and Lewes Prison in England. He was freed from prison as part of the amnesty in June, 1917 but re-arrested in August, 1917. He died in September, 1917 after participating in a hunger strike.

Breen, Dan: A member of both the Irish Republican Brotherhood and the Irish Volunteers, the British had a £10,000 price on his head. During the Irish Civil War, Breen took the Anti-Treaty (Republican) side and was arrested for his activities by the Pro-Treaty (Irish Free State) army.

Brugha, Cathal: An Irish revolutionary who became Chief of Staff in the Irish Republican Army. He served during the Irish War of Independence and presided over the First *Dáil Éireann* in 1919. During the Irish Civil War, he took the Anti-Treaty side and during the Battle of Dublin, while he ordered his men to surrender, he refused to do so himself and died of gunshot wounds sustained at that time.

Casement, Sir Roger: A diplomat and Irish nationalist, he worked for the British Foreign Office. In 1916 he attempted to bring German guns to Ireland to aid in the Easter Rising, but was arrested and ultimately executed for high treason, after first being stripped of his knighthood.

Clarke, Tom: As an active member of the Irish Republican Brotherhood (IRB), Clarke was a driving force behind the Easter Rising. While he did not have an official role in the Irish Volunteers (formed in 1913), the IRB had great control over the activities of the two organizations, and as Treasurer in the IRB, Clarke was very influential and was recognized as one of the commanders of the Rising. He was one of the seven signatories of the Proclamation of the Republic. He was executed for his part in the Rising.

Collins, Michael: A member of the Irish Republican Brotherhood (IRB), he served as financial advisor to Count George Plunkett where he engaged in preparing to arm for the Rising. He served as aide-de-camp for Joseph Plunkett at the General Post Office in Dublin during The Easter Rising in 1916, where he fought side by side with Patrick Pearse and James Connolly. He was interned in Fongoch Internment Camp for his part in the Rising where he began to form ties with many other republicans from all over Ireland. After being released, Collins became a key player in the War of Independence, resulting in the British offering a £10,000 price for his capture. After the 1921 ceasefire, Collins served as a delegate on the Anglo-Irish Treaty, the signing of which produced the Irish Free State. After signing, he famously remarked to F.E. Smith "I may have signed my actual death warrant." This statement proved prophetic, as he was shot and killed in an ambush in August, 1922.

Connolly, James: A Scottish-born Irish republican and socialist leader, he, together with James Larkin, formed the Irish Citizen Army (ICA). During the Easter Rising, Connolly served as Commandant of the Dublin Brigade. Connolly was sentenced to death for his role in the Rising; Connolly had been badly injured during the fighting, and needed to be carried out on a stretcher and tied to a chair to be shot.

deValera, Eamon: During the 1916 Easter Rising, he led forces in the defence of the southeastern approaches to Dublin. He was sentenced to death for his part in the Rising, but his sentence was commuted to penal servitude for life. He was one of the few republican leaders that was not executed; in part due to the intervention by the U.S. Consulate in Dublin who protested that he was an American citizen. He was freed as part of the June 1917 amnesty and in July, 1917 was elected Member of Parliament and President of the Sinn Féin party. In 1919 deValera travelled to America to raise support for Ireland, leaving Michael Collins to run the day-to-day governing of the country. Later deValera and Collins would become opponents in the Irish Civil War.

Deasy, Liam: During the Irish War of Independence, Deasy was the Adjutant of the 3rd Cork Brigade. During the Irish Civil War, he took the Anti-Treaty (Republican) side and was in command of the men who ambushed and shot Michael Collins; however, he himself was not a part of the ambush.

Ennis, Tom: A member of the Irish Volunteers, he fought with the GPO Garrison during the Easter Rising. He was interned at Fongoch Internment Camp in Wales before being released in August, 1916. He resumed active duty, participating in several operations, perhaps most famously leading the burning of the Custom House. He escaped that operation, surviving a gunshot wound to the leg. During the Civil War, he took the Pro-Treaty ('Free-State') side. Ennis rose to the rank of Major-General before retiring to civilian life. He died in 1945 of natural causes.

Flood, Frank: A 1st Lieutenant in the Dublin Brigade, he was a student at University College Dublin when he was captured while attacking a lorry load of Dublin Metropolitan Police. He was executed in Mountjoy Prison in 1921. He was 19 years old.

Gifford, Grace: An Irish artist and cartoonist, Gifford married her sweetheart, Joseph Plunkett hours before he was executed in Kilmainham Gaol.

Griffith, Arthur: As a newspaper editor and politician, he founded the political party Sinn Féin. In 1921 he led the Irish delegation which resulted in the contentious Anglo-Irish Treaty. He died of natural causes ten days before the assassination of Michael Collins in August, 1922.

Lawless, Frank: Battalion Quartermaster under Thomas Ashe, he led a section in the Battle of Ashbourne during the 1916 Easter Rising. He was sentenced to death for his part in the Rising, but the sentence was commuted to ten years' penal servitude. He was subsequently released in the amnesty of 1917 and later elected as part of the First *Dáil Éireann*.

Lawless, James (sometimes known as JV Lawless): A brother of Frank Lawless, he was Battalion Adjutant and led a section during the Battle of Ashbourne.

Lawless, Joseph: A son of Frank Lawless; at the age of 20, he served as Brigade Engineering Officer and led a section of Volunteers during the Battle of Ashbourne. He was sent to Knutsford Prison in England and then Fongoch Internment Camp in Wales before being released in December, 1916.

MacCurtain, Tomás: A commander of Irish Volunteers during the Easter Rising from County Cork who was interned in Frongoch Internment camp for his part in the Rising. After being released during the amnesty, he returned to active duty as a Commandant of what became the Irish Republican Army. In March, 1920, MacCurtain was assassinated by members of the Royal Irish Constabulary (RIC).

MacDonagh, Thomas: Commandant of the 2nd Battalion, Dublin Brigade, he was one of the seven leaders of the Easter Rising and a signatory of the Proclamation of the Irish Republic. He was executed for his part in the Rising.

MacNeill, Eoin: He established the Irish Volunteers in 1913 and served as its Chief-Of-Staff. In 1916, when he heard of Roger Casement's arrest, he countermanded Patrick Pearse's instructions to the Irish Republican Brotherhood for the Easter Monday Rising by placing a last-minute advertisement advising Volunteers not to take part. He was later elected to the First *Dáil Éireann* (Assembly of Ireland) as a member of Sinn Féin.

Markievicz, Countess Georgine: She was an Irish politician and revolutionary who was elected to the position of Minister of Labour in the First *Dáil Éireann* (Assembly of Ireland). Countess Markievicz was a founding member of the *Cumann na mBan* (The Women's Council) and the Irish Citizen Army. She fought in St. Stephen's Green during the Easter Rising in 1916 and was sentenced to death for her role; however, the sentence was commuted to life due to her sex and she was sent to Aylesbury

Prison in England. Markievicz was released in 1917 as part of the amnesty.

McAteer, Hugh: A leader of the Irish Republican Army in the North, McAteer participated in the Easter commemoration of the Rising at the Broadway Cinema, Falls Road, Belfast in 1943.

Mulcahy, Richard: He was Second-In-Command to Thomas Ashe during the Battle of Ashbourne and was interned at Knutsford and at Frongoch Internment Camp for his part in the Rising. He was released in December, 1916. Mulcahy subsequently supported the Anglo-Irish Treaty and ordered the execution of 77 Anti-Treaty prisoners during the Irish Civil War.

O'Connell, Daniel: An Irish political leader from the early nineteenth century, sometimes known as 'The Emancipator' for his work to emancipate Irish Catholics.

Parnell, Charles Stewart: An Irish nationalist who served to further the Home Rule efforts in his positions as the leader of the Irish Parliamentary Party (1882 – 1891) and Leader of the Home Rule League (1889 – 1892).

Pearse, Patrick: A member of the Irish Republican Brotherhood (IRB), Pearse was a leader of the Easter Rising in 1916. On behalf of the IRB, he read the Proclamation of the Irish Republic outside the General Post Office (the headquarters of the Rising) on Easter Monday, April 24, 1916, marking the start of the Rising. Pearse was executed for his part in the Rising.

Plunkett, Count George Noble: Father of Joseph Plunkett, George Plunkett was created a Papal Count in 1884. It is believed that his son, Joseph swore him into the IRB some time before the Rising.

Plunkett, Joseph: One of the original members of the Irish Republican Brotherhood (IRB) and thus very involved in the planning of the Easter Rising. Plunkett suffered from tuberculosis at a young age and was in frail health, leaving his hospital bed to take part. His aide-de-camp was Michael Collins. Plunkett was executed for his part in the Rising, and married his sweetheart, Grace Gifford, in Kilmainham Gael hours before his death in 1916.

Steele, Jimmy: A member of the Irish Republican Army from Belfast, Steele participated in the Easter commemoration of the Rising at the Broadway Cinema, Falls Road, Belfast in 1943.

Traynor, Oscar: An Irish Volunteer who was the leader of the Metropole Hotel garrison during the Easter Rising. In the Irish Civil War Traynor took the Anti-Treaty (Republican) side and was in charge of the Barry's Hotel garrison during the Battle of Dublin.

Weston, Charlie: A section commander in the 5th Brigade during the Battle of Ashbourne.

Part I

Emmet Ryan

1

Ashbourne, County Meath, March 1916

Emmet Ryan sat next to his best pal Liam Kelly on the damp grass looking out on the view of the village of Ashbourne spread below the green hill.

Liam nudged Emmet. "Your Ma still giving you a hard time about spending time with the Volunteers?"

Emmet cradled the wooden rifle he had carved himself. "Yeh. I don't know why. She doesn't give Da or Michael and Kevin grief and they spend more time than me." Emmet cocked his head and mimicked his mother's voice: 'Emmet, you should be spending more time on your studies, and not out playing at soldiers. You won't get into college that way.' He shook his head. "As if the Fingal Volunteers is some kind of game. Just because I'm sixteen doesn't mean I don't believe in Ireland's Cause just as much as Da and the boys."

Liam snorted. "It's because you're the youngest. She wants to keep you tied to her."

Emmet raised an eyebrow. "You're very wise sounding."

"Well, can you imagine her saying something to your Da or brothers?" Liam wagged his finger. "Ned Ryan, don't you take those boys out to the Volunteers tonight. I want you home by your fireside."

Emmet laughed. "I can just see Da's face."

"Women. They're all the same. They want to keep you tied to their apron strings. I won't have it."

Emmet nodded. Liam's mother had long given up trying to control him. She had younger children to look after, while Emmet was the youngest in his family. He chafed to have the freedom that Liam had sometimes.

It rained overnight and the sky was still a bruised green-grey but it was dry, so the boys had the assignment to 'keep watch'.

Liam plucked a blade of grass and then tossed it aside. "What exactly are we supposed to watch for?"

Emmet studied his friend. Liam's shock of red hair and freckled face gave him a well-deserved look of mischief. Emmet could see that Liam was bored. Liam always got twitchy and restless when he sat for too long.

He shrugged in response to Liam's question. "The enemy." Out of habit, Emmet kept his answers short, still nervous that his voice would betray him and crack, although in fact his voice had deepened to a man's timbre, so like his father's.

Liam snorted. "And who's that, then? Some say the Brits and some say the Germans."

Emmet slanted his eyes towards his friend. "You've got an uncle over in France, now don't you?"

Liam nodded, looking down at the ground and plucking again at the old brown grass.

"Do you ever hear from him?"

Liam frowned. "My aunt's heard from him. He doesn't say much."

Emmet scrubbed his hand across his head, still getting used to the feel of the short crop of his curls.

Liam grinned and tackled Emmet, sitting on his chest, and rubbed his hands over Emmet's hair, all the while mimicking the voice of the girl from last weekend's dance. "Ooh, Emmet. I wish I had such beautiful curls as you."

"Feck off." Emmet twisted and shoved Liam off. The girl's comments triggered Emmet to shear off his curls and now he regretted the rash move which showed off his sticky-out ears. He had only the vaguest sense that the combination of his blue eyes and black hair was quite striking. He didn't think of himself as handsome, but he knew he didn't like the way his short hair accentuated his ears, so he was keen for it to grow out again.

Emmet stood, brushing off the dampness from the seat of his pants. He looked down at Liam. Emmet understood that Liam had tackled him to change the conversation. He could see that Liam wore his shame like a dirty vest under a clean shirt. The shame of having an uncle fighting with the Brits. Emmet knew many Irishmen joined the British in the war in France and Belgium, but his Da said they shouldn't be there fighting an English war. They should be at home looking after their own. Emmet read in the paper accounts for both sides of the argument. 'It provided work and the men could send money home' was one point of view. Emmet understood that. Liam's uncle's seven children looked better fed and clothed over the past year than Emmet had ever seen them, but still, his Da's words stuck in his mind.

Liam stood as well. "Come on. Surely, we've stood watch long enough. Let's go back and see what's up."

Emmet nodded. "There might be a cup of tea to be had."

They raced down the hill and back to Murphy's barn. The outer wall stones showed through the peeling whitewash, and the roof thatch needed repair where grass grew in large patches. Emmet followed Liam inside and smiled at the two Murphy horses in their stalls along one short end of the barn He could swear that the old grey smiled back, flickering his ears and shaking his head. The horses were used to men coming and going and didn't seem to mind the intrusion. Along the long walls were bales of hay stacked to the ceiling, except for one gap where the bales had been shoved aside and a wooden board was nailed to the old barn board wall. At the other short end, various implements hung or rested against the wall. Three men grouped together in the open area between the hay bales studying a map laid out on a table of bales. The conversation stopped when the boys came in and Seamus Murphy folded up the map. He nodded to the boys. "All right, boys?"

Emmet felt his jaw tighten. He didn't like to be considered a boy. *I'm ready to give up my life just as much as anyone else is.*

He held his temper, though. Murphy was his leader and due his respect. "Good. Nothing unusual to report."

Liam had flung himself down on a bench. "We're parched, though. Anything to drink?"

Pat Heeney lifted an eyebrow. He was only four years older than Emmet and Liam but behaved like he was a generation older. "What did you have in mind?"

Liam grinned. "What's on offer?"

Emmet shook his head. "A cup of tea would be grand."

Murphy nodded to the group. "Let's go in, lads. Mary'll have something waiting for us by now." He rested his hand on Emmet's shoulder as they walked to the house. "You're doing important work, keeping an eye on what's happening around the area. Don't think you aren't."

Emmet took the chance to speak his mind. "But we watch day after day and nothing happens. When is it all to begin?"

Murphy nodded. "Soon enough. Soon enough." He tapped the side of his nose. "I can't say more, but just stay diligent, my boyo."

Emmet sighed and followed Murphy into the house to join in the chat about the local hurling team and wondered if the revolution would ever really happen.

2

Ashbourne, County Meath, April 1916

The 24th of April was damp, just as most of the month had been so far. The sky was a bruised grey on grey, tinged here and there with purple and yellow. In Ashbourne, it was dull but not quite raining. It was Easter Monday, and Emmet had thought he'd cycle out to visit a cousin who lived in Ratoath.

He pulled himself out of bed, enjoying the extra sleep the holiday had allowed. He pulled on his knickerbockers, slipping the braces over his clean blue shirt and then yawned his way to the kitchen where his mother was stirring the pot of porridge on the big Aga cooker. Her broad back was swathed in a pinny, saving her dress from the cooking and cleaning stains.

She turned, using the wooden spoon to point to him. "I thought you'd have been out long ago, meeting up with all your pals from the Volunteers."

"Why? I'm allowed a little lie-in on Easter Monday, surely?"

"Your Da and brothers are gone long since to see what's going on."

She put a steaming bowl in front of him and filled a cup with fresh milk.

Emmet dug his spoon in, hardly paying attention as his mother went on.

"It seems as though there's the usual chaos amongst all that gang."

He paused now between mouthfuls. "What gang?"

"Your lot. The Fingal Volunteers. No one seems sure about what they're supposed to be doing. There's a Rising. No, there's no Rising."

Emmet jumped up, almost knocking his half-full cup of milk over. "The Rising's begun? And me sleeping through it? Why did no one call me?"

"Sit down and finish your breakfast. As I said, no one knows if it's on or not on or what. Michael said he'll come back and get you as soon as he knows something."

Emmet gulped down the last of his breakfast and ran back up to his room, taking the steps two at a time. He grabbed his jacket, carefully securing the tin pin on his lapel that he'd received when he joined the Volunteers. He usually didn't wear it, afraid to lose it, but today was the day. The day he'd been waiting for. He hesitated for a moment, considering whether he should change into his Sunday long trousers instead of the knickerbockers that he and Liam still usually wore. *Ah no. I'm comfortable and there's no time to waste.*

His mother called out after him as he flung his leg over the saddle of his bicycle. "Don't be back late for your tea. Let your Da and brothers know, too."

He shook his head as he pedalled away, hearing her shout something about a ham. *What is she thinking? How can anyone care about their tea when the whole country was rising up?*

Emmet was halfway to Murphy's when he spied Liam trotting along the road ahead. "Liam."

Liam turned and grinned. "Give us a lift."

Emmet held the bike steady as Liam balanced himself on the back rack. "What have you heard?"

Liam spoke loudly over the sound of the tires crunching on the road. "Not much. Just that we're all called out."

Emmet needed all his breath for cycling with the extra burden, but they were there in minutes. Liam slid off the back while the bike was still coming to a stop. Emmet dropped the bike near the tangle of other bicycles and followed steps behind Liam. They slipped in behind the group of about a dozen men, all calling out comments and questions.

Emmet nudged his way closer to the front and saw Murphy tacking a map to the wooden board on the wall. It looked to be the same map that Emmet had seen a couple of weeks earlier. *He was telling the truth. It's all happening.*

Emmet saw his father and two brothers standing on the other side of the group. His Da never spoke about being involved and yet here he was. Emmet felt himself flush when he thought of the times he'd spoken about the drilling and other activities he'd been involved in. *They must think I'm just a boy, not to be trusted, the way I've blathered on.*

Emmet's oldest brother Michael stood, tall and thin, his shirt collar looking loose around his neck. He had the same large ears as Emmet and his hairline looked like it was already receding even at only twenty years old. He nodded to Emmet and Emmet nodded back. Emmet's other brother Kevin stood the same height as Da, his thick head of hair a burnished dark copper, his deep-set eyes dark brown. He inherited Da's cleft chin, and there were always a few reddish bristles on his chin because he didn't take enough care with his shaving. Emmet knew that Kevin, at eighteen, was popular with the girls at the dances, and even here as he stood completely focused on what Murphy was saying, Emmet could see the small smile that was Kevin's natural look.

Murphy held up a hand. He was wearing a proper uniform with his Sam Browne belt and strapped bandoliers across his chest. The crowd quieted down.

"You'll have heard conflicting messages by now."

A rumble went through the room in agreement.

"It's true that we've had a couple of major blows." Murphy held up a finger, hands red and hard looking. Farmer's hands. "One. The German ship bringing us arms has been captured. Casement has been taken away to London."

A groan of disappointment went through the group, although most of them had already heard this news from two days earlier.

"Two." Murphy held up a second finger. "MacNeill has put out an order telling us to abort."

This was news and a louder groan went around the room. Now Murphy held up his hand to silence the barrage of questions and comments being shouted out.

"Now lads. Quiet down."

Emmet's father stepped forward and faced the group. "Quiet." His deep voice cut through the noise and the chattering eased off.

Emmet felt a shiver of pride. *Da's got some say here. He may just be a post office worker, but he's respected.*

Murphy nodded. "Good man, Ryan." He took a deep breath and Emmet could feel the men holding their breath along with Murphy.

"Despite these setbacks, we're going ahead, men."

Ah, this was more like it. Men nodded, and Emmet could see some of them clenching their fists.

Murphy stepped up to the map, but before he turned to it, he pulled a piece of paper from his breast pocket. "There was an emergency meeting of the Military Council and the order is to go ahead." Murphy lifted his eyes from the paper and looked slowly around the room, pinning each man with his gaze. "As we stand here, men, the Dublin Volunteer units have assembled and marched. They are seizing the following key strategic targets."

There wasn't a sound in the room now as Murphy intoned one by one the names of the places that the Volunteers were moving on, including the General Post Office and the Four Courts. Emmet himself didn't often get down into the city of Dublin, but he could see that for these men, the names evoked a picture of places they knew and could visualize.

When Murphy finished, the silence held for a moment and then he said, "We pray for their success." Murphy crossed himself, folded the paper and put it back into his pocket. He nodded to the group and pointed to the map. "Gather close, men, and let's look at our own targets."

The men jostled each other to get close to the map while Emmet held back. Liam moved in beside him.

Liam's eyes were bright, and he blinked rapidly. "Come on. I can't see from back here."

Emmet wasn't sure they were meant to be included. He could see his father through the crowd and his Da nodded at him and lifted his chin as if to pull Emmet forward, closer to the map.

Emmet nodded. "Go. I'm right behind you."

Liam squeezed through between the burly farmers with Emmet directly behind him until they could see and hear.

Emmet heard someone call out: "Will Thomas Ashe be coming to lead us?"

Murphy nodded. "He's already on the ground. He and Mulcahy are here, but what they're doing and where they are is strictly on a need-to-know basis. Listen up now while I take you through our orders."

They crowded around as Murphy explained how the Fingal Volunteers were being split into four columns. They were part of the fourth column under Joe Lawless.

"So men, go home now. Get whatever weapons you've got stashed, put some food in your pockets and we'll meet back here as quick as you can. Some of you may be deployed to Dublin itself, so be prepared for anything. This is it, boys. The day we've been waiting for our whole lives. The day we begin our emancipation from the yoke of the Brits. Godspeed."

———————————

Emmet joined his father and two brothers cycling home. They burst in on their mother with a clatter of noise.

She wiped her hands on her apron and smiled at Emmet. "You found them all, then?"

Emmet's father put a hand on her shoulder. "Kathleen, make up some packages of sandwiches for each of us. We'll be leaving again in a few minutes and I don't know when we'll be back."

She put her hand to her mouth. "It's not true. You're not really going to fight?"

"We are. Is there any food ready right now that we could have a quick hot meal?"

She stood with her hand still pressed to her mouth and then glanced over to her youngest son. "Not Emmet as well?"

Emmet felt his chest swell when he heard his father. "Emmet's old enough to make his own decision."

She came near him and reached out her hand as though to hold him fast, but Emmet nodded. "Me too, Mam."

She wiped her eyes with a corner of her apron and then went to the cooker. Her voice was thick with tears and defeat. "The spuds aren't ready, but you'll each have a cut of ham on bread with onions and gravy before you go anywhere."

The plates were on the table, steam rising in a fragrant plume, when Michael and Kevin came back into the kitchen. Michael, carried a shotgun while Kevin clutched a hatchet. They set their weapons down near the door before sitting down to tea. They ate quickly with little conversation, while Emmet's mother cut more thick slices of fresh bread to make into sandwiches.

As she finished wrapping the lunches for the four of them, Emmet's father went out to the shed behind the house, returning with a revolver and long knife in a leather holder that he used for skinning rabbits.

"For God's sake, where did the gun come from, Ned?"

"Shush, woman." He nodded to the wrapped sandwiches. "Are they ready now?"

Before taking the lunch from his wife, Emmet's father handed the knife to Emmet. "For Jaysus' sake, don't slice yourself with this."

Each of the men kissed Kathleen as they took their lunch from her. Tears slid unchecked down her cheeks. "Ned Ryan, you bring them home safe to me."

Ned took one backward glance before lifting himself onto his bicycle. "I'll do my best, my girl."

When they got back to the rendezvous, most of the men had already returned. Emmet sought out Liam standing at the fringe of the group. Liam's freckled face was flushed and his voice high and animated. "I'll go to Dublin. Do you want me to go with them, sir?"

Murphy was selecting men to be sent over to join Captain Coleman with orders to march to Dublin City.

"No, I need you here, son."

Emmet nudged Liam. "You should wait for your orders, not jump in like that."

Liam frowned. "Why not? I'm ready for the action. I want to get into the thick of it, not hang about here."

Before Emmet could respond, Murphy turned to the two boys. "I need scouts that can fit in easily and not look threatening. It'll take courage and you'll need to be able to think on your feet in case you come face to face with those brave men of the Royal Irish Constabulary." His voice was thick with sarcasm as he gave the full name instead of just calling them the RIC as everyone usually did.

Liam heaved a deep sigh. "More of the 'watch and wait', then."

Murphy put his hand on Liam's shoulder. "Seriously now, lad. Men are being lifted everywhere and being thrown in prison for just walking along the wrong road. If the RIC come your way, you'll need to be convincing that you're up to nothing dangerous and then get back to your leader as quick as you can with your report. If you or anyone of us ends up being taken, that's a man down that we can't afford. Can you lads do that?"

Emmet spoke for both of them. "We can, sir."

Murphy nodded. "Right, then."

The briefing went on with men being assigned to various points where the order was to deliver 'harassing actions' for the rest of the day. Tomorrow they would reconvene, and new orders issued based on the reports coming in from Dublin and from their own efforts.

Emmet and Liam were each assigned to a different troop. Liam went along to Swords while Emmet went to Saint Margaret's. Their job was to serve as lookouts and messengers working closely with their leaders. Emmet cycled directly behind his leader, James Lawless. Like the Ryans, Frank Lawless and both his boys were all engaged with the Fingal Volunteers. Frank and the two sons, Joseph and James, were all leaders of sections or columns. Frank wore a bushy handlebar moustache, but the two boys were clean shaven. Joseph reminded Emmet of his own brother Kevin, with his fair hair and mischievous grin. James was dark-haired and sombre, and Emmet was glad to follow him now, trusting him to lead with care. They took the less direct route which took them through Greenogue. When they reached the crossroads at Surgalstown Lawless stopped the troop. He gestured to Emmet who rode up beside him.

Lawless pointed ahead. "Right now, lad. Ride on ahead and make sure there's no RIC between here and St. Margaret's. We'll wait fifteen minutes and if we don't see you return, we'll figure the way is safe."

Emmet's heart raced as he cycled along the quiet road into the town. The two-and-a-half miles seemed much farther to him, but aside from a black Labrador Retriever running out from a laneway and barking furiously as Emmet passed, the way was quiet. Heavy rain-grey clouds hung over the road as he pedalled through the countryside. High hedges shrouded old stone walls and blocked his view as he wound his way along the road into St. Margaret's. On the outskirts of town, he passed the entrance to St. Margaret's Cemetery. He felt a shiver trace along his spine at the sight of the large white-spotted Celtic Cross, looming near the ruins of the ancient church. He pedalled harder until he was past. He knew it was foolish, but he heaved a sigh of relief when it was behind him. He pulled over and stopped to catch his breath. His instructions had been to go into town and cycle all the way through and then back along the side lanes and roads. If he saw anything concerning, his orders were to go back to a farm on Kilreesk Lane, owned by a comrade who would know exactly where to find Lawless. Meanwhile the troop was working on cutting communication lines along several key stretches.

The hours passed slowly for Emmet. He cycled along past St. Margaret's Church to the end where the houses trailed off, and then circled back. There really was no village to speak of and after the initial excitement wore off, the time dragged. He cycled up to Dunsoghly Castle and sat resting against the centuries-old stone to eat the sandwich Mam had given him. The sun had broken through the clouds. His eyes were heavy, and he closed them for a moment. He was on the edge of dozing off when he heard voices. His eyes sprang open. *Jaysus.*

Two RIC constables cycled up the pathway towards him. Despite the heat, the hair on his arms rose in goosebumps. He swallowed as his cheese and pickle sandwich threatened to rise in his throat. He sat frozen until one of the constables spotted him. After a muttered word, the two men stopped, dismounted and rested their bicycles against a crumbling wall. One went off around the corner of the old chapel while the other approached Emmet. Emmet stood up. He was the same height as the man sweating in front of him, but the constable's flat-topped peak-hat made him seem taller.

The constable stroked his heavy black moustache. "What are you up to then, boyo?"

Emmet's heart pounded at the arrogant tone. "Nothing. Only minding my own business."

"And what business would that be?"

The other constable came back, still buttoning up his fly.

Emmet glanced at him and then turned back to his interrogator. "Just having a bit of lunch."

"But why here?" The man turned to his partner. "Take a walk around and see if this fella has any pals lurking."

Emmet stopped himself from licking his lip, not wanting to look nervous. "Is there a law against it?"

The second constable made a half-hearted stroll to the corner of the tower for a quick look and then came back. "Ah, leave it Joe. There's nothing. Probably just skiving."

Emmet breathed deeply through his nose to slow his breathing. He clenched his teeth as the constable hesitated while his partner returned to his bicycle. The black moustache twitched as the man sneered. "I should write you up. I can tell you're up to no good, but I'm feeling generous today. What's your name?"

Emmet picked a name from Irish history and put it together with the constable's own name "Joe Parnell."

"Well Joe Parnell, I'll remember you if I hear of any trouble around here."

The man's partner rested a foot on his pedal, ready to push off. "Come on, Joe. We need to do another patrol around Donabate and then get back to barracks and out of this heat."

Emmet stood until they disappeared down the path and out onto the road before he slid down the wall to sit on the ground again. *Thank God he didn't ask me where I live. I should have had something prepared. Jaysus, how stupid am I?*

Emmet sat for another moment and then rose to climb on his own bicycle. He needed to report this. There were RIC in the area! His legs felt like rubber for a few moments and then the adrenalin kicked in again and he flew along the way to the meeting place on Kilreesk Lane. He knew he was early for the three o'clock meeting time so Joe Lawless may not even be there, but he'd try anyway.

He cycled in through the gate, half-hidden behind a copse of trees, and climbed off his bicycle in the farmyard. He rested his bike against the stone wall of the barn. It was quiet in the yard and chickens scattered before him as he walked to the door of the house. *Is this the right place? How will I explain myself if I'm wrong? I can't just ask for Jim Lawless.*

Emmet's stomach churned, but as he raised his hand to knock, the door opened, and a woman stepped out. She reminded Emmet of his mother in her pinny, although her face was closed as she stood in front of him, drying her hands on a tea-towel.

"Yes?"

"My name's Emmet."

From inside the house, Emmet heard the voice of Lawless. "Let him in, Alana."

She turned, and Emmet followed the woman into the house. She nodded through an open door into a sitting room. "In there."

Lawless was sitting at a table with three other men, two of whom Emmet recognized from their troop. They had cups of tea in front of them and looked like they had been there a while.

Lawless looked up at Emmet, his heavy jowls wreathed in a grin. "All quiet, soldier?"

Emmet felt a sudden lump in his throat. *A soldier. I've done a soldier's work today.* Emmet straightened his shoulders. "No, sir."

Lawless straightened up. "Oh? What is it?"

Emmet recounted his meeting with the two RIC constables.

"Did they ask who you were?"

Emmet nodded. "I said Joe Parnell."

Lawless grinned. "Parnell. You have big shoes to fill, but I'd say you're well on your way."

Emmet felt himself grow warm with the praise.

"And you think they were from the barracks in Donabate?"

"They were. I heard the one say they should head back there."

"Right, so. That's the opposite direction and the others should be well on their way now so there'll be no danger of running into them. Sit and have a cuppa and we'll give those two a chance to clear the area."

Lawless pushed a chair back from the table for Emmet to sit down and then he continued the conversation he had been having with the other men. "So, a grand day. Highly successful."

Emmet pulled the knitted green cozy off the pot and poured himself a cup of tea, soaking up every word that his leader was saying.

Lawless nodded to the man Emmet didn't know. "Thank you for having us here. This was an ideal headquarters for today's actions and the information you gave about the layout of the telegraph lines was invaluable."

The man's ears flushed red. "Come back when you need to. Anytime."

The men chatted for another half hour and then Lawless stood. Emmet gulped down the last of his tea. Everyone rose and Lawless held his hand up to hold everyone in the room while he walked down the hall to the kitchen. Emmet could hear him talking. "Thank you, Missus. God Bless all in this true Republican house."

He came back down the hall and they went outside. Emmet mounted his bicycle and waited while the others fetched their bicycles from the barn. Lawless seemed in great form and he waved cheerfully to the farmer and his wife standing at the door of the house. As he pushed off, he called out to Emmet and the two other men. "Let's hope they have some food ready. I could eat the hind leg of an ass."

Emmet laughed along with the others as they wheeled out of the farmyard.

———

They were back at Murphy's barn before dark and then he was told to go home for the night but be back at daybreak. Others had already gone home before him. Emmet didn't see Liam or his own brothers but went home gratefully. The adrenalin that coursed through him for most of the day had left him exhausted. He cycled home and found that Kevin had arrived in before him.

His mother hugged Emmet as he came through the door. "Ah, son. Come in and have a hot cup of tea. I'll get your tea out for you now."

Kevin looked up after scraping his own plate clean. "You all right, then?"

"Grand. Tired, though."

"See anything of interest?"

Emmet shrugged to be nonchalant, but he knew his voice gave him away as he told his story. His mother turned from the cooker and crossed herself as she listened to him speak.

When he finished his story, Emmet nodded to his brother "What about you?"

Kevin sat back and waited until their mother had finished serving out Emmet's dinner. "I didn't see anything of the RIC, but saw Ashe go by on that Hunter motorbike of his. You can hear it putt-putting a mile off."

Emmet felt his eyes widen as he chewed his food, waiting for Kevin to go on.

Kevin nodded. "He went past and then Mulcahy and some others pedalled like mad men to keep up followed behind."

Kevin and Emmet were both laughing at the image when their father and Michael walked in. Immediately they both stopped laughing and waited in silence to hear what Da might have to say.

Kathleen helped her husband take his jacket off. "You're all home then, thanks be to God."

Ned nodded. "We'll get a few hours sleep and then go back." He pulled his lunch out of his pocket and set it on the counter. "That'll do me for tomorrow. I didn't need it."

The three boys all looked at each other. They had all found time to eat their sandwiches.

Kathleen nudged her husband and Michael to the table. "Sit down now and I'll get you a hot meal."

Emmet shifted in his chair and then burst out. "What's the news, Da? Did you see any action?"

Kathleen set the two plates down for Ned and Michael. "Let your father eat in peace."

Ned nodded as he sliced into a bite of ham and potato. "We went out and cut some of the telegraph lines."

Emmet heard his mother's quick intake of breath.

Ned glanced at her. "Don't worry. There really was no danger. Snip, snip and we were away again on to the next one."

Now Michael joined in. "Tomorrow will be the telling day. They'll have had time to start organizing themselves, so we'll see some resistance tomorrow, I predict."

Kevin nodded. "The Fifth Battalion may not have a lot in the way of weapons, but we have heart. We'll show them what's what."

Kathleen sat down with a cup of tea for herself. "You aren't to take foolish chances, though. Isn't that so, Ned?"

24

Emmet's father nodded. "Don't worry. We won't be sent into something futile. We'll keep the boys safe." This last statement was directed to his wife and she gave a trembling smile in return.

Emmet went to bed and tossed and turned, imagining various scenarios where he figured as a hero of the Rising. When he remembered his jolt of fear at the sight of the two constables though, his last conscious thought was *will I be brave enough?*

3

Ashbourne, County Meath, April 25th, 1916

It was still dark when Kevin shook Emmet to wake him up. "Come on. It's time."

Emmet couldn't believe that he had slept so soundly. When he fell into bed his mind had been so full of the day that had passed and speculation about the coming day, he thought he'd never sleep and yet at the end, exhaustion had won out.

He jumped out of bed, doing his ablutions and dressing in record time. There'd be no school for him for the foreseeable future. In passing, he thought about a math test scheduled for the first day back after Easter holiday. *They'll have to reschedule. Surely no one will be in school.*

He put everything else out of his mind aside from dressing warmly and strapping the leather knife holder onto his belt.

The empty bowls and cups showed that his father and Michael were already gone. Kevin was eating his breakfast while his mother dished out a bowl of porridge for Emmet.

She looked at him with pleading eyes as she set the bowl down. "You don't have to go again, you know."

Before Emmet could respond, Kevin stood up. "Leave him be, Mam. He's not a boy anymore." Kevin turned to Emmet. "Eat up. I'll wait for you."

Emmet had never eaten so fast in his life, lifting the bowl to just under his chin to spoon the food into his mouth.

They took their sandwich packets along with the small whiskey bottles that Kathleen had filled with milk, stuffing the food and drink into their deep jacket pockets. They each put on their caps and hugged their mother. Kathleen clung to Emmet until he pulled back. "We have to go, Mam."

The two young men climbed onto their bicycles and headed off into the darkness. The last of the quarter moon was setting and cast ghostly shadows on the road but gave enough light to see the way. Emmet shivered as a fox screamed out a warning to a rival.

The sliver of light coming from the open crack of the barn door welcomed them. Emmet was glad to be there; happy to leave the night sounds behind.

Emmet saw that his father and Michael stood at the map with Murphy and another man. Ned nodded and followed a line with his finger, tracing the route. Emmet looked around the room; most of the men wore ties, some with bandoliers across their shoulders, most just with brown belts.

Emmet felt a nudge with an elbow in his side and turned to see Liam beside him. "You made it out of bed then, Liam."

Liam grinned. "I hardly went to sleep. I slept on the settee to make sure I got up on time. Mam and Da didn't want me to come, but they would have had to lock me up in the shed to keep me away."

"Your folks don't agree that Ireland should be free?"

"They think we should just keep our heads down and work hard and we'll get our reward in heaven."

Emmet nodded. *Sounds like what the priests say.*

Liam waved over to the map. "So, what's the plan?"

Emmet shrugged. "Just waiting to hear. More of the same, I suppose."

Liam shook his head. "Not for me. I'll get my hands on a gun today. I promise you that."

"Will you really use it?"

"No problem."

At that moment Ned called Emmet over. "Emmet, you're with me."

Liam followed behind Emmet to stand close to the map. "What about me? Where should I go?"

Murphy nodded to the other man standing by the map. "Liam, do you know Joe Lawless?"

Joe nodded to Liam. "I've seen you before. You're Sean Kelly's boy, aren't you?"

Liam grinned. "I am, but don't hold that against me."

Joe frowned. "This is serious business, lad."

Emmet saw the grin slide from Liam's face and a flush rise to his cheeks. "Yes, sir. I know."

Joe studied Liam for a moment and then nodded at Murphy. "All right, I'll take him along."

Emmet turned his attention to his father's voice. "We'll be moving along here to meet up with others from the Battalion." His finger again traced a route that ran between Ashbourne and Donabate. "Our goal today is to raid the barracks, here."

Emmet swallowed. This was the real thing. *A raid.* Michael was being sent to another column to move towards Swords, but Emmet and Kevin were to stay with Ned as they joined up with the other handful of Volunteers assigned to this target.

Ned pierced first Kevin and then Emmet with a look. "Are you ready?"

Both nodded. Emmet felt the largeness of the moment as his heart raced.

Ned stepped over and had a last few quiet words with Murphy and then he turned and waved to the four men who were with him, including his two sons. "Right, let's go."

The sun had risen as they each climbed on their bicycles. In the early dawn, Emmet heard the song of a blackbird. Repeating again and one last time, Emmet thought he had never heard anything so lovely. *Is it an omen? Three times for luck for the three of us Ryans here at this moment?* Emmet felt a sudden wave of love for, not only his family, but the other men with whom he had drilled and joked for the past five months. *We're in this together. Someone could die today. Is it worth it?* They cycled on without speaking, each intent on his own thoughts.

As they crossed from County Meath into County Dublin, Ned had everyone pull off the road.

Ned pointed. "Okay, boys. Take cover behind those rocks. I'll go ahead and see if the others are waiting."

Emmet and Kevin chatted quietly with one of the men, Seamus Flynn, while the fourth man stretched himself out higher on the hill to keep watch along the road.

Kevin played on the local hurling team with Seamus. Emmet listened to them discuss the strengths and weaknesses of their team as compared to the team from Garristown. Their voices lulled Emmet into a trance-like feeling. *I could just go to sleep here and now. How can I be tired with the day that's in it?*

Emmet snapped awake. The lookout had whistled one sharp 'tweet' and all talk stopped. They froze waiting to hear or see what was happening. The lookout crept back to where Emmet, Kevin and Seamus were crouched behind their boulder.

"It's Ned, back again."

They all rose and went back to the road to meet Emmet's father. Ned stopped his bicycle but didn't dismount. "Come on, boys. The others are up ahead waiting for us."

The five of them cycled ahead to meet with the other group, men that Emmet didn't know. There was no talk or called greetings between the two groups; only a few nods to acknowledge each other. Ned held up his hand to stop his detachment while the others mounted their bicycles and then they all started forward, but now Ned was just one of the twelve-man unit, led by someone else.

They pedalled forward, each man knowing that their large group was now at risk for being spotted. Emmet wished he could ask his father some questions. *Who is that man in charge? Do you trust him to know what he's doing?* Instead he cycled on in silence, the ghostly group slipping through the morning past a landscape that Emmet didn't know. *I'll just trust they know what they're doing.*

When they reached the outskirts of Donabate they pulled off the road into a well-treed area and Emmet finally heard the leader, Charlie Weston, introduce himself.

Weston pointed out two of his own men. "You two are going to take the pickaxe and sledge and burst in the door." He looked then at Emmet's group. "I need another strong lad to take the crowbar and help with that."

Seamus stepped forward before anyone else could speak. "I'm your man, sir."

Ned nodded his agreement and then looked back to Weston. "Have you a crowbar with you?"

"We do. We'll want two more to go along and rush the door. It'll be a pig to get it open and speed will be of the essence." Kevin and another man were assigned. Weston himself would lead the charge.

Weston took a stick and used it to draw in the soft earth under the trees. "Now, we want three men here, and three there."

Weston pointed out men and told them where he wanted them. Emmet was to stay close to his father and be ready to charge in through the open door. It was possible he'd be needed to help stand guard of prisoners.

They remounted the bicycles and drew closer to the barracks. When the grey, two-storey rectangular building was in sight, they left their bicycles and slowly crept closer, using trees and bushes to cover their advance as far as they could. The barracks was silent. Emmet kept staring at the row of windows on the main and second floor, like so many blank staring eyes,

Weston held up his hand as he studied the building, surrounded by the whitewashed stone wall. A police bicycle rested against the wall near the open gate.

Emmet's teeth were chattering, and he clenched his jaw to still them.

Suddenly Weston's arm dropped. "Go!"

The six men rushed through the gate to the door. Emmet heard Weston shout out: "On behalf of the Irish Republic, surrender now or we'll break down the door."

The air cracked with a volley of gunshot exploding from a top floor window.

Emmet's ears were blasted by the answering fire from the men around him who had shotguns. He clapped his hands over his ears and watched as the window shattered, raining glass and splinters down on the men below.

The six men at the door fought to break it down. The hammering of the sledge against the thick timber boomed. Emmet heard a jumble of words as the men at the door shouted to each other.

"Here, throw it here."

And "Get the prise in here."

"Now lads, give it all you've got."

Emmet glanced over to his father who had risen to a crouch as he kept his shotgun trained on the building. Emmet looked back to the men working at the door, so he didn't notice as the shooter on the top floor changed his angle and let loose with a hail of bullets. He gasped as his father stood and returned fire, but the shot went wild, thudding into the wall between windows, sending flakes and chips of brick and mortar flying.

Surprised at the miss, Emmet turned his head to see if his father would try again. He heard his own voice shriek, high with shock. "Da!"

His father lay on his back. His face was already chalky as the blood seeped through his jacket.

Emmet vomited, wiping his mouth with the back of his hand as he crabbed his way across the few feet separating them. "Da."

Ned opened his eyes, blinking rapidly. "I'm all right. Stay down. Keep low."

Emmet gulped and tried to calm his voice. "You're not all right. You're bleeding."

One of the other men, a fellow called Paddy, crept up on the other side of Emmet's father. "You all right, Ned?"

"Feckin shoulder's gone."

The man pulled out a dressing from his backpack and pulled open Ned's jacket. He pressed the pad down against the wound and nodded to Emmet. "Hold that."

Emmet lay his hand down against the dressing, not wanting to hurt his father further.

"Hard. Press hard to stop the bleeding."

Emmet pressed down harder, smelling the copper smell of warm blood. The man had pulled out a strip of cotton and wound it across the pad and around Ned's chest and shoulder. "Looks like it went right through."

Ned spoke through gritted teeth. "Grand."

At that moment there was a cry from the men at the door as the frame gave way. The door toppled in, but inside there was another door.

Despite himself, Emmet looked up and could see that the second door was of iron or some sort of heavy black metal. For a moment Emmet's heart sank. *They can't breech it. This is all for nothing.* As the sledge again started thumping, a shout came from within.

Surrender! The men inside were surrendering. A rifle was thrown out through the top window as a token of their surrender.

Ned flapped his hand. "Go. Paddy, take the lead. Emmet go, go, go."

Emmet bit his lip. "I want to stay with you."

His father's voice was weak, but firm. "I'll be fine. This is why you're here."

Everything in Emmet cried out to stay where he was; to hold Da in his arms, and yet he rose, hesitated for another second and then rushed forward behind the others where they surrounded the entry in case there were any attempts of escape.

The iron door opened, and Weston pulled a revolver out of his holster and shouted to the men inside. "Step back. Back against the wall with your hands in the air, all of you."

Emmet held his breath. They had so many weapons inside. *What's to stop them from firing on us now?*

The half dozen RIC did as they were instructed and backed against the wall with their arms up. All the Volunteers were now inside and those with guns kept them trained on the constables.

Emmet tried to make his way over to his brother, but it was too crowded in the small room. He saw Kevin look around, his brow furrowed, and Emmet knew he was looking for Da. At that moment, he saw Paddy draw Weston aside for a quiet word. Weston frowned, and Emmet knew they must be talking about his father.

Weston pointed to Emmet's brother. "Ryan, you can drive a motor, can't you?"

"Yes, sir."

"Your father's been wounded. I saw a motor behind the barracks. Get your father to a doctor quick as you can. Then come back here with the motor."

Emmet saw Kevin's eyes widen. "Yes, sir." He hustled out, throwing a worried look at Emmet as he left.

He heard a muttered 'Jaysus' and he turned to see the two from the previous day. If Emmet had been feeling less sick and worried, he might have smiled. The one he knew as Joe narrowed his eyes. "Joe Parnell. I knew you were a bloody troublemaker."

Weston raised an eyebrow at Emmet and Emmet shrugged.

One of the RIC had his hand wrapped in a bloody towel.

Weston directed Paddy, as the appointed medic, to the injured constable. "See to him. Can he survive until help comes?"

Paddy nodded, and Weston had the other members of the RIC herded down into their own cells.

Weston pointed to Emmet and another man. "You two start collecting all the weapons and ammo that you can find."

As Emmet lifted down rifles from the gun rack he heard Paddy ask the injured constable what had happened to him.

"I was the one at the window so one of you beggars shot me."

"That'll teach you."

Paddy pulled out another dressing from his pocket and used it to bandage up the constable's hand.

"He'll be fine."

Weston nodded. "Right. Take him to join his mates, then."

While the others collected the weapons and took them outside, Weston went through the paperwork and files.

"Jaysus. Look at this."

Emmet wished he had gone along to look after his father, but he kept quiet and followed orders. Weston flipped through the pages of a thick file and his voice was shocked. "They've got intelligence on everyone in the area. Names. Dates of parades. They've got eyes and ears everywhere."

Kevin was back just as they finished, and he stopped beside Emmet on his way to report to Weston. "Da's fine. He was all for coming back with me, but the doctor gave him a sedative and said he'd bring him over when he rested up a bit."

Emmet shook his head. "But all that blood."

"It looked worse than it was."

Kevin moved on to report in to Weston.

Weston nodded. "Good. We'll leave the motor here. It's too obvious and will be a dead giveaway."

They cleared out all the weapons, ammunition, and files of relevance and went back to their bicycles. The whole episode had taken less than two hours, but as Emmet climbed back on his bicycle, loaded now with a heavy tin box on the back, he felt as though an entire day had passed. They were heading back to make camp partway between Ashbourne and Garristown, and Emmet wasn't sure he'd make it.

Kevin pedalled up beside him. "How are you doing?"

Emmet nodded. "I'm all right. Tired." Emmet didn't tell his brother that the sight of Da bleeding had made him throw up. Even the memory of the image made him queasy.

Kevin sat up straight on his bike, letting go of the handlebars to lift his arms in victory. "I'm just the opposite. Now that I know Da's all right I say let's go get 'em somewhere else."

Emmet forced a grin at his brother and then watched as Kevin sped up to catch up to his pal Seamus.

He's right. Christ, we just took a barracks. He felt a little more energy come into his legs. He sat up straighter and let the weak April sun warm him. As he sucked in deep gulps of fresh spring air, the tension left his muscles. He realized he'd been shivering. *The whole time? Did anyone see that I was shaking the whole time? But I'm OK. I didn't shame myself or Da.*

They followed Weston to the camp. Others were already there, some seated on the ground eating from bowls. Others in line waited for theirs to be dished out from a large cooking pot hung over an open fire. They left the line and came over to greet the new arrivals.

Weston faced the men behind him. "Take all weapons and ammo and hand it in to Frank Lawless in the barn where the Battalion Quartermaster is set up."

Emmet unstrapped the box of ammo from his bike carrier and joined the others of his group.

While he was walking over, his oldest brother came over to join him.

Michael put his hand on Emmet's shoulder and gave it a squeeze. "I heard about Da. You came back in one piece, though. Are you all right?"

Emmet tried to smile. "Yeh. I'm all right, but when I thought that Da was...."

Michael nodded. "I know. I'd have been the same, but it's the chance we all take." Michael paused, his hand still resting on Emmet's shoulder. "You know that, right?"

Emmet frowned and twitched Michael's hand away. "I do, of course. But knowing it and believing it. It's different."

Michael nodded again. "I know." He hesitated and then went on. "You know you can go home. No one would blame you."

Emmet straightened his shoulders. "I'll go home when you go home."

Michael grinned. "So tell me about the operation, then. It was a great success, I hear."

Emmet tried to keep his voice calm. "Yeh, good. We took the barracks and you can see, we took a good haul. What about you?"

Michael nodded. "Victory all around, then. We walked away with half a dozen carbines, so not a bad day's work."

Michael suddenly grinned at a commotion behind Emmet as men moved aside and called out 'hurrah'. "Look who's here."

Emmet turned. "Da!"

He was wearing a uniform jacket that someone had given him, his ruined jacket gone.

Kevin came trotting over when he saw his father.

Ned was still pale, and his voice sounded groggy, but he looked a hundred percent better than when Emmet had last seen him. "I'm fine, boys. No need to make a fuss now."

Michael grasped his father's good elbow for an instant. "Are you sure you should be here, Da?"

Ned's voice was gruff. "Where else would I be? By tomorrow I'll be fine. Nothing more than a flesh wound."

"Well, then. It's good to see you. Have you seen Weston already?"

"I have. Now, let's get something to eat, lads. There'll be a briefing in an hour."

Michael left Emmet to hand in his ammo and went off with his father to talk further.

As Emmet handed in his tin box and watched Frank record the contents on a record of their arsenal, he felt his heart swell. Frank simply took the box without comment. *I'm just one of the men. No one looks twice at me to wonder why a boy is here. I look like I belong.*

Emmet left the barn and made his way to the field kitchen to get his supper. When he had a bowl and spoon he looked around for a place to sit and saw Liam sitting on his own eating his meal.

"Mind if I join you?"

Liam looked up. "Emmet. Sit man, sit." His eyes were wide. "Tell me about it. I heard that you saw some action."

Emmet sat down on the damp ground. "We did."

"Well what happened? Did you use a gun, yourself?"

Emmet made a wry face. "No, but I had my knife, and you can be sure if any of those beggars tried to make a run for it, I was ready to use it."

"But there was shooting?"

"There was. They weren't ready to surrender without a fight."

Emmet went on to describe in detail what had happened. Now that he had seen with his own eyes that his father would be all right, he could relax and enjoy the telling of the story, with a few embellishments here and there.

Liam shook his head. "I wish I had been there."

"What about you? You weren't sitting around doing nothing today."

"No, we had a good day as well. We went all over the county cutting telegraph lines."

"Sure, that was important work as well." Emmet was glad that he could tell a more exciting story of his day. *But if we had the day Liam had, Da wouldn't have been shot.*

They finished their food and then wandered around stopping here and there to listen to the stories of the different forays until it was time to gather in the barn for their briefing.

The forty-odd men gathered in the barn and then two men in actual uniforms went to the front where a large map was tacked to the wall. It was the first time that Emmet had seen either the Battalion Commandant, Thomas Ashe or his second in command, Lieutenant Richard Mulcahy.

Emmet, standing with Liam, bit his bottom lip, almost holding his breath, waiting for Ashe to speak.

Liam nudged him and whispered in Emmet's ear: "Grand-looking uniforms. How do we get our hands on some like that?"

Emmet frowned at Liam, not answering.

Ashe had an unruly head of curls and a wide, waxed moustache that gave him the look of a dandy, but when he spoke, Emmet was entranced. "We've had an extraordinary day today, men. Well done to all of you."

Emmet looked around the group of rough farmers and working men and saw the glow of pride on their faces.

Ashe nodded and went on. "We've made a good start. Today the barracks at Swords and Donabate were both taken, significantly adding to our arsenal. Add these successes to the major disruption that's been delivered to the communication systems and we can say that the Fifth Battalion can hold its head high. The troops in Dublin will be grateful for the help that's been given with these actions."

Heads were nodding around the barn.

Ashe turned to his second in command. "Lieutenant, please take the men through the next phases of our work."

Now Richard Mulcahy stepped forward. Emmet had heard his Da talk of this man before because he also worked for the Post Office, but he had never seen him. He was about the same age as his Da, so in his late thirties or early forties. He was tall and lean with a square chin and chiselled face; deep lines marking his cheekbones and exaggerating his deep-set eyes. His collar was loose around his long neck.

Mulcahy took off his fedora and wiped his brow with his sleeve before replacing his hat. "After we finish the briefing you should all try to get some sleep because we'll be going to Garristown tonight for a raid. We'll pack up camp, so take everything along with you."

Mulcahy gestured for the men to gather close to the map as he pointed with a long stick, the route that they planned to take. "It will still be dark, lads. Study the map so you know where you're going."

When the briefing was finished, and assignments made clear to each detachment, men settled down to sleep as they could. Jackets were rolled under heads as pillows or thrown over themselves to keep the damp April night dew from them. The four Ryans instinctively gathered together to try to sleep.

Emmet saw Liam standing, studying the map. "Liam, come away now and lie down for a bit."

Liam joined the Ryans. "I won't sleep."

Emmet nodded. "I know, but we should try anyway."

They lay down side by side, the two youngest members in the group. Emmet closed his eyes and felt the comfort of having his father and brothers around him. Unbidden, he had the vision again of his father lying on his back, blood seeping, and once again he felt his gorge rise. *I want to be a part of this. I need to be a part of winning Ireland's freedom, but do I have the stomach for it? It's so different than what I expected.*

The thought was the last one Emmet had before exhaustion sent him to sleep.

———

Emmet's eyes snapped open. *Where am I?* Then he remembered everything and sat up. His father had already left his place, but his brothers and Liam were all still sleeping. Perhaps his father's departure had woken him.

Someone came into the barn carrying a lantern. "Time to rise and shine."

There were groans as the men stretched sore muscles.

The lantern carrier called out over the sounds of the coughing and snuffling. "There's tea and bread waiting for you. Get your breakfast as quick as you can and then get ready to move out."

Liam rubbed his eyes. "What time is it, anyway?"

Emmet peered at his watch, trying to focus in the dim light. "One-thirty."

"Jaysus"

Emmet stumbled outside, the dampness clinging like a cobweb. It was a dark night, the moon just a sliver of light high above him.

He was drawn to the fire along with everyone else. Tin mugs with sweet tea were handed out and he inhaled the steam gratefully. There was a queue to get a thick cut of buttered bread, which he joined.

Kevin came in behind him. "Did you get any sleep?"

"I didn't think I would, but I did."

Liam joined them, yawning and twisting his head first one way and then the other. "God, I've got a desperate kink in my neck."

Emmet rolled his shoulders. "Funny enough, I feel good."

Kevin smiled. "The sleep of the righteous."

They all received their breakfast and ate standing up. Mulcahy walked amongst the men having a word here and there, checking that everyone was well and ready to move out. The barracks in Garristown should yield another good haul for their arsenal and everyone was excited to add to their successes of yesterday.

Liam's voice was high-pitched, and he spoke very fast, the words tripping over themselves when Mulcahy stopped by his side. "Will we all be issued guns, sir? I've used one before. My uncle has a shotgun that he's let me use out hunting."

Mulcahy held up his hand to stop Liam's barrage of questions. "Weapons will be issued to those that require them, son."

Liam persisted. "Should I go and check with the Quarter Master? Does he have a list of names?"

At that moment the Commandant called for Mulcahy. Mulcahy shook his head to Liam. "If you needed one, you would have it now." With that he hurried away.

Liam turned to Emmet. "So much for being soldiers. What are we doing here?"

Emmet touched Liam's arm. "Don't fuss. Soldiers do what's needed and that's what we'll do, too. Who knows what the day will bring?"

Kevin nodded. "Emmet's right. It'll be a long day and every one of us will have a job to do."

Liam scowled. "You can say that. You've got a gun."

Kevin shook his head. "Settle down, Liam. Come on, it looks like we're getting ready to go."

Joe Lawless came striding over to them. "There you are. You're with me again, Liam."

Liam nodded. "Right behind you, sir."

Emmet frowned at Liam and got a grin in return just before Liam set off behind Joe.

They mounted their bicycles and headed off in the semi-darkness. The line of bicycles strung out along the road formed a surreal chain.

An hour later the men were in place surrounding the Garristown barracks. Again, the door was rushed in the same fashion as Emmet had seen in the previous day's attack at Donabate. This time there was no answering fire or even shouts from within. The men breeched the door only to find that the barracks had been abandoned. There were signs of a hurried departure.

By then most of the men were crowding around the door and Emmet heard Mulcahy curse. "Dammit. They must have heard about the raids yesterday and took everything worth taking and deserted."

There was a conference between the leaders and they decided to make camp a short distance off and get some more sleep. In the morning they planned to destroy the Midland Great Western Railway.

It was a subdued group that set up camp to try to get a few more hours' sleep.

***

Friday dawned clear with the promise of a sunny day. The men gathered around Ashe and Mulcahy for the morning briefing.

Ashe's voice carried through the stillness of the morning. "We're reorganizing, so listen up for your new assignments." He looked around the group to ensure everyone was paying attention. "I'm splitting you into four sections. We've had some intelligence that makes us believe that British troop reinforcements are being sent from Athlone into Dublin. We need to help our comrades who are holding on as well as they can in Dublin, so we need to sabotage the rail lines to stop the troops from getting to Dublin."

Ashe handed the briefing over to Mulcahy to go through the exact instructions and assignments. "So, sections one to three – be prepared to leave at ten o'clock. You men of Section Four will be with Jim Lawless to guard the camp and help Frank Lawless gather supplies and food. Be ready to come in as support if necessary."

Emmet had already been told that he'd be with Section One, commanded by Weston again and would act as courier to deliver messages between the various sections. Ashe needed to know exactly how things were going at all times in order to shift men as needed.

The briefing ended, and Emmet caught up with Liam before they mounted their bicycles. Liam grinned as he pointed to the long thin Martini Henry carbine now strapped to the bar of his bike.

Emmet nodded. "You got your gun, then."

"A beaut, isn't she?"

"You're with Section Three, with Joe again?"

"I am. Joe thought I should have a weapon as well." Liam's voice was proud.

"Well, we're off, then. Good luck today. I'll see you later."

Liam mounted his bike, his hand caressing the dark wooden stalk of the weapon.

Emmet smiled at him and went to find his own bicycle. He didn't care that he didn't have a gun. In fact, he was secretly glad of it. He patted the leather knife pouch strapped to his belt. *This will do.*

They lined up in order of section. Section Four was going to hold back, but the other thirty plus men pushed off on their bicycles, silent now that they were on the way. In the rear, the only motor car would follow, driven by the medical officer, Dr. Hayes.

The convoy was led by two scouts from Section One who went ahead to act as spotters. Ashe and Mulcahy were in Section Two. They headed off along the Dublin-Slane road, which would take them close to Rath Cross, north of Ashbourne.

The plan was to check if the barracks on the way to Ashbourne was still in use. If so, Section One would lead the raid to capture the arsenal. Emmet found his teeth starting to chatter again as they rode towards Ashbourne. He was in Section One. As soon as the spotters came back to report, the section would move on. This was his home neighbourhood. Even the RIC were familiar faces to him. *Please God, let them just surrender.*

The three sections followed the spotters, detouring towards Ashbourne. They were on the main road and the barracks was in sight. Emmet stiffened his back and craned his head to look ahead. Soldiers! There were two men building a barricade in front of the barracks.

Weston waved his men to a stop and they watched as the scouts raced forward.

Emmet could hear the shouts from the two scouts as they waved their weapons aggressively at the two RIC soldiers. "Hand over your weapons or we'll shoot!"

Emmet watched with wide eyes as the soldiers did as they were told.

Emmet heard the closest man behind let out a soft cheer. "Good man, Niall."

The two scouts took possession of the soldiers' weapons and marched them along the column of Volunteers, taking their prisoners to the rear of the convoy.

The raid would go forward now. Ashe ordered all the men off their bicycles. "Sections Two and Three, take cover."

The men dismounted and took cover close to the edge of the by-road. They were just north of the crossroads called Rath Cross.

Ashe and Mulcahy came forward to join Weston and Section One. Ashe led the men, creeping forward to take positions behind an embankment just across the road from the barracks.

Emmet's father moved stiffly but otherwise seemed better today. Ned pointed to an area on the edge of the group. "Emmet, get over to the flank there and hold until the door is breeched. Come forward then. We'll need every man to help guard and collect the weapons."

Emmet crept along the embankment to a slope where he could clearly see what was happening both at the barracks and his own section.

Ashe bellied up to the top of the embankment, with Mulcahy on one side and Weston on his other. Along the top ridge of the embankment, the rest of the men trained their rifles on the barracks. The building was larger than Donabate, but otherwise looked the same. The whitewash on the stone walls was newer but still weathered and chipped. Ashe lifted his head above the top of the grassy hill. His voice rang out, clear and loud in the still morning. "In the name of The Irish Republic, surrender now or pay the price."

A volley of rifle fire came from the barracks, aimed at Ashe. Spurts of dirt exploded from the hill as Ashe dove for cover. He shouted to Section One, "Fire at will!"

The men returned fire on the barracks. A barrage of bullets was aimed at the windows and an explosion of glass and splintered wood flew through the air.

Ashe and Mulcahy slid back down the embankment, directing the men to take positions. Emmet's eyes were stretched as he watched some of the Volunteers sprint for the protection of the wall in front of the barracks. They dodged the bullets as they made it to the footpath along the road.

Emmet clenched his fists. *Dear God, they'll never make it. It's madness.* But they did. Others rushed out to take positions north of the barracks.

The noise made Emmet's ears ring. The smell of cordite hung in the air, making his eyes sting. And then Emmet watched as his own father made a dash to dive in behind a wall just south of the barracks. Emmet almost cried out 'no' when he saw his father leaving the safety of the embankment, but held himself in check.

Now there was only a handful of them left behind the hill, but they held there on the instructions of Weston. They would wait to move forward when the door was breeched. Meanwhile the two who had rifles continued to fire at the windows and door.

Emmet had a moment to wonder what Sections Two and Three were doing. *Will they come forward?* And then he forgot about them again as he continued to watch what was happening in front of him.

For the next half hour, the police in the barracks exchanged fire with the Volunteers. Finally, Emmet watched as one of the Volunteers stood up and threw a homemade canister grenade at the barracks. He did it quickly and bobbed back down behind the wall before he could be shot. The grenade landed short of the barracks. Dirt flew up in a spray of grass tufts, pebbles and mud, leaving a small crater in front of the barracks.

A shout went up from the Volunteers. "Surrender! They're surrendering!"

From one of the upstairs windows a white cloth was displayed. An old towel draped over a wooden stick protruded outside the window.

Around Emmet, the men moved into a crouch, ready to dash forward when the door opened. One of his comrades glanced over to Emmet. "Get ready, lad. We'll be going in."

Emmet heard Ashe's voice over the din of the continuing potshots. "Cease Fire. Cease Fire."

On both sides, the firing stopped. The volunteers crept closer to the door, waiting for the RIC to emerge.

A shot rang out. Emmet slid back down a little behind the cover of the embankment. *It's a trick.* Emmet looked towards the barracks to see if they had resumed shooting, but no. It was silent, and still the white cloth hung loosely from the window.

He heard another shot. It was coming from the crossroads. At that moment Ashe appeared behind the embankment beside Emmet. "Go, lad. Find out what's happening. Just look and come back to report."

Emmet rose to a crouch and dashed off, bent over, keeping down behind the embankment, but making his way around to a spot where he had a view of the crossroads.

Dear God. Emmet took a long enough look to burn the scene onto his brain and then scurried back to Ashe who was waiting with Mulcahy to see if the police from inside the barracks would emerge.

Emmet flopped down on his belly beside Ashe. "Sir." He gasped for air, struggling to get the words out.

"Well?"

"A convoy of police cars, sir."

"How many?"

"I counted twenty-four."

"Our men?"

"It looks like they're in control, sir. Several of the police have left their vehicles and taken cover in the ditches. Our men are giving them hell, sir."

Ashe nodded to Mulcahy. "Come on." He waved his hand towards the barracks. "They won't come out now. They know reinforcements are coming."

Ashe pointed to Emmet. "You're with me. I may need a runner."

Emmet's heart pounded as he followed Ashe, slipping on the grassy hill as he ran in a crouch behind the fast-moving men. Mulcahy stopped for a moment to brief Weston on what was happening. Weston nodded and held his hand up pointing to two of his men, directing them to hold their places. He then waved at the others from around the barracks, directing them to move forward to the crossroads.

When Emmet arrived back at the crossroads, he could see two men lying in the road, blood seeping from wounds. He could also see the driver from the lead car, lying across his steering wheel.

Dead? Certainly wounded. He swallowed hard, feeling the vomit rise in his throat. *The real thing. This is the real thing. I can't do it.*

Ashe and Mulcahy were in a huddle while Weston led his men up the western side of the road. The Volunteers from Section One began firing into the convoy and Emmet watched as the police were pinned down under the motorcars or in the ditches on the eastern side of the road.

Ashe gestured to Emmet. "Quick as you can, take this order back to Section Four to come now."

Emmet took the order, stuffing it into his pocket. "Right, sir." He ran back to his bicycle and jumped on, pedalling with all his might to get back to the camp he had left only two hours previously. He was hardly aware of the road under his wheels as his mind tried to process all he had seen so far this morning. *I wish I had time to see Da before I left. Please let him, Michael and Kevin come out of this day all right.* He hadn't seen Liam for the past hour so didn't know if he'd had a chance to fire his gun yet. *He'll see the action he wants today, for sure.*

Emmet was back at the camp faster than he thought even possible. He thrust the note into the hand of Frank Lawless, and as Frank scanned the note quickly, Emmet bent over resting his hands on his knees, sucking in deep breaths.

Frank shouted as he dashed to get his bicycle. "Mount up, men. Follow me. We're needed."

Emmet waited until the dozen men furiously took off and then he too mounted back on his bicycle, following as fast as he could. His heart was still pounding from the ride to the camp. His legs felt like rubber as he tried now to keep up with the group riding back towards the crossroads.

As they pulled close to the RIC barracks, Emmet conjured up a burst of energy, flying up to the front to come abreast of Frank. Emmet pointed to the embankment. "The bikes are all there."

Frank nodded and waved his men to the side of the road and Emmet led them to where everyone else had left their bicycles behind the cover of the hill. The sound of heavy gunfire echoed around the hills.

Emmet pointed up the road. "Shall I take you to where I left Commandant Ashe?"

Lawless nodded. "Good lad."

Within minutes they came upon Mulcahy, who had been watching for them. Emmet fell to the back of the group as Mulcahy led them northward towards the Garristown Road. They crept forward and suddenly they were under fire.

Emmet flattened himself into a ditch while the others returned fire. *Zing.* Emmet thought the bullet almost grazed him. He kept his face pressed against the cold mud of the ditch.

Then he heard shouting. Someone was yelling, but it wasn't the police. It was Mulcahy. "Hold your fire. Hold your fire."

The bullets slowly stopping whizzing past and the men around Emmet cautiously raised themselves up.

Emmet heard Frank Lawless. "Dear God. It's our own men. We've been feckin' shooting at our own men."

Mulcahy waved his revolver to Frank. "Go. Take the men north to get above the convoy. I'll find Ashe."

Emmet stayed with Frank and the men as they continued. It wasn't until much later that Emmet heard that the 'friendly fire' incident had wounded two men from Section Two who had been moving, along with Section three to reinforce Section One.

Section Four moved slowly, watching for men of either side as they tried to get into position to outflank the police.

As Section Four came abreast of the tail end of the convoy, Emmet saw a policeman who looked like a senior man, given the braid on his shoulders and the way he was shouting orders, stand up from his spot behind his vehicle. When the man stood, he saw the Volunteers of Section Four moving along parallel to the road.

Emmet took a breath to shout a warning. Too late. The shot found its target and a Volunteer fell, clutching his chest, blood seeping between his fingers. Frank Lawless lifted his revolver. The policeman dropped to his death, even as he was still waving his arms to rally his men to stand up and fight.

There was a shocked silence and then a rifle was thrown from the ditch. Surrender! All along the road the trapped RIC men threw down their weapons and surrendered. As the Volunteers came down and began collecting the weapons, Emmet watched for his father and brothers. *Yes. There they are. Michael, Da, Kevin. Ah, and there. There's Liam. All fine.* Emmet stood on the hill and looked down at the road. It was littered with wounded and dead men but none of them Volunteers. Only the one man from Section Four.

Ashe and Mulcahy walked along the road, checking on each of the wounded. Ashe turned and saw Emmet. He gestured to him in a 'come here' motion. Emmet ran down the hill to Ashe's side.

"Go to the parish and fetch the priest."

"Aye, sir."

Safe now that all shooting had ceased, Emmet ran along the road to where his bicycle was. He stopped for a moment when he saw the stream of police coming out of the barracks with their hands in the air. He counted fifteen men who were being led by their Volunteer guards to join the other prisoners.

Emmet pushed himself to cover the half mile to the town of Ashbourne as fast as he could. He pulled open the heavy wooden door in the Church of the Immaculate Conception. An old woman sitting in silent prayer glared at his noisy entrance.

The stone walls echoed with his shout. "Father Dillon. You're needed."

"Hush, son. What is it?"

"Have you not heard? There's been a great battle just up the road. There's dead and dying waiting for you."

The old woman cried out and crossed herself.

The priest also crossed himself. "I'll get my things and Father Murphy. Where exactly? We'll go in the motor."

Emmet waved his arm in the direction from which he had just come. "Rath Cross."

"We'll be there directly."

Emmet once again mounted his bicycle, covering the short distance back to the battleground in minutes. Since the area was secured, he rode all the way to the crossroads to find Ashe. "The two priests will be here in a moment, Sir."

Ashe nodded. "Good, good." He turned away from Emmet then, giving instructions to men along the way. "Can you drive? Yes? Good, you'll help to take the wounded to the infirmary in Navan."

Between Mulcahy and Ashe, they quickly arranged for all the wounded to be loaded into the police motor cars and sent them off to be tended.

Emmet saw a man he knew who hadn't been involved in any shooting loading dead men into a cart. "John, shall I help you?"

John Austen who worked at the local post office nodded. "Two of the RIC are helping as well, but yes, I could use your help."

They walked along the road to where a man lay in the road. The car he had been driving was gone, used to transport the wounded. The body looked strange, lying alone in the middle of the road. Emmet reached down to take hold of his legs, the police boots still shiny as if the man had given them a good buff before leaving for work that morning.

Again, Emmet's stomach recoiled as he touched a dead body for the first time in his life. He hesitated before grasping the dead man's legs and then gritted his teeth as his hands closed around the legs. "Jaysus, he's heavy."

John nodded. "People don't realize how much heavier a dead man is, than a live one who's helping to move himself."

Emmet wanted to treat the man with care, but by the time they managed to lift him up to the cart, it was all he could do to get the body fully on top of the ones already there. The body landed with a thud, and flies scattered from the blood-covered face of the previous body.

Emmet ran to the ditch and heaved, the breakfast he had eaten so long ago, coming back up. He wiped his mouth and then rejoined John.

John shook his head. "Go on. I'll get one of the police to help me."

Emmet straightened his shoulders. "No. I'm fine. Let's get on with it."

By the time they were done, there were eight dead men in the cart.

Emmet joined Liam near the back of the group of Volunteers. He looked at his friend's carbine resting on his shoulder. "Did you use it?"

"Of course I did. What do you think?"

"And?"

"And did I kill anyone?"

Emmet nodded.

Liam shrugged. "Who knows? We were all firing like mad, so I don't know." He sniffed and tilted his chin up. "Probably. I think I probably did."

Emmet bit his lip. "Well, I guess that's what you were supposed to do."

Liam frowned. "You don't think I'm sorry, do you?"

Emmet was saved from responding when Ashe began to speak. There were about eighty prisoners assembled at the crossroads.

"Men, it was your membership in the Royal Irish Constabulary that led to this battle today. It is not our wish to fight and kill fellow countrymen."

There was a silence as the prisoners waited to hear what their fate would be.

"On behalf of the Provisional Government of the Irish Republic, you are all hereby pardoned. If ever, however, you are seen again bearing arms against the Republic, you will..be..shot. Make no mistake about that."

Emmet heard Liam muttering beside him. "I'll be watching."

Emmet glanced at the scowl on Liam's face as the prisoners were dismissed and told to go home. *I can't tell if he's bloodthirsty or just wants everyone to think he is.*

When the prisoners had all dispersed, their weapons and ammunition were loaded into the remaining vehicles to take them to their new camp in Kilsallaghan.

Emmet cycled beside his father. "I was worried for you, Da. How's the shoulder?"

Ned was riding with only one hand on his handlebars while the other was tucked against himself. "A bit stiff but not too bad."

"It seemed like Section One was really taking a beating."

His father's teeth shone white through the grime on his face in the fading light of dusk. "We gave the beating, son. I was in no real danger."

Emmet was mostly silent on the ten-kilometre ride to the new camp as his father discussed the operation.

As the Volunteers set about making camp, Emmet overheard men around him talking. "We'll be marching down to Dublin tomorrow. Mark my words."

"Aye, we've got a good arsenal now to take with us."

Emmet joined Liam in the line waiting for food. "Will our lives ever go back to normal, do you think?"

Liam swelled out his chest. "This is normal now, me boyo."

"And what about your family? They must be worried about you." *And Mam. Poor Mam must be out of her mind by now.*

"Sure, I'm a man now. My family'll be glad of one less mouth to feed."

"I don't believe that."

"Believe it."

"Are you done with school, then?"

"The school of life will teach me more than the Brothers ever could."

Emmet accepted a dish of mutton stew and wandered over to sit beside his two brothers, his mind on Liam for a moment. *He's found his calling.* He sat down beside his oldest brother, drawing comfort from Michael's warmth. "What happens now, does anybody know?"

Michael scraped his bowl clean and then set it aside. "We're waiting for orders."

Kevin looked at Michael, who seemed to be well-informed. "What's the news from Dublin?"

Michael shrugged. "I heard they're holding on, but barely. The city is burning."

Emmet frowned. "So it's just a matter of time before they are taken over?"

Michael nodded. "It was always just a matter of time."

"There was never any hope of winning?"

Kevin coughed a short bark of a laugh. "Emmet, are you mad? The Brits aren't about to hand over the country they've been lord and master over for hundreds of years, without an almighty fight."

Emmet felt himself flush. "But there must be some kind of hope, otherwise what's it all for?"

Michael reached over and tousled Emmet's hair. "You're right. There's hope, of course. It just won't be easy. This is just the start of a long fight."

Emmet sighed. *No college for me, then. Life is changed forever.* He felt dizzy at the thought. *Blood and death. But if that's what it takes, so be it.*

Later, when they were all stretched out on the floor of the old barn, Emmet raised himself up on his elbow to look down at his father who was lying beside him.

His father opened his eyes, looking up at his youngest son. "What is it?"

"Does Mam know we're all fine?"

"She does. I managed a quick ride out to the house earlier on."

Emmet nodded. "That's good."

"Was there something else?"

"I guess I'm done with school."

His father raised himself up on his good elbow as well. "Why is that?"

"Well, the Republic needs me."

"The Republic will always need you. Not every man needs to carry a gun to be useful. The country needs educated men and women, trained in every skill and trade."

Emmet blinked. "So you think I should continue on in school?"

"Without question, if that's what you want."

Emmet bit his lip, trying to imagine how it could work. His father and brothers out fighting with the Volunteers, and him home with his mother.

His father seemed to follow Emmet's thoughts. "Son, this battle has almost run its course. Life will go back to what it was, but with a difference. The Brits now know that we aren't prepared to settle for the status quo any longer."

Emmet nodded.

His father lowered himself back to the floor and closed his eyes. "For now, though, let's get some sleep and we'll leave tomorrow to tomorrow."

———

On Friday morning, the men walked restlessly around the camp, chatting, smoking and drinking tea. At one point Emmet saw Ashe and Mulcahy studying some papers and then Mulcahy left, riding Ashe's Hudson motorcycle.

Emmet walked from group to group listening to the speculation. Last night's excitement after the success of the Battle of Ashbourne, as it was already being called, was wearing off. "The police have been spotted regrouping. They'll catch us like fish in a barrel here."

"No, we're being disbanded and reassigned to other battalions."

And "We're going down to reinforce Dublin." That rumour was the most prevalent.

The coughing sputter of the motorbike had everyone watching when Mulcahy returned and spoke to Ashe. After a short discussion between the two of them, Ashe called everyone together for a briefing.

The men gathered close together to hear what was coming.

The smell of a week's worth of unwashed bodies mingled with the damp wool of their jackets and the acrid smell of turf smoke. Emmet inhaled as he glanced around the group. It was a unique smell of this moment, of this group. And Emmet knew that he would remember it always.

Ashe took a deep breath, his face a frowning mask before he spoke. "Men. The orders are in. Lieutenant Mulcahy has verified the orders, so there's no point in denying them or protesting."

The man standing beside Emmet shifted uneasily from foot to foot.

Ashe continued. "I have here an order, signed by our Commander-in-Chief, Padraig Pearse, instructing us to surrender."

A moan of pain and disbelief went through the group.

Ashe held up his hand. "I will read the order in full."

Emmet looked at his father and saw tears running down his face. It was the first time he had ever seen his father cry. Emmet felt a sob building in his own throat and swallowed hard, listening as Ashe read.

In order to prevent further slaughter of the civil population and in the hope of saving the lives of our followers, the members of the Provisional Government present at headquarters have decided on an unconditional surrender, and commandants or officers commanding districts will order their commands to lay down arms.

Ashe now looked up, took a deep breath and gulped, his Adam's apple jumping visibly. "The order is signed P.H. Pearse, Dublin, this twenty-ninth day of April, 1916."

One of the Volunteers shouted out. "Feck it! That's all right for Dublin City, but why do we need to surrender?"

Ashe straightened his shoulders, his moment of deep emotion conquered. "Because our Commander-In-Chief has ordered it."

A rumble went through the group; men muttered protests and folded their arms across their chests, scowling.

Ashe continued. "What we have accomplished will be written in history. The Fifth Battalion has done the Republic proud, and you, each and every one of you, will hold your head high as we follow our orders. Know that we will fight another day and know that one day complete and absolute victory will be ours when we see our children and grandchildren live as free Irishmen and women."

Ashe turned to Mulcahy. Everyone could hear as Ashe ordered him to go and arrange the surrender to the British cavalry.

Ashe ordered the Section leaders to form up their sections to await their official surrender.

Liam stopped beside Emmet as they were moving into place. "It's a fecking fiasco. We should just get the hell out of here now, before the Brits show up."

Emmet shook his head. "You go if you want to, but I'll do as my Commander-In-Chief orders."

Liam grimaced and moved away to join his section.

They were told to sit in formation and wait. Emmet was glad he was in the same Section as his father and Kevin. His stomach was twisting. *What now? What happens now? Will they shoot us for treason?*

It seemed hours, but wasn't, before the ground vibrated with the approach of boots on the ground.

Ashe came out of the barn with his briefcase. The weapons and ammunition had already been gathered and were stacked ready to be confiscated.

Ashe nodded to the section leaders.

The orders rang out. "Men, *atten-tion*."

Everyone rose and stood straight, arms by their sides.

The Lawless brothers each turned, backs to their sections, to face the enemy now coming towards them with rifles and fixed bayonets.

Emmet heard the man behind him mutter. "Just yesterday we were the ones taking prisoners." His voice was dazed as if he couldn't imagine how this turn of events had happened.

They watched as Ashe and Mulcahy officially surrendered to the senior British officer, and then the order was given to "Quick, march."

During the long march to Richmond Barracks in Dublin, Emmet's mind jumped from one thought to another. Small details took on great importance as his brain tried to come to grips with his arrest. *What will happen to my bicycle? It'll be stolen probably. Will Mam be told?* He tried to think of what his classmates would be working on during the coming week. He tried everything to keep the fear from gripping him. *Now what? Now what?*

As they approached Dublin, Emmet's fear gave way to shock as citizens of Dublin City jeered them. Children ran alongside, laughing and pointing. Women shouted "Youse ought to be ashamed."

We fought for them. How can they act this way? Don't they want to live as free Irish citizens? Emmet felt the fear melt away from him to be replaced by anger. *What's wrong with them?* He pushed back his shoulders. Ashe had told them to hold their heads high.

By God I will.

They marched on, approaching the high, grey-mottled stone walls of the barracks. As he marched under the high archway leading into the barracks courtyard, he slanted his eyes to the man marching beside him. Emmet could see that he too, marched with his chin up, his cap square on his head. Emmet felt his heart contract. *I love these men. Whatever happens, we did it for the right reasons and that will get me through.*

4

Richmond Barracks, Dublin, May 1916

In the two weeks following the internment of the Fingal Volunteers, Emmet learned more about Irish history than he had in his entire eleven years of schooling. He listened in awe to men like Eamon de Valera as they talked of their experience during the days of the Rising. de Valera had been at Boland's Mill. Like the Fifth Battalion, he hadn't believed the surrender order.

"When O'Connor and I got the message, I sent Elizabeth O'Farrell out again to get the order counter-signed by my own Commanding Officer. She went, God love her, but even without MacDonagh's signature we were forced to believe it when we heard the silence falling everywhere."

Emmet and Liam sat cross-legged in the warm sun of the courtyard. The sun didn't last long. The tall stone walls on four sides made the space gloomy and damp for most of the day, but for these moments, Emmet couldn't think of a better place to be.

They talked of the tragedy following the surrender. de Valera shook his head. "Pearse, Clarke and MacDonagh. All gone now. The bastards will pay one day for shooting them."

Day after day, more men were taken out to Kilmainham Jail to be executed. And then, on May eighth, de Valera, Ashe and four others were taken for trial.

Emmet walked around the large yard with his father. "Da, what do you think will happen? Will they execute all of us?"

His father draped his arm around Emmet's shoulders and gave him a quick hug. "No, they won't. They're going after all the leaders, but the rest of us will have to do time."

Emmet turned his head to look in his father's face. "So far everyone that gets taken away never comes back."

"I know. It's hard to see. You have to stay strong, son."

When his father dropped his arm again, Emmet felt the loss of the connection. "You're not considered a leader, sure, you aren't?"

"I'm no one's leader outside of the family, and even then, not always."

Emmet tried to smile at the weak joke. "Michael's not easily led."

"No, he never was, but it's made him into a fine, independent man."

By the end of that day they got the news. Both Ashe and de Valera sentenced to death. They were taken to Kilmainham Jail to await their execution.

The men left at Richmond Barracks had little appetite for their supper. For the Fingal Volunteers, this was now very personal as Ashe, their leader, the man they had all known and with whom they had fought side-by-side, waited to die. As he sat with the others at a long table in the mess hall, Emmet found he could hardly choke down his bread when he thought of Ashe saying his last prayers in Kilmainham Jail.

Liam tried to talk to Emmet. "What do you think he's thinking about?"

Emmet shrugged, unable to even talk.

"Would he be thinking of his family, or about the Cause?"

Emmet stood and walked away from friend. "I don't know, Liam. I can't bear to think of it."

Emmet looked up as Kevin came striding into the room. The excitement on his brother's face had the small groups of two and threes all turn to hear what Kevin had to say.

"The sentence has been changed."

"What? What's happened?" the demands for more news went around as they crowded close to Kevin.

"I just heard it from one of the guards. Ashe, de Valera and the others. It's been changed to penal servitude for life."

Men crossed themselves in thanks. "What's changed?" One of the Volunteers looked to Kevin for the answer.

"The guard told me that there's been a huge backlash after the executions. The British government is afraid to execute any more prisoners." Kevin shrugged. "That's what the guard said, anyway."

Some of the men left to try and discover more information. Emmet joined Kevin as the crowd thinned. "Do you think that's an end to the executions, Kevin?"

"It's impossible to know. Tomorrow they could change their minds again, but it wouldn't surprise me. Remember we've been hearing that people are starting to complain?"

Emmet nodded. Someone usually managed to get their hands on a newspaper which would make the rounds amongst the internees, so they had read reports of a changing attitude amongst Dubliners. Where they had made cups of tea for the British soldiers during the week of the rising, they were now coming out to protest.

"Ashe is safe. And de Valera. It's great news."

Kevin nodded. "They'll be here to lead us into the next phase of the revolution."

Emmet frowned. "They can hardly do that from jail."

Kevin smiled. "You think not? Wait and see, little brother."

Emmet felt more hopeful and went in search of Liam. He stepped out into the yard. Near the end, by the gates, a crowd gathered. He frowned. Visitors were allowed between eleven in the morning and one in the afternoon. By now they should all be gone. He quickened his pace and joined the edge of the gathering crowd.

He craned to see what was in the centre of the group. "What's going on?"

A burly man in a flat cap spoke over his shoulder to answer Emmet's question. "Fight."

Emmet started to back away. He'd seen enough fighting for now, but then he heard a shout of encouragement. "Come on, Liam! That's it."

Liam. It might be another man with the same name, but Emmet felt his stomach churn. He pushed his way forward despite the complaints and shoves he received.

Oh God, no. It is Liam. He wanted to call out to him to stop but knew it would be hopeless. He could only wait until it was over and try to offer his friend comfort.

Liam stood with his fists raised, his lip already cut and bleeding, his cap in the dust nearby. "You bastard. You'd sell out your own mother, wouldn't you?"

Liam's opponent was taller and older, but he was thin, with bad buckteeth, giving him the look of a weasel.

The weasel-man jabbed at Liam. "I didn't sell out anyone."

"I saw you. You were getting all cozy with the guards." Liam jerked his head towards one of the guards standing close by, whose rifle with fixed bayonet rested casually on the ground. Beside him stood another guard. It seemed to Emmet that the two were making bets on the outcome of the fight, and they weren't alone. This was great sport in a place where boredom reigned.

Liam danced around the weasel-man, bouncing from foot to foot and suddenly he moved in. He struck a fist into the man's stomach. A sympathetic groan rumbled through the crowd as the thin man doubled over with a grunt of pain. Liam kneed him in the face while the man was bent over, but instead of striking the nose, the man turned at the last second, taking the blow on the side of his jaw. He straightened quickly, taking Liam by surprise and then it was Liam's face taking the blows. The weasel man punched and then struck again, ignoring the spurt of blood exploding from Liam's nose. Liam fell back, but the weasel-man clutched at him with his left arm, using his right fist to smack him again and one more time before Liam crumpled. Weasel-man aimed a kick at Liam's ribs and then the guard stepped in.

"All right. That's enough. Disperse now. Fun's over."

Slowly men in the crowd exchanged cigarettes and coins, conceding that despite Liam's youth and strength, he had lost.

Most men wandered away, but one older man stood watching as Liam struggled to his feet. Emmet was about to rush forward, and the man gripped his arm. "Is he your pal?"

Emmet nodded, wanted to shake the man free to go and help Liam.

"He's a good scrapper but needs some finesse. If he wants some tips, tell him to come see me. I'm in F Block. George Noble Plunkett."

Emmet's eyes widened. "Count Plunkett? Joseph Plunkett's father?"

He nodded.

Emmet put out his hand to shake the older man's. "I'm so sorry about your son, Sir. He was a hero to us all."

"Thank you." He closed his eyes and paused for an instant before he continued. My other boys, Jack and George can do some training with your friend if he's interested."

Emmet looked at Liam where he stood dizzily weaving, looking for his cap. "I'll tell him."

The man walked away, and Emmet went to help Liam back to his cot. "Liam. What was that all about?"

Liam wiped the blood from his face with his sleeve and spoke though swelling lips. "That bastard is getting favours from the guards for information. I've been watching him, and I've seen him get cigarettes and food from the guards. He's a grass."

"Jaysus Liam. It's not your job to deal with him."

"Why not? I'm the one that's seen him. It's my job just as much as anyone's."

Emmet kept his arm around Liam as his friend tried to pull away in his rage. "Ah, you're right of course. Listen now while I tell you about this fella that was watching you."

Liam slumped back to lean on Emmet as they made their way down to their block. "Who?"

"Only Joseph Plunkett's father."

Liam stopped and looked into Emmet's face. "Go away."

"Yup. He said for me to tell you that you're a great scrapper and he and his two sons can give you some tips."

Liam pulled away again and straightened. "Where is he? Where do I find him?"

Emmet put his hand on Liam's back and nudged him towards their barracks. "Not now. Tomorrow. He's in F Block."

Over the next few days Liam's bruises slowly healed, although he earned a few new ones from the daily training with the Plunkett boys. Emmet went along and enjoyed talking to Count Plunkett while the training went on in the yard. The older man and Emmet talked about the future of the political landscape in Ireland, while Liam learned the art of delivering an upper cut and a hook.

On May 13th, Emmet, Liam and Kevin were all released and told to go home.

A few of the older Volunteers who had farms to run were also released. Emmet hugged his brother Michael and then his father. "Da, I'll write to you and let you know how everything is."

His father stood back and gripped his son by his arms. "I expect you to go back to school. You'll help Kevin and your Ma of course, I know you will, but the main thing is that you need to keep going with your studies."

Emmet nodded. "I'll get a job to help out as well."

"That'll be grand. As long as your studies come first. Promise me now."

"I promise."

His father drew him close in one more hug. "That's for your Mam, now. You give her that from me."

Emmet swallowed hard. "I will, Da."

Kevin nudged Emmet. "We're going now."

They joined the men marching out under guard. Over the sound of their boots on cobblestones, Emmet heard his father call out. "God Bless, boys."

His bicycle hadn't been stolen after all. After the surrender, locals had gathered together to return any personal belongings to their homes. Emmet and Kevin saw their bicycles in their rightful places as they walked up the garden path.

The door flew open and their mother burst out, pulling her apron up to wipe her tears. "Oh, thank you, God for returning my boys to me."

She grabbed each of them around the neck and pulled them down, Kevin and Emmet knocking heads as they were gripped in a vice-like embrace. They stood like that for a few seconds, the three of them hunched into a bundle. Over her shoulder, Emmet could see Liam hesitating by the garden gate, not moving as he watched the reunion.

Emmet pulled himself free, leaving Kevin to continue to comfort their mother.

Emmet called out to Liam. "Did you want to come in for a cuppa before going home?"

Liam seemed to consider it before shaking his head. "I better get on."

Emmet was glad. He wanted to rest in the comfort of his own family and just his family. "Right, then."

Liam waved and walked on with slow steps, as if reluctant to leave the joyful celebration in the Ryan home.

Kathleen led the way into the house. "Come in, boys and tell me everything. Oh, I had so hoped that all four of you would be coming together, but I'm so pleased to see the two of you anyway."

As his mother was putting on the kettle, Emmet stooped down to give her another hug. "That's from Da. He told me to deliver that to you."

Her eyes filled with tears again. "Are they all right? They aren't being beaten or anything?"

Kevin was setting cups out on the table. "Mam, they're fine. Look at us two. Not a mark on us and Da and Michael are just the same."

She turned her back to them as she fussed with the teapot. "I've been that worried over you all."

Emmet rubbed her back. "We know, Mam."

Kathleen sliced thick cuts of bread and set them out, along with butter and a dish of strawberry jam.

She poured out the tea and the boys dug in.

Between mouthfuls, Kevin prodded his mother. "So, tell us all the news from the outside world."

She took a sip of her tea. "It's a terrible business. So many lives destroyed. That man, James Connolly, so injured that he was executed in a chair. Shocking. Absolutely shocking. And what's to happen now to your Da and Michael?"

Kevin shook his head. "We don't know, Mam. It looks like they're trying to empty out Richmond Barracks, so they'll probably be moved somewhere else."

"What's to become of us? I've only been managing with the help of neighbours and the little emergency fund your Da and I had put by."

Kevin put his hand over hers. "Emmet and I are going to look after things until Da and Michael come back home. Don't you worry."

Emmet's mother turned to look at him. "What about school?"

"I'll have some catching up to do, but I will."

She nodded and pursed her lips. "Then I best get on with ironing your uniform for tomorrow."

Emmet was about to protest and tell her to relax, but he caught the warning look from Kevin. Kevin patted her on the arm. "That's a good idea, Mam. We better all get on with things. I'm going to run down to talk to Mr. McNamara to see if he needs any extra hands on the job site."

Emmet stood as well. "Kev, ask him for me as well, will you? I can come right after school if he's got anything."

"I'll check. Meanwhile you better pop down to school and see if you can get the assignments you've missed."

Emmet nodded. Only two years older than Emmet, Kevin was donning his mantle of responsibility like a cloak.

They settled into their new lives. Kevin worked full time and Emmet part time. Kathleen got a dozen turkey chicks to raise. "They'll be great to sell at Christmas."

The three of them went about their business, trying not to speak too often about those in internment. Instead they had more general discussions about the state of Ireland, and the support it was getting, especially from the United States.

Liam had left school and worked on a farm, but he routinely came over after the weekly hurling match on Sundays.

Liam felt that the Americans would be their saviours. "I'm going there one day. Did ya read in the paper about the pressures the Americans are putting on Britain to release the prisoners?"

Emmet nodded. "But how much power do they really have? They can complain and protest, but at the end of the day, the Brits always do as they please."

"The Brits will listen to the Americans. They want the Yankee munitions to fight the war in France."

Liam was right in that. Emmet picked up the newspaper from the previous week. "There's a great bit in the paper about American-Irish groups pressuring their own government to do something about the 'Irish problem.'"

Liam took the paper from Emmet. "I wish I could get over there. I think I have some second cousin or something in Boston."

Emmet shook his head. "You don't even know them. How could you go so far away from everyone you care about?"

"*Hmph*. Easy. I could be doing something better over there."

"Better, how?"

"This farm work is desperate. I need something more interesting."

"Maybe you should be thinking about going back to school?"

"That's not the answer." Liam hurried to add "It's fine for you. You like studying. I'm no good at it."

Liam sighed. "The battle of Ashbourne, 'twas grand, wasn't it? Do you remember how they just threw down their weapons when they knew they were beaten?"

Emmet smiled and opened his text book. "I do."

Liam sat back, his eyes glazed. "I could have taken some more shots if there hadn't been a ceasefire."

Emmet glanced at his friend. "Liam, I really need to study."

Liam grimaced, stood and wandered away, hands stuffed in his pockets.

―――――

The turkeys were ready, and all had been reserved by neighbours, aside for one Kathleen was keeping for their own Christmas dinner.

She threw out a handful of corn to the birds and they clamoured around her looking for more. For most of their lives they simply grazed in the back garden, eating grass, weeds and whatever, but now, as Christmas approached she had taken to supplementing their diet.

Emmet stood watching. "It'll be hard to part with them, I'm thinking."

Kathleen turned and saw her son watching. She wiped her hands on her apron and came to stand with him. "The secret is to not give them names."

He smiled. "Which one is ours?"

She pointed to the smallest. "With only the three of us, we won't need a big one."

Emmet was sorry he had mentioned it. He put his arm around her shoulder. "Come on inside, Mam. It's cold out here."

They went in and Emmet sat at the kitchen table while Kathleen put on the kettle for a pot of tea. Emmet picked up the newspaper from December 7th, a couple of days previously. "So Lloyd George is the new Prime Minister."

"Will it make any difference to us?"

Emmet had taken to reading everything about history and politics that he could lay his hands on and had become the family expert.

"It might. He's spoken in favour of Home Rule. Mind you it's a coalition, so he may not get much done."

She sniffed. "They're all the same to me."

"We have to stay positive, Mam, otherwise what's it all for?"

Kathleen nodded. "That's a good question."

———

The days went by and Christmas came closer. Kevin and Emmet delivered the turkeys as everyone made ready for the holiday.

Two days before Christmas Emmet was trying to convince Kathleen that they should do some decorating. "We always gather holly, Mam. We should keep up the traditions."

She was staring out of the kitchen window looking at the grey fields behind the house. "I don't have the heart for it. You and Kevin go on."

"Kevin doesn't have time. Come on, Mam."

"No, honestly. I'm that tired I just couldn't think of it."

They had been so engrossed in their conversation that neither had heard the front door open. From behind them a voice had them swivelling in shock.

"That's a fine welcome home for a man and his son, when there isn't a decoration to be seen."

Kathleen threw her arms out, reaching for her husband as she ran the few steps to cross the room. "Dear God, are you really here?"

Emmet was right behind his mother and reached out to hug his brother Michael as his mother and father stood embracing each other, she, sobbing against his chest.

Emmet felt the bony hardness of his brother that seven months in prison had wrought. "How is it possible? How are you here?"

Kathleen stepped back and put her hand to her mouth. "You didn't escape, sure you didn't?"

Michael grinned. "Don't worry, Mam. You aren't harbouring fugitives."

She touched her husband's arm. "Ned, tell me."

"Hush, Kathleen. You haven't heard then. Lloyd George has declared a Christmas amnesty and any one of us who weren't out-and-out leaders have been released."

She crossed herself then. "It's a Christmas miracle."

Emmet felt his own tears clog his throat. "It is, Mam."

She whirled then and scurried around the kitchen heating up some soup and getting the kettle going.

The three men sat and talked about all that had happened since they had last seen each other. His father looked Emmet up and down. "You're a bit thin. You're still at the studies I hope?"

Emmet laughed. "I am still at the studies, and that's the pot calling the kettle black, saying that I'm thin."

Kathleen set some food down in front of her husband and oldest son. "We'll start fattening you up again immediately."

She turned to Emmet. "Run down to meet Kevin to make sure he doesn't delay coming home."

Emmet nodded, grabbed his jacket from the hook by the door and threw his cap on. As he mounted his bicycle to go down and head Kevin off before his brother settled in to the pub after work, he threw a glance back at the house. *It's a home again.*

He cycled almost all the way to Kevin's job site before he saw his brother coming towards him.

Kevin saw him approach. "What is it? What's wrong?"

Emmet grinned. "Nothing wrong but we've got a full house and Mam wants you home."

Kevin put his feet down while he waited for Emmet to get his bike turned around. "So who's there that I'm needed in such a panic?"

Emmet considered drawing it out but couldn't. "It's Da and Michael. They're home."

Kevin's eyes widened. "The amnesty. It's true, then?"

Emmet nodded. "It is. They got out early this morning and walked the whole way. They've only just arrived."

Kevin pushed hard on the pedals and took off in a spit of gravel.

Emmet laughed and pushed himself to keep up with his brother.

Kevin's breath was short with the exertion, but still he shouted out questions. "Are they all right?"

"Seem to be."

"And in their spirits?"

"They're happy to be home. That's all I could tell so far."

Emmet cautioned as they turned into their own gate. "They're skinny as rakes and are shaggy looking. Mam'll have the hair clippers at them by tomorrow, I'll bet."

Kevin dropped his bicycle at the front door and flung the door open. Emmet parked his bike and then picked up Kevin's and parked it as well.

Emmet could hear Kevin through the open door. "Da! Michael! By God, it's good to see you both!"

Emmet came into the kitchen and saw his father giving Kevin a hug. Michael was patting Kevin's shoulder while his mother stood by the cooker watching the scene with tears running down her cheeks.

It was over. For her at least, it was over.

5

Ashbourne, December 1918

Emmet was home from college for the Christmas break. The elections were coming up in two days; the first elections in eight years and the newspapers were full of news about it.

Supper was finished, but they all continued to sit in the kitchen, as usual; Emmet and Kevin at the table with the newspaper in front of them, Michael and his Da on the old horsehair settee under the window and Mam in a chair by the cooker, mending. Emmet was reading pieces out of the paper to the family. "It says here that it's expected that the number of people eligible to vote in Ireland this time has gone up from seven hundred thousand to about two million. Damn, I wish I was older."

Kathleen responded automatically. "No need to curse, Emmet."

"Sorry, Mam."

Kevin nodded. "How do you think I feel? A couple more months I'll be 21 and I'd be able to vote. As it is I'll have to wait."

Michael grinned. "Poor boys. Never mind, I'll cast my vote for you both."

Emmet turned to his father. "Will de Valera get anywhere, do you think?"

Ned shrugged. "I think he will. At the annual conference he was elected leader of the party with great support all around."

Emmet sighed and tossed the paper aside. "He's a great favourite around the college."

Kathleen looked up at the mention of college. "When will you get your exam results?"

Emmet stood and went to look at the calendar on the kitchen wall. "They're supposed to be mailed out this week, so probably next week."

Michael picked up the discarded newspaper. "It'll be a competition in the Ryan house to see what's a bigger news item – the election results or Emmet's exam results."

Ned frowned. "Just because you only have politics and women on your mind doesn't mean you should scoff."

Michael flushed. "I'm not. Emmet, you know I'm just taking the mickey."

Emmet smiled. "I do, of course."

Michael stood. "Speaking of women, I'm away to the church dance. Anyone going with me?"

Kathleen furrowed her brow. "Are you sure it's still on? I heard they might cancel it, on account of the influenza. So many people are getting it."

Michael nodded. "It's desperate, all right. I saw Father Kenney earlier and he said they were going ahead but there may be no one there."

Kevin stood. "I might as well."

"Emmet?"

"No, I told Liam I'd go down and have a pint with him."

Kathleen raised her eyebrows. "He's home, then?"

"He is."

"Well that's a blessing."

Michael pulled on his jacket. "We may join you if the dance is a bust. Will you ould ones be all right without us?"

His mother threw a sock at Michael. "Go on. Ould ones indeed."

The boys all went outside together. Emmet watched his brothers walk away and then climbed onto his bicycle to go in the opposite direction to Ashbourne House for a pint with Liam.

Emmet shook the few snow flurries from his cap after he parked his bike in the courtyard in front of the long two-storey white building. He went in through the arched doorway and wheeled left to go through to bar. The lounge, where women were permitted, was on the right, but he knew he was most likely to find

Liam in the men-only bar. He looked around and spied Liam sitting on his own in the corner by the fireplace.

"Liam. Great to see you."

Liam rose, reached over and punched Emmet lightly in the shoulder. "And you."

Emmet nodded to the half pint of Guinness that sat in front of Liam. "Are you ready for another?"

Liam lifted the glass and drank most of the contents without taking a breath. "Make it a pint."

Emmet smiled and shook his head. "Sure."

Liam was thinner than when Emmet had last seen him. He had hollows below his eyes and his cheeks were sunken. His red mop of hair looked faded. *It's hard to imagine he's been in the British army over in France. Do I talk about it or just carry on as if nothing's happened?*

When Emmet brought back the two drinks he saluted Liam with his glass. "Good luck."

Liam nodded and clinked his glass to Emmet's. "Sláinte"

Emmet took a deep breath. "You were de-mobbed pretty quickly. How did you manage that?"

Liam shrugged. "I was already in England in November, so that bumped me up. Maybe they wanted rid of the Paddies as quick as possible."

Emmet frowned. "Why were you in England?"

Liam hesitated before setting his glass down. He shoved the sweater sleeve on his left arm up and Emmet saw an angry red scar running from the elbow up towards the shoulder. There was a puckered one-inch indentation in his forearm with white lines spidering off around his arm.

Emmet blinked. "Oh my God."

Liam pulled down his sleeve again.

"Jaysus. What happened?"

"Shrapnel."

Emmet had a childish desire to touch it, the partially healed hole. "You're lucky you didn't lose the arm, I guess."

Liam nodded. "Believe me, this is nothing compared to the other fellows in the hospital."

Emmet shook his head. "Was it worth it? I know you went because you were broke, but at the end of it all, was it really worth it?" Emmet clenched his fist on the table. Every time he thought about Liam joining the British army, he felt the bile rise in his throat.

Liam grinned and Emmet took a deep breath as he saw his boyhood pal in Liam's face again.

Liam lowered his voice. "The Brits taught me some great skills. Luckily it was my left arm injured and not my right. I'll have to use something other than my left arm as a prop if I'm doing any target practice in the near future, but I was one of the squad's best snipers."

Emmet smiled. "I was afraid you'd have changed."

"Not me, boyo. Listen, the dosh I sent home kept Mam going, and I put some away as well. Between that and the pension the Brits are so kind as to give me, I'm free to get on with my real business, so yes. It was worth it."

Liam stood. "You want another one?"

"Go on."

When he returned, already taking a sip as he walked back to the table, Liam clearly wanted to change the subject. "So, you're looking very scholarly these days. Are you enjoying University College Dublin?"

Emmet nodded. "I am. I meet interesting people with great ideas."

Liam laughed. "There's no shortage of great ideas in Ireland."

Emmet frowned. "I mean ideas that can really make a difference. Writers and people studying law."

"Tell me again what you're going to do with all this education?"

"I plan to be a journalist."

"Oh yeh. That's right. I remember now."

Emmet narrowed his eyes at the sound of Liam's voice. The slight sneer he felt in the tone. "I know college wouldn't be for you, but I like it."

Liam shrugged. "I was always more of an action-oriented person".

There was an awkward silence as they ran out of words. The easy camaraderie of their boyhood had been left behind in the trenches of France.

"We're not all like you, Liam."

Liam sat back with his arms resting on the table. "Very true."

Emmet felt the flush rise in his face. "I'm not a coward." He knew his voice was raised when the fellows at the next table both turned to glance over.

Liam frowned. "I didn't say you were. Don't read so much into everything. You do your bit and I do mine."

Emmet finished his pint. Liam stood as Emmet did. "Are you leaving already?"

"Yes, I'm beat, and I said I'd help Da cut turf tomorrow."

"Your soft hands won't find that easy."

Emmet forced a smile. "You're right, so I better at least get a good night's sleep."

Liam stuck his hand out. "Will you shake the hand of a former British soldier?"

Emmet cocked his head at the uncertainty in Liam's voice. He suddenly understood that Liam's comments were more bravado than insults aimed at Emmet. He shook Liam's hand. "Of course. We're still friends, Liam, no matter how much I don't agree with what you did. It's in the past now."

Liam nodded. "I'm glad. You're more like a brother to me than my brother is."

Liam followed him outside and they both stopped as the cold air engulfed them.

Emmet shivered. "Jaysus. I should have had a pish before I left."

Liam tugged on Emmet's sleeve and steered him into the deep shadows between the hotel wall and the house next door. Emmet smiled and closed his eyes as the two of them stood side by side and relieved themselves in the peace of the dark snowy night. *We're taking different paths, but we're connected for life.*

———

The election was over, and Emmet was ecstatic.

He and his father sat side-by-side at the table reading the results from the paper. Emmet pointed to the final numbers. "Can you believe it? Sinn Féin won seventy-three seats out of a hundred and five."

His father shook his head. No one in the Ryan household needed the explanation that this party, which literally meant 'We Ourselves', had never had a significant role to play in the political landscape of Ireland.

"It's unbelievable. You see, lad, mighty oaks from little acorns grow."

"You mean that the Easter Rising didn't look like it achieved much when it happened, but now we're seeing the results, right?"

Ned nodded. "The country's with us now."

Emmet leaned his elbows on the table, hunched over the paper to read every word again. "A hundred and four men and one woman. Brilliant, isn't it?"

"It is indeed. Now we'll really see the republic stand up on the world stage as a country separate from Britain."

"Sinn Féin will work with the British parliament to move Ireland's independence, won't they?"

Ned smiled. "They will, of course. It's just a matter of time now."

Emmet folded up the paper to save it. "It'll be a great Christmas and New Year this year."

———

Emmet was back in school, so he was in Dublin for the historical first meeting of the Irish Parliament on the twenty-first of January. The Sinn Féin members had refused to take their seats in the Parliament of the United Kingdom, instead meeting in the Mansion House in Dublin.

Emmet knew this day would be extraordinary. He barely felt the cold wind ghosting around the great stones of the university. In the gardens behind Earlsfort Terrace, he grabbed the arm of Sean Flynn, his friend from his Social History class. "And did you get in to listen to the speeches?"

Sean grinned. "I was right there in the Round Room when the Proclamation was read out."

"You're a lucky man. I wish I could have been there."

"I'll try and get you a part-time job with me on the paper. That'll get you places in the future."

"That'd be grand. Tell me again what you heard."

Sean flipped open his notebook. "I tried to scribble as much as I could. They said there'll be copies printed out that we can get later, so I'll be sure to get you one."

Emmet nodded, still waiting to hear some of the words that Sean had heard.

Sean stopped and turned to face Emmet, reading from his notes "Here's a piece I liked:

"to ensure peace at home and goodwill with all nations and to constitute a national policy based upon the people's will with equal right and equal opportunity for every citizen

Emmet nodded, repeating some of the words. "peace at home and goodwill with all nations"

Sean went on. "Or how about this: "we ask His divine blessing on this the last stage of the struggle we have pledged ourselves to carry through to Freedom"

Sean's voice was choked with emotion by the end.

Emmet patted his arm and they resumed walking. "Isn't it fantastic to be a part of it and to know that from here on, we'll be united as a republic?"

Sean nodded. "It is, my friend. It surely is."

———

Emmet joined the Literary and Historical Society. This was the college's debating union, and every Saturday night members would read papers after which a debate would be held on questions of general interest. Many of the topics were of a political nature and Emmet loved being a part of it all. On his first night, he met his mentor.

The red-haired student looked very young. His chin showed no sign of a beard yet. "Hiya. I'm Frank Flood."

Emmet shook his hand. "I'm Emmet Ryan."

The handsome boy grinned. "I'm going to teach you everything you need to know about debating."

Emmet gave a mock salute. "I'm ready to learn. I haven't seen you in class. What are you studying?"

"Engineering. I hear you're taking up the pen."

Emmet nodded. "I am."

Frank told Emmet how to get to his house, and as he walked away, Emmet thought: *This is going to be fun.*

At times Frank would come to Emmet's room and on other days Emmet would go to Frank's family home. Even though Frank's father was a policeman, the Flood family were passionately republican.

One Friday evening they were in Emmet's room. Frank stood as he demonstrated the nuances of the art of debating. "See, you always make your key point first and then you continue to enumerate all the other points." His back was straight, and he used his hands to accentuate his points. He continued: "First I'd like to assert, as we have heard from the paper just presented, that Daniel O'Connell is the greatest Irish leader this country has ever known. He has not been named 'The Liberator' on a whim."

Frank turned to Emmet. "You see. Be strong. Make your statement with all your heart. And then follow it up."

Emmet nodded. "I can do that bit. It's when I have to rebut that I get a bit flummoxed."

"Right. So when your man on the other side goes through his argument to assert that Charles Stewart Parnell is in fact the greatest leader, here's what you do." Frank stood with his head down slowly shaking it.

Emmet grinned.

As if he had finished listening to someone speaking, Frank straightened. "I wonder if you realize that..and then you go on to get your point in. Don't be rude of course, but don't let him away with it."

The two young men opened bottles of beer that Emmet had brought in for the evening to go along with some cheese and brown bread. Emmet had heard rumours that Frank was part of the Dublin Brigade of the IRA but didn't want to ask. Instead, he asked about someone else. "You're friends with Kevin Barry, aren't you?"

Frank's face was quizzical. Kevin Barry was known to be active in the IRA. He only hesitated for a heartbeat. "He's a sound man. Yes, I'm proud to say we are good friends."

Emmet nodded. "I was with the Fingal Volunteers in '16."

Frank brightened. "Were you? They have a great reputation. Ah, the Easter Rebellion was only one small battle in the fight, wasn't it, Emmet?"

"So it seems."

"The past couple of years haven't brought us much closer, but as long as there are men like Barry, you and me who will continue the struggle, we'll get there in the end."

Emmet was quiet for a moment. "It's why I've gone into journalism. I hope to inspire and challenge, using my words."

Frank nodded slowly. "Words may not be enough, my friend." He drained his bottle of beer. "Come. Let's give you some practice at oration so you can shine tomorrow night for your first public debate."

6

Dublin, November 1920

Emmet settled into the warmth of Davy Byrne's snug, off Grafton Street. He nodded to Liam. "Hard to believe it's been almost a year since I saw you."

Liam shook back the hair that flopped into his eyes. His eyes shifted around the pub, watchful in a way he never was before.

Emmet picked up the pint that Liam set in front of him. "Cheers. So what have you been doing with yourself since I last saw you?"

Liam shrugged. "This and that."

Emmet shook his head and heard the sarcasm in his own voice. "Are you telling me that your new skills are useful?"

"Michael Collins thinks so."

Emmet took a long swallow of Guinness. "It doesn't bother you that you may run into some of your old Regimental pals?"

"I didn't make any pals. I just did my job and took my money."

Emmet studied Liam. The slim boy of their youth had long since disappeared. This man was tough, and there was something Emmet couldn't put his finger on. Something he didn't quite trust or understand. There was a darkness in Liam's eyes instead of the mischievous sparkle he had always known.

Changing the topic, he waved his hand in the direction of Liam's home. "So, are you back living at home?"

Liam shrugged. "I go where I'm wanted. Now I'm home, but tomorrow I could be on my way to Belfast. Yes, I'm a wanted man now." His mouth crooked in a sardonic grin. He took a deep sip of the pint.

Emmet took a sip of his own and then set it down, determined not to try and keep up with Liam. "It was a sad day in September when the Dáil Éireann was declared illegal", using the Irish name for the parliament.

Liam nodded. "You had to know letting us keep our parliament wasn't going to be easy. None of this is easy."

Emmet sighed. "I know. I'm writing part-time for the paper now. I know it isn't easy, but still, it's disappointing."

Liam up-ended his pint and finished it. "You can fight the fight with your pen and leave the hard work to men like me."

Emmet flushed. "This again. I'm prepared to fight if necessary."

Liam bit his lip. "I know you are. Sorry. I got carried away there."

Emmet nodded to the empty glass. "You're ready for another?"

"Why not?"

Emmet went to the bar to get a pint for Liam and a half pint for himself.

Liam took the glass and clinked it against Emmet's. "Don't mind me. You're my friend and I have few enough real friends. I didn't mean any harm."

Emmet nodded. "I know. And I know that it may look like I'm not in the fight any more, but there are more ways to get the message across than with a gun."

"You're right, of course."

"I'm not sure my brother always agrees with me. He's more like you. He thinks action is what's wanted, not words."

"Ah, yes. Did I hear that Kevin's gone to Cork?"

"Yes. He went down for the funeral of Tomas MacCurtain in March and hasn't come back yet."

Liam drummed his fingers on the table. "The murder of the Lord Mayor of Cork won't go unanswered."

Emmet nodded. "Yes, that was terrible, and now things are heating up even more with all these new RIC recruits that are arriving from England every day."

"You mean the Black and Tans?"

Emmet nodded. "I've heard them called that."

Liam grinned. "At least they make themselves easy to spot in those uniforms."

Emmet sighed. "I thought this would be the year that we'd see some real progress. Now that we have a parliament in Dublin and even courts, but it's like we have one step forward and then two steps back when you hear about the rioting in Belfast."

"They're a different kettle of fish altogether."

Emmet raised his eyebrows. "Why do you say that? Wasn't that the point? That all of Ireland should be united and that all us fish are in one kettle?"

Liam sat back in his chair studying Emmet. "You're a true believer, aren't you?"

Emmet scowled. "Aren't you?"

"I'm a believer and a realist."

"What does that mean? Have you given up on the idea of a united Ireland? Free from the tyranny of Britain?" Emmet stood up, his fists clenching.

Liam slid Emmet's drink back in front of Emmet. "Sit down and finish your pint. I'm not saying that I've given up on the idea."

Emmet sat back down. "What are you saying when you call yourself a realist?"

Liam shrugged. "I just think that a goal like that will take a long time to come about and there will be a lot of bloodshed in the meanwhile."

Emmet took a drink. He felt his racing heart slow down. "I'm not saying it will be easy."

Liam nodded. "Look, the rioting in Belfast happens every year when all the Orange parades come out and trample around. You know there's more going on there than just British presence in the city. There are men who consider themselves Irish who play along with that malarkey. It's the Protestants against the Catholics there, so whether you like it or not, they are a different situation."

Emmet had calmed down again. "Fair enough."

"Tell me what the latest news is with the football. Did I hear that Owens blew out his knee?"

They turned the conversation to sports, leaving the more contentious subjects alone. They left the pub when it closed, each taking his separate way home, leaving Emmet to think.

Why did I get so angry with Liam? I could have punched him.

Emmet relived the conversation and realized how defensive he had been when he thought that his dream was being mocked. His long-held vision of a united Ireland living in peace was a part of him.

It's like Liam was making fun of the vision and therefore making fun of me.

———

Emmet and Sean walked together along North Circular Road towards Croke Park. They'd eaten in the Arthur Conan Doyle and opted for a half-hour walk to work off the meal.

Emmet had his hands stuffed into his jacket pockets. "You'd think it was January instead of the twenty-first of November, it's that cold."

Sean laughed. "We'll get you jumping up and down at the match. You'll soon warm up."

Emmet nodded. "True. It promises to be a great game. We'd better step it out if we want to be there in time for the kick-off."

Sean lengthened his stride to keep up. "You're right. We don't want to miss a minute of Tipperary's great victory over Dublin."

Emmet snorted. "Ha. You'll be lucky."

As they got close, they had to press close to the walls of the shops to let a convoy of troops drive past.

Sean frowned. "What are they up to?"

Emmet turned to watch them drive south towards the canal end of the park. "Could be they're still nervous after all the hue and cry from Kevin Barry's execution."

Sean shook his head. "Barry'll go down in history as a martyr for the cause and it was grand that so many rioted in support, but that was three weeks ago. I don't believe they'd be out in force like this because of that."

There were other men walking along as they were, and Emmet called out to one who cursed at the passing vehicles. "What's going on? Do you know?"

"It's probably because of all the shootings this morning."

Emmet and Sean looked at each other. They had been together studying before going out for lunch. Even at the pub they had taken a table in a quiet corner and hadn't spoken to anyone other than to place their orders.

They hurried to catch up to the man. They walked on either side of him and Emmet prompted him. "We haven't heard the news. Tell us."

"Jaysus, you must be the only two in Dublin who don't know. Collins ordered the execution of somewhere around thirty British agents."

Sean crossed himself. "Good God."

Emmet's eyes were wide. "Here in Dublin?"

"Aye. All over the city."

Sean stopped. "I should get down to the paper."

Emmet looked at the gate of Croke Park. "Come to the match until half-time and then we'll both leave. Maybe I can be of some use running copy to the editors or some such."

Sean hesitated and then agreed. "Right. We'll go down to the south end so we can slip out easily at half-time."

They made their way past the ticket sellers and wove their way around to the stands near the canal end of the park.

Sean looked at his watch. "Three-ten and the match not started. This lot would be late for their own funerals."

Emmet pointed. "They're starting now. Half an hour late isn't too bad by Irish standards."

They cheered along with everyone else when the match finally got underway at three-fifteen. Much later, Emmet remembered that they enjoyed ten minutes of exciting football before he heard the first staccato *rat-tat-tat*.

Sean stood to see what was happening. It was three-twenty-five.

A volley of shots thundered from the turnstile entrance. Emmet didn't need to stand to see armed men pouring into the park. The crowd started pushing and running towards the far end gates. Panic, pure panic flamed through the crowd with a life of its own as the gunfire continued.

Sean fell over, crumpling heavily on top of Emmet. Emmet grunted and nudged Sean to move, but his friend lay heavily against him. Pushing the weight off, he looked into Sean's face and saw the staring eyes. Emmet groaned. "Oh God, oh God, oh God. Sean. Come on Sean, wake up." Emmet's mind flashed back to the vision of his father when he saw the bloom of red spreading across Sean's chest. *But Da was all right. Sean will be too.* And then Emmet knew this was different. The wide-open eyes told the story. He put his shaking fingers to Sean's neck. Nothing. No pulse. Emmet groaned, stunned, gathering close and rocking his friend's body in his arms. The rifle fire seemed to go on and on, but Emmet was frozen where he was. Others were hunched down in the stands. Fathers lay on top of their children as they tried to protect them with their own bodies. Women screamed and clung to each other.

And then it was over. The gunfire stopped after long minutes of shouting. Emmet heard someone shouting over and over, "Cease Fire! Cease Fire!"

At the other end of the park shots continued for a few seconds after the south end had stopped. The screaming and moaning continued.

Emmet laid Sean's body down, stood up and others followed suit. He took one last look at the young man, who moments earlier had been cheering and laughing. Forever after Emmet would see Sean's broken, blood-stained watch stopped at three twenty-five.

There was nothing he could do for Sean now. To his left two women were clinging to each other, bleeding. Below him a father raised himself and cradled his crying son. To his right a man sat holding his head in his hands, moaning. Emmet moved off to see to one of the women on his left who was sobbing, blood pouring from one arm.

He felt unnaturally calm. He heard his own voice as if it came from someone else. He took his handkerchief and wound it around her forearm which had a large gash. "All right, you're all right now."

Emmet gently shook another woman who was sitting close to the wounded woman. "Come, now. Your friend needs you. See to your friend now."

He moved on when he saw the dazed woman shuffle close to her friend and wrap her arm around the woman's shoulder.

Emmet moved among the wounded, trying to help as he could. On the field, a crowd of people surrounded two players. He heard a cry go up. "Hogan! They've killed Hogan." The Tipperary team ran to see to their fallen captain, but it was too late for him. Like Sean, there was nothing to be done for him.

The next hours passed in a blur. By dusk the park had been cleared out and Emmet made his way to the offices of the *Freeman's Journal,* which was the newspaper where Sean had worked.

The office was in chaos with the stories of the earlier shootings of the British agents, and now the massacre at Croke Park.

Emmet found the editor to give him the news. "Mr. Hooper, I'm sorry to tell you." He stopped to take a deep breath, the words sticking in his throat. "Sean Flynn is dead."

Patrick Hooper stared at him, running a hand through his thinning hair. "What happened?"

"We were at Croke Park."

"Dear God. And you were with him, son?"

Emmet nodded. He didn't trust himself to speak. He closed his eyes for a second and the vision of Sean's bloody watch loomed before him. He opened his eyes, and shook his head to clear the image.

Hooper put his hand on Emmet's back, propelling him into his office. He pushed Emmet onto a hard-wooden chair and then went around to his desk, pulled open a drawer and took out a bottle of whiskey. He poured out two shots into empty tea mugs and handed one to Emmet. "Here. Get this down."

Emmet took the drink and swallowed it without stopping. He coughed and felt the blood rushing to his face.

Hooper sat down across from Emmet. Tell me what happened."

Emmet opened his mouth to speak and then Hooper held up his hand. "Wait."

He stood up again and went to the door of his office. "O'Dowd. Get in here with your notebook."

A reporter came trotting in and sat in the other chair.

Hooper introduced them. "He was there. Tell me your name again?"

"Emmet Ryan."

"I've seen you around here, haven't I?"

Emmet nodded. "I sometimes work here part-time. Copy boy."

"Right. Okay, go ahead."

Emmet just stared at Hooper for a moment. "It's my fault. He wanted to come here, but I convinced him to go until half-time. It's my fault he's dead." His eyes burned, and he blinked rapidly.

Hooper held up his hand. "This is in no way your fault. Take a breath and tell us everything."

Emmet coughed and then started from the beginning as the reporter scribbled notes on Emmet's impressions, starting from when they saw the convoys going past. Retelling it brought him some peace. Putting himself into the role of journalist helped to distance himself from the events. He spoke dispassionately about the father clinging to his crying son and the woman whom he had bandaged.

Hooper and O'Dowd interrupted with questions for clarification, but otherwise let him tell it at his own pace.

Finally, when they were through, Emmet stood. "I need to reach his family. I don't know how to do that. I should send a telegram."

Hooper shook his head. "You've done enough now. We'll do that. He worked here. We've got the information on file somewhere. It's time for you to go home."

Emmet nodded. *Yes. I'll go to Ashbourne. Being with family is the only way.*

7

Dublin, March 1921

Emmet left his room on Wynnsward Park at six o'clock in the morning on Monday March 14th. It took him just over half an hour to cycle up to the north end of the city and, by then, the crowds were already gathering outside Mountjoy Gaol. He chained his bike to a post on the grounds of the Mater hospital and navigated his way on foot around the high stone walls of the prison until he could see the imposing granite-block front gates. He waved his official Freeman's Journal identity card and people grudgingly gave way until Emmet stood just to the right of the heavy black wooden doors. He saw guards peering out of the narrow, barred windows on either side of the doors. An armoured car was parked nearby, and troops stood, helmeted and with bayonets fixed, ringed along the front walls.

Women and some men too, were already sobbing. Everyone waited for the official announcement, but the crowd knew that the six prisoners were expected to hang this morning.

A man next to Emmet sucked the last of his cigarette, holding the burning end pinched between his thumb and forefinger. He dropped the butt, grinding it with unnecessary pressure, as if imagining he was stomping on one of his enemies. He picked a fragment of tobacco from his lip and flicked it away before nodding to Emmet. "Any chance for a reprieve, do you think?"

Emmet blinked, feeling his eyes burn. "Unlikely, I fear." He couldn't help himself then. He needed to talk. "I know one of them."

"Do you?"

Emmet nodded. "We're in the Literature and Historical Society at college. Frank Flood. He's only nineteen."

The man put his hand on Emmet's shoulder. "He's young. They may pardon him yet."

"Please, God."

The crowed continued to build and Emmet was separated from the man. He hadn't asked what brought him there. *I should be asking questions; making notes.* He couldn't bring himself to it. He stood, more and more squeezed as more people arrived and pressed forward.

Emmet looked at his watch again. Eight-twenty-five. A cry was raised as the gates opened. Quiet! Quiet! The noise level rose as people kept shouting for quiet.

A man in a suit read out the news. All six IRA volunteers had been hung for their activities in various ambushes. The announcement was as brief as it could be. Emmet shook his head. The man didn't detail again that Frank Flood was captured on the 21st of January when he along with four others attacked a lorry load of police in Drumcondra. There was no need, since the papers, including the Freeman's Journal, had been full of the news and would print it again after today's executions.

The piece of paper trembled in the official's hand as he read the brief announcement and then he scurried back inside, the gates slamming behind him. No one pounded on the gate. No one turned on the troops. Instead, there was a palpable sadness. A low moan washed through the people and became a swell of sound as the tears of the relatives mingled with the taking up of a rosary.

Emmet fingered the beads in his own pocket, tears sliding down his cheeks unashamedly. His heart seemed to throb in harmony with the prayers. The image of Frank; the sharp parting in his fair hair, and the ever-present half smile, filled his mind.

The troops began to nudge and push against the crowd. "Go home now. There's nothing for you here." Little by little the people left the area.

By the time Emmet retrieved his bicycle, the paper boys were already out, crying out the news of the executions, along with the instruction issued by the Labour movement for a general strike as protest. Emmet was amazed at the quick action. He was just a copy-boy so hadn't realized that everything was ready to go the moment the announcement was made that the hangings were done. The papers also called the day a national day of mourning. As Emmet pedalled his way home, he watched as the city ground to a halt. The buses came to a stop, bewildered and angry passengers pouring out onto the pavement. Shops put up their shutters and closed. Even the pubs closed their doors.

A surreal quiet settled over the city as the citizens went home, locking doors and windows as they waited to see what would happen in retaliation for the hangings.

Emmet went to the office of the Journal and pounded on the door to be admitted. He found the editor, Patrick Hooper, looking harassed in shirt sleeves and tie askew.

In response to Emmet's offer "Can I help?", he was put to work running copy up and down the stairs from journalist to editor and back again. He made cups of tea and even went to the home of one of the staff to have the man's wife make up a plate of sandwiches.

By seven in the evening, Mr. Hooper told Emmet to go home. "You want to be home well before the nine o'clock curfew, young man."

"Yes Sir." Emmet didn't argue. He climbed on his bicycle, his legs feeling wobbly with exhaustion. He rode through the strangely silent streets, passing armoured cars and British troops as though travelling through a nightmare-induced landscape.

He had the best of intentions to write in his journal when he got home. Instead, he barely made it up the three flights of steps to his bed-sitting room, pulling himself along using the handrail. He sat on the edge of his bed to yank off his boots. *I'll just lie back for ten minutes and then I'll make myself a cup of tea.* The image of Frank Flood, pounding his fist on the debating society's podium as he emphasized his argument, was the last thing Emmet saw.

I'll carry your message on, Frank.

8

Dublin, March 1921

Emmet leaned forward, his hand cradling his pint. He had to speak up over the noise in the busy pub but the Gravedigger's on a Friday night was always packed solid. "I'm telling you Liam, with Michael Collins in for de Valera, Lloyd George and all of the British Parliament will soon be on their heels."

Liam sat back shaking his head. "Forget it. He doesn't stand a chance."

Emmet sighed. "You're always so negative. Between Collins and Arthur Griffith, they can be very persuasive."

Liam balled his fist as it rested on the table beside his glass. "How can there be any hope of negotiating with the likes of those who just executed the six Volunteers last week?"

Emmet nodded. "God, it was appalling. I went out to Mountjoy Gaol in the morning. There were thousands and thousands of people, I mean forty thousand. I've never seen a massive crowd like that. It was truly awful, Liam.. When they opened the gates and announced the executions, there was a wave of crying. I can't describe it any other way. A huge tidal wave of tears." He hesitated because even now he got choked up at the memory. "I was friends with Frank Flood."

Liam nodded in sympathy and then crooked his mouth. "They got more than they bargained for when the general strike and day of mourning were called. I was with the Third Battalion on March

14th. We went out that night, close to the nine o'clock curfew. We had orders to attack any police or military target we could find."

"Jaysus, I didn't know you were a part of that. Were you part of the ambush on Great Brunswick Street?"

Liam put his finger to his lips. "I'm alive." He crossed himself. "But I can tell you that I saw civilians mowed down by the Vickers machine gun that the Auxiliaries had in their armoured car."

Emmet bit his lip. "What a bloody business. Every day brings another shooting. People are afraid to go about their daily business. I write the stories, but it seems so futile. That's why I'm pinning my hopes on Collins with the negotiations. I have a good feeling about it. Just watch."

With a shake of his head, Liam changed the subject. "I'd rather watch that girl over there."

Emmet turned to see a stunning girl with red hair cascading in waves down her back. Emmet turned to face Liam. "She's gorgeous. Will you go and have a word?"

"No. No point. I'm not interested in starting anything. I'm never sure where I'll be from one day to the next."

Emmet swivelled again to take a quick look as the girl took two half pints of Guinness back to a table where she sat with another girl.

Liam grinned. "Go on. I saw her first, but I'll let you have her."

Emmet snorted. "You'll let me, will you?"

"I will."

Emmet stood up. "You're just about ready for another drink anyway, aren't you?"

"Always."

Emmet stopped at the table of the two girls on his way to the bar. "Hello, ladies. Can I interest you in another drink? You'd be welcome to join my friend and me." Emmet nodded towards Liam who waved.

The dark-haired girl smiled towards Liam before turning to the girl with the red hair. "What do you say, Bridie?"

"I have a drink."

Emmet smiled at her, feeling his heart race. "Sure, you could drink it at our table just as well as here."

She seemed to consider that and then nodded. "All right, then."

The two girls picked up their coats and drinks and went to join Liam while Emmet got two more pints.

Emmet was delighted to see that Liam was making a concerted effort at chatting with the dark-haired girl. When he sat down, he introduced himself. "I'm Emmet Ryan and this is Liam Kelly."

The red-haired girl smiled. "I'm Bridie Mallon and this is Eleanor Collins."

Emmet grinned. "We were just talking about Collins. Are you related to him, Eleanor?"

"No, not that I know of, anyway."

Bridie raised one eyebrow. "Are you a fan of his?"

Emmet and Bridie became immersed in discussing the possible treaty for Irish independence while Liam and Eleanor talked about all the development going on in the local neighbourhood.

Before Emmet knew it, it was closing time. He looked at his watch when the bar man started calling "Time. Drink up, now."

Emmet's eyes widened when he looked at his watch. "Good Lord, I had no idea it was so late. I'll have to hustle to make curfew."

Bridie nodded. "We meant to just come in for one drink."

Emmet pulled out the little notebook he always carried. "Can I be so bold as to ask for your address, Bridie? I'd love to see you again."

Bridie bit her lip and then took the book and pencil from him and wrote out her address.

He felt himself flush as he took the book back from her, knowing that he would study her handwriting later. "Perhaps on Sunday afternoon? Could I take you for tea?"

She nodded. "I'd like that. After mass. You can come by the house to get me at three o'clock unless you want to meet me somewhere?"

"No, I'll come by the house. I'd like that."

———

Emmet stood on the pavement in front of Bridie's house on Finglas Road. The red brick house was rather grand looking with its front bow windows and stained-glass fanlight above the blue-painted front door. He took a deep breath, feeling constricted in his stiff white Sunday collar and black tie. Releasing his breath, Emmet opened the wrought iron gate that led into an actual garden with roses along the pathway and stepped smartly to the door. He knocked, and Bridie came to the door immediately, making him think that she must have been watching from behind the lace curtains.

Emmet felt his heart race as he stood in front of her. She was even prettier than he remembered.

She stepped back into the foyer. "You'll have to come in for a minute, I'm afraid. Mammy and Daddy want to meet you."

Emmet nodded. "That'd be grand."

She sighed, and Emmet wondered if she regretted her impulsive agreement to have tea with him.

Just before she opened the frosted glass door to what must be the sitting room, he touched her shoulder and she turned back to him. "Would you rather I go?"

She blushed. "No, no. I'm just a bit annoyed that they're putting you through this."

"I'm not bothered."

She smiled at him, looking relieved. "Right, then."

She opened the door and Emmet followed her into a large room. The two windows facing the street framed the fireplace and each had a brown leather chair in front, facing the room. In one, to the left of the fireplace, sat a man wearing a three-piece sat, folding up his newspaper as Bridie and Emmet walked in. There was a long floral-pattern sofa in soft colours; greens and browns, along the wall facing the door through which they had come and another shorter settee at right angle to it. To the left of the door was a piano. Emmet absorbed all this in a glance, but his focus was on the woman who sat on the sofa with two young girls on either side of her.

Bridie led Emmet to her mother. "Emmet Ryan, this is my mother, Mary Mallon."

"Mrs. Mallon, I'm pleased to meet you." Emmet shook her hand. Her faded red hair was piled high in a complex style that

Emmet suspected the woman would wear until the day she died, despite any styles and fads that may come and go between now and then.

Mrs. Mallon's grip was firm, and she nodded. "Mr. Ryan."

Bridie gestured to one girl and then the other. "And these are my sisters, Tess and Kate."

The two teen-aged girls smiled shyly. Both had the chestnut hair of their father and Emmet thought that Bridie was the beauty in the family. Emmet nodded to each in turn. "Hello."

By then the man had stood and stepped nearer and Bridie introduced them. "Daddy, this is Emmet Ryan. Emmet, my father Dermot Mallon."

Emmet reached out and shook his hand. "A pleasure, Mr. Mallon."

Her father stood and looked down at Emmet. His callous-free hand suggested a business man and he wore a heavy, neatly trimmed moustache. His dark hair was receding, leaving a high forehead and piercing grey eyes.

"So you're taking our Bridie out for tea, is it?"

"Yes, sir." Emmet wished he could say something bright and intelligent, but his mind froze, and he remained silent. *Don't blather.*

Mr. Mallon studied Emmet for a moment before turning to his daughter. "Don't be too late, dear."

"I won't, Daddy."

With this, Bridie turned and led Emmet out of the living room. He turned in the sitting room doorway and nodded to Bridie's mother. "Good-bye. It was nice to meet you all."

He stood at the door in the foyer while she took her hat and shawl from the coat stand. She pinned on her hat without looking and flung on the brown shawl and then nodded to Emmet who opened the door for her.

She led the way out through the gate and waited while he latched it behind them.

She smiled at him. "That wasn't too bad, was it?"

He laughed. "Not at all. I don't blame them for wanting to see the fellow that's taking you off for the afternoon."

They walked along, and he longed to offer his arm but was afraid he'd appear too bold. "Where would you like to go?"

She smiled up at him from under her embroidered yellow Tam O'Shanter hat. "Up past Kavanaugh's there's a place that looks out on the Botanical Gardens. Is that all right?"

He nodded. They walked side-by-side along Prospect Avenue, chatting about the pub where they met; he called it Gravedigger's, she called it Kavanaugh's, about her friend and about Liam. *She's easy to talk to.*

She led him, without seeming to, inside the small cozy room. There were only five tables, two of which were in front of the tall, narrow windows. It was to one of these that they gravitated and sat. He was quiet while they waited for the serving girl to come to them. From the trolley, they both selected a slice of apple cake with custard sauce, along with a pot of tea to share.

While they waited for their order, Emmet tried to think of an uncontroversial topic to discuss, but before he could say anything, Bridie burst out. "So, what do you make of the treaty talks?"

His eyes widened. "Jaysus, I can think of nothing else. Rumours have it that it might not include all of Ireland. The Brits want to keep the north. That would be wrong. So very wrong."

She blinked. "Do you think so? Isn't it better to have Home Rule for the majority and then keep working towards ultimate freedom for everyone?"

He shook his head. "No. It's giving in to the usual British tricks."

Bridie frowned. "But maybe Ulster wants to stay with Britain. If that's true, how is it wrong?"

Emmet bit his lip. He didn't want to argue with this pretty girl, but he couldn't keep his opinions to himself. "It should be all of Ireland, not pieces."

The tea came, and they were quiet as they ate and drank. She looked at him over the rim of her tea cup. "You're very passionate about it all."

His heart melted as her blue eyes pierced him. "I am. I know I am. I've been involved since I was a boy and I believe what I believe."

She nodded and set her cup down. Her hand slid across the table and touched his lightly. "I like that in a man."

Emmet swallowed hard, his heart pounding.

She pulled her hand away again but kept smiling at him. "Tell me more. My parents aren't very political, so maybe I don't know all the facts."

They sat for an hour talking. He ordered another pot of tea. "Are you sure you don't mind me blathering on like this?"

She shook her head. "I live amongst it every day but know only what I read in the papers. When I read about the killings last November, first by the Michael Collins' Volunteers in the morning, and then later in the day by the Black and Tans at Croke Park, it was hard to know what was happening. It's like living in the middle of an American story of cowboys and Indians."

He nodded. "I was there in Croke Park."

She put her hands up in front of her mouth. "Oh, God. That must have been awful."

Emmet felt his throat close as he remembered Sean. He took a deep breath to regain control. "Yes. It was. I lost a very good friend that day."

"So much violence. It's confusing to know what's right."

"I know it's hard, but if you just keep one thing in mind, you'll be all right."

"What's that, then?"

His voice was soft. "Ireland should belong to the Irish. Period."

She nodded. "When you put it like that, I can't argue with it."

He smiled. "That's grand. I don't want to argue with you."

She licked her lip. "Are you never uncertain, though?"

"About?"

"The method of getting there, I suppose."

He sighed. "It's hard. I understand that. I contribute with my pen now that I'm working full time for the *Freeman's Journal*, but sometimes I wonder if it's enough."

She glanced over her shoulder and lowered her voice. "Do you know any of those Volunteers personally?"

He hesitated before answering. "Let's talk of something more cheerful. When can I see you again?"

She smiled and let it go. "When would you like to see me again?"

"Sure, I'd like to see you tomorrow, but between my work and yours in the shop, I'd say I may have to wait until the weekend to see you again."

"Then let's make a plan. Next Sunday?"

He grinned and nodded. "Next Sunday."

They left the tea shop and Emmet felt like singing. He walked her home and she slipped her hand in the crook of his arm. Emmet's heart beat faster and he straightened his shoulders as he matched his long stride to her shorter one.

They chose a different tea shop the following week, but to Emmet he might as well have been drinking tea on the moon for all he noticed. They ordered and then again spent more time getting to know each other.

He watched as she poured out the tea for each of them. "Your parents don't mind you coming out with me?"

She tossed her curls back out of her eyes. "I'm twenty years old. They don't say anything. They probably think I'm overdue for settling down. It's my sisters that are all giggles and gossip when they see me getting ready to go out."

He saw a small 'v' form on her forehead and she turned to look out the window, quiet for a moment. "What is it, Bridie? Is your family teasing you over the likes of me?"

She turned back, her eyes shiny with tears. "No, nothing like that."

"What then? Something's wrong."

"I was just thinking of my other sister."

Emmet frowned. "I thought you only had the two."

"I do. I had another who was two years older than me. Maureen was her name."

"You never mentioned her before now."

A tear spilled down her cheek. "I can't bear to talk of her. We were the best of friends. She was taken by the Spanish influenza three years ago."

He leaned across and touched her arm. "I'm that sorry, Bridie."

Bridie pulled a hankie from her small embroidered handbag and touched it to the corner of her eye. She looked back out the window and Emmet had to strain to hear her. "She was fine. We were all fine. She went to play cards with three other women on a Wednesday afternoon and by the following Wednesday three of those women were dead."

Emmet crossed himself. "Dear God."

Bridie took a deep breath and exhaled, seeming to steady herself. "I'm sorry for bringing you down. We were having such a nice time, but she's always with me, you know? I imagine what she'd think of you or of what she'd say when I tell her this or that. It just isn't right that she isn't here. She was my best friend."

He didn't say anything, just squeezed her arm one last time before leaning back again to pick up his tea.

She gave him a small smile. "Tell me about your family."

Emmet smiled. "My oldest brother Michael is married now. My next brother Kevin seems to be too busy going here and there to settle down."

She tilted her head. "Going where?"

"He spends quite a bit of time down around Cork these days, but he's also gone up to Belfast. One never knows where he'll be found."

"Does he travel for work?"

Emmet nodded. "You could say that." Changing topics, he pointed to a pamphlet she had put on the table. "What do you have there?"

"After we talked last week, I started to read more about it all."

He smiled. "Good."

She slid the pamphlet over to him. "It's about the Women's Movement."

He read the title. "*Cumann na mBan*. Ah, you've been looking into the Irishwomen's Council."

She took the small booklet back again and flipped through it. "It's quite fascinating. They are very active and the Countess Markievicz is the leader."

"Yes, I know."

She looked at him. "They're like you. Ireland for the Irish."

He nodded. "True patriots."

"I'm thinking I might look into joining."

He bit his lip. "Don't do this for me. You have to believe in what it all stands for."

"I do. As I'm reading more and understanding it now, I find I do agree."

He took her small hand in his and pressed it quickly. "You'll find that when you are with people who think like you do, who believe in the same things you do, you'll feel a kinship to them like no other."

She flushed, and he released her hand. "I think you're right. I can well imagine it."

"Will your family be upset?"

She shrugged. "I'm not sure I'd really talk to them about this."

He grinned. "You have *me* now. You can talk to me to your heart's content. You can talk to me about anything."

He loved the pink blush that settled in her face. He felt a heat in his own cheeks in response. He wondered if it was true; that he could talk to her about anything.

9

Dublin, May 1921

Emmet was surprised to have Kevin show up at his room one evening. He opened the door wide to let his brother in.

Kevin held up two bottles of beer. "I come bearing gifts."

Emmet grinned. "You're welcome any time but even more so when you bring gifts."

His flat held just a bed, two easy chairs placed in front of a coal fireplace and a small pine press cupboard. The press held some crockery on its two shelves, and on one sat half a loaf of bread, a waxed paper containing butter and a small pot of jam.

Emmet found his bottle opener but didn't offer a glass. "So, what brings you my way?"

Kevin held up his bottle in a toast. "I wanted to talk to you."

Emmet raised his eyebrows. "What about? Are Mam and Da all right?"

Kevin nodded. "They're fine. Everyone's fine."

"What, then?"

Kevin took another sip of beer as Emmet waited in silence. His brother seemed to be studying Emmet before speaking. "Are you still as keen as you were about the cause?"

Emmet frowned. "Of course. Do you need to ask?"

Kevin shrugged. "People change."

"Sure, don't you read any of the pieces I write?"

Kevin nodded. "Words are easy."

Now it was Emmet's turn to study his brother. "Why do you say that? What am I missing here? Why would you think I'm, as you say, less keen?"

Kevin shook his head. "I'm not accusing you of anything. I'm just making sure."

Emmet scowled. "So now you're sure."

Kevin nodded. "Now I'm sure." He took another drink. "There's something coming up and we're looking for men."

Emmet's heart beat faster. "What is it?"

Still Kevin hesitated. "Are you in?"

"I need to agree before I even know what it's about?"

"I think so. Yes."

Emmet sucked in his breath, exhaling slowly. *I thought I was done with that side of things. I can't say that out loud. I'm not a coward.* "Then I'm in. You can count on me."

"That's what I told them."

Emmet tilted his head. "So? What did I just sign up for?"

"We're going to take the Custom House."

"Jaysus. For real?"

Kevin nodded.

"Tell me more."

Kevin set his bottle on the floor and leaned forward, his elbows resting on his knees. "You can't say anything, to anyone at all."

"Obviously."

"I know you've got a girlfriend now. Not her, not Liam, no one."

"Is Liam not signed up?"

Kevin shrugged. "Liam has his own things he's up to."

Emmet nodded. Different cells. Different assignments. "I get it. Talk to no one."

"It'll be a strike against the alien tyrant."

Kevin and Emmet spoke for an hour about the plans for the coming action.

The beer was long finished before Kevin looked at his watch. "I have to go now. I'll see you at the pub on the twenty-fifth, then."

Emmet went to bed after Kevin left, tossing and turning. *This is it. Did I jump too quickly because Kevin doubted me? Dear God, what have I agreed to?*

He had to talk to Bridie. He believed in his heart he could tell her anything, and yet Kevin had been clear. *I may not even survive and yet I can't talk to her. I have to be loyal to the cause, meaning, not a word to her, no matter how much I want to.*

———

The weather was lovely, so Emmet and Bridie met at Fusiliers' Arch to wander through St. Stephen's Green before finding a shady spot by the water. Bridie shook out the blanket that she had brought with her and they sat down. Emmet pulled out two bottles of ginger ale from his jacket pocket.

Bridie smiled. "You've very organized."

He stroked the blanket. "No more than you."

She nodded. "We make a good team, I think."

He took her hand and smiled. He nodded but didn't say anything.

She gave his hand a gentle squeeze. "So why do you look so down?"

He sighed. "It's a mess, Bridie."

She bit her lip. "Us?"

"No. The ongoing occupation of our land. This never-ending war of independence. We get hopeful and then everything seems to stall."

He released her hand and wrapped his arms around his bent knees, hunching himself together.

She tilted her head. "What's different about now versus a few weeks ago?"

He shook his head. "You've been to a few of the *Cumann na mBan* meetings now. You must realize how strong the feelings are running."

She nodded. "You're right, but what's to be done?"

"What's not to be done is just to *settle*. People won't. Even the elections show that. All one hundred and twenty-four Sinn Fein candidates were returned in the election. We can't just give up and let our country be partitioned like this. It's wrong."

Bridie pulled at some blades of grass.

Emmet watched her and then, still hugging himself he took a deep breath. "Bridie, I think we should stop seeing each other."

She swivelled her head quickly, her eyes wide. "Why? Are you angry because you think I'm not as involved as you?"

He chewed his top lip for a few seconds. "I may be called on to help more."

She frowned. "You're a junior journalist. What can you do? And whatever it is, why does it mean we can't see each other any more?"

"I can't really talk about it. I just think that after today, we'll take a break until I can focus on us again."

"But I just don't understand." She scowled. "Is there someone else?"

He stretched out his legs and took her hand again. "No. Only my country."

Now tears rolled down her cheeks. "I don't understand why you can't have room in your life for both your country and me."

When he didn't respond, she choked out her question. "So how long a break are you talking about?"

He shrugged. "I wish I knew."

She stared at him, blue eyes swimming.

He licked his lips. "I'm sorry, Bridie. I know this isn't fair to you. In fact, if you found someone else, I'll understand and wouldn't blame you."

"I don't want someone else. I want you."

He felt a lump in his throat. *I wish I could tell her everything, but it's not possible. I can't even tell her about Kevin coming to see me last week. She'll hear soon enough.*

He scooted closer and draped his arm around her. She sat rigidly in his embrace, sniffing. He had no words to offer her comfort.

"Can you trust me, Bridie?"

"How can I know when you won't explain anything?"

"I promise you'll understand soon."

He felt her body sag and lean into him. Her words were muffled against the rough fabric of his jacket. "Then I have no choice but to trust you."

10

Dublin, May 25th, 1921

At eleven o'clock Emmet met his brother Kevin at Mulligan's for something to eat and a pint. It was a beautiful summer's morning.

Kevin ate a big meal of roast beef, but Emmet only ordered a bowl of potato and leek soup and a cheese sandwich. Even that made his stomach turn. He watched Kevin eat. "How can you eat all that?"

Kevin shrugged. "Don't know when we'll eat again, so I've learned to make the most of the chance."

Emmet sighed. "You're probably right, but I can't manage it."

Kevin nodded. "You'll wish you had, later."

Emmet pushed his plate aside, part of the sandwich left behind. He looked at his watch. "Twelve-fifteen. We should go, shouldn't we?"

Kevin held up his half-full glass. "In a minute. We don't want to be too early. People get edgy when they see fellows hanging about."

Emmet nodded.

Kevin took another sip, seeming to study Emmet over the top of his glass. "You're not having second thoughts, are you?"

Emmet shook his head. "No. Just nerves. It's been a long time since I've been involved in this way."

"You'll be fine."

When Kevin finished his drink, they both made a quick visit to the toilet, and headed out. They walked along Poolbeg Street and then turned left towards George's Quay. Crossing the Liffey, they turned right, walking along the river towards the Custom House.

Emmet took a deep breath. "I've been thinking it all out, and I'm still a bit confused about what happens after."

Kevin looked at him. "After?"

"I understand the plan about getting in, the fire, all of that. But after we've made a success of it, explain again what happens next. The place is blazing. Is there an escape plan for us?"

Kevin had a way of crooking up the right side of his mouth in half a smile. A sardonic smile. "We hope to mingle with the prisoners as they leave the building to safety. The idea is that we melt into the crowd."

Emmet tried to picture it. "Do you think that will work?"

Kevin shrugged. "It's worked in the past."

Emmet nodded. "Right. Okay. I just wanted to know in case we get separated, you know?"

Kevin rested his hand on Emmet's shoulder. "No one should get hurt."

Emmet twitched his shoulder and Kevin let his hand fall. "I'm not worried about getting hurt." An image of the bloom of blood on his father's jacket came to his mind. He didn't tell Kevin *I'm worried about you getting hurt.*

"Whatever happens, it'll be fine. We're striking a blow here. It's meant to make a statement. Whatever price we pay for that, it'll be worth it."

Emmet nodded. "Yeh, sure. You're right."

They made their way to Sean Connolly Hall where others were already waiting. It was twelve-forty-five. They went into the building. Kevin pointed out the leader and led Emmet across the floor.

Kevin introduced Emmet to Tom Ennis. "Tom, I know you've heard me mention my brother Emmet before. He's part of the Ashbourne Volunteers along with me."

Ennis was about thirty years old, his sandy coloured hair thick and unruly, the left parting barely visible in the shaggy curls. Emmet smiled to see that Ennis had the same sticking-out ears as himself.

Tom shook Emmet's hand. "I've heard of you, and I'm familiar with your writing. I'm glad to have you here. You'll be able to chronicle the operation first-hand."

Emmet nodded and felt a glow of pride. His doubts vanished. He shook Tom's hand. "I'm happy to be here, serving with your Dublin Brigade."

Tom pulled his rucksack off his back and slipped each of them a revolver and six bullets. "Here's your job." He spelled out their instructions. "You'll go up to the second floor and bring down any staff you find. All prisoners down to the main hall." Tom continued as Emmet committed the words to memory. He made a mental note to write it all down later in his little notebook. He'd have to leave out any names just in case the book was confiscated. Emmet blinked and refocused as Tom asked if they understood.

Both Kevin and Emmet nodded, and Tom moved on to other newcomers.

At one o'clock a lorry pulled up in front of the building, loaded with tins of petrol. The men left the hall and queued up behind the lorry where two men handed out the petrol. Kevin and Emmet were given one between them. As soon as they were given the tin, they hustled away to be replaced by other young men. The hundred and twenty men were surprisingly quiet. The smell of nervous sweat mingled with petrol fumes.

Kevin was a few steps ahead of Emmet when they rushed in through the front entrance. They took the stairs to the second floor two at a time, Emmet carrying the petrol while Kevin kept his revolver out and ready to fire. They burst into the first office.

Inside the office were four men and a lady having tea. One of the men stood up. "Who are you?"

Kevin waved the gun. "We are the IRA and are occupying this building. Come along now. You'll have to go down and join everyone else down in the main hall."

The man stepped closer to Kevin and folded his arms across his chest. "Why would we do that?"

Keven jerked his head towards Emmet. "We're going to set fire to the office."

Now they all stood. The woman pointed to her coat hanging on a stand at the far side of the room. "May I get my coat?"

Kevin frowned. "Hurry it up."

She picked up her purse, hurried over to the rack and threw her coat over her arm and then joined the others as Kevin herded them out.

Kevin nodded to his brother and Emmet nodded back. Emmet heard Kevin tell the group to 'move it'. As soon as the room was cleared, Emmet started to fling petrol around the office. *Goodbye, you symbol of tyranny. It's time for Ireland to take hold of her own destiny.* As he worked to cover the papers on the desks with petrol, he had a brief memory of himself behind the hill, surrounded by gunfire. *This is for you, Commander Ashe.*

Emmet went back out into the hallway and saw others like himself coming out of the offices. The staff had all been taken away now.

The stench of petrol lay over him and his eyes watered. He heard, muffled through the thick stone walls a deep *boom* from somewhere outside. The building seemed to vibrate, and Emmet heard rifle fire popping from the street out front. It wasn't until much later that he heard about the young Volunteer who threw a hand grenade at a lorry of police, before being gunned down.

The minutes seemed to crawl. Emmet felt his heart pounding and he tried to take some deep breaths. Through burning eyes, he glanced at his watch and then, at last, he heard it.

Tweeeet. The whistle! It was the signal to set everything ablaze. Emmet stood frozen for a second.

Then, up and down the hall there were shouts from the Volunteers. "That's it, lads!" And "Light her up!"

Emmet turned back into the office he had soaked with petrol. His hand shook as he struck the match. It flared and died again just as quickly. *Damn.* He could smell smoke now drifting down the hall. He struck a second one and this time the match flared and caught. Emmet tossed it on to the desk and leaped back as the desk erupted. The papers curled and burned and then the fumes carried the flames from the desk to a chair and the room exploded in flame.

Emmet felt the blast of heat against his face. He smelled burning hair and thought his hair or eyebrows were singed. He spun and ran out into the hallway, his feet pounding down the stairs, following the men before him, with others right behind.

In the main hall, the prisoners were lying down. Emmet saw Volunteers crouching and moving through the civilians, pushing anyone taking too long down on the floor. "Down. Lie down. It's for your own safety. Lie down, lie down."

At the sound of a burst of machine-gun fire from outside, some of the women screamed. Emmet heard prayers and moans. He spied Kevin at a position by one of the tall windows facing the quay and ran over to join him. They crouched down, huddling behind the stone wall and covered their heads with their arms as a hail of bullets shattered the window. Glass rained down on the floor where seconds before they had crouched. Wind from the river Liffey blew in through the open window frame, and carried the sound of shouting and gunfire as the military and auxiliaries fought to regain control.

Kevin shook his head. "They don't give a damn that there are civilians in here."

The Volunteers broke more windows and returned fire. It was the first time that Emmet had fired a gun. Aside from the hunting knife his father had given him during the 1916 rebellion, his weapon had always been the cutting words he used in his articles. When he fired his first shot, Emmet was shocked as the recoil caused his arm to jerk upwards, sending the shot wild. He now understood why most men used two hands to steady themselves against the kick. His six bullets were gone before he knew it. *I should have saved them. I should have waited until I saw a specific target.*

Emmet was expecting the fire to spread through the building, but it hadn't yet reached the lower level as far as he could see.

He moved away from the window, crawling towards the centre of the main hall. Most of the Volunteers had depleted their ammunition. The sound of gunfire slowed as the police realized they were not being fired upon.

Kevin nudged him and they both watched as the commander, Tom Ennis, started shouting orders. "Up! Get up on your feet!"

Many of the women seemed frozen as they lay crying. Now Ennis's men walked through, helping people up instead of pushing them down. "Come on. It's over. Get up. Time to go."

The civilians were lined up. Tom opened the door and they were marched out with their hands raised. The Volunteers and the staff all shouted a continual chorus of "Don't shoot, don't shoot!"

For a moment it appeared that the hostages would make it to safety without further incident and then Emmet watched in horror as a team of Auxiliaries charged in while the civilians made their way outside, shooting as they came in. Several men fell, wounded. Emmet watched as a group of three civilian clerks all fell, hit by rifle fire. Emmet grasped Kevin's arm. "What the feck are they doing? Oh my God."

Slowly the gunfire stopped. Kevin and Emmet joined the line of men walking out with their hands raised.

Emmet's eyes widened as he saw their leader make a run for it. He grunted in sympathy when he saw Tom get hit, and then, limping heavily, he was swallowed up by the crowd of onlookers. Some Black and Tans tried to give chase, but no one dared fire into the crowd, and the soldiers came back empty-handed.

Emmet heard Kevin. "He made it away. Good."

The line of men shuffled forward as the Auxiliaries marshalled them outside.

One of the leaders of the police walked along the line of men with the head customs official. "Now then sir, please identify your employees."

The official pointed out the employees one by one. "Him, yes and him. Her and these two."

As they were identified the employees could leave.

The two men stepped up to Emmet and Kevin. The official shook his head and they walked on. Emmet bit his lip. He had known what the risk was when he agreed to participate in the operation. There was never any doubt that it would end like this. *I'm going to jail this time for certain.*

He shifted from foot to foot as they waited for the identification parade to finish. By the end Emmet estimated there were close to a hundred people left. Some were fellows he knew but there were others that he had never seen. *Who are they?*

As they were marched off to the waiting lorries, Emmet kept close to Kevin. *Maybe we'll be put together in a cell.*

The lorries took most of them to Arbour Hill detention barracks where they were held for two days for processing and then most were sent to Kilmainham Jail. The brothers did not end up in the same cell, but as it happened, Emmet was content with how things worked out. His cell mate was a man about twenty years his senior. Michael Rourke was from Balbriggan and regaled Emmet with stories of past exploits, including the burning down of several R.I.C. barracks. He had long dark hair that he flipped out of his eyes while tugging at the matching dark moustache he did his best to keep neatly trimmed. He had a floppy newsboy cap that he always wore outside of the cell and Emmet suspected Michael worried he was going bald. They had to sign up for work details and Emmet was put with Michael in the garden.

Michael leaned back against the stone wall, looking as comfortable as if he had been lounging on a sofa at home. "You should be keeping a journal, son."

Emmet bit his lip. "You're right. I don't know why I didn't think of it."

"That lass of yours will be coming to visit again. Tell her to bring you a notebook."

"I will. Did you ever keep a journal?"

Michael laughed. "No, not me. I'm not one for holding on to things. Books, clothes, women. I never seem to have them for long."

Emmet nodded. "You travel light."

Michael nodded. "Have to."

After work they walked out to the yard together. They were allowed free time for exercise and it was during this time that Emmet could meet with his brother and other friends.

Emmet found Kevin sitting on his own with his back against a wall, warming his face in the sun. "Imagining you are on holiday somewhere?"

Kevin opened his eyes, his hand shading the sun. "No place I'd rather be than here."

Emmet sat down beside him. "Does it bother you at all that Tom Ennis isn't here with us?"

Kevin leaned forward, wrapping his arms around his knees. "Not at all. Why? Does it bother you?"

Emmet shrugged. "I don't know. Sometimes yes, most times no."

Kevin frowned. "If I had my way there'd be no one other than me here."

Emmet studied his brother. "You'd like to be a hero?"

"That has nothing to do with it." He waved his hand at the group that was mingling around the yard. "As long as all these men are here, they're less able to work for the movement."

Emmet nodded. "I didn't look at it that way."

Kevin grinned and tousled his brother's hair. "So what have you been learning from your roommate?"

"He suggested I keep a journal."

Kevin nodded. "Great idea. We need as many of you scholars as possible to chronicle what's happening."

Emmet stood up and Kevin followed him, rolling his shoulders. He put his arm around Emmet's shoulders. "I'm serious, you know. We're part of history here. We need a record. The words of Connolly, Pearse and Clarke. They've been put down for all to see in the future, but the likes of you and I, the likes of Tom Ennis. These are the moments that need to be recorded. We're fighting for every person of Ireland and it's of them and for them that we need to record it all."

Emmet felt a lump in his throat. "I will. I'll do my best."

"Good man. Come now and let's see what the latest rumours are all about."

11

Dublin, July 1921

On July 9, Emmet wrote in his journal:

The word went from mouth to ear like falling dominoes. It's a truce. Will we be let out? Some say yes, some say no, some say some. The bigger question is what happens now? The country divided. Is this what we've fought for? What good men died for?

Emmet paused, listening to the babble of discussion around him as he sat alone at the end of a long table in the dining hall. He heard the debates and speculation and tried to think about how he felt about it all. *God, I can't wait for Mam's cooking. A real meal with food that smells and tastes like something I can recognize. A lamb roast. Small spuds fresh from the garden.*

He thought of the last meal he had eaten as a free man. *A cheese sandwich. Kevin was right, of course. I should have had something more memorable.*

As if he had conjured him up, Emmet saw Kevin coming towards him. In only six weeks his brother seemed to have shrunk; his jacket hung on him as if it belonged to another man. *But sure, aren't we all different men now?* Emmet closed his journal. His heart wasn't into deep thoughts.

Kevin sat down across from Emmet. "Did you hear the latest, then?"

Emmet shrugged. "I've heard everything from we're going free to we're being shipped off to England or Wales."

Kevin nodded. "I've heard all that as well." He hesitated and leaned in close to his brother. Kevin's breath made warm puffs in Emmet's ear. "We're going home. I'm sure of it."

Emmet didn't question how he knew that. Kevin just knew things. True things. He closed his eyes for a moment, feeling his heart pound the blood in his temples. He opened them to turn his gaze on his brother. "My God. When?"

Kevin sat back and grinned. "That I don't know. Soon, though."

On July 11 the truce was official. Ireland and England were no longer at war.

On July 12th, Kevin and Emmet were on their way home. They only had the clothes on their backs to carry and Emmet's notebook and pencil. A lorry took them as far as Finglas and from there, they walked. A farmer with a horse pulling a hay wagon picked them up at Kilshane Cross and for half an hour they lay back in the sun-warmed hay to rest, but then they had to walk again. After giving the farmer some heartfelt thanks, Kevin seemed to find a new energy and he set off at a march, arms swinging.

Emmet had to put all he had into it to keep up with Kevin. "Are we in a race, then?"

Kevin held up his arms as if to touch the sky which had turned grey with a light drizzle. "I'm keen to get home out of the wet. Are you not?"

"I am, of course. I'm just savouring it."

"Being soaked to the skin?"

"Freedom."

"And have you thought about what you'll do with the freedom?"

"Go back to work, I hope."

"And what about that lass of yours?"

"Yes, that's playing on my mind. I haven't seen her for a few weeks now. Maybe she's found someone new by now. "

Visitors were allowed to talk to prisoners between eleven in the morning and one in the afternoon and many had come each day to crowd at the fence where, with luck and cooperation, they could visit through the chain link. Bridie had been a regular and had successfully coaxed a guard to take the notebook and pen from her to give to Emmet. Many of the guards had been good that way.

Kevin put his arm around Emmet's shoulder. "I saw the look in her eye when she was with you. I don't believe she's found someone new."

Emmet shrugged, and Kevin's arm fell away. "We'll see."

"She'll stick by you. I know it."

Emmet smiled. "And you're always right, I suppose?"

Kevin lifted his hands. "When am I not?"

This time the homecoming was expected, and all the family greeted the boys with hugs, including Emmet's two-year-old nephew in the arms of Michael. Mam had made a lamb roast, just as Emmet had longed for, and the end of the war was celebrated, none of them realizing how short-lived it would be.

———

Emmet gave himself plenty of time to cycle from Ashbourne to St. Stephen's Green. He had sent a note to Bridie to suggest they meet there and her response confirmed she'd be there but seemed cryptic. A simple 'yes, I'll be there.' As he rode along, he relished the sun on his back, but wished it were cooler so he wouldn't sweat so much.

He parked his bicycle at the gate and walked to their meeting place by the pond. His stomach churned almost as much as when he had raced into the Customs House. *She's through with me. I know it, and sure, she's probably right. I'll just bring her heartache. The Cause will be my life and I'll leave the romance for others.*

He watched the swans swimming gracefully in pairs. He tried to steel himself but then he turned and saw her. His heart pounded, and his eyes burned when he saw the look on her face.

12

Dublin, July 1921

He watched her approach. Even at a distance he saw the tears on her face. As she got close he noticed that her eyes, normally blue, looked grey, filled as they were with tears.

She's done with me. At least she's here to tell me in person. Don't blub. He felt his own eyes burn.

And then she was there and reaching for him despite the open and public place. Her wide brimmed hat got in the way and she pushed it back so that it hung around her neck and she kissed him full on the mouth. She pulled away and they both took a breath.

She straightened her hat. "Emmet, you're as thin as a rail. We'll have to fatten you up."

He took her hand and led her to a shady spot. Slipping off his light jacket, he laid it on the grass for her. "Don't worry yourself. I'm fine and my mother is working hard to put the meat back on me."

There was a silence as they sat side by side. He plucked a blade of grass, playing with it as he spoke. "Why did you not come to see me at the end, Bridie?"

"It wasn't because I didn't want to."

He threw away the grass and turned to look at her. "Why, then?"

"My parents."

"Have they set against me now?"

She shook her head. "Not really. It's just they decided it wasn't seemly for me to be going to that place."

"And that's the only reason?"

"It is."

Emmet's voice was low. "I thought maybe you had found someone else."

Her voice was choked. "There's no one else."

He took her hand in his and it felt comfortable and safe captured in his.

He studied her. He felt his Adam's apple bobbing up and down as he swallowed. "I don't know what I'd do without you, Bridie, but if you want to finish it with me, for whatever reason, I understand."

She shook her head. "I don't."

He heaved a heavy sigh, as if he was exhaling the worries of the world. "That's all right then. I fretted when I didn't see you anymore and didn't hear anything. How bad is it with your folks?"

She shrugged. "They aren't happy. They think I can do better."

"I don't blame them. I wouldn't want someone troublesome for my daughter either." He patted her hand and then released it.

She smiled. "You'll have to prove to them you aren't troublesome, won't you?"

"I'll do my best, I promise."

She took a deep breath. "It's time to think of the future. What will you do now?"

He turned back to her, shifting a little to be able to talk to her face to face. He hesitated and bit his bottom lip. "There's a rumour out that they'll be looking for some men to go to America."

She frowned. "Who's they?"

He glanced around as if to see that no one was near by. It was an automatic reaction. Something he picked up in Kilmainham. "The party. Michael Collins."

"What does that mean to you?"

He looked away then, watching the swans before speaking again. "I've put my name forward."

She flinched and leaned away from him. "America? You're going to America?"

He shrugged. "I put my name forward. That doesn't mean I'll be chosen."

Bridie stood, brushing her hands down her skirt to smooth the wrinkles.

He stood as well and reached out both his hands to grasp hers. "Bridie. Sit down again. Hear me out." He heard the pleading in his own voice. He needed her to understand. He couldn't just walk away. Not now.

"I can't sit on the damp ground. It's creasing my dress."

"Don't be cross."

She pulled her hands away from him. "You said that if I wanted to finish with you, you'd understand. Perhaps what you were really saying is that you want to finish with *me*."

His hands dropped and hung loosely by his side. "No, not at all. The thought of you is what's kept me strong all these weeks. I need you, Bridie. I need you to believe in me and stand by my side as we try to make the vision of a united Ireland come true."

She stared at him, as if trying to understand what he wanted from her. "America." It was all she could say.

He picked up his jacket and shook it out before draping it over his left arm. He offered his right arm to her, but she ignored it and they walked on to the path that led around the lake, the gap between them feeling greater than it was.

She sighed. "Tell me, then."

His voice was almost feverish as he explained how he and Liam wanted to go together to help raise funds for the Cause.

"So how long would you be away, then?"

"Not more than a few months."

"And what would you do? How do you raise funds?"

His heart raced as he talked about it. "I would mostly be writing. I'll write speeches, pieces for the American papers as well as send articles home for the papers here."

Bridie shook her head. "I thought that once you were released we'd get to spend more time together."

"It isn't forever."

"My friend Mary is engaged." Bridie flushed.

"I know it's asking a lot of you to wait for me, but it's important. You see that, don't you?"

She hesitated. "I see that you think so."

He tried to find the words that would explain. "It's for Ireland. There's more work to do and I know I have the skills to do that work."

She stopped and turned to look up at him. "Here's what I know. I know that my parents are heartsick at the loss of that beautiful building that you helped burn down. I know that they don't want me to see you anymore because you're dangerous."

He stared at her. "I didn't realize you were getting such a hard time from your parents."

"Well, now you know. But it isn't even that. I can tolerate the remarks and disapproving looks. I could tolerate it when I thought that you cared for me.."

He protested. "I do care for you."

She held up her hand, her eyes narrowed. "When I thought you cared *enough* for me that you were worth the hard times. Now, it seems that I was mistaken about how much you cared. Clearly with you it will always be Ireland first and me second."

She turned and strode off.

He trotted after her and tried to lay his hand on her shoulder.

She twitched her shoulder and pulled away from him. She spit the words out. "Leave me alone, Emmet Ryan. Don't follow me. Go to America and I wish you joy with it." Her angry words were punctuated with tears.

He stood helplessly and watched her go. It seemed so easy to make these plans when he was far away from her. The Cause was everything when he was in Kilmainham. Now, it didn't seem so straightforward. *I love her.* His breath caught with the realization. *What do I do now?*

13

Dublin, September 1921

In early September Emmet, Liam and two other men crossed the ocean to America on the S.S. Columbia which landed in Ellis Island, New York. The trip took five days, and while Liam and one of the others, Joseph, a bandy-legged man with wild dark hair, were sick for most of the trip, Emmet and the fourth man, Paul, a bespectacled fair man, quickly got their sea legs and enjoyed wandering the ship. They were in second class where the four of them shared a cabin and the trip was paid for by de Valera's fund, as all the expenses of travel and accommodation were. Emmet loved wandering around the ship and talking to people. He wrote pages in his journal about the stories of people on board, crafting articles that he intended to send back for publication. These stories captured the whole range of emotions from excitement of the single men for the adventure ahead to the fear and worry of the family of eight who left only because they had no other options when the jobs and money ran out.

Emmet chronicled every leg of the journey in letters to Bridie. He had seen her only once after their blow-up in St. Stephen's Green, and while she hadn't said she was prepared to wait for him, she had grudgingly agreed to have tea with him, and when he told her that he would write to her she hadn't told him not to. Emmet took that as a hopeful sign and wrote as if they were still good friends.

After the whirlwind of landing, the four men were picked up and then assigned jobs, which is how Emmet came to be on a train heading from New York to Chicago. The train jerked and swayed, but still Emmet managed to work on his letter.

Dear Bridie,

I'm on the train as I write this, so don't mind the odd squiggle in the writing. We are going to Chicago to the offices of the AARIR. You may remember me mentioning that organization last year when I read about de Valera's trip here. They are the American Association for Recognition of the Irish Republic. That's a grand name altogether, isn't it? There are three of us going to Chicago and the others are going to Washington. We were given tickets for the train, (people call it 'the most famous train in the world.' No one's told me why, but that's the American way – everything is the biggest and best.) It's an express that left Grand Central Terminal and goes all the way to Chicago, with no changing trains anywhere along the way. The price of the ticket was fifty-one dollars American for each of us and for that we get a Pullman sleeping berth (I haven't seen it yet, but I gather the seats fold down to make a bed with a curtain to draw over for privacy). It's all very luxurious and I'd say you won't find any farmers taking their chickens to market on this train! The seats are a dark green velvet with carved wood throughout. There are toilets at either end of the car (one for men and one for women). As soon as I finish this letter, Liam and I are off to discover the dining car. Naturally he's choking for a pint.

We left New York at four this afternoon and expect to arrive in Chicago tomorrow morning around nine o'clock. I'm told that I'll be put to work writing pamphlets to help drum up support for the Irish cause. Liam and Joseph will go about to different places to help talk it up. They love the old accent here, so Liam lays it on for good measure.

My head's in a spin sometimes, imagining that I've gone from jail only a short time ago to this.

I only wish you were here to see it all with me. Perhaps one day.

Write to me, care of the AARIR, Visitation Assembly Hall, 900 West Garfield Boulevard, Chicago IL, U.S.A. I expect to be there for the next while and not move around anymore, although I understand that Boston is where the real action is. If it looks like I'm being relocated, I'll let you know.

Emmet

In October, while Emmet was in Chicago, he did, at last, get a letter from Bridie.

When it was delivered to his desk, he put it away to savour later when he was alone in his room. There were too many people around him to afford him the privacy and quiet he wanted.

Maybe she's forgiven me.

Maybe she'll tell me to stop writing.

Instead of opening his letter, he concentrated on reviewing the paper he had written which would be given the next day at a social at the Visitation Sodality Hall. The speech was to be read by the council president, John Conroy, but Liam and Joseph would each take a turn at speaking from the heart as well.

Emmet made sure to mention that the Catholic Daughters of America had purchased a one-hundred-dollar bond, in the hopes of inspiring other groups to step up and match the donation.

When he was finished and put the final paper in an envelope for delivery to Conroy, he stretched his back muscles and rotated his shoulders. After tomorrow's event he would write a piece to send home for his paper to print. *I'm a bridge between the two worlds.*

He walked over to the lunchroom where Liam and Joseph debated how they should talk about the delegation going to London to discuss a treaty.

Joseph sat with his arms crossed, his black hair a frizzy halo around his head. Liam, his red hair combed and brilliantined, leaned forward, pressing his point.

"Collins should be in charge of the delegation, not Griffith." Liam was adamant.

"Griffith is the politician and the man with the fine words. He'll keep his cool. Besides, it doesn't matter a damn what we think. The point is, there's a delegation going over to meet with the Brits and that's positive news that we can talk about."

Liam sat back. "Yeh, all right. You talk about Griffith then since you're such a fan, and then I'll close with a final push about what great things the money is doing and how we couldn't manage without it."

Emmet sat down with them. "I'm done and am heading back to the house." They had rooms in a boarding house nearby.

Liam stood up. "I'm going for a pint. Will you come along, Emmet?"

Joseph closed his notebook where they had captured their notes for tomorrow's talk. "Aye. We're all going. Come along."

Emmet shook his head. "Maybe later. I told Mrs. Doherty I'd be there for supper tonight."

Liam shrugged. "Ah, well. You know where to find us. I know a dark-haired beauty who will be severely disappointed you aren't there."

Emmet flushed and glanced through the open lunchroom door towards the office. "I'm sure you clowns are enough entertainment for Maggie without me sticking my oar in."

Liam and Joseph laughed. They both knew that the girl who worked as a typist for the AARIR was smitten with Emmet.

Liam rested his hand on Emmet's shoulder. "She only has eyes for you, my son."

"Go on, the pair of you."

Still laughing, Liam and Joseph went to their desks to scoop up their jackets. They walked out together, Emmet heading in the opposite direction from his friends.

Emmet liked the house where the boys boarded. They each had their own room in the three-storey red-brick house and in some ways it made him think of a stand-alone version of the houses in Drumcondra with the bow windows and bright red painted front door. The widow landlady prepared hearty meals from home, with plenty of spuds and cabbage.

He climbed the stairs to his second-floor room and took off his jacket and topcoat, hanging them up on the hooks on the back of the door. He sat on the edge of his bed and tapped the envelope on his knee. *Maybe I should leave it until later.* An image of Maggie with her dark hair sleeked into shiny finger waves crossed his mind. He looked back to the envelope and sighed. He stood and put the envelope on the dresser, unopened.

He put his jacket back on and went down to the dining room. "Am I too early for supper, Mrs. Doherty?"

She wore her apron much like his own mother might and when she looked up from laying the cutlery on the table, she grinned. "You're in a hurry tonight, Mr. Ryan."

"The smell of your fine cooking makes me hungry."

She smiled. "You're a grand one for telling stories. Go on and sit. I'll dish you up a plate, but if the spuds are still a bit hard, you've only yourself to blame."

Emmet ate his supper alone, looking out the window, haunted by the letter on his dresser. *If she tells me to stop writing, I'll be friendlier to Maggie.* I'll go out to O'Hanlan's Pub after all. They'll all still be there. Maggie will be there. He knew that the quick touches she gave him on his arm, and the smiles she gave him were flirtatious and that he enjoyed it. He remembered just that very morning when he gave her his article to type, he had stood close enough to her to feel the warmth of her arm against his sleeve. If he closed his eyes he could conjure up the scent of her, while he couldn't do the same with Bridie. When he thought of Bridie's scent, he had an impression of clean, not perfume. But when he thought of Bridie's red hair falling in waves to her shoulders and sparkling blue eyes, he felt his heart pound and his breath catch.

I can't go out without knowing.

The other boarders were just coming in when he finished his supper. "Thank you, Missus. That was lovely."

Mrs. Doherty set two plates down in front of the young men and wiped her hands on her apron. "Will you not have a sweet?"

"Ah, no. Thank you. I said I'd meet some friends down at O'Hanlan's."

"All right, then. Have a good evening."

Emmet went back up to his room and once more picked up the letter, sliding his paper knife under the flap to slice it open.

———

Emmet walked into the bar and saw Maggie sitting facing the door at a corner table. She waved to him, her face lighting up with a smile, teeth shining whitely against the contrast of her red lipstick. Emmet wove between the tables to the corner. Joseph sat across from Maggie and it seemed to Emmet that he scowled slightly when he noticed Emmet standing beside him.

Emmet pointed to the drinks. "Can I get anyone a refill?"

Joseph nodded. "I thought you weren't coming out?"

Emmet shrugged. "Changed my mind."

Maggie smiled. "And we're glad you did. Mine's a gin and tonic."

Emmet pushed in next to Liam at the bar. "Can I get you another?"

Liam grinned. "It's himself arrived in." He held up his glass to the bartender who nodded.

Emmet stood and waited as the pints of Guinness he ordered settled. "I decided to come out. Did I miss anything?"

Liam shook his head. "I came over here to get away from Joe for a bit. He wears me out."

"Not the Collins versus Griffith discussion again?"

"More like a discussion about where and how the most good can be done. I thought I'd be able to do great things here, but now I'm here, I think I'm best at home."

Emmet nodded. "I understand. For what it's worth, I think you're doing great things. You bring a passion to the talks that we can't all do. That's why it's always best when you finish the night, and not Joseph or one of the local politicians. And you know that yourself."

Liam took a swallow of his drink. "I know. I can get the crowd going when someone helps me with the right words. I just think I'd be more useful at home doing work that no one else has heart for."

Emmet bit his lip. "Liam, that sort of work may just about be over. When the treaty is worked out and signed, we'll be able to put the guns behind us."

Liam raised an eyebrow. "You really believe that?"

Emmet pulled back and frowned. "Of course. Don't you?"

Liam shrugged.

The bartender put the drinks in front of Emmet and took the money.

"Help me carry these over and come sit for a while. Let's put it all aside and talk about what we'll do on Sunday."

Liam picked up the gin and tonic along with his own drink. "Joe won't be best pleased that you're here."

"Why not?"

"I think he fancied his chances with Maggie, but now you're here, that'll go out the window."

Emmet crooked a half smile in understanding.

When they were all sitting around the small round table, Emmet pulled his letter from his inside pocket. "I'm in great form this evening which is why I decided to come out to celebrate with a drink."

Joseph raised his eyebrows. "Why is that, then?"

"My girlfriend has forgiven me for coming all this way."

Maggie froze with her glass halfway to her mouth. "I didn't realize you had a girlfriend at home."

Emmet smiled. "I wasn't sure that I had one. When I told her I was coming to America, she was raging, but time has done its healing and she's softened towards me."

Liam slapped Emmet on the back. "That's brilliant. You don't deserve her."

"Probably not."

Maggie took a large sip of her drink. "Well, that's lovely for you."

"Thank you, Maggie. So, what's everyone doing on Sunday after we have our big success tomorrow night at the social?"

14

Dublin, December 1921

The fundraising tour had been a great success, and Emmet and Liam were released to go home. Joseph opted to stay on to continue working for the AARIR and it looked to be a permanent position now that he and Maggie were an item.

The trip home was uneventful; even Liam found his sea legs after the first two days. They sat out on the deck when it wasn't too cold and windy. Liam especially loved the fresh sea air. "God, it's great to get the city blown out of my system."

Emmet laughed. "You love Dublin with all her grubby streets. What's different about Chicago?"

"Everything. The smell, the sounds, the feel of the cobbles under my feet. Don't tell me you don't feel just the same as me."

Emmet nodded. "I do, of course. I can't wait to get home. You're right about the smell. The smell of a turf fire on a damp evening just cries out a welcome like nothing else."

Liam poked Emmet. "You have the added bonus of coming home to Bridie. Will you make an honest woman of her now?"

"If she'll have me."

Liam frowned. "I thought you two were sound now?"

"I hope so. Until we're together I won't know for certain. Her Da doesn't like me."

"Was there ever a Da who does like the fella that takes his daughter away?"

"If that's all it was, I'll be all right."

"Is he still bothered because of your history?"

"Bridie doesn't say much, but that was the case before I went away in September. I can't imagine that being away in America would have endeared me to him much in the meanwhile."

"Bridie doesn't strike me as a girl to blindly do as her parents tell her."

Emmet grinned. "I suspect you're right there, but it would be easier if they liked me."

"You'll be home for Christmas. Did you let her know?"

"I wrote just before leaving, but I'm not sure the letter will get there any sooner than I will myself. If the Captain is right, we'll be in Dublin for Christmas Eve, and Bridie's house is my first stop. I'll drop by before I head home to Ashbourne."

They watched the heaving sea for a while, each with his own thoughts, and then headed inside, Emmet to their cabin to reread the last letter from Bridie and Liam to find a card game.

———

It was close to nine o'clock when Emmet arrived at Bridie's house on Christmas Eve. The family had moved to Portobello, a lovely area of Dublin, but quieter, where people didn't just drop in. Bridie had written that they planned to have house guests for the Christmas holiday. An old friend of Bridie's mother had come with her husband, daughters and an English niece named Elizabeth.

It was late, and Emmet hesitated before knocking, but he just couldn't go home without at least seeing Bridie for a few moments. He bit his lip, took a deep breath and lifted the knocker.

Emmet tried not to look surprised to see a servant girl open the door to him. *They're moving up in the world. That's not good for me.* "Hello. Emmet Ryan to see Bridie if possible."

"Step in and wait here a minute while I check."

From his spot in the foyer, he heard Mr. Mallon's voice "Who can be calling at this hour?"

He heard his name given by the girl and then Mrs. Mallon "Show him in then, Bella."

Emmet gave the girl his coat and hat to hang and then followed her into the parlour. His eyes found Bridie first and feasted on her flushed face and wide eyes. He had the sense that she was perched on the edge of the sofa, ready to leap up to meet him.

He stood posed in the doorway. "Good evening, Mr. and Mrs. Mallon. Thank you for allowing me to stop in at this late hour."

He turned then to Bridie. "Did you get my letter? You knew I was coming?"

Bridie pulled an envelope from her pocket. "It just came today. I haven't had a chance to look at it yet."

Emmet's mouth turned down. "Ah." And then he smiled "Well, here's a Christmas surprise, then."

Mrs. Mallon nodded to a chair. "Please sit down."

Emmet glanced around the room. "I know you have visitors. I won't stay. I only wanted to stop in to say hello."

Bridie rose then and walked to his side to steer him around the room, introducing him to the group. She gave a little information about each of their house guests, leaving a tall, slim young woman until the end. "And this is Elizabeth. We've become great friends now, haven't we Elizabeth?"

Elizabeth rose to shake hands with Emmet. "Yes, we have."

Emmet blinked as he heard the English accent but recovered himself quickly. "Then I'm sure we too will be great friends."

Elizabeth nodded. "I hope so."

The introductions complete, Bridie made her way back to her seat on the sofa.

Mrs. Mallon waved her hand in the direction of the kitchen. "Shall we have tea? Emmet, would you like a cup?"

He hesitated and glanced towards Bridie. Bridie widened her eyes and gave a tiny nod which he interpreted as *Please stay.*

As if he heard her thoughts, Emmet nodded. "I'd like that if you're sure I'm not intruding."

Bridie's youngest sister, Katie grinned. "I, for one, am dying to hear about America. Won't you tell us all about it?"

Emmet smiled. "That would take more than one cup of tea, I'm afraid."

Mr. Carson leaned forward. "What took you to America, young man?"

"Unity, Sir."

Mr. Carson frowned. "Meaning what?"

Bridie burst out before Emmet could continue. "Emmet is a writer, Mr. Carson. He's been travelling with the group who have been in America raising funds for the cause of bringing Ireland together as thirty-two counties."

Emmet saw the frown crease Mrs. Carson's face, but Bridie continued to tell them about some of the articles that had been published in the Dublin papers. Emmet felt his heart swell as he heard the pride in her voice.

Mrs. Carson paled. "Isn't that rather, well, radical?"

Emmet smiled. "Not so very much. I simply recorded the speeches and wrote short articles explaining our position for various local American newspapers."

Katie shook her curls. "Never mind all that political stuff. Tell us about what you saw there. Is everything so large, and the people all so rich as we always hear?"

Emmet shook his head. "There are just as many poor in America as there are here. But you're right about everything being large."

While they sat and drank tea, Emmet regaled them with stories of the countryside and long train rides between cities.

Before he wanted to, Emmet stood and shook hands with the men. He made a small bow to Bridie's mother and Mrs. Carson. "Again, forgive the intrusion and thank you for the tea."

He glanced at Bridie but before she could stand to walk him to the door, Mrs. Mallon called out for Bella.

Emmet took away the smile she gave him before he turned to leave. It was enough to tell him what was in her heart.

15

Dublin, January 1922

Emmet's reputation had grown while he was in America. He was promoted into a full-time writing position which meant that he was making enough of a wage to think of the future.

With the money he had saved up in America, he bought a ring. He went to West's on Grafton only to leave again quickly, shocked at the prices. He wanted to buy the best, but in the end, his brother Michael steered him to a local shop in Ashbourne where the rings suited his budget. Before asking Bridie, he knew he had to get her Da's approval, so in the first week of January, he sent a note to Mr. Mallon and asked to meet at the Bleeding Horse on Camden Street. Emmet made sure he was there early so that he could select a quiet corner.

When Bridie's father came in, Emmet rose to greet him. He held his hand out to shake the older man's hand. "Thank you for meeting me, sir."

Mr. Mallon nodded.

"What can I get you?"

"A Jameson's with water on the side, please."

Emmet went to fetch the drink and a half pint of Guinness for himself.

"Thank you." Mr. Mallon raised his eyebrows. "A half?"

Emmet shrugged and smiled. "Best to keep a clear head, I think."

"That sounds ominous. Are you going back to work later?"

"No, I'm finished for the day."

"You're busy chronicling the Provisional Government activities to do with the Treaty, I suppose."

Emmet tried not to frown. "Yes, there's a lot going on at the moment."

"You must be happy now that there's a treaty in place. I know you've got a keen interest in politics."

Emmet gritted his teeth. "As a journalist I try to maintain a degree of neutrality, but quite honestly it isn't the outcome that I would wish for." Before they became embroiled on the merits of the treaty, Emmet hastened ahead. "You may be wondering why I asked to meet with you, Mr. Mallon."

Bridie's father sighed. "I have my suspicions."

"Then perhaps it won't come as a surprise to you that I'd like your permission to ask Bridie to marry me."

Emmet's heart pounded as he waited as the silence stretched.

Mr. Mallon took a large sip of his drink. "Son, you're a well-educated, sincere man. Of that I have no doubt."

Emmet eyes widened. He felt it coming.

"But there is no way I can encourage you to continue this pursuit of my daughter's hand."

Emmet felt the sweat prickling under his arms and he took a deep breath to calm down. "I see. May I ask why not?"

Mr. Mallon looked him in the eye. "Quite frankly, I believe you to be a troublemaker. You've been in prison more than once, you have radical opinions and you have a job that can hardly support yourself, let alone a wife and family."

Emmet had an urge to punch him in the nose. He gritted his teeth and did his best to modulate his voice, willing it not to quaver. "I believe you have a skewed vision of me, sir. In fact, I have recently been promoted, so that I believe I do have the income to look after my wife. As far as being a troublemaker, many, many people have been interned in these troubled times, men who are now taking a leadership role in our new government. Surely you don't view them as troublemakers as well?"

"That's irrelevant to this discussion."

"I don't believe it is. I have not been in prison for a crime such as theft or assault. I worked for the freedom of our country and am proud to be in good company in that regard. As far as my radical opinions go, again, I'm not alone in wanting to see our country free and united."

Mr. Mallon waved his hand as if to brush aside these arguments.

Emmet's breath came fast and short. "May I ask why, given your feelings, you have allowed Bridie and me to walk out together? What did you think would happen after a time?"

The older man finished his drink and waved to the bartender to bring over two more drinks despite the half glass that Emmet still had in front of him. "Honestly, I hoped that you would just stay in America, or at least that you and Bridie would forget about each other while you were away. It seemed hopeful."

Emmet drained his drink and then immediately felt queasy. "I love her, and she loves me."

Mr. Mallon grimaced. "Grow up, son. That isn't enough."

"Are you forbidding me to continue to see her?"

"I wish I could, but Bridie is too much of her own person for that. We lost one daughter to the Spanish flu, I won't lose another one by being heavy-handed." He leaned forward and placed his hand on Emmet's arm. "Don't get me wrong. I don't dislike you. Far from it. I just believe that Bridie deserves someone who will be better suited to her. Someone to take her to nice places. A man of whom she can be proud."

"I believe she's proud of me."

"Show me that you are deserving of that pride."

Emmet nodded. "All right. I will."

Again Mr. Mallon finished his drink in one swallow and then he stood. Emmet had a full drink in front of him. "Stay and finish your drink. I'm getting these. I believe I've said everything I need to say."

Emmet stood as well. "I invited you here. I am paying for the drinks."

Bridie's father nodded. "Very well. Thank you."

Emmet held out his hand. "I appreciate you taking the time to meet me."

They shook hands and Emmet sat down to finish his drink. *Damn you.* His jaw ached from clenching his teeth together. *I'll prove myself, Mr. High and Mighty. I'll show you that I'm deserving of Bridie's pride. You'll eat your feckin' words.*

16

Dublin, January 1922

Emmet noted in his diary: *January 16th will go down as one of the most important days ever known in Irish history.* It was the day that Dublin Castle and the machinery of government was handed over from the British to the Provisional Government of Ireland. It was a cold Monday morning and the handover from the Viceroy of Ireland to Michael Collins was scheduled to take place at noon.

Crowds had begun to gather at daybreak and by noon, thousands of people had collected, stretching in both directions along Dame Street. While no one other than the people involved in the handover were permitted in the Privy Council Chamber itself, journalists, officials, soldiers and some invited members of the public were assembled in the courtyard. From here, they could witness the arrival of Collins and his party and then view the events taking place in the well-lit chamber through the windows, as though watching a silent theatre production. Emmet was one of the journalists lucky enough to be included in this momentous event. He selected a spot close to the northeast corner of the yard by the Chief Secretary's Office. He knew it was through this door that Collins and his party would enter and leave the building.

At noon word went out amongst the waiting crowd in the courtyard that Collins was running late. Emmet used the time to describe in detail the feel of the waiting crowd. He filled page after page in his little notebook as he talked to men and women around him.

The wife of one government official was in tears as she spoke. "I never believed I would see this day. I was always happy that my Patrick." she glanced at the man beside her sporting a large black moustache, "had such a good, steady job. Our children have never gone without shoes, thanks be to God, but now, it's beyond wonderful. He'll be working for the good of our own people, for our very own government."

"But how do you feel, knowing that the Treaty doesn't incorporate all of Ireland. Some people think we've sold out."

She shook her head. "It's a start. Of course, I want all of Ireland included. Who wouldn't? But let's get this going and then we can negotiate for the rest of Ireland to reunite with us."

With conversations like this, the time passed quickly and then at 1:40 Emmet heard the cheering from outside the courtyard and knew that Collins must be arriving. With some luck he'd be able to ask him a question or two as Collins went in.

Three taxi cabs pulled in to great cheering and applause within the yard. Collins and the other seven members of his party quickly strode from the cabs to the door and were in and gone with no chance for questions. Emmet shifted so he could peer up to the three tall windows of the Privy Council Chamber, located above the archway. Within a moment he saw the men moving around. The King's representative, the Viceroy of Ireland, Lord FitzAlan-Howard must have been informed of Collins arrival because several moments later he too arrived.

Emmet glanced around and saw the police lining the yard poised and ready, but the courtyard was subdued as he arrived and there were no problems. *The last ever Viceroy of Ireland.*

Having been to see the Privy Council on other occasions, Emmet knew that it was a grand-looking room with great brass chandeliers and in the centre of the room stood a great table, usually covered in a red cloth. He wondered if Collins and the others were impressed.

The window afforded a reasonable view of what was happening. Emmet saw that the Viceroy stood at the fireplace, while Michael Collins took a seat on the right-hand side of the Lord Lieutenant's Chair. He looked at ease. The Viceroy took something that Collins handed him and Emmet knew it must be a copy of the Treaty which was the official document authorizing the handover. As the crowd outside watched the group in the chamber moving about, it seemed that Collins was introducing the members of his government and then it was obvious that the Viceroy made a short speech.

By 2:25, it was all over, and Emmet pressed back into his spot by the door when he saw that people were leaving the Council Chamber. The Chief Secretary's Office door opened, and two members of the new Free State Government emerged, followed by Collins.

Emmet called out: "Mr. Collins. How do you feel, sir?"

Collins hesitated, grinned and responded quietly, yet loudly enough for Emmet, almost standing right beside Collins, to hear: "It was a hell of a different visit from the last time I was here, disguised as the driver of a coal-cart, with a price on my head."

As Collins hustled forward to his waiting taxi, Emmet immediately transcribed what Collins had said. The triumph and joy ringing through those words, brought a lump to his throat.

Emmet stood rereading his notes as the crowd dispersed and then he retrieved his bicycle where it was chained near the Palace Street Gate. He navigated through the lingering groups of people as quickly as he could back to Westmoreland Street to his office at the *Freeman's Journal*. He spent several hours writing and rewriting his piece about the handover, including the impromptu comment by Collins before showing it to Mr. Hooper.

Hooper sat with his elbows on his desk reading Emmet's piece. He looked up where Emmet stood nervously waiting. "By God, you've done a great job on this, Ryan. You've captured the mood completely. That's the sign of a top-class journalist. I'm putting your name to this as a byline."

Emmet swallowed. "Thank you, sir. I want all the people of Ireland to feel the magnitude of the event. Even for those who don't believe in the Treaty, it was a momentous occasion."

Hooper nodded. "It is indeed. Well done." He wrote Emmet's name at the top of the article and then carried the papers to the door of his office. He shouted 'copy', whereby a young man dashed over to take the pages away for printing. Hooper rested a hand on Emmet's shoulder. "Go home. You've done good work today."

The next morning Emmet stopped at the newsagent. His jaw dropped as he stood before the display of papers as he recognized his own article, with the promised byline announcing that he, Emmet Ryan, had written it. He bought a copy of both the *Irish Examiner* and the *Irish Independent*. The Independent had it as a small piece in the bottom corner and it continued on page three. Their own in-house political commentator had a large piece of his own, but with a different flavour, providing a glowing report of how the Viceroy wished the new government well, and would stay on to support the transition until the end of the year. Still, there was Emmet's own piece with his name, right there on the front page of the two large dailies as well as his own *Freeman's Journal*.

Emmet carried all three papers to the office under his arm. He walked in to a smattering of applause and congratulations from his co-workers. "Well done, Emmet. Grand job, Ryan." He smiled and thanked them as he walked on. When he sat down alone in his office, he allowed the grin he'd been stifling to break out. He read each paper to see if they had taken the whole piece. The Examiner had, but the Independent had edited it down to cut out about a third of the word count, but they all had his quote from Collins. It's what made the article.

Hooper walked in and grinned. "You've seen them, then."

"I have indeed."

"You're a big man about town now, boyo."

Hooper sat down across from Emmet and continued. "Seriously, Ryan. You did great work in America and our readership went up as people followed the campaign there. You have a way of putting a human face to the story. Now this. Your spot is secure here, young man."

Emmet had a hard time focusing on his work after Hooper left. *I have to see Bridie tonight. Maybe she'll come out for a celebratory tea.* He dashed off a short note to her with an invitation to go out and took it out to one of the many delivery boys who hung about waiting for a message to run.

"Take this and wait for the response if the lady is at home. If not, just come back and let me know she wasn't there, right?" He gave the boy 5 pence and watched him jump on his bicycle.

The return message was delivered to Emmet in his office by a copy boy.

I'd love to go out with you. I'll be ready at six o'clock. We're all a-buzz with the excitement of your piece in the Independent!

Emmet took a deep breath. *Better and better. Her Da must have seen it.*

———

Emmet had made a reservation at Jammet's. He knew it would be far more expensive than anywhere he'd ever eaten, but he threw caution to the wind. Emmet would manage it. He started with a brandy for himself and a sherry for Bridie.

He felt the warmth of the brandy coursing through him. "Bridie, I wish I could bring you to places like this all the time."

She reached over and put her hand over his. "This is far too grand for the likes of us, Emmet. I'm perfectly content with John Kavanaugh's."

They both smiled, recalling the pub where they met.

"Are you saying you'd like to leave?"

"Not on your life. I'll make the most of this." She held up her glass of sherry to clink it against his crystal glass of brandy. "Congratulations, Emmet. I was that proud of you today when I saw your name as the byline in the Independent, I nearly cried."

"Did your Da see it?"

"He did, of course."

"Did he say anything?"

She tilted her head. "No. I know he read it through though, and then he showed Mammy."

"Did he?"

"Why the interest in what Da thought?"

He heaved a sigh. "Well, I'll tell you. I met your Da last week. I wanted to talk to him."

She frowned. "He never said."

"Here it is. Bridie, I love you."

She blushed and glanced around to see if anyone had heard.

He continued. "You've been so patient waiting for me. I'm now able to ask for your hand in marriage and that's why I met with your father. I asked him."

Her mouth fell open, and she covered it with her hand. "I didn't know."

"He said no."

Her eyes widened. "What?"

He nodded. "He wouldn't allow me to ask you to marry me."

Her eyebrows came together, and her lips formed a thin line. "How dare he?"

"I'm not being very noble by telling you this, but I'm not giving up. That's why I'm curious about what his reaction was to my article."

She bit her lip. "Emmet Ryan, I won't be told by my father what I can and cannot do."

"Ah, Bridie. You must. I won't have us starting out in life being estranged from your family." He smiled then. "I'll woo him. I'm patient."

She gave him a small smile. "You are."

"It's enough for me to know that you are willing even if your Da isn't."

She shook her head. "I don't want to waste more time waiting. I've waited long enough."

He reached across the table and took her hand. "A little bit longer. Meanwhile he hasn't forbidden us to see each other, so we'll continue as we are for now. I wish I could just ask you here and now, but let's do it right. I would rather have the blessing from your parents."

"And if they don't give it?"

He stroked the back of her hand with his thumb. "Let's face that if it happens." Emmet smiled and lifted his glass of wine to hers. "To us." His heart thumped at the smile she shone on him as she clinked his glass.

"To us." She agreed.

17

Dublin, February 1922

It was billed as a celebration of the Irish Free State Agreement Act which had been brought to the British House of Commons. It was also a dinner dance where awards were handed out to those who were seen to have helped the Cause that led to the agreement, and so Emmet's name had been put forward for his work in America and the piece that made his name a household word at the Government handover. It was a ball at the Mansion House. The official residence of the Lord Mayor of Dublin, and the current meeting place of the Dáil, or the Assembly was also the premier place for fancy events and Emmet never imagined he'd be invited to attend something there.

Emmet read the invitation and tossed it into the wastepaper can beside his desk.

When Hooper came in a few moments later, the editor stooped and retrieved the invitation. "What are you doing? I had a hand in getting you nominated for this. Are you thinking of not attending?"

"I don't think this sell-out of an agreement is anything to celebrate."

Hooper frowned. "Listen son, this is a big step forward for the country and whether you are for the treaty or against it, as a journalist you need to be at every historic event you can manage to get into." He slapped the invitation on the desk. "Go and enjoy the free food and drink and I'll look forward to your piece about the glamour of the new government afterwards."

Emmet saluted. "Yes, sir."

Emmet sent the official invitation over to Bridie. With its embossed paper and invitation to the supper and awards, to be followed by a ball in the Round Room of the Mansion, Emmet knew it was impressive and hoped her father would think so as well.

———

When Emmet walked into the Mansion the night of the ball, he was glad he came. Bridie was stunning in a long satin dress with full white skirt covered by a black cutaway overskirt and black strapless bodice. Her long white gloves made her arms and shoulders appear translucent. With her red hair brushed back from her face in an elaborate swept-up style pinned in place with a pearl comb, he thought she looked like a queen.

He kept stealing glances at her. "God, you're gorgeous."

She smiled at him and brushed a tiny piece of lint from his hired black dinner suit. "You're not so bad yourself."

A photographer roamed the room and took their photograph, after which Emmet gave him his card and asked for a copy to be sent to him.

The photographer glanced at the name and smiled. "I will, of course. Good luck with the awards tonight."

Bridie whispered in Emmet's ear. "He knew who you were."

Emmet smiled at the pride in her voice.

Later, after a supper that involved too many forks, and an awards ceremony that saw a different reporter win, Emmet danced Bridie around the room. "I'm going back to your father, Bridie. I'm not waiting any longer for you and me to be married."

He felt her gloved fingers on his neck and his heart clenched at the smile that she beamed on him.

———

This time Mr. Mallon sat across from Emmet in Emmet's office. It had been a risk, asking Bridie's father to come to him. Emmet knew he may take it as a summons, which would be seen as an impertinence of the highest order, but Emmet positioned it that Mr. Mallon could come at any time that suited him, which may have made it more palatable.

When the older man was shown into Emmet's office, he seemed less sure of himself in the unfamiliar surroundings.

Emmet stood and came from behind his desk to shake Mr. Mallon's hand. "Thank you so much for coming to meet with me, sir."

Bridie's father took the chair that Emmet guided him to and then Emmet took the other one in front of the desk rather than retreat back to his own seat.

"Can I have tea ordered?"

Mr. Mallon waved his hand. "Don't trouble yourself. I know you have work to do."

Emmet nodded. "The last time we met, you told me that I needed to prove myself."

"Yes."

Emmet licked his lips, feeling the dryness make them stick; stopping the words from coming. "Since that time, I have achieved great exposure with my own byline which was, as you may know, picked up by the *Irish Examiner* and other papers. That success in turn, has prompted my paper to reprint some of my American pieces."

Mr. Mallon crossed his legs and flicked a piece of lint from his trouser leg. "Indeed?"

Emmet felt the heat rise in his face. He knew that Mr. Mallon knew this. "Yes. I have been promoted..." Emmet spread his hands to gesture at his office "and I have been nominated for an award for my work."

"Which you did not win."

Emmet gritted his teeth. "As you know, I was invited to the recent ball at the Mansion. I am engaged in important work, Mr. Mallon. Bridie is proud of me."

Bridie's father remained silent and Emmet felt his heart race.

"Mr. Mallon. I may not have won the award, but I will not fail to win something far more important, and that is, Bridie's hand in marriage. We love each other, and I can provide a good life for her."

Mr. Mallon raised one eyebrow. "Was there anything else you wish to say to me?"

Emmet took a deep breath. "I would again like to ask for your blessing and agreement that we become engaged."

Mr. Mallon studied Emmet for a moment. "Very well." He smiled then and Emmet felt the blood pound in his head. "I know when I am beaten."

He stood, and Emmet jumped up to grasp his hand. "Thank you, Mr. Mallon. You won't regret it."

Bridie's father nodded. "Be sure that I don't."

18

Dublin, May 1922

Bridie met Emmet in front of the General Post Office. The GPO had taken a beating during the 1916 Rising but it was looking good again. It continued to be a favourite meeting place, perhaps because of its place in the history of Ireland. The scarred building stood proud on O'Connell Street.

Bridie linked her arm through Emmet's and they walked towards the market on Moore Street. "I have been instructed not to come back without strawberries."

"Strawberries? Are they already available?"

"I hope so. Mammy has it in mind to create some sort of fancy confectionary masterpiece for the desert table."

Emmet nodded. "My mother is going a bit mad as well. I think she's a little worried that your family will look down on mine because they're from the country."

Bridie stopped to look at Emmet. "But that's silly. They've met several times now and everyone's gotten along so well."

Emmet rolled his eyes. "I know. That's what I've told her, but now she's in a dither about the wedding lunch."

"But your parents are bringing the ham and the chicken. They're doing more than their part. I know Daddy has said something about feeling guilty at accepting so much kindness from them because it should be him paying for everything."

"Now that's nonsense. Perhaps we should have eloped. We could have gone to America."

"Don't even joke about that. I don't want you ever going to America again. The first time was your last time."

Emmet patted her hand resting on his arm. "Yes, dear."

She pinched his arm. "I mean it."

"And what if Michael Collins calls upon me to go again?"

Bridie frowned. "You'll just have to send him to me. I will tell him that you have too many responsibilities as a married man and can't just be running off whenever it suits you."

Emmet smiled. "Right, then. I'll do just that. Send him to you."

"Family comes first, Mr. Ryan."

They reached the market. Emmet pointed out a display of fruit including a basket of strawberries. "There now. Will those do?"

Bridie did her shopping with Emmet by her side. They knew many of the vendors, who all wished them well on their wedding day and picked out the best produce to give Bridie.

Walking home, Bridie squeezed his arm. "Emmet, I don't know how I'd manage if you weren't there at home with me every evening."

He slipped his arm around her waist. "Shush now. I'll always be there for you."

"Will you, though?"

"Of course, I will."

She bit her lip. "So, you agree that the family always comes first?"

There was a hesitation before he answered. "Family comes first, but sometimes the bigger picture affects the family, so we always need to be able to look at that. We need to be able to see what the best for the family will be. Don't you think so?"

She sighed. "Yes, I suppose that's true."

"It's not always one or the other, right?"

"Hmm."

He squeezed her. "Now don't upset yourself about trying to think through every possibility that might come to us. As long as you and I are together, we'll find a way through."

She nodded. "You're right. I'll stop being a miserable git now. Let's get these things home and then we can sit out with a cup of tea before you have to go."

Emmet leaned in to kiss her temple beneath her straw hat. "And then next time I'm with you, I won't be going anywhere without you."

Bridie's smile seemed shaky.

Emmet seemed to feel her thoughts. "Are you nervous?"

She shrugged. "A wee bit."

"Me too."

She looked at him. "Really? I thought men were all brave and strong and never afraid."

Emmet laughed. "You can't be serious. I can't tell you how many times I've known fear, and I think the idea of being married is one of the most fearful."

"Why? Do you not want to be with me?"

He stopped and set the shopping basket on the ground. He took both her hands in his. "Bridie. How can you think that even for a second? I want to be with you more than anything I've ever wanted. I'm afraid of making a bollocks of it."

She cheeks grew pink at the curse, but she left her hands resting in his.

He went on. "I see how my Mam and Da are together and I want to be like that. I want to be good to you and make you happy, but I'm not sure I know how."

She smiled and squeezed his hands. "We'll figure it out together."

———

The wedding day dawned with a grey drizzle, but Emmet felt the day perfect. Liam was there to serve as best man. Emmet had taken on a proper flat in Drumcondra and it seemed too big and strange to him. He missed his little bed-sit.

Liam clapped him on the shoulder. "Are you ready?"

Emmet nodded.

"You don't want me to hire a cab and we'll make a run for it? I know places up in the hills where we can hide for weeks, no questions asked."

Emmet grinned. "I can imagine. Probably a cache of guns under the bed so that we could fight off the whole of the Mallon clan when they track us down?"

"You've got it."

"No, you're all right. I can't wait to start my new life with my wife."

Liam pulled a small flask from inside his jacket. "One last drink as my bachelor friend." He took a deep sip and handed the flask to Emmet.

Emmet took a long draw and then coughed. "Jaysus. What is this?"

"Poteen of the finest."

Emmet took another small sip. The illicit liquor made from potatoes burned its way down his throat and made his eyes water. "From the stills of your mountain pals?"

Liam smiled. He took the flask back and capped it after taking another sip himself.

"Right, so. Let's go."

———

The organ played, and Emmet turned to watch.

Bridie's sister Katie walked down the aisle in front of Bridie who followed in a beautiful ankle-length dress that fell straight from her shoulders, simple in its elegance, with lace trim at the shoulders and hem and with a matching lace ribbon below her waist. She wore a long veil that fell across her shoulders and was pinned to her red hair.

Bridie held tight to her father's arm. Emmet watched as Bridie glanced at her mother in the front row and saw his bride's eyes fill with tears. She looked away from her mother to Emmet, and he felt the heat and knew his ears must be turning deep red. He locked eyes with her, seeming to pull her towards him. Bridie loosened her grip on her father's arm as they reached the altar, slipping her hand away, and transferred her grasp to Emmet's arm. He felt strong and warm under her touch.

The solemn words were spoken and then they walked together back up the aisle, as husband and wife. Friends reached out to greet them as they passed. The drizzle had cleared, and they stood in the sun of the early summer's day surrounded by family and friends.

Bridie leaned in and brushed Emmet's ear with her lips. "My heart feels like it will burst."

"When can I take you away to be alone with you?"

She laughed. "Not for a long time yet. Look, we are gathering for a photograph."

They crowded together; their two families mashed together as tightly as they could get while the photographer that her father had hired kept calling out instructions to *squeeze in* and *stand still now.*

They all laughed when Emmet's brother Kevin muttered "Jaysus, when can I take this jacket off?" His gripe was loud in one of those moments of silence that sometimes happen.

They made their way back to the Mallon house and then the jackets came off and cool drinks were served. The plan was that Bridie and Emmet would take a cab to the Shelbourne Hotel for the night. It was expensive, but Emmet had been saving money from his trip to America for the wedding trip.

At Bridie's house, the men all gathered in the garden to drink pints of porter. Mr. Mallon had gotten in barrels for the occasion. Emmet had a drink with his brothers and father, and while his oldest brother and father became embroiled in a discussion about the likelihood of Kilkenny making it to the hurling finals this year, he and Kevin moved to a quiet corner of the garden.

Kevin clinked his glass against Emmet's. "Slainte, brother."

"Sláinteagad-sa."

Kevin grinned. "We've had some adventures, you and I."

"We have, that."

Kevin nodded. "You're done with all that now, but you're starting a whole new adventure now."

Emmet tilted his head. "I'm not giving up on my beliefs."

"Ah, no. I didn't mean that. I meant that I promise I won't call on you to drag you into mischief."

Emmet smiled. "You'll have to look after yourself without my steadying influence."

"I'll do my best. I'll miss you, but I'm happy for you. She's a lovely lass."

Emmet drained his drink. "She is, and I think it's high time I find her."

He gave his brother a quick hug and then turned away to find his wife. He spied her in a corner of the room with her friend Elizabeth who had come with the Carsons for the wedding. It was always a bit of a shock to Emmet to hear Elizabeth's English accent, but he knew Bridie and her friend were close, so he liked the girl for that reason.

He joined them in time to hear Bridie say to Elizabeth: "I'm so glad you all came down for this."

Emmet nodded. "I am too, Elizabeth."

Elizabeth straightened a fold of lace on Bridie's shoulder. "I'm very glad as well. Bridie, I consider you one of my dearest friends by now and I'm delighted to be here to help you celebrate."

Bridie reached for Elizabeth's hand. "What are your plans now? We haven't had five minutes to really catch up since you've been here."

Emmet wondered if he should leave the two girls to talk. "I should go have a drink with my brothers."

Elizabeth rested her hand on his arm. "Don't leave on my account. You're both my friends now." She turned back to Bridie. "I have been pleading with my father to let me come home."

Bridie frowned. "Oh, no. That's not what I want to hear. Are you not happy with the Carsons?"

"I'm happy enough, but it really doesn't feel like home. They've been so very kind to me, but they have their own busy lives, and I feel that it's time I go back to my own."

"You'll be twenty-one in another month, won't you?"

"Yes, and that means that I have a small inheritance coming to me. I have a dream to set myself up in a little business."

"A business? What sort of business?"

"I plan to tutor young ladies in the arts. I can play piano reasonably well, and I can paint."

"You aren't going to be a governess, are you?"

"No, my inheritance should allow me enough independence to live a quiet life in some rented rooms where I could live and work from. Perhaps for some people I would go to their homes to give the lessons."

"What about your father? Could you not live with him?"

Elizabeth furrowed her forehead. "No, I think not. He prefers to live at his club and quite honestly, I think I prefer to live independently. I love him and miss him. I hope to see him often, but I would rather live alone."

"How brave you are."

Elizabeth squeezed Bridie's hand. "You helped to show me what was possible with your work at the shop."

Emmet felt a glow of pride. "Our Bridie is an inspiration."

Elizabeth nodded. "She is that. Go on now, the pair of you. Everyone wants to chat with you. I'm going to help in the kitchen."

Bridie linked her arm through Emmet's. "It's time for the men to come in and sit down to lunch. Come. We'll go fetch them in."

Emmet nodded and tilted his glass to finish his drink. His head swam a little and he realized he'd had more to drink already than he usually drank. "Right. Lead the way, wife of mine."

Bridie raised an eyebrow. "Are you all right?"

"Never better."

They went out and called for those in the garden to come for lunch and then led their way in to the long table that had been set up. The table spanned the length of the house by opening the French doors between the parlour and living room. Emmet heard laughter from the far end of the table as his brothers and the girls squeezed into their places.

To start, Bridie's father made a speech to welcome Emmet to the family and to thank all the guests for coming to share the day.

Emmet felt a lump in his throat as he listened to his father-in-law's voice, thick with emotion. Once Mr. Mallon had consented to the marriage, he never expressed doubt again. He ended by lifting his glass to the group. "Please lift your glasses to Mr. and Mrs. Emmet Ryan and wish them a long and happy life together."

The toast was repeated along the length of the table while Bridie turned to Emmet. "To a long and happy life together."

He smiled and clinked his glass to hers. "To a long and happy life together." He drank down half the glass of wine in one gulp.

Bridie leaned over to touch her father's hand. "Thank you, Daddy."

He shook his head and turned away, his eyes shiny with wetness.

Next Mr. Ryan stood and welcomed Bridie to the family. "We have been blessed with gaining one daughter already when our Michael was married, and now we have a second one to make our family even more complete."

Finally, Emmet rose to thank everyone. He thanked her parents for hosting the day. Then his parents for their contributions. After that, the other guests for joining in the celebration and finally he looked down at Bridie sitting beside him. "And last but not least." He shifted unsteadily on his feet. "My beautiful bride. I must thank her for having the patience to wait for me while I travelled to America and.."

Liam called out from where he sat on Emmet's other side. "She'll be running out of patience if you blather on much longer, as will we all. I'm starving."

Everyone laughed. Emmet lifted his glass, abandoning the rest of his speech. "To my lovely Bridie."

Emmet looked proud of his pun, linking the notion of his bride with Bridie's name.

Bridie shook her head but smiled and clinked her glass against his.

Bridie picked at her lunch. A piece of ham stuck in her throat and she coughed. Emmet handed her a glass of wine.

Bridie shook her head as the coughing subsided. "I've had enough to drink."

Emmet lifted his glass and drained it. "It's a celebration, love. Let's enjoy the day."

Liam immediately came around to Emmet and refilled his glass. Bridie rested her hand under the table on Emmet's thigh. "I just don't want to overdo things."

The evening was drawing in as the guests finally drifted away. Emmet and Bridie stood at the door wishing everyone safe home. Emmet wished he could stretch out on the settee for a nap. Liam was one of the last to leave. He gave Bridie a hug. "You're a lovely girl and Emmet's a lucky man."

Bridie smiled. "Thank you, Liam. I hope you know that you'll always be welcome in our home."

Liam nodded. "That's a blessing and an invitation I'll be sure to take you up on."

He turned then to Emmet. "Will you not come for one small drink to the pub?"

Emmet grinned and nearly stumbled into Liam's arms. "I better not."

Liam nodded. "You're probably right. I'll run down to the corner to get a cab for you, will I?"

Emmet blinked. "I can do it." but Bridie quickly answered. "Will you, Liam? That would be grand. Thank you."

When Emmet closed the door behind Liam, Bridie pointed to the suitcases that her father had brought to the front hall. "Will you be able to manage?"

"Are we on our way, then?"

"Yes, I think it's time. Don't you?"

"I thought one more drink would be in order."

Emmet's father stood in the doorway of the parlour along with Mr. Mallon. The Ryans would head for home as soon as Emmet and Bridie were gone. He stepped forward and put his arm around Emmet's shoulders. "Time for all of us to go now, Emmet. You've kept your lovely wife waiting long enough for your company."

"Right, Da."

A cab pulled up then and together Emmet's father and Bridie's carried out the cases while Bridie's mother came to give her one final hug.

"I'll see you soon, Mam."

"Of course, you will. Sure, you're only going to Wexford for a few days and then I'll come and see you in your new flat."

"Thank you for this day. It's been perfect."

Mrs. Mallon kissed her daughter on the forehead. "Go on now, Mrs. Ryan."

Emmet listened to the exchange between Bridie and her mother. His mouth felt dry and his tongue like flannel. He wanted to thank his mother-in-law as well but struggled to form the sentences.

The cab arrived and Emmet went outside, longing for fresh air. He stood leaning on the car and waited for Bridie.

Both fathers carried the cases to the cab and gave them to the cabbie. Emmet watched as Bridie gave her father a quick hug and then Emmet's father pulled her close.

Emmet frowned when he heard his father's quiet words: "Be patient with him tonight. He's not much of a drinker, I'm afraid."

Bridie smiled and climbed in. Emmet seemed to fall into the seat beside his wife and then he developed hiccups. With every noisy spasm, he apologized. "Sorry, sorry."

Bridie patted his hand.

The drive to the hotel only took ten minutes and then Emmet struggled to clamber out again. His legs felt like rubber.

A hotel porter pulled Emmet out while another unloaded the suitcases.

Emmet put his arm around her as they walked in. "It's very posh, isn't it?"

Bridie cringed. "Not so loud, Emmet."

Emmet's eyes widened. "Am I loud? Sorry."

They followed the porter up to their room, Bridie clutching Emmet around his waist, keeping him from stumbling.

The porter hovered after he put their suitcases down and Bridie nudged Emmet. "Have you a coin for the man, Em?"

Emmet felt himself flush and rooted in his pocket to give the man a tip.

The door closed and then they were alone. Emmet sat down on the end of the bed, feeling lost and woozy.

Bridie went across to look out the window. "There's a lovely view from here over St. Stephen's Green."

"Is there?"

Bridie turned to look at Emmet. She shook her head and tut-tutted. "Look at the state of you, Emmet Ryan."

He gazed at her blankly.

She went to him and kneeled to unlace his shoes.

He patted her head. "I think I need a little lie-down, Bridie."

"Yes, I think you do."

She helped him shrug off his good jacket and pulled off his shoes. "Can you stand for a moment?"

He pushed himself off the bed and stood, wavering, while she undid the buttons on his shirt. "You'll have to take your own trousers off."

Bridie turned her back on him and pulled down the cover and blanket. The sheet was crisp and white. Emmet dropped his trousers to the floor.

Bridie turned back to him and she put her arm around his waist. "Come and lie down."

He collapsed in the bed, knowing he should remove his socks but unable to make the effort. Bridie pulled the covers over him.

His tongue was thick and fuzzy. "Sorry, Bridie."

He felt her cool hand brush his hair from his forehead and heard her soft words. "For better or worse, my love."

19

Dublin, 28 June 1922

The pounding on the door of their flat shocked them awake. Bridie sat bolt upright while Emmet leaped out of their bed, grabbing his dressing gown in passing.

Emmet growled at the boy who thrust a note into his hand. "What is it?"

"From the paper, sir. I was told to fetch you because Collins is bombing The Four Courts."

Emmet tore open the note from his editor. It simply said. "Civil War. Get in as quick as you can."

Emmet frowned at the boy. "When did it start?"

The boy's voice was high pitched and frantic sounding. "I don't know. I was just told to run and knock you up so you could record it all."

Emmet pulled open a drawer in the small table by the door where he kept loose change. He gave the boy a penny. "Right, so. You did well. Run on back now. I'll be there directly."

As soon as the door closed, Bridie hastened to Emmet's side. "What is it? What's happened?"

Emmet pulled her in against his chest. "The Government is bombing the anti-treaty garrison at the Four Courts."

Bridie pulled back and peered into his face. "Ah, no. It surely hasn't come to this. Collins wouldn't."

Emmet sighed and then walked quickly back to the bedroom to throw on his clothes. "He'll do what he has to do to keep order. I know Churchill has been putting pressure on him to resolve the Four Courts."

"But they've been there since April. Why now?"

Emmet pulled on his jacket. The Brits have been threatening to come back in.

"Dear God. How will it end?"

Emmet shook his head. "With bloodshed."

Bridie clung to him at the door. "Let it not be your blood."

He kissed her. "My days of being in the middle of the fight are done. I fight with my words now."

"But who's in the wrong here? How will you write it up?"

He closed the door without answering her question.

Emmet rode his bicycle downtown to the temporary office of the Freeman's Journal, not having the patience to wait for the tram. Since the presses had been destroyed by the Anti-Treaty I.R.A. in March, they had been operating from a flat above a shop on St. Augustine Street. He crossed the Liffey, coughing in the cloud of smoke that engulfed him.

The boom from the 18-pounder cannons shook the very streets and plant pots fell crashing to the pavement from window sills.

Emmet came into the office and joined the reporters, editors and copy-boys, all talking at once.

"Ryan. Good. You're here. I want you out there. Get some firsthand impressions of what's going on."

"When did this start?"

Hooper wiped his brow. "Around four o'clock. I believe Collins gave the order, but no one will confirm it. All I know is that The Free-Staters have got British weapons backing them. Those hooligans in the Four Courts will finally be routed out. They should never have been allowed to dig in like they have."

Emmet bit his lip at Hooper's tone. "They were peaceful. It's pretty extreme to take cannons to them."

Hooper's eyes popped wide open. "Peaceful?" He waved his arms around the small office space. "You think destroying our premises and presses was peaceful? We're only in this poxy place because of those fellas. They deserve what they get."

Emmet nodded. "Right. I'll get out there and see what people are saying."

"Make sure you get the story in and finalized before three o'clock so we have time to get it over to the press."

"I'll make sure." Emmet knew they were renting time on another paper's press until they could get their own back up and running, so they were limited in the time they had in order to get out an evening paper.

Emmet walked down Lower Bridge Street and turned right on Merchant's Quay and then the way was blocked by men in uniform. The noise of the shelling was deafening. Lorries raced along the quay on the other side of the Liffey from where Emmet stood, taking men and supplies to the battle to reinforce the Provisional Government troops.

Emmet turned back and crossed over the Liffey and cycled in a wide circle to try to get closer to the Four Courts. He stopped regularly to talk to people. He watched as British troops delivered two more cannons to the Free State troops and spoke with a captain who told him that Collins had been offered 60 pound howitzers by the British, along with the offer to bomb from the air, but Collins had refused on the grounds of the risk to the civilian population.

Emmet shook his head. "My God. Not long ago we were all standing shoulder to shoulder and now the Brits are providing the means for Irishman to kill Irishman."

The captain wiped a sleeve across his forehead. "It's madness, I know, but what can we do?"

A little after two o'clock in the afternoon there was a huge explosion that sent a thick grey mushroom cloud into the air.

At the barricade Emmet threw himself to the ground. His eyes stung with smoke. He wiped his face with his handkerchief and it came away black with soot.

Emmet crawled over to a trooper who studied the scene through binoculars. "What the hell was that?"

"Looks like the Records Office just exploded."

"Surely an 18-pounder wouldn't do that?"

"No. They've booby-trapped the whole area around the building with explosives. We must have hit one of those spots."

Alarm bells clanged as ambulances made their way back from the area carrying wounded Free State troops. Emmet helped to lift the wooden barricade out of the way to allow an ambulance to race past. He wished he could get closer to the Four Courts but knew it was too dangerous. His heart went out to the men and women holding the building, fire now raging.

He knew he had to get back and write his story to make it into the paper in time, so he reluctantly climbed back on his bicycle and cycled through the falling silt and smoke back to the office.

The story he wrote focused on the human element of the fight. He wrote about the men who felt driven to the extreme action of occupying the Four Courts by their sense of betrayal with the Treaty, and how the British may have lost the War of Independence, but they were now getting their revenge by pitting the Irish against each other.

When Hooper read the story he came into Emmet's office and threw down the notes. "What is this?"

Emmet straightened his shoulders. "It's the way I see it."

Hooper tore the pages in half. "Write it again. You're a damn journalist. Report the news, don't offer your personal point of view."

Hooper marched out and Emmet sighed. He wasn't entirely surprised. He looked at his watch, understood he had very little time and pulled a clean sheet of paper out. The story was half the length and kept to the bare facts of weapons deployed, explosions witnessed and the current state of the situation.

Emmet read it through.

There's no heart to it but if this is what the editor wants, so be it.

———

Emmet slept in his office for a few hours. Before that he went out and back again twice but after another huge explosion around five o'clock things quietened down somewhat for the evening. He had sent a note to Bridie to tell her that he'd be home when he could be, but it may not be for another day. He felt grimy and longed to go home for a bath and change of clothes, but he didn't dare. Too much was happening.

The battle had spread to encompass a much wider area outside of the region of the Four Courts. It now stretched over to

O'Connell Street. The Anti-Treaty Dublin Brigade had taken over several key buildings, including several hotels. He knew that the Four Courts would need to be surrendered soon and he was torn between waiting nearby to witness that or to move to where the battle was now most active. There were plenty of his colleagues keeping watch over the Four Courts, amongst the crowds of general population watching the activity.

He waved at another reporter from the Journal and pointed towards Sackville Street. The man touched his hat in a brief salute to acknowledge he understood that Emmet was leaving. *They can chronicle the surrender.*

He decided to get as close to the Gresham Hotel as he could to get a look there. If he could get into any of those buildings, he knew he could get to all of them safely because he heard that the Brigade had mouse-holed between the buildings, cutting passages through the walls to facilitate movement between them.

Maybe I can find Liam. Emmet knew Liam was with the Dublin Brigade. *I'm glad Kevin went to Cork a few weeks back.*

He cycled along the Liffey, crossed over the river and turned north up Sackville Street. He stopped for a moment to gaze up the street. His mouth fell open when he saw the devastation already created. Shop windows were smashed and debris lying out in the street. Broken chairs lay upside down on the pavement amidst bricks, wood panelling, pots and boxes. Shards of window glass crunched underfoot as men bolted from one side of the street to the other. Torn awnings and drapes flapped in the wind as they hung by corners and shredded bits of fabric. He started forward again, keeping a watchful eye for signs of snipers or soldiers. He passed the General Post Office, the scene of so much action during the 1916 rebellion and then he left his bicycle on Cathedral Street, to continue by foot up Thomas's Lane around to the back of the Gresham.

A man from the Citizen Army, dressed in his everyday woollen jacket over a once-white collarless shirt, with his flat cap pulled low over his eyes, stepped out from a doorway and threatened him with an old rifle, probably kept in hiding since 1916. "Who are you? You can't go any farther."

Emmet showed his press identification. "I need to get closer. I need to tell the story as it's happening. Let me go in and let people know the truth."

The man frowned. "Are ye for us or against us?"

Emmet hesitated. "In theory, I'm neutral but if you're asking am I a spy, I'll tell you no. You've nothing to fear from me."

The soldier nodded and lowered his rifle. "Follow me, then."

Emmet followed his escort along Thomas's Lane and in through a back door into the Gresham Hotel. He was led to an upper room where an officer wearing a dust-covered uniform and bandoliers crossed against his chest stood peering out the window.

The soldier called out: "Comander Holohan? I found this man out back. He's a journalist."

Holohan turned, ran his hand through his dark hair and glared at Emmet. "Who are you?"

Emmet showed his identification again.

Holohan growled. "I've no time for entertaining the press."

"Let me just stand back and make notes."

Holohan turned back to the window to peer up the street. "Just stay out of the way, but I can't guarantee your safety."

"Of course not."

Emmet retreated to a back corner of the room while his escort nodded to him and left, presumably back to his post. After a few moments, Emmet left the room to explore. He stopped to speak to the defenders at their posts by the windows, and others deep in the maze of broken hallways as they restocked supplies or as they took a rest. He was surprised by how many women were there, not just in the capacity of preparing food and rolling bandages but returning fire side by side with their male counterparts.

He found a spot in an empty room and sat down to write. The story he wrote resonated with heartfelt interviews, but even as he wrote it, he knew it would never be published by the Freeman's Journal, and yet he was driven to write it. Like in 1916, the Anti-Treaty, or Republicans understood that they were not going to win this battle, but they felt compelled to stand up for their beliefs. Emmet wanted to capture their names and where they were from, these men and women who put their lives on the line for their beliefs. The battle for the block of buildings where Emmet spent the rest of the day and into the next became more desperate as the Free State army blasted their positions with heavy firepower.

On July fifth the Republicans surrendered. The Gresham Hotel was crumbling and on fire, but the defenders did their best to help the senior men to escape.

Emmet stumbled down the steps in exhaustion to the back entrance. He intended to make his way back to his office to write up his stories when two Republican snipers caught up with him. Everyone knew him by now.

One soot-blackened man rested his hand on Emmet's shoulder. "Take a look and see, is it clear?"

Emmet cracked open the back door, and seeing no one there, he opened it farther. "It looks clear, lads."

He held the door open wide for the two soldiers to pass by him. They had just left the blazing building when they heard shouts from the end of the lane by Cathedral Street. Emmet jumped out and stood in the middle of the laneway, waving his arms with his identification held in one hand. "Run, boys!" he called over his shoulder.

He heard the pounding footsteps of the two escaping soldiers as three Free State soldiers shouted for him to get out of the way.

Emmet bit his lip and felt his stomach and sphincter muscles clenching as he kept waving his arms. He resisted the urge to close his eyes as he waited for the bullets to strike him. "Don't shoot! I'm a journalist!"

By the time the three reached him, the two Republicans had disappeared.

One of the soldiers yanked his identification from Emmet. "Jaysus, you almost got yourself killed. You're under arrest for aiding the escape of an enemy."

Another soldier pushed him forward. "That's treason. You'll be shot."

Emmet licked his lips. "I'm sorry. I didn't mean to get in your way. I'm just doing my job, getting the story, like."

"Yeh. Tell it to the judge."

They pushed him along to a waiting vehicle, and then he was driven to the police station. Emmet's thoughts were on Bridie, and he asked the desk Sergeant if he could send a note to his wife.

The Sergeant nodded, and Emmet pulled a page from his notebook.

Dear Bridie,

Don't worry. I'm fine but I've been arrested. As soon as I know anything I'll let you know. I've been taken to the Castle."

He signed his name and after the Sergeant read it, he was given an envelope and the Sergeant walked to the door and shouted into the courtyard for a boy to come and take the note for delivery.

"Can I send a note to my editor as well? He'll need to know I'm here."

"Go ahead but be quick. I have to process you and get to the others."

More prisoners were being brought in every minute.

Emmet addressed a short note to Mr. Hooper and gave that to the delivery boy as well who stood looking up at Emmet.

Emmet pulled out a tuppence and gave it to the boy who disappeared at a trot.

"Empty your pockets into this box."

"Can I keep my notebook and pen?"

"No. Everything in here. Can't have you making notes about how to blow this place up next."

Emmet sighed. "I didn't blow anything up."

"That's what they all say."

Emmet was taken to a large cell and shoved in with several other exhausted, grimy, soot-covered men. He found a space on the floor and sat down on the cold stone beside a man in his thirties who still wore his oversized flat cap, long grey trench coat, and incongruously, his tie. "Well, boys. You did your best and stood up for Ireland."

The man narrowed his eyes. "Who are you? I don't know you." He looked around the group. "Anyone know him?"

A few shook their heads and a grumble of 'no' from others.

Emmet held up his hands. "They took my identification away, but my name's Emmet Ryan. I'm a journalist."

One man called out. "I know that name. Are you the fella that wrote the piece when Michael Collins took over?"

"I did."

More grumbling. "So, you favour the Treaty?"

"I don't. As a journalist I have to try not to take sides, though."

The man with the trench coat frowned. "I say he's a spy."

Emmet felt his heart race. "I'm no spy. I just spent the past two days side by side with Holohan and Traynor's men at the Gresham."

Trench coat stood up, swaying with exhaustion. "Collecting evidence? And now you're here to find out who the leaders are and what we know? Is that it?"

Emmet saw the man ball his fists. More men struggled to their feet. "No. Jaysus, men." Now Emmet stood as well. "I'm no bloody spy. I was in the Finglas Volunteers in '16 and I did my part as well at the Custom House."

Trench coat narrowed his eyes. "We all have that sort of history. It's the side you're on now that counts."

A swarthy man, his jaw blackened with a week's dark stubble, leaned against the wall and spoke up. "Tell us about the Battle of Ashbourne, so. I'm in the mood for a story."

"Sure, he'd know all about it from writing his news reports."

Emmet sucked in a deep breath and pointed at the man who'd made that comment. "I know what happened because I was there. As was my father, my two brothers and my closest pal, Liam Kelly. My Da was shot and wounded the day before the battle, but we all were there on the day it went down and went to serve our time in Kilmainham afterwards. That's how I know what you're feeling right now. You feel betrayed. You wonder what it was all for when you had to surrender. You're so tired you can barely stand, so let's all sit down again, and I'll tell you what it was like for me that day when I followed Thomas Ashe into battle."

A few men crossed themselves at Ashe's name, and slowly they sat again. The one leaning on the back wall nodded. "You know Liam Kelly?"

Emmet nodded. "We're still friends. I thought I might see him over the last few days. I know he's here somewhere."

The man against the wall gave a small nod. "I say he's all right."

Trench coat sat down and folded his arms across his chest. He grunted but didn't say anything further.

Emmet sighed and looked at the blackened, grimy ceiling. "I believe in a united Ireland. There isn't much more I can say."

The fight seemed to go out of Trench coat. "It's hard to know who to trust these days."

Emmet nodded. "Fair enough. The reason I'm in here with you now is because I got in the way when two of your men were getting out the back door of the Gresham. The Free Staters weren't best pleased when they couldn't fire at the escapees since I was standing there waving my press identification at them."

There were some tired chuckles. "And did they get away, then?"

Emmet nodded. "As far as I know."

"Well that's something, anyway."

Emmet held his hand out to Trench coat. "Let's start again. I'm Emmet Ryan."

"Sean."

Emmet knew the man still didn't trust him, but at least the feeling of imminent danger had passed. A few more men muttered their names as Emmet looked at them. Some simply closed their eyes to avoid further discussion. When Emmet looked up at the swarthy man, still leaning against the wall, the man nodded. "Dan Breen."

Emmet rose to his feet. "Of course. I should have recognized you. It's an honour to meet you."

Breen crooked a ghost of a smile. "Recognize me from the Wanted Posters the Brits had plastered everywhere, you mean?"

Emmet returned the smile. "I was thinking of your recent nomination in the elections."

"Right." Breen slid down the wall and tipped his cap low over his eyes. Conversation was at an end.

Emmet wasn't lucky enough to have a wall to lean against and sat feeling his backside get numb with his arms wrapped around his knees and forehead resting against them. *What happens now? Not back to jail. God, I hope not. Bridie doesn't deserve that.*

20

Dublin, 5 July 1922

Emmet must have dozed off because when they came, banging nightsticks against the bars, he leapt up, heart pounding.

"Up, up. Come on now. Arms out so we can cuff you as you come out." Police guards stood, guns cocked and ready as the prisoners rose and lined up, ready to leave the cell.

Breen shouted over the muttering and groaning of the shuffling men. "Where are you taking us?"

Emmet took his place in line and inched forward as one by one the men were cuffed and shoved forward in the passageway.

Breen called out again. "Well? We have a right to know."

The officer in charge responded. "You're going to Wellington Barracks. You're the army's problem now."

When Emmet was next in line to be cuffed, the officer in charge poked him in the chest with his night stick. "Ryan?"

"Yes."

"Not you."

Sean with the trench coat was already in the lineup, handcuffed and waiting to move forward. He turned and threw a glare in Emmet's direction.

Emmet saw it and gritted his teeth. "I'm not a fecking spy."

Sean turned and walked away.

Emmet stepped back into the cell and watched the others leave. The officer in charge gestured him to come along. Emmet came to the cell door again and held out his hands, but the officer shook his head. No cuffs.

"Follow me."

Emmet resisted the temptation to ask questions. *Maybe Mr. Hooper is here to get me out.*

He walked behind the broad back of the Civic Guard officer, the man's black boots and belt shining in the pools of light along the hallways. It was the middle of the night, yet the dark uniform was well turned out.

He was taken into an office where an older man wearing the chevrons of a sergeant sat behind a desk, an open file in front of him.

The officer escorting Emmet saluted. "The prisoner Ryan, as requested, Sergeant Kelly."

The sergeant nodded. "That will be all. Thank you."

Another crisp salute and the officer swivelled and left, closing the door behind him.

Emmet remained standing as the sergeant turned pages in the file. Finally, he looked up. "All right, sit down."

Emmet felt the sweat prickling under his arms. He sat down.

The sergeant crossed his arms across his chest. "Do you know who I am?"

Emmet frowned, a glimmer of recognition crossing his mind. "I've met you before."

"Yes." He pulled an envelope from under the file and withdrew a single sheet of notepaper. He unfolded that and flattened the crease.

From his side of the desk Emmet tried to read what the note said or at least figure out who it was from. It wasn't Freeman's Journal letterhead. *Not Hooper then.* Then it came to him. He couldn't read the words, but he recognized his father-in-law's writing.

Emmet muttered. "Kelly."

"Yes. Sergeant John Kelly at your service."

Emmet's mouth fell open. "You're Bridie's uncle. Her mother's brother. You were at our wedding."

"I was. It was a happy day. I didn't expect to see you here in front of me, Ryan."

"No."

"We are now in unhappy times. Irishman against Irishman. Sad, and dangerous times."

"I agree."

"I've had a note from my sister's husband." Sergeant Kelly slid the note across for Emmet to read.

After reading the plea for help, Emmet shook his head. "Bridie shouldn't have asked her parents to send this. I understand the position it's putting you in."

"Do you? Do you really understand? You have a bit of a history, boyo. I can't easily just let you go."

Emmet nodded. "In my defence, I have to say that we were all on the same side when I experienced my *history*, as you call it. Now, I'm simply doing my job. I wasn't taking sides, I was just getting as close to the action as I could to get the story. I could have stood with the rest of the crowd, watching the bullets fly, but that's not what a real journalist does. Anything that happened was just a case of wrong place at the wrong time." Emmet prayed that no one had looked at his notes which would clearly show where his sympathies lay.

Sergeant Kelly removed his reading glasses and rubbed his nose. "The fact is, you abetted two escaping Republicans, whether you intended to or not."

Emmet licked his lips but remained quiet. He knew that Kelly was deciding his future and it was best if he let the man think rather than continue to plead his case.

Kelly put his glasses on. "I'm letting you off with a warning."

Emmet didn't realize he was holding his breath until he expelled it. "Thank you."

Kelly waved a finger at Emmet. "This is the first and last time. I'm doing that for my sister and for my niece, of whom I am very fond. Don't let me hear your name again."

"No, Sergeant."

Kelly's face softened then. "Unless it's for an invitation to a baptism."

Emmet smiled. "That may not be for a while, but I'll remember."

It was mid-morning when Emmet got home. He held Bridie as she sobbed against his shoulder. At last, he led her to the kitchen and she grew calm as she went through the familiar tasks of making tea and getting a breakfast of rashers and eggs with brown bread ready. She showed him the note her uncle had sent to her mother as they waited together in her parents' home for word.

Dermot,

Emmet has been arrested for aiding and abetting criminals. During the final round-up of the anti-treaty militants, it is alleged that Emmet helped two men escape through the kitchen of the Gresham Hotel. They were spotted coming out of a rear door with Emmet stepping out first and then standing in the way, preventing the capture or prevention of escape of the two Republicans.

I have interviewed Emmet and am giving him the benefit of the doubt in this incident.

Given the small amount of evidence against him, I have made the case to the Commanding Officer to release Emmet with a warning. He will be processed and his name now on record, but he should be able to go home in the morning.

Regards to my sister

John Kelly

Emmet set the note aside and watched Bridie moving around the kitchen. "I'm sorry you had to go through that."

He saw her shoulders stiffen, but she didn't respond.

"It's over now, Bridie."

She turned the thick slices of bacon and then swivelled to him. "I thought when we got married, you would put your family first. That's what you promised me."

"This is my job. Do you expect me to just stand with the crowd of women and children who watched the fighting from behind the barriers like they were watching some sort of performance at the Abbey Theater?"

His wife turned back to the sizzling rashers. She cracked an egg into the frying pan and cut a thick slice of bread while the egg cooked. She said nothing as she put everything out on the plate and set it in front of Emmet.

He grasped her hand after she laid down the plate. His voice felt thick in his throat. "Bridie, love. Please, let's not row. I was never in any real danger, but I can't just stand back. That's not who I am. As it is, I just spent the night amongst men who thought me a spy."

He dropped her hand and picked up his knife and fork.

She made a pot of tea and poured out a cup for each of them and then sat across from him as he ate. "Who thought you were a spy?"

He looked up. "Most of the men in the cell."

She set down her cup. "That must have been hard for you."

He closed his eyes briefly. "First Michael Collins, and then the men I think of as comrades think me a spy." He heaved a long sigh. "It breaks my heart."

Tears slid down Bridie's cheeks. "And then I berate you."

Emmet pushed the empty plate away. "Hush. I'm just exhausted, but I'll need to go in and file the story."

She stood and took his plate and cup away. "You'll have a wash and a sleep first."

He nodded and stood, weaving on his feet, feeling almost too tired to even make it to the bedroom.

She came and looped her arm around his waist. "Come, love. Hold on to me. You know I didn't mean anything earlier. I was just afraid."

He leaned on her. "I know." He felt stronger with the warmth of her arm around him.

The worst is over.

21

Dublin, 6 July 1922

He woke to her finger stroking his cheek and for a moment longer kept his eyes closed, enjoying the touch and sound of her voice. "Emmet? Are you awake?"

He opened his eyes and sat up. "I am."

"You said to waken you at noon."

"Right. I'm awake now. I'll be out directly."

"I made some soup."

"Lovely. Thank you. Where would I be without you?"

She smiled and left him to get ready.

He had his lunch and then set off on his bicycle to get into the office. Dublin was a very different place than it was just yesterday. The percussion of heavy artillery and *rat-a-tat-tat* of smaller guns were replaced by the sounds of hammers and saws as demolition and reconstruction began. Packs of children dashed across the road armed with sticks as they replayed elaborate battle scenes in place of rifle-toting men.

Emmet arrived at the office and shook his head at the good-natured comments thrown at him, teasing him about his time in jail.

He went first to his editor's office. He knocked and entered at Hooper's "Come."

Hooper sat back and laced his fingers behind his head. "They've released you, then."

"Let me off with a warning."

"What were you thinking to get between soldiers and escaping Republicans?"

Emmet raised his eyebrows. "So you've heard the details, then?"

"I have my sources, Ryan."

"Of course. Well, I just wanted to let you know I'm back and I'll write up my notes from the last couple of days."

Hooper sniffed. "I'm not sure we'll use them. It's rather after the fact now, wouldn't you agree?"

Emmet felt the chill from his boss. "I'll write it anyway and you can see."

Hooper folded his arms across his chest. "Remember what I told you before. I don't want a whole sad story about this pack of renegades fighting a just fight. The people voted. We're a Free State now and that's the position we support, right?"

Emmet felt heat rise in his neck and face. "So, it's all right to write something less neutral as long as the slant is in the direction of the Free-Staters?"

"That's the side of the law, Ryan. We are for the law, and if you don't see it that way, maybe you shouldn't be working here at all. Maybe you should find some place that suits you better."

Emmet felt the sweat prickle under his arms and his palms were sweaty where he gripped his leather briefcase. "Maybe I should."

Hooper waved his hand towards the door. "Don't let me stop you. You're a fine writer, Ryan, but I don't think you fit in here anymore."

Emmet hesitated for another second. "Right, then. I'll clear out my desk."

Hooper stood. "I'll let payroll know. You can pick up your final pay on your way out."

Emmet blinked. *What have I just done?* He turned and went across to his own office.

———

Bridie sat on the sofa and cried. "Oh, Emmet. What will happen to us now? You need a job."

Emmet took a deep breath. "I know I need a job, Bridie. I'll find another one. It was bound to happen one of these days. The paper is barely struggling on after they had the presses destroyed. The poxy little office they're in and renting time on other presses are all signs that the paper's struggling. I'll find a better job. Don't worry yourself so."

Emmet rubbed his eyes. It was only six in the evening, but it seemed like the day was endless. *I just want to sleep for a week.* He drank his tea and watched as Bridie picked up a piece of fabric and continued the sewing she'd been working on for the past few days.

He saw the tears spilling down her cheeks. "What are you working on?"

She looked up, eyes wide as if searching for an answer, but before she responded there was a knock at the door.

Emmet sighed. "Whoever it is, don't offer them a cup of tea. I'm just too tired to be sociable."

Bridie set her sewing into her basket and went to answer the door.

Emmet stood when he saw Liam. "Come in and sit down. Jaysus Liam, you look worse than I feel. You look completely banjaxed."

Liam's eyes were circled with dark purple shadows. He had scrapes and scratches on his face, neck and hands. He was clean but hadn't shaved in several days.

Bridie stood behind Liam and raised her eyebrows to ask Emmet silently if she should offer tea or not. Emmet nodded, and she touched Liam's arm. "Will you have a cup of tea?"

Liam hadn't said anything after his initial hello but looked Emmet steadily in the eyes. He turned to look at Bridie. "You wouldn't have a drop of brandy, would you?"

Bridie frowned. "I'll get out the whiskey."

Liam nodded and stepped towards Emmet. He reached up and grasped Emmet's shoulders with both his hands.

Emmet pulled back, wary at Liam's solemn expression. "What is it, Liam? I thought I'd see you over the past couple of days. You must have been in the thick of things by the look of you."

Bridie came back with three glasses and the bottle of Jameson's whiskey and set the tray down on the small round table beside the sofa.

Still gripping Emmet's shoulders, Liam finally spoke. "I was in the thick of it, but I'm not the only one."

Emmet pulled away and poured out 3 measures of whiskey. "I know that. I was in the Gresham."

Liam nodded. "I heard." He bit his lip. "Emmet. This isn't a social call. I'm here on behalf of the Dublin Brigade."

Emmet stood holding two glasses. "What does that mean?"

Liam took the glasses and set them back down. "Emmet, there's no easy way to tell you this. Your brother.."

Goosebumps shivered up Emmet's spine.

"Your brother, Kevin was involved. He was up at the outpost in the YMCA."

Emmet shook his head. "No, he's in Cork."

"He *was* in Cork."

Bridie moved to Emmet's side and put her arm around his waist.

Emmet shook his head again.

Liam continued. "I'm sorry to have to tell you this, but Kevin was killed in the fighting when the Free State troops tunnelled into the building."

Emmet remained standing for another second and then stumbled to a chair to collapse. "I don't believe it." Even as he spoke the words, he knew Liam wouldn't say it unless he knew it was true.

Liam picked up the whiskey and shoved it into Emmet's hand. "Drink."

Emmet tipped his glass to drink the whole measure. It served to unlock the anguish that gripped him. He put the glass on the floor between his feet and hid his face in his hands, elbows pressed into his knees. He tried to hold the sob inside, but at the feel of Bridie's hand on his back, he groaned. "No, no, no."

Liam crouched down in front of Emmet. "He died doing what he believed in. He died as a brave and true Irishman."

Emmet looked up, his face inches from Liam's. "I thought he was safe. I never thought to look for him."

Liam shook his head. "He didn't want you to know he was back. He knew you'd worry. There was nothing you could have done. You did your job, chronicling the fight. He did his job. You both did what you had to do."

Bridie perched on the arm of Emmet's chair and rubbed his back.

Tears burned Emmet's eyes. "It wasn't enough. I should have been by his side."

Bridie squeezed his shoulder. "Where would I be, then?"

Liam nodded. "Listen to Bridie."

Emmet jumped up. "My parents. I need to let them know."

Liam shook his head. "No. We're doing that. Right now, Kevin is on his way home. Two of our boys borrowed an ambulance and they're taking him back to Ashbourne."

Emmet stood, his arms hanging by his side, tears smearing his face. "What do I do now? I should be doing something."

Liam moved to Emmet's side. "Right now we are going to finish this bottle of whiskey. Then you are going to bed and in the morning, you'll go home to be with your family." Liam refilled their glasses.

Emmet sat down again and took the glass that Liam put back in his hand.

Liam lifted his and Emmet and Bridie both lifted theirs to clink the three glasses together. "To a fine man and a good, good friend."

Bridie spoke through her tears: "To Kevin."

"To Kevin." They chorused.

Bridie went to the kitchen and set her glass on the work top, not finishing the drink. She cut some bread, cheese and cold chicken and took the platter out to the living room for Liam and Emmet to pick at during the long evening ahead.

Later when the bottle was finished and most of the food gone, Liam helped Bridie get Emmet to the bedroom and lay him on the bed. He heard Bridie walk Liam to the door and while he knew they were talking, their voices came as if through a heavy fog. Muffled sounds. He thought he heard Liam say 'congratulations' but knew that couldn't be right. There was nothing to celebrate tonight. Emmet felt his life crumbling around him. *No job. Kevin dead. It's all gone badly wrong.* It was his last thought before exhaustion overcame him.

22

Ashbourne, July 1922

After the funeral, people crowded into the old farmhouse. Emmet's mother sat by the Aga cooker in the kitchen most of the time, her face white and her blue eyes rimmed with red and swimming with restrained tears. His father circulated with bottles of whiskey and Emmet poured pints of Guinness from a keg they'd gotten from the hotel.

Emmet watched his brother Michael for a moment. Michael stood looking out the window holding his young son on his hip. The child must have sensed his father's distress because the small hand kept rubbing his father's neck, as he'd no doubt, felt his mother do for him when he suffered a childish hurt. Emmet turned his eyes away, feeling a sob build in his throat.

Bridie appeared beside him. "Shall I take over pouring pints? Why don't you take a break? Maybe sit with your mam for a bit?"

He shook his head. "I'm not strong enough."

Bridie touched his cheek. "You are. She needs you."

He nodded and left her there to go and join his mother. "Mam. Can I get you anything? A drink or sandwich?"

"Ah, no. Thank you, though."

He pulled a chair close to her and took her hand in his two. He stroked her hand, feeling the frailty of it. And feeling the strength of it.

She turned her fingers to grasp his hand. "It's hard to go on, isn't it?"

He nodded.

"There's always a feeling of guilt that those of us left behind feel. I think about what I could have done differently to change the outcome."

He frowned. "Mam. There's nothing you could have done. You taught him to think about what he believed in, and to stand up for those beliefs."

She nodded. "I know, but it's human to imagine we might have done something, isn't it?"

He closed his eyes. "Yes. I guess it is."

She squeezed his hand again. "But there's nothing either of us could have done."

He sighed. "No, nothing."

She leaned over and kissed his cheek. "Remember that, so."

He swallowed, trying to dislodge the lump in his throat.

She smiled. "It's time for you to think of the future. What will you do now that you aren't with the Journal?"

He shrugged. "Look around for something else."

She narrowed her eyes. "Don't take long about it."

"We're all right. We have some savings."

"Ah."

"What does that mean? Ah?"

She stood up. "I better go and talk to some of our neighbours. And you, you better talk to your wife."

Emmet shook his head as he watched her move into the sitting room. He followed her, looking around for Bridie. Michael had taken over at the keg and she sat with Michael's wife, with the child on her lap. He wandered over and rested his hand on her shoulder.

She smiled up at him. "All right?"

He shrugged. "Mystified."

"Oh?"

"Mam told me to come talk to you."

Bridie exchanged glances with Michael's wife. She stood and handed the child back to his mother and then led Emmet outside into the garden.

Bridie linked her arm through Emmet's. "Your mother is a wise woman. Even at a time like this, she misses nothing."

Emmet wrinkled his forehead. "What am I missing?"

She stopped and turned to face him. "I've been waiting for the right time, but maybe indeed this is it. The right time."

He stared at her.

"Emmet. I'm pregnant."

For what felt like the hundredth time that day, Emmet's eyes burned with tears. "In death, there is life."

She nodded. "I know it isn't ideal, with you out of work, but I thought I could take in some sewing."

He pulled her to him in a close hug. He kissed her hair. "It's time for a new start. I'll find work, no matter what it is."

Emmet heard the door open and Liam's voice. "Out here canoodling, are you?"

He released Bridie but kept his arm around her shoulder as he turned to face Liam. "And why not? Why shouldn't I give the mother of my child a hug if I like?"

Liam smiled. "Ah, that's brilliant. It's great to hear something good right now."

Emmet had a feeling that his best friend wasn't entirely surprised, but let it go. "I just wish.."

Liam stepped forward to shake Emmet's hand and to kiss Bridie's cheek. "Never mind wishing. Kevin would have been over the moon for you, and you've got a pack of other people in the house that could use some cheering up right now."

Emmet looked down at his wife. "Can we tell people already?"

"Yes. I've been to the doctor already and all is well."

Emmet shook his head. "I've been so focused on everything else that I didn't pay attention to what was happening in my own home. I'm sorry. Things will be different from now on."

She smiled and gave him a gentle push towards the house.

They held hands as they went first to tell his mother. Kathleen smiled when she saw them and nodded. "You've told him, then."

Emmet's father blinked away tears when they told him. "It's a blessing." He looked up and crossed himself, as if saying a silent prayer.

Emmet hugged his father. "Da, I'll have a hard time being a father as good as you've been."

His father patted him on the back. "Just follow your instincts, son." His father then called out for quiet in the room. "We've had enough sadness for the day. My son Emmet and his wife Bridie are just after telling me that they are expecting their first child, and we know that Kevin will be an angel above watching over this happy news. Who will give us a song for Kevin and for the baby to come?"

Someone pulled out a fiddle from under a chair. Another man took out a harmonica and they started up the music. Drinks were refilled, and voices joined the music in song.

As women crowded around Bridie to talk about pregnancy and babies, Emmet went back outside in the dusk. He looked out over the green patchwork hills as they faded to browns and yellows in the fading sun.

A child. I'll be a father.

He was still trying to imagine it when Liam came to join him.

His friend put a glass of whiskey in his hand. "Congratulations, my friend. You're an adult now."

Emmet looked at the pale gold liquid in his glass. "You're always magically showing up with whiskey when I need one."

"That's my job."

"And what's my job? What's it all been for, Liam? Starting with 1916 and here we are six years later, still fighting and losing the same battles. Kevin lost his life, and for what?"

Liam sighed and took a drink of his whiskey. "If it was easy, it would have been done a couple of centuries ago."

Emmet tilted his head as he looked at Liam.

"Freedom for Ireland. That's always been the goal, Emmet. It's what Kevin died for. It's my job and it's yours."

Emmet took another sip. "I don't think anything I do can make a difference."

Liam rested his hand on Emmet's shoulder. "Of course, it does. Probably what you do even more so than anything I can do."

Emmet frowned. "Why do you say that?"

Liam gripped Emmet's shoulder. "I've told you before. Your words. They can touch people in a way I can't. Just tell your stories. You show ordinary citizens why this makes sense for them, and for their children."

Liam dropped his hand and they finished their drinks in silence.

Finally, as the last of the sun's rays faded to darkness, Emmet murmured. "For our children."

23

Dublin, July 1922

Bridie raised the subject of getting work again. "Emmet, perhaps I should take in some sewing."

Emmet looked up from the desk where he was writing letters. "Nonsense, Bridie."

"But how will we manage?"

"I'll get something. It isn't for you to worry about."

Her voice was sarcastic. "I wonder would the former Minister of Labour agree with that notion."

Emmet felt himself flush. "I hope you don't intend to follow in the footsteps of the Countess Markievicz."

Bridie smiled. "I'm not quite that ambitious, but at the same time, she is a model for all Irish women to admire."

Emmet threw down his pen and held up his hands in surrender. "All right, all right. If you have something you feel you should do, then I won't hold you back."

Now that Bridie had won the argument, she didn't seem keen on the idea of taking in sewing. "I'll give it some thought."

Emmet folded the letter he had now completed. "Meanwhile, I'm off to meet someone that might be helpful to us."

Bridie kissed him at the door. "Good luck."

Several hours later Emmet returned. He rocked unsteadily in front of Bridie with a grin on his face.

Bridie grimaced. "Have you been celebrating or drowning your sorrows?"

He leaned in to kiss her.

She leaned back and waved her hand in front of her face. "You'll have me drunk just from your fumes."

He pulled her close and kissed her despite her complaints. "Good news. I am once again a working man."

"Truly, Emmet?"

"Truly."

She wriggled out of his arms and pulled him by the hand to sit down. "Tell me."

"It's that new paper called *Poblacht na hÉireann.*"

She nodded. "Of course. The Republican paper."

"That's it. That's the right place for me."

She smiled. "It is."

Two weeks later Emmet came home from work to find Bridie singing as she stirred a pot on the cooker.

He kissed her neck. "You seem in good form. Are you feeling better?"

She tipped her head forward and Emmet kissed her neck again, enjoying the salty summer sweat that was the taste of her.

She turned then with a smile. "The morning sickness is almost gone, but I'm in good form because I have work."

"Oh?"

She set down her wooden spoon and led him to the sofa. "Let me tell you what happened today." She proceeded to tell Emmet about her conversation with Mr. Riley who owned the dry goods shop down the street. She apparently impressed him when she tallied up what she owed him in her head as he was still noting down on paper the various items and prices. He called her a marvel when she put the exact money on the counter before he could add it up. He then went on to say he wished he had her talent because he was always in a muddle with his bookkeeping.

With a triumphant grin Bridie finished the story. "So the upshot is, I'm to do his books as a regular thing. For now, I'll go to the shop two mornings a week, but once the baby comes, I can do the work here at home. Either I'll pick up the receipts or he'll bring them to me. What do you think of that?"

Emmet took her hands and kissed each of them. "I think Mr. Riley knows a good thing when he sees it. You are a marvel with numbers. No question."

She smiled. "Well, this marvel better see to the dinner."

He went in to lay the table and slice some bread. He was still heartsore at the loss of his brother, but he was learning to live with the constant ache. Despite it, he found himself smiling more than he had in a very long time.

They went on to talk about his day. Every day was exciting for Emmet now that he didn't have to curtail his true feelings. He interviewed politicians and soldiers. He went to functions and listened to arguments in Parliament. He often went to Dublin Castle, something that both he and Bridie found amazing after all the years of British rule.

Emmet finished the last of his dinner. "It's sad to see Michael Collins standing on one side and de Valera on the other. After everything we've been through, they should be standing shoulder to shoulder."

Bridie nodded. "It is. I hope they can come together somehow, but with the North opting out of the Free State, it's hard to know how they will ever agree again."

Emmet drained the last of his tea. "Did I tell you I heard from Liam?"

"No. Where is he and what's he up to?"

"Not really sure. He just said he's up in Belfast at the moment but expects he'll be going to Cork next month. When he's in the south he hopes to come by and say hello."

"I couldn't see myself going here and there like he does. He never stays home."

Emmet smiled. "He doesn't have a home to stay in."

Bridie wrinkled her forehead. "That's true, isn't it. How sad."

"He would say that a united Ireland is his home, so until that happens he can't settle anywhere."

Bridie was silent for a moment. "And if it never happens?"

Emmet shook his head. "Don't even think that. The day will come. It won't be easy though, especially when I see how complacent most people are."

Bridie reached across the table to rest her hand on his. "As long as the battle you fight from now on is only with your words."

Emmet put his free hand over hers. "I understand that I was lucky that your uncle helped me out. Don't worry, my love."

Bridie pursed her lips. Emmet suspected it wasn't enough of a promise, but it was all he could give her.

24

Dublin, August 1922

The headlines screamed the news. *Michael Collins Assassinated*

The country was embroiled in a civil war. Emmet worked long hours to capture the hour- by-hour news, but he was paid very little for the effort.

Bridie counted the pay packet. "Oh, Emmet. It's hardly worth all the hours you put into it."

Emmet paced from table to sofa to window and back again. "Bridie, we're part of history here, don't you see? How can we put a monetary value on that?"

Bridie felt weighed down, pressed into the chair. She leaned her elbows on the table, looking again at the few shillings that lay in front of her. She could hear the tiredness in her own voice. "Every day that we live becomes part of history, Emmet."

He walked back again to look out the window to the quiet street below. "Not like this, Bridie. I'm writing the words that will be read by generations to come when we are all living in a free and united Ireland."

She pushed herself up using the table. He felt her behind him as she wrapped her arms around him, the swell of her growing belly nestled against him. "I know that, and I'm so very proud of you. I just wish they would pay you more. You put your heart and soul into it. It should be worth more. That's all I'm saying."

He turned and held her close. "It'll all come right. Imagine the day somewhere in the future when we can say to our children that *we were there, and we helped to make it happen.*"

She smiled. "Yes, that will be a grand day."

———

The months seemed to fly as the baby grew within Bridie. Emmet loved to sit late in the evening with a drink and rest his hand on her to feel the child moving. Most nights he was too tired to talk much, so he listened as she talked of her days.

"Mama hates that I'm working, of course."

He smiled. "I'm not surprised. I'm not happy about it myself."

"I don't mind. It takes my mind off the things."

"What things?" He sat up straight. "Are you worried about the baby?"

She sighed. "Not worried about having a baby, or about the health of him."

"Or her."

"Or her." She agreed. "I just wonder about the world we're bringing a child into. When brother is fighting against brother, it's just so awful. We got what we wanted for the most part. We have our own government. Isn't it time to let things settle?"

Emmet took a deep breath. "No. That's the problem. That's what the treaty did. Settled." He stood to pace the small sitting room.

"I'm sorry, Emmet. Don't get angry."

He came back to sit down. "I'm not angry with you, but I'm frustrated that I'm not doing enough to make people understand. If my own wife isn't convinced that we need to carry on with the fight, how in God's name can I hope to influence anyone?"

She was pale, and Emmet bit his lip. "Never mind, Bridie. I asked what you were worried about and I'm glad you told me. Let's put it out of our minds for now. Tell me more about how the visit with your family went."

Part II

Maeve Ryan

25

Dublin, February 1923

On February 14th, 1923, on a blustery night with the sleet smearing the bedroom window, Bridie gave birth to a baby girl. The midwife washed the baby and laid the swaddled tiny bundle in her mother's arms.

Her mam finished sponging Bridie's face and combing out her wavy hair, so it lay like a copper mantle over her shoulders. "Shall I go and fetch Emmet?"

"Do, Mammy."

Bridie watched her mother leave the bedroom. She could picture her husband's face when her mother said "Emmet, come in and meet your daughter."

Emmet came in and closed the door. He perched on the edge of the bed as if afraid of disturbing them.

Bridie pushed down the soft white flannel wrapping the tiny baby to reveal her face. "Well Dadda, what do you think?"

Emmet licked his lips and tried to speak. His Adam's apple bobbed up and down as he swallowed two or three times. He blinked very quickly, but it wasn't enough to hide the tears. Finally, in a whisper, "She's perfect."

Bridie smiled her agreement. "It's Valentine's Day. Shall we call her Valentine?"

Emmet looked dazed. "No, nothing so frivolous. She's—"He searched for the words. "Important and grand. A symbol of our unity. Can we call her Maeve?"

Bridie studied him. *Important and grand. Like her father and his work for our country.* "I think that's a lovely name for her. And what about Katherine for her middle name, for my sister?"

"Maeve Katherine Ryan." He touched the baby's nose with his finger. "It suits her."

Bridie held the bundle towards him. "Will you hold her, Dadda?"

He took the tiny blanketed child in his arms. He stared down into her face, seeming to be mesmerized. "Maeve Katherine Ryan. My own girl. We'll be the best of friends, you and I."

Bridie leaned in to see the baby resting in Emmet's arms. "Are you planning already to take her to football matches?"

"I'm planning to take her everywhere. Football and rowing. Concerts and lectures. Cups of tea at Bewley's on Westmoreland and lemonade in St. Stephen's Green."

"Sure, you won't have time to work with all of that."

Emmet looked into Bridie's eyes. "I'll find time. I'll make time."

There was a tap on the door and Bridie's mother came back in. "Your father is dying to get a peek at his granddaughter."

Emmet handed the baby back to Bridie.

Bridie settled the baby and then nodded to her mother. "Let him come and then Emmet and Papa will wet the baby's head. There's a new bottle of Jameson's in the sideboard."

Bridie's father must have been hovering right behind the door because as soon as Bridie gave the word, he came in to look.

Emmet squeezed past his father-in-law. "I'll be out here getting the drinks when you're ready."

Her father stroked the baby's cheek. "She a lovely little lass. She'll have red hair by the look of it. She'll be a firebrand. You have your work cut out for you there."

Bridie smiled. "My goodness, what a dire prediction for such a tiny creature."

He smiled. "You're well able for whatever mischief she brings you. You're a strong girl and I've always been very proud of you."

Bridie felt herself grow hot. "Thank you, Daddy."

Her mother gave her husband a gentle shove towards the door. "Emmet's waiting for you. Go on now and celebrate, the two of you. Bridie needs her sleep. I'll sit here with her while you two relax and right the wrongs of the world."

———

Bridie finished feeding the baby and sat in the easy chair pulled up near the window. The wind blew papers and old brown leaves around. The grey skies threatened rain and Bridie rested her head against the back of the chair, enjoying the feeling of her baby sleeping on her lap.

Emmet's voice woke her. "A letter for you, Bridie. From your friend in England."

Bridie started and saw the baby's face pucker up for a cry before settling again peacefully. Bridie held out her hand for the proffered envelope. "I haven't heard from her in a long while. I was so glad she came to our wedding, but that seems like such a long time ago now."

Emmet stood, admiring the sight of his sleeping daughter. His voice was quiet. "Sorry, I didn't realize you two were asleep."

Bridie shook her head. "I shouldn't have been. I should be taking advantage of her sleeping and get the accounting caught up for Mr. Riley."

"Shall I put her in bed for you?"

Bridie knew Emmet longed to pick up his daughter for a cuddle. "Go on, then."

He bent over and expertly lifted her into his arms. "Hush, hush now." Maeve opened her dark blue eyes momentarily and then fell asleep again.

Bridie watched Emmet walk to the bedroom to put the child in her cradle.

I'll enjoy my letter from Elizabeth before starting work. Bridie read the first few sentences and jumped up, all grogginess gone in her excitement.

"Emmet. You'll never guess."

Emmet trotted into the sitting room, closing the bedroom door softly behind him. "What is it?"

"Elizabeth is also expecting a baby. She's due next month."

Emmet gave a small smile, as if to ask, 'is that all?'

Bridie waved the letter in the air. "That's so wonderful for her. She got married so quietly, it seemed like it was hardly even an event. This will be something that can truly be celebrated."

Emmet kissed Bridie's forehead and then turned to go to his desk. Over his shoulder he threw the wry comment. "You just felt left out since we weren't invited to the wedding."

"It's not that. It was a very small affair because she was still mourning for her mother. I understood that."

"Hmm. But to hear of it after the fact, miffed you."

Bridie shrugged. "Perhaps. I was glad to hear that her beau waited for her, though. She deserves some happiness."

Emmet opened his portfolio and immersed himself in his work.

Bridie reread the letter before putting it away. She laid out the ledgers on the kitchen table and set to work, humming softly.

Life was good for them. Emmet worked in a job he loved, baby Maeve was healthy and thriving. And now it looked as though the brutal killings might stop.

The birth of their baby meant that Emmet didn't talk as much about his work when he was at home, but Bridie read the stories. The anti-treaty Republicans were losing the fight and when their leader, Liam Deasy was captured, he called for the Republicans to end their campaign. He encouraged his men to work with the Free State to find a solution.

It was a blow for Emmet, but secretly Bridie thanked God. The end was in sight. The end of her worry about violence touching their family.

26

Dublin, November 1927

Bridie threw a critical eye over four-year old Maeve. "Pull your socks up, sweetheart."

Maeve sighed and as she bent down to pull up her sagging white socks, Emmet winked at Bridie.

Bridie heard her daughter mutter, "They'll only fall down again," and she tried not to laugh.

As the child straightened, she held out her hand to Emmet. "Can we go now, Daddy?"

He grasped her hand and held out the other one to his two-year-old son. "Ready, Robert?"

The small boy toddled over to his father to grasp the outstretched hand.

Bridie smiled at the trio. "Daddy, are you sure you should be taking them to such a fine place as Bewley's?"

"Why not? Ryan children are not hooligans." He looked sternly from one to the other. "Are you?"

Bridie doubted that Robert even understood the question, but as his beloved big sister said, "No Daddy," so did he.

"Right, so. Let's go and let your mammy have some peace and quiet. Unless you changed your mind and want to come along?"

Bridie shook her head. "No, no. This is a special outing just for you three." She rested her hand on the swell of the new baby beneath her dress. "This little one is very active today. A rest would be lovely."

After watching the trio toddle their way to the tram stop, from the front room window of their terrace house on St. Peter's Court, Bridie put the kettle on for a cup of tea. She was knitting for the new baby. She could reuse most of her old baby things, but the new baby deserved some new things of his or her own as well.

Bridie let her mind wander as she knitted. The movements came automatically; knit one, purl one. The tiny sleeves of the sweater made her smile. They grew so fast, she knew the sweater would be abandoned in only a couple of months but that was all right. She tried to remember when Maeve had been small enough to fit into a sweater like this. In some ways it was so long ago and, in some ways, just yesterday.

Her hands fell still as she looked around the sitting room and compared it in her mind's eye to the sitting room in their old flat. *God, it was so tiny. However did we manage?*

Bridie recalled the day that Emmet came home with the news that he'd gotten hired on to the *Dublin Opinion*. She smiled to remember the celebrations they had enjoyed. A lovely dinner and too many drinks. She was convinced that the result of that night was young Robert. The extra money that came from his increased wages were soon eaten up with this, a larger house and a new baby. Bridie didn't have any more money at the end of the week than before, but never mind.

Katie was married now, and Bridie enjoyed the walk to visit her sister. Life was good. She missed the work she used to do for Mr. Riley, but once they moved, it wasn't feasible. Perhaps she'd find work again in the future, but at the moment her hands were full with family things and that's how she liked it.

Rap, rap, rap. A knock on the front door startled her from her reverie.

Struggling to rise from her relaxed slump in the easy chair, Bridie took a few moments to regain her feet and make it to the door.

Rap, rap, rap. The knuckles on wood sounded again. Her heart pounded. *An accident?*

She was breathless as she opened the door, to be engulfed in a bear hug. It took her a second to adjust to the knowledge that nothing was wrong.

Bridie pushed back out of the hug and she grinned. "Liam Kelly, what brings you to our door unannounced like this?"

"Must I have a formal announcement in order to be welcomed?"

"God, no. Where are my manners? Come in and sit yourself down. I'll put the kettle on for a fresh pot."

Liam followed her to the kitchen. "Where's himself, then?"

"Out with the children. Taken them to the new Bewley's on Grafton, if you can imagine it."

Liam raised his eyebrows. "I can't imagine my father taking me anywhere other than the back shed with the switch in his hand when I was a boy."

Bridie smiled. "Emmet has really taken to being Daddy. He's definitely more involved than my father ever was either."

Liam carried the tea things into the sitting room and set the tray down on the small table. "It's a good thing he likes being a father." He glanced meaningfully at her belly.

She rubbed her stomach and nodded. "Indeed. So, what's going on with you? We haven't seen you since Robert's baptism."

He shrugged. "You know. I've been with de Valera working for the new Fianna Fáil."

"Have you? That's exciting. Now that they are one of the major parties and did so well in the election, you must be quite satisfied."

Liam bit his lip. "There's so much yet to be done. We're no further ahead with a united Ireland as far as I can see."

Bridie tilted her head. "But with Dev and the Fianna Fáil recognizing the legitimacy of the Free State we have peace. It's all political now, isn't it?"

Liam pursed his lips. "There's no Fianna Fáil in the North."

Bridie frowned. "Is it your hope that the party gets established there too?"

Liam shook his head and then smiled. "I don't know, Bridie. I'm no politician. All I know is that it seems like the cause that I believed in ten years ago has all but petered out here." Liam shook his head as if to banish the dark thoughts. "Never mind that now. Show me around this grand house of yours. Our Emmet must be doing well to have set you all up here."

Bridie smiled and got to her feet again. "He is, Liam. You know he's with the Dublin Opinion now. He works with all sorts of people he admires. Even Grace Gifford."

He followed her as she led the way out into the back garden. "It's a lovely spot you have here. Even a garden for the kids to kick around a ball. That's brilliant."

She shivered, and they went back inside. "Emmet shouldn't be too much longer. Do you want another cup of tea or would you rather go off to the pub and I'll send him down to see you when he gets here?"

"I don't want you thinking I'm not enjoying your company."

"Go on. I know you men. You're parched for a pint. Why don't you go down to Toner's on Baggot? It's one of his favourites."

Liam stood, still hesitant. "You don't mind?"

Bridie shook her head. "Of course not, but you'll come back with him for your supper."

Liam nodded. "That sounds lovely. Then I can see these children as well."

Liam left, and Bridie considered what she should make for supper. The simple potato-leek soup and bread that she had planned would wait until tomorrow. *There's nothing for it, but I'll have to go out after all.*

She put on her coat, squeezed her swollen feet into her shoes, wrapped her head in a warm scarf, picked up her basket and braved the cold wind to do some shopping.

———

Later that night, Bridie shifted in bed to find a comfortable position. "It was nice seeing Liam again. It's a shame he wouldn't stay overnight. You two could have spent your Sunday together and gone to the match."

Emmet was quiet for moment. Bridie wondered if he had fallen asleep until she felt him turn towards her.

"It *was* nice seeing him again."

Bridie prompted him. "But?"

Emmet sighed. "But it wasn't purely a social call."

Bridie turned her head on the pillow, her eyes searching through the dark gloom of the room to see him. "What was he looking for?"

"I'm not sure I should even be talking to you about it."

"Well, you've started now, so you can't leave it at this."

Emmet pushed himself up to lean on one elbow. "He asked if occasionally he could leave some packages with me."

Bridie's heart raced. "Packages?"

"I didn't ask for more details. I don't want to know."

Bridie knew that packages was another word for guns or explosives. "The war is over."

"Liam's isn't."

"Oh, Emmet. I hope you said no."

Again, the ominous silence.

"Emmet? Did you tell him no?"

"I said I have family now and they are my first priority."

"That isn't an answer."

"It was the only answer I could give."

"What did he say?"

"He agreed that he would make every effort not to call on me."

Bridie clenched her fist. "How dare he even ask it of you. Had I known what he was about, I wouldn't have made him so welcome."

Emmet reached over and stroked her face. "Bridie, Liam knows very well that I agree with him. A divided Ireland was never what we wanted when we signed up."

"But you aren't *signed up* anymore."

"Am I not? When the country is divided?"

"We wanted to get out from under British rule. And that's been achieved. We live in a free country now. You *did* get what you fought for."

"We got part of what we wanted, but when part of the country is still under British rule, how can we just rest and leave them to it?"

"They voted. It's what they want."

"Bridie, you can't believe that. It's what some wanted because they don't want to lose the power they have, but it certainly isn't what should have happened. Ireland for Irish men and women. That's what we want."

Bridie felt the blood pounding in her temples. "Emmet, don't get involved. Don't put everything we have at risk."

He lay back down and took her hand in his. "I won't. Don't worry yourself. It isn't good for baby Ryan or for you. I'm quite sure we won't hear from Liam for years again. Nothing will come of it."

He continued to speak softly of other things and slowly Bridie calmed down. She heard him tell again of the visit to the tearoom with the children. He would do anything to protect them. She fell asleep feeling comforted. *He won't endanger us.*

27

Dublin, October 1930

Emmet and Liam sat upstairs in the snug in the Brian Boru pub. It was Liam's birthday and Emmet toasted his boyhood friend, clinking his pint of Guinness against Liam's glass.

"Happy birthday, my friend."

"Thirty years old. It's crazy, isn't it?"

Emmet nodded. "Don't I know it?"

"You've got a lovely family to show for the years, though. What do I have?"

Emmet shrugged. "It's not too late."

"Ah, sure, maybe not in years, but in experience it is."

Emmet nodded. He saw the worn look on Liam's face. "You need a holiday."

Liam shook his head and barked a laugh. "Can you see me lying stretched out like a flounder on a beach somewhere?"

Emmet grinned. "No, I can't."

"No. I'm working with de Valera and the Fianna Fáil at the moment, but I'm not sure it's for me."

"Why not?"

Liam sighed. "It's all gone, Emmet. All collapsed. We've less than two thousand members now, so I thought I'd give this political route a try."

"I know how you feel, Liam. People aren't interested in the old ways any more. It's politics now and I think Dev's got the right idea. Without the people on side, what other option is there?"

"We've all come around to your way of doing things, Emmet." Liam laughed. "You were ahead of the times in your approach."

Emmet heard the bitter sound in Liam's voice. "Don't sell yourself short, Liam. We needed your kind of work *and* mine to get where we are today. We have a proper political party now to represent our position."

Liam tipped his glass up and drank the rest of his pint down. "I'm not giving up. My Ireland includes all four provinces."

Emmet nodded. "I agree with you." He stood. "Ready for another?"

"Go on."

They stayed until closing and hugged before parting. Emmet gripped Liam's arms. "Will you not come with me and sleep on the sofa?"

"Not at all. I'm in the mood for a walk and my own bed awaits. I paid good money to rent that kip."

"Don't be such a stranger. The children adore you."

"What about Bridie?"

"Any worries she once had about you are long behind us."

"I take it she doesn't know about the time last year when you held a package for me in your garden shed."

"No, she does not. And as I told you then, I can't do it again. I can't risk the young ones finding anything."

Liam held up his hands. "I know, I know. There's hardly a need for it these days anyway. I told you; I'm a reformed man. I'm all talk now."

Emmet smiled. "Tell it to someone else, Liam."

Liam grinned, tipped his fedora low over one eye and turned to stride off down Phibsborough Road.

28

Dublin, October 1935

Twelve-year-old Maeve opened the sitting room door and peeked inside. She crept in and picked up the empty cup and saucer from the round table beside her father's chair. She stood for a moment looking at him to see if he would wake up. She wished he would. He could tell her a story. Sometimes when she listened to him, her heart raced, and she got goosebumps. He told the best stories of kings and queens and myths from Irish history.

She listened to him snore softly and considered what she could do to accidentally waken him.

Emmet was slumped in his overstuffed, worn blue corduroy chair with his legs stretched out towards the fire, the leather of his boots emitting a faint smell that reminded Maeve of a farmyard; the odour not unpleasant as it mingled with the acrid smell of the turf fire, and lingering yeasty aroma of the bread Mam had baked earlier. He was long and thin, stretched out like this. His black curls held threads of grey and were kept under control with brilliantine. A greasy brilliantine mark sat on the cotton antimacassar Mam used to protect the chairs. Even with Da's hands folded on his stomach, Maeve saw the black blotchy tattoos on his first two fingers and thumb which told of days spent with pens and nibs and bottles of ink.

The room was quiet save for the typical sounds of a 1935 Dublin autumn evening. The clatter of carts on cobblestones and the electric trams on nearby Cabra Road were muffled, which is why, Maeve knew, her father loved to come here for a nap after tea.

Maeve set the cup back down and picked up the fireplace shovel. Metal scraped against stone as she pushed some embers that had fallen to the stone hearth, further back under the iron grate. She straightened up and glanced in the mirror above the fireplace. Her father hadn't moved. *Ah sure, he's just pretending now. You couldn't sleep through that noise.* She hesitated another moment, moving her focus to the two framed photographs resting on the thin stone slab mantel. One was of her parents on their wedding day and the other was of herself along with her two younger brothers. The photo had been taken a few weeks earlier by a famous photographer as her family crossed O'Connell Bridge. Her long curly hair was blowing in the wind that came off the Liffey and partially obscured her face. Only her wide, watchful eyes were visible while her nose and mouth were masked by her hair, giving her, Maeve fancied, the look of a young female highwayman, ready to cry out 'stand and deliver'. Beside her the boys grinned, acting the clown.

Maeve turned and sighed as she picked up the cup and saucer again. She was just about to open the door when she heard her mother's distinctive tread in the hall. Mammy's hard shoes tic-tacked on the wooden floors and in the next instant the door opened.

Somehow Mammy looked taller than her five foot and seven inches, as she stood framed in the doorway. Maeve had a second to admire the way her treasured tortoise shell clasp held back her fading copper hair, scraping it sleek against her scalp. She had removed her apron which meant she was done with her chores.

Her mother looked startled to see Maeve. "There you are. I wondered where you'd gotten to. You haven't finished the washing up and the boys are standing by idle waiting for you."

Maeve heard her father shift in his chair and knew he was well and truly awake now. "I was just getting Da's teacup."

"Off you go, then."

She stepped into the hall and her mother closed the door behind her. Maeve knew it was wrong but she couldn't help herself. She stood with her ear pressed against the door and smiled when she heard her mother cough. *Making sure he's awake.*

Maeve imagined her father glancing up at the painting of Jesus on the wall. He didn't seem to realize that he always did that when he felt he needed to muster his patience. She heard him speak.

"Bridie, please let's not do this again."

Maeve heard the whoosh of air from the cushion as her mother plunked herself in the matching chair on the other side of the fire. "Don't put me off again."

"I'm not putting you off. I just don't know what there is to discuss."

"The pension, the bloody pension."

There was a silence and then her father's voice dropped, as if he suspected Maeve was just outside the door, listening. "You know how I feel about that. I'm not taking it." He paused. "It's thirty pieces of silver. You know that."

"I don't know that. What I know is that we need the money."

Her father didn't respond and then Maeve heard her mother sigh and make a *tsk* of impatience with her tongue. "Emmet, I'm not asking you to give up on your dream of a free and united Ireland. I'm only asking you to put your family first."

Maeve didn't want to hear any more. This was something private between her parents and she slipped down the hall to the kitchen where her brothers Robert and Malachy were sitting at the table making games with the salt and pepper shakers.

Robert stood up. "Where have you been? We want to go outside but we had to wait to finish the washing-up."

She frowned at him. "I had to get Daddy's cup."

"All this time?"

Maeve ignored his complaints as she thrust her hands into the dishwater. "Ouch." Maeve snatched her hand out of the water and saw blood seeping from her thumb.

She glared at Robert. "Who put the bread knife in there?"

"Mammy."

She put the bleeding thumb in her mouth.

Malachy made a gagging sound. "Ugh. Don't let Daddy see you do that. He'd be sick."

Maeve pulled the thumb out of her mouth and waved it at her brother. "You're just like him. You can't stand the sight of blood any more than he can."

Malachy turned away, not denying it.

The cut had stopped seeping and Maeve dumped the water down the drain. She wiped down the big Aga cooker and wooden worktop with the damp kitchen rag.

Maeve heard the sitting room door open and her father growl. "I'm going to the pub. There's nothing more to be said."

Maeve stepped over to the open kitchen door and looked down the hall where her mother partially obscured her father. Mam moved as if to put her hand on his arm. To stop him.

Maeve felt a lump in her throat as she saw her father step away from her mother, wheeling right to retrieve his jacket and cap from the hook by the front door. He shrugged them on as he walked out.

Maeve scooped her cardigan from the back of a kitchen chair and went out by the back door before her mother came back. She felt the eyes of her brothers on her, so she turned in the open doorway, saw the two boys in their short pants, Robert tall for his ten years of age, and eight-year old Malachy, whose dimpled knees spoke of his indulgence for jam, and smiled at them before closing the door, hoping they wouldn't say anything right away to her mother.

She made her way through the garden and out through the gate to the laneway where she ran down to the end and left to catch up with her father. She was at the junction before him. He must have stopped to adjust his cap in the outside alcove of their red brick terrace house. Maeve stood still and watched him walk towards her. His hands were stuffed in his pockets and he walked slowly, his eyes lowered. He appeared to be deep in thought, so he didn't see Maeve until he was almost beside her.

"Da."

Emmet started, looking up. "Jaysus. Where did you appear from?"

She tucked her hand in the crook of his arm. "What are you and Mam rowing about?"

He slanted his eyes at her. "Nothing you need to concern yourself with, madam."

She persisted. "It's to do with your time in the Irish Republican Brotherhood isn't it? She should be proud of you and not harass you."

He pulled his hands from his pockets and gave her a quick hug. "Now, Maeve. You know that we very rarely disagree, your Mam and I. This time we just have a different opinion."

Maeve frowned. "You fought in the Irish Rebellion and were a hero. People shouldn't argue with you."

He took her hand and they walked on in the cool evening air. "Ahh, Maeve, I wasn't a hero. I just tried to do my bit. It's too complicated to explain it all to you now, but one day I will. You're too young right now."

Maeve persisted. "Tell me just a little about what it was like."

Emmet gave a ghost of a smile. "It was like nothing else. The comrades I made; knowing we were all in it together. It was a grand and glorious time."

Maeve glanced at her father's face and could see that faraway look he got when he was remembering the past, so she walked by his side quietly, satisfied for the moment to walk together in silence. When he was ready, she knew he would tell her. He was like a history book, only better.

"Tell me a story about an Irish warrior woman, then."

"Ahh. Well, let me tell you about Muirisc. She was a great beauty and among other things was a sea captain."

They walked in the Dublin evening and talked of bold and daring achievements of Irish women. Maeve saw her father's shoulders drop and felt the tension in his arm against her linked arm relax, and she smiled to know of her own power.

29

Dublin, June 1936

Thirteen-year-old Maeve was mesmerized by Uncle Liam. She knew that technically he wasn't an uncle but he was Daddy's boyhood pal and so they were to call him Uncle as a sign of respect. She had real uncles including Michael who was Daddy's brother. Then there was Great-Uncle John who was very old, maybe fifty or sixty at least. Great Uncle John had somehow saved Daddy once, according to Nana, but Maeve wasn't sure what that meant. She had made up various versions to tell her brothers, but they were all just from her own imagination. When she had asked her Nana to explain, Grandpa had frowned and Nana had said it wasn't important.

Uncle Liam was staying overnight and Maeve was being very quiet sitting on the top step, listening to the talk that floated up to her. She heard Mammy try to hush them a couple of times, but the whiskey made them talk louder. Even Mammy seemed to give up after a while and Maeve heard her voice go up in pitch when she joined in the conversation, which Maeve understood meant she was a bit giddy.

Maeve couldn't really make out the details of what they were saying. She just loved the sound of Uncle Liam's voice. Although he and Daddy came from the same place, Uncle Liam had developed a slightly northern accent.

She heard his raised voice now. "Even Dev's Fianna Fáil are letting us down now. He's banned the IRA, Emmet."

Maeve heard his voice grow even louder as he repeated his last words. "Banned us."

The voices grew quiet again and Maeve knew her mother must have shushed him. Maeve strained to hear what was happening now when the sitting room door was suddenly thrown open. Her eyes widened as Uncle Liam stepped into the hallway on his way to the toilet. His face lifted, and he pinned her with his gaze.

He grinned and lifted a finger to his lips. Maeve smiled. He wouldn't give her away.

When Liam came back, he winked at her and went back into the sitting room, leaving the door open.

Maeve heard him clearly when he mentioned her. "Emmet, did you tell me that Maeve is a lovely singer?"

Her Daddy's voice was proud. "She sings like an angel. You should hear her. We should have asked her for a song before she went to bed."

Uncle Liam's voice held laughter when he responded. "Perhaps she's still awake."

Maeve heard her mother. "Emmet Ryan, don't you wake the children. The stories you two told at supper were enough to get them up to high doh. I don't want them kept awake half the night."

Uncle Liam stepped back into the hall. "Ah, look who's awake. Come down and give us a song, girl."

Maeve saw her mother poke her head out the door. "Maeve Katherine. What are you doing up?"

Maeve stood, watching her mother's face. "I only just woke, Mammy. I wanted a glass of water."

Her mother's eyes were disbelieving, but not angry. "Well, seeing as you're awake anyway, come in and give your Uncle Liam a song."

Maeve bounced down the steps, buttoning up her favourite green cardigan she had pulled over her long white nightdress when she came out to sit on the steps.

Maeve took a place in the centre of the room. She sang in church and in school and loved the attention. She straightened her shoulders. "What shall I sing, Daddy?"

"How about *Foggy Dew*?"

Maeve filled her lungs, steadied herself and then let the song flow. In her mind's eye she followed the images created by the lyrics, blind to her small audience. She surfaced to her surroundings when Uncle Liam swiped his hand across his eyes.

*Oh, had they died by _Pearse's_ side or fought with _Cathal Brugha_*

Their graves we'd keep where the _Fenians_ sleep, 'neath the shroud of the foggy dew.

She finished the song, her heart racing.

The three grown-ups applauded, and Maeve felt the flush come to her face.

Uncle Liam shook his head. "Beautiful. Just beautiful. Sing us another." He turned to Maeve's mother. "Is that all right?"

Maeve saw the proud smile on her mother's face, and the nod she gave.

Without asking for suggestions, Maeve took a half step back, so she was turned to face her mother. She had been practising this song for just such an occasion. She had heard it on the wireless at her friend's house and loved the song.

She began with the opening lines.

There's a spot in my heart which no colleen may own there's a depth in my soul never sounded or known

"Ah, Mother Machree." Emmet leaned over and took Bridie's hand in hers.

When Maeve finished, Emmet stood and gave his daughter a hug. "That was lovely."

Bridie rose and put her arm around Maeve. "Thank you, sweetheart. That was very special."

Maeve hugged her mother in return. The words her mother spoke may not have been gushing, but the hug said it all.

Bridie released her daughter and then gave her a gentle push towards the door. "Right now. Get your glass of water and then back to bed."

Uncle Liam called out. "Thank you for the songs. You have a true feeling for the music of Ireland."

Maeve went to bed humming.

———

Uncle Liam left the next morning but in the days that followed Maeve remembered his shouted words. *They've banned us.*

At school, she asked the nun who was her teacher about what it meant that the IRA was banned by the government.

Sister Mary patted her on the shoulder. "It's good news, Maeve."

Maeve wrinkled her forehead. "Is it?"

Her teacher smiled. "Definitely. It means that those violent troublemakers are now marked as the criminals they are."

Maeve took her books and left the classroom, closing the door behind her.

She scowled when she came into the hall to find a tall freckled girl standing in the hall, hands on her hips. "Are you listening in on private conversations Emer O'Reilly?"

The girl narrowed her eyes, leaned forward and poked a finger hard at Maeve's chest, just under the collarbone. "Why are you asking about the IRA? Your Da is one of them hooligans. I heard my mammy say so."

Maeve felt herself grow hot. "He's not a hooligan. You take that back."

Emer stabbed Maeve with her finger again. "I won't. He writes all those stories that glorify murder."

Maeve recognized that her tormentor must have heard those words from someone else. "You O'Reillys never stood up for anything in your life." Maeve drew herself up, dropped her books on the floor and shoved the other girl who stumbled back against the wall.

Emer's eyes widened, her face went from white to a deep red. She dropped her book sack and leaped on Maeve, yanking the yellow ribbon out of her hair.

Maeve shrieked "Give that back!" She made a grab for the ribbon, the heel of her hand thumping against Emer's nose.

A spurt of blood shocked both girls into jumping apart, the ribbon dangling, forgotten, from Emer's hand.

"Ahhhh!" Emer's wail brought the teacher running into the hall.

"What in the world is going on here? I thought there were banshees shrieking."

Emer had dropped the ribbon and pulled her handkerchief from her pocket. "Maeve Ryan attacked me!"

Sister Mary lifted the handkerchief from Emer's nose and dabbed for a moment. "All right Emer, calm down. You're going to be fine. I'm sure your nose isn't broken."

She turned to Maeve who stood wide-eyed looking at the bloody handkerchief. "She started it, Sister. She called my Da names."

Muffled by the sodden handkerchief, Emer mumbled. "I only said the truth."

Sister Mary sighed. "Whatever it was, I don't want to hear any more about it. You can be sure that the headmistress with be speaking with both of your parents. Maeve Ryan, I'm very surprised at your behaviour," she turned to pin Emer with her gaze, "whatever the provocation was."

Maeve straightened her shoulders. "I had to stand up for what's right, Sister."

"Go home now, the both of you. You haven't heard the last of this." She stooped to pick up the ribbon. "Is this yours, Maeve?"

"It is, Sister.

She handed over the ribbon. "Go on away home now, Maeve. Emer, you come with me and we'll wash some of that blood off your face first."

Maeve gathered up her books and trotted out into the fresh air. Her friends had gone on without her, but that was fine. Maeve wanted to think.

Uncle Liam is a criminal. That's not right. He doesn't seem like a bad man. And what about Daddy? Uncle Liam clearly said 'us'.

When Maeve got home, her mother was busy peeling potatoes. Maeve sat down at the kitchen table, fussing with her books.

Her mother turned to study Maeve. "Why the long face?" She narrowed her eyes. "Maeve Katherine, what's happened?"

Maeve bit her lip. "Mammy, is Uncle Liam a criminal?"

Her mother wiped her hands dry on her apron and took the chair beside Maeve. "Now what makes you ask that?"

"My teacher said that anyone in the IRA is a criminal and it's good that the government has banned them."

Bridie sighed. "It's all rather complicated, Maeve."

Maeve sat patiently, waiting for more.

"The IRA, the Irish Republican Army, had a purpose when we were fighting to get out from under British rule, but many people believe that their purpose has now been served, so the time has come for them to disband."

Maeve nodded. "So Uncle Liam isn't a bad man, then."

"No, he isn't. He just believes very passionately in a united Ireland."

Maeve hesitated. "What about Daddy?'

"What about him?"

"Is he in the IRA?"

Bridie stood and went back to the potatoes. "Maeve, you know very well that Daddy works as a journalist for the Irish Press. And before that he was with the Dublin Opinion, so that's the end of any talk of Daddy and the IRA."

"Emer O'Reilly said he's a hooligan."

Her mother turned to Maeve again. "What?"

"She did, Mammy. And I had to defend him, didn't I?"

Again, she put down the potato and wiped her hands. She stared at Maeve. "Tell me what happened."

The story spilled out, but Maeve kept her chin held high. "I did the right thing Mammy, didn't I?"

"Oh, Maeve. You should have walked away. This isn't your fight."

"I'm not sorry."

"I suppose we'll be hearing from the Head. Oh dear." She shook her head. "It's done now. Run up and change out of your school clothes. You can help me heel and toe the beans."

Maeve's heart was less heavy, but as she changed into her daily dress, she thought about her mother's explanations. *It does seem complicated. Uncle Liam seemed really angry at the government, but other people, like her teacher seem happy with the way things were being run. Who's right?*

Maeve studied her father at supper as he talked to her mother about work. She could tell that Mammy hadn't told him about her fight. She'd probably wait until after the boys were in bed.

Emmet speared a potato and then held it poised while he continued to talk. "I miss Gallagher. Of course, I do. He was the first editor the paper had, and he was great at it."

Her mother prompted. "But?"

"But the scope has broadened. We aren't just a mouthpiece for de Valera and Fianna Fáil anymore. Just look at this series that we're working on now."

Bridie pointed to the potato. "Your supper's getting cold."

Emmet ate a few bites and then resumed. "The slums in this and other cities in Ireland are truly shocking. The government spends more effort on rural constituents and less on urban. Bridie, you should see some of the photos that have been taken of these tenements."

Bridie tilted her head. "So, are you happy that the paper is now targeting Fianna Fáil?"

Maeve listened, eyes wide for his answer.

Emmet finished eating and pushed his plate aside. "I think that Dev has fallen into the same trap that so many politicians fall into. He's complacent and forgotten the goals he fought for. Remember, I helped raise money for Dev, but it wasn't so he could let politics get the better of him."

Maeve spoke without thinking. "That's what Uncle Liam thinks, isn't it?"

Emmet started, as if he had forgotten that the children were still at the table. "Uncle Liam and I agree on many things but not everything."

Maeve swivelled her gaze from her father to her mother when Bridie snorted.

Emmet frowned. "What's that for?"

Robert took advantage of the distraction between his parents and kicked Maeve under the table. Rather than cry out, Maeve glared at him to keep him quiet. She was all ears.

Bridie stood and picked up the bowl with a few crumbly potatoes at the bottom. "We'll save these bits of spud. No money to waste in this house. Not when you continue to refuse to take the pension."

This was the old argument that Maeve had heard before. It was one of the few things about which her parents argued. The pension. She wanted it and he didn't. That's all Maeve knew.

Emmet shook his head. "Not this again. You know that the pension is nothing more than a government bribe."

Bridie stood at the counter and then spun to face her husband again. "Liam takes it. It doesn't mean he compromised his beliefs. He's just pragmatic enough to take the money that's offered."

Maeve just couldn't help it. "Why is the pension a bribe, Daddy?"

Emmet looked at Bridie and then back to Maeve. "It's offered to anyone who had service in the Civil War."

"Well, that's you, isn't it?"

Maeve's mother made a satisfied *hmmph* sound. "Out of the mouths of babes."

Emmet sighed. "Yes, that's me. I believe, though, that by taking the pension, I'm as good as agreeing with them about the way things are."

Maeve nodded. "You mean that we don't have a united Ireland?"

"Exactly."

Maeve frowned. She opened her mouth to speak again, but her mother was quicker.

"Maeve, please clear the table. Boys, please go and get your workbooks and Daddy will look over your lessons."

———

After the boys were in bed, Maeve hovered at the top of the steps to listen to the muffled sound of her parents arguing in the kitchen.

Finally the door opened and her father called for her. "Maeve, get down here."

I'm for it now.

She crept into the kitchen and stood beside the table. Her father was seated in his normal place and Mammy stood leaning against the worktop with her arms folded across her chest.

Daddy frowned at her. "I'm quite shocked at your behaviour, young lady."

Maeve stared down at her shoes as tears slid down her cheeks.

"Look at me, now."

She forced her eyes up to her father's. "I'm sorry Da, but I was defending you. I had to stand up for what's right. Isn't that what you always do?"

Her father's ears reddened. Maeve saw her mother shoot a look at her father. "I never imagined *uh, um.*" He coughed. "There's a big difference in standing up for a grand cause and getting into a brawl in the school hallways like a street urchin."

She looked back down to her shoes.

He sighed. "I'm sure your heart was in the right place."

Her mother took over then. "Tomorrow morning you and I will go early to school, so you can apologize to the Head, and then to Sister Mary and finally to Emer."

Maeve scowled and looked at her mother. "But she started it."

Mammy snapped. "And you continued it."

"Yes, Mammy, Maeve's bottom lip quivered."

Mammy pursed her lips as she pierced Maeve with her look. "Now, up you go and get out your Bible. I want you to read all of Matthew, chapter five and then go to bed and meditate about turning the other cheek."

"Yes, Mammy."

Her father murmured as she turned to leave. "Goodnight love," and then her heart didn't feel quite so broken.

30

Dublin, June 1939

On the 11th of June, when Maeve was 16, Emmet took her to watch the quarter-final match between the Gaelic football teams of Wexford and Longford at Croke Park.

Robert and Malachy had complained mightily about Maeve going alone with him, but Emmet promised to take them to the Finals of the Leinster Championship in July.

Robert continued to protest, even as Emmet and Maeve put their jackets on to go. "She doesn't even like football. Why does she get to go?"

Bridie stood with a hand on each shoulder of her two sons. "Don't whinge, Robert. We'll walk out in a little and find the ice cream man."

Emmet pulled the door closed behind him and they set off to walk the half-hour journey to Croke Park.

As they walked along North Circular Road, Maeve touched her father's sleeve. "Da?"

"Yes, lovey?"

"Why *are* you taking me to the match?"

He smiled at her. "Are you not glad to be going out with your old Da?"

She linked his arm. "Of course, I am, but I would have been just as happy going out for tea or something."

He patted her hand resting on his arm. "Years ago, I told you that one day I'd tell you more about some of my experiences. Now that you're sixteen, that's what I'm doing."

She nodded. "I loved hearing all about how when you were my age, you went with Papa, Uncle Michael and Uncle Kevin to fight in the War of Independence. It was exciting to hear all about the Battle of Ashbourne. What does football have to do with it, though?"

"It's not football so much, as Croke Park. I haven't been back there in many years because it was just too hard for me, but now, with you by my side, I'll take you to where I was on Bloody Sunday."

He told the story of what he had gone through in 1920 and the loss of his friend Sean.

By the time they were close to the stadium, Maeve was in tears. She released her father's arm to root about in her red embroidered bag for her handkerchief.

They sat in the same section in which Emmet and Sean had sat. The events were still clear, years later as if they had happened recently. By the time the match started, Emmet was drained with the retelling. "I haven't been back to Croke Park since then."

The teams were out now and warming up. Maeve blew her nose and put her handkerchief away. "Thank you for telling me about Sean and what happened, Da." She touched his cheek where his own tears dried. "Now it's our time. Let's make a new memory."

He blinked and smiled. "Yes. That's right. It's behind us now, but I promised I'd tell you and now I have."

They turned their attention to the match, and although Emmet knew that Maeve had little interest in sports, he grinned to watch as she cheered on the Longford team. She chose that team because he cheered for Wexford and although he had to explain the rules of the game, she seemed to enjoy the afternoon.

On the walk home, they were confronted by a group of men and women carrying signs that read *Boycott British Goods*.

Maeve shifted closer to Emmet. "Da, there's even a nun with a sign."

Emmet nodded. Yes, lots of people are passionate about this."

"We didn't see these people when we went in to the match. How come they're all here now?"

"Since so many men will go to the pub now, they want to remind everyone not to buy Bass ale."

"Do you drink Bass ale?"

"Good Lord, no. I don't need reminding. This is still the same fight we've been having all these years, Maeve."

"So even now, people stand up for what's right."

"They do. It's good to see."

Emmet and Maeve waved at a group of women holding signs, and the women smiled and waved back.

Maeve was quiet for most of the walk home and Emmet was content to let her be alone with her thoughts. He knew that his afternoon with the boys at Croke Park would be very different than this had been. His daughter was the only one interested in the history, and Emmet suspected that even when his sons reached sixteen years of age, he wouldn't have a day like this with them.

As they walked in companionable silence, Emmet thought about his dreams for his daughter.

Maybe she'll be a writer, with her love of the history. Not a journalist like me. My words are here today and wrapping up the fish tomorrow. Maybe she'll be a Joyce or O'Casey.

He smiled to imagine it and was content.

31

Dublin, Summer 1941

Eighteen-year-old Maeve was having a serious talk with her brother Robert, who, at fifteen, was excited about the German bombing. He didn't seem at all upset or sympathetic about the damage done.

Maeve waved her finger at Robert. "No. Do not take Malachy to see the damage. These are people's homes we're talking about. Mammy will throttle you if you two go down there."

Robert was sullen, and Maeve could tell he regretted telling her that they planned to cycle down to North Strand to see where the bombs had fallen a few days ago.

"Sure, we'll be back before lunch. Mammy doesn't even have to know." He looked meaningfully at his sister. He kept her secrets often enough.

Maeve had a sudden change of heart. "Oh, go on then. Who am I to tell you? I'm not giving you permission, mind. I still don't think it's a good idea."

Maeve decided to walk down to the newspaper offices where her father worked. She would take him a flask with tea.

When she walked into the offices of The Irish Press, the staff all greeted Maeve warmly. "Hiya, Maeve. How's it going, Maeve?"

Her father looked up from his desk when she walked in. "This is a lovely surprise."

She handed over the flask. "A cup of tea for you."

"Ah, you're a darling."

She looked at the notes and clippings on his desk. "What are you working on?"

"Lambasting the government for not yet sending a formal protest to the German government for the bombings."

"Why are they bombing us? We're neutral."

Emmet shrugged. "It might just be pilot error."

"Might?"

Emmet pushed back in his chair and poured out a cup of tea from the flask. "No. I don't really think that, but it's what the public explanation is. I say *might* because it may also be a warning to us, the Republic."

"What sort of warning?"

"To stay out of the war. After de Valera's speech in April about the bombings in Belfast, there are rumours that the Germans weren't best pleased."

Maeve nodded. "After he proclaimed that *they are our people.*"

Emmet nodded. "That's it."

Maeve sat down opposite Emmet's desk. "Will we get embroiled in this awful war?"

Emmet reached over and patted her hand. "No. Don't worry. Dev will make his protest and that'll be an end to it."

He leaned back again and changed the subject. "Did your Mam talk to you about our house guests?"

Maeve brightened. "She did. This is the woman from England that she's known forever, right?"

Emmet smiled. "Not quite forever, but yes they've been friends since they were about your age."

She tilted her head. "Isn't it strange that she's friends with an English person?"

"They're not all enemies. Most people are just like you and I, trying to live their lives. But aside from that, I think you know that Elizabeth is half Irish."

"Oh, that's right. Her father is Irish."

"Yes, and now they're coming here because their home has been damaged. The Carsons can't have them. They've left Belfast and gone to stay with some distant family living in Donegal. Buncrana or some such hole in the wall."

Maeve laughed. "It's probably quite lovely."

Emmet grimaced. "And what would you know about these little villages? You're a town girl."

"I've stayed with Nana and Gramps in Ashbourne before. Or does that not count because it's *your* little village?"

Emmet grinned. "Ashbourne is very civilized."

Maeve shook her head and returned to the subject of the house guests. "So there's just Mammy's friend and the son coming, right?"

"Yes, he's her only child. The husband died quite young in an accident of some sort. I think the two of them lived with her father for a while, but from what I understand, he's actually working with the government now in some capacity to do with the war office."

Maeve nodded. "The boys will enjoy having a young man around to pester with questions about living in war."

"Actually, I think that's part of the reason they're coming here."

Maeve frowned. "Why?"

"It seems as though he wants to sign up and Elizabeth is in the horrors that he'll disobey her and run off to join the army."

"But he must be too young?"

"He's a few months younger than you, so he's seventeen."

"So he could easily join if he wanted to."

Emmet nodded. "I'm sure he could, but it sounds like he's coming here, so that will keep him busy for now. We'll see how long he stays."

———

Robert and Malachy weren't wild about sharing a bed, but the excitement of having the English boy Daniel in the room made up for the inconvenience. Robert and Malachy would bunk together in Malachy's bed and Daniel would get Robert's. The tiny storage room had been made over with a second-hand bed to accommodate Elizabeth.

Maeve had expected Daniel to be sullen and awkward. That was the way many of the boys she knew were. Instead, he had a natural full-lipped smile. He was tall; about five feet ten and he held himself straight and at the same time, relaxed. He liked to stand with his hands in his pockets with a casual ease that exuded confidence. His dark hair was wavy and combed back from his face. He had a long elegant neck, but his most striking feature was his hazel eyes. They seemed to pierce Maeve when he fixed his gaze on her. Maeve loved that Daniel had lovely manners and was very attentive to his mother. She felt her heart flutter the first time he shook her hand.

School was out for summer break. Maeve's brothers were always looking for adventure so they were delighted when they could convince Daniel to go along with them. They cycled off to hurling matches, even though Daniel didn't know the first thing about hurling. He preferred to kick the ball around in a spontaneous game of football. Daniel's real passion was rugby. Maeve was gobsmacked when he recited part of a poem about rugby by Louis MacNeice to the boys.

They were all sitting in the parlour after tea one evening. The boys and Emmet were debating the speed and excitement of Gaelic football to rugby when Daniel stood up, his hands clasped before him chest high, in a stance such as a singer might adopt and in a clear, strong voice recited:

> Lansdowne Road - the swirl of flags and faces
> Gilbert and Sullivan music, emerald jerseys;
> Spire and crane beyond remind the mind on furlough
> of Mersey's cod and Rome's.

Daniel lifted his arms above his head in a gesture of triumph and continued:

> Eccentric scoring - Nicholson, Marshall and Unwin,
> Replies by Bailey and Daly;
> Rugs around our shins, the effortless place-kick
> Gaily carving the goalposts.

He grinned and sat down to a round of clapping.

Maeve could have listened to him for hours. "Is that the whole poem? Is there more?"

Daniel shrugged. "There is more, but I don't remember it."

"That was lovely."

Maeve's mother raised her eyebrows "Have you become a fan of rugby all of a sudden then, Maeve?"

Maeve felt herself grow hot. "Of course not, but I can appreciate poetry about any subject."

Robert grinned. "That was grand, Daniel."

Daniel dipped his head in a mock bow. "Do I have you convinced that rugby is the superior sport? Surely you have no poems about your football."

The debate continued with Malachy protesting that real sports didn't need poetry, just good, fast men.

Maeve stopped listening but later, in the quiet of her room, she tried to remember the poem to copy in her journal. She underlined the date to remind herself in the future about what a nice day it had been.

———

It was a clear August morning. Daniel had declined to go along with the boys to the zoo. "I think I'll stay behind this time."

Maeve sat out in the back garden with a book when he came out to join her. She shaded her eyes to look up at him. "You look restless. You should have gone along with Robert and Malachy."

He shook his head. "I've had enough small boy adventures."

Maeve raised her eyebrows. "Oh?"

"May I sit?"

"Yes, of course."

Daniel pulled over another chair, angling it so Maeve wouldn't have to look into the sun. "What are you reading?"

Maeve held up the cover of her book for him. "It's a biography about the Countess Markievicz."

Daniel frowned. "I've heard the name but don't know her. Is she some Russian?"

Maeve felt herself grow hot but took a breath before answering. "No. She's the greatest Irish woman who ever lived."

Daniel's eyes widened. "Oh. Sorry."

Maeve could see he wasn't sure what to say next. She also saw that his startling hazel eyes had chocolate flecks. Yes, they were the most beautiful eyes she had ever seen. "Sorry. I didn't mean to come across so strongly. She's my heroine."

"Tell me about her."

Maeve sketched out the highlights of her life, concluding with "She died before she could take up her seat after the '27 elections."

"Right, now I do remember hearing about her."

"She was the first woman to be elected to the British House of Commons, so even if you don't know much about Irish history, that's how you might have heard about her."

Daniel nodded. "You sound very passionate when you talk of her."

"She had such an impact on our country."

"Yes, I see that." He hesitated and then continued. "I'll bet you could make that kind of impact."

"Me?" Maeve closed the book and laughed.

"Certainly. Why not?"

Maeve shrugged. "True. Why not, indeed."

Daniel stood. "Let's go for a walk."

Maeve stood. "All right. We'll go down to St. Stephen's Green. Give me a minute to get my hat."

It seemed to Maeve that the walk to St. Stephen's had never been covered so quickly. It was usually at least a twenty-minute journey for her, and perhaps it was this time as well, but Maeve didn't feel it. During the walk they spoke of the houses, gardens and churches they passed. Daniel told her about where he lived and the destruction of so much that had been familiar to him.

Before she knew it, they were wandering through the park, and finally when they spotted an empty bench, as of one mind, they moved towards it and sat side by side to watch the children playing ball. When they sat down, Maeve had almost forgotten the conversation they had been having earlier, in her own garden, and she had to think for a moment when she heard him speak.

Daniel voice was carried on a sigh, so that she almost didn't hear him. "I want to do great things as well."

Maeve smiled at him. "What sort of great things?"

His beautiful eyes were serious when he turned to her. "I should be joining the army and fighting."

"The British Army."

He frowned. "Yes, of course the British Army."

She nodded. "Since you and your mother have been here, I've almost forgotten that you are British."

He had a trick of raising one eyebrow when he wanted more information.

She looked away. "For all my life I've learned that the British Army were our enemies." She turned quickly and saw his face colour. "I'm sorry. I don't mean that you're my enemy, and of course, you're partly Irish."

His voice was stiff. "I've never felt partly Irish. I've only ever been British."

"Oh. Even now that you've been here in Dublin for a while? Do you still feel the same?"

"England is still my home."

She tried to get back to the comfortable way they had been. "I'm sorry. I interrupted you. You feel that you should be over in France or wherever fighting."

She heard his intake of breath and knew he was also trying to regain the ease of a few moments before.

He nodded. "I have schoolmates who have gone."

Despite herself, she felt a catch in her throat. "How awful."

He shook his head. "They are standing up for what's right. That's what I should be doing. Not here with my mother, hiding. I feel like a coward."

Maeve looked at him with new eyes. He had seemed so young until now. *He's a man, not a boy.*

She touched his sleeve. "I don't think the war is going to be over tomorrow. Your mother wants to keep you safe as long as she can."

At her touch he flushed again, his cheeks firing red. "I know, and I am trying to be kind to her and not harass her, but when I'm eighteen, I can do as I think best."

She nodded. "I, for one, hope that you find something worthwhile to do, other than join the British army."

"Such as?"

"You told me that you love the sciences. Perhaps being a doctor would be worthwhile?"

He sniffed. "Now you sound like her, like my mother."

Maeve frowned and pursed her lips. "Oh no. I don't want to sound like your mother."

There it was again. The raised eyebrow.

Now it was Maeve's turn to feel the colour rise in her face. "I don't mean there's anything wrong with your mother. I just mean I don't feel like a mother to you." *Dear God, just stop talking.*

She stood quickly. "We should go back."

Daniel stood, and this time offered his arm to her. Maeve took it, trying to imagine any boy that she knew of her own age behaving like this. *He's different. Maybe because his Da died so young. He grew up fast.*

They walked in companionable silence for a few minutes.

He glanced at her. "When I go home, would you write to me?"

She nodded. "That would be fun. I can keep working to convince you to go to medical school."

"Yes, you can try. That is, if you have time to write. You'll be starting college yourself in a few weeks."

"That's true. I'm so excited to be going to University College Dublin. It's a great school."

"What will the study of literature and history get for you though? Anything practical?

"I expect I'll teach."

Maeve wanted to walk past the house just to continue their conversation. She slipped her hand from his arm before getting close to the house. *No point in giving the boys something to tease me about.*

———

Daniel spent less and less time with the boys and more time with Maeve. She knew people noticed but didn't care.

Today they were at the Municipal Gallery to see the Lady Lavery Bequest.

They wandered around the old townhouse which housed the gallery. Maeve stopped in front of a portrait of Lady Lavery. "She was beautiful, wasn't she?"

Daniel studied the painting. "She certainly was. There's a real elegance about her, isn't there?"

Maeve looked around and lowered her voice. "They say that she was in love with Michael Collins, you know."

He turned to stare at her. "The man who negotiated the treaty?"

She nodded. "I heard she was heartbroken when he was assassinated."

"My goodness. Who would guess that such a fine English lady would fall in love with an Irish rebel?"

"There have actually been many cases of relationships between English and Irish."

He smiled and the way his eyes sparkled at her made Maeve's heart race. "So it's not always contentious between us then?"

She tilted her head, feeling bold. "No, not always."

He nodded. "There's something fascinating about the Irish. You bring such enthusiasm to everything. That's very different from the understated ways I'm used to. You're very different than any girl I've ever met, Maeve."

She felt sweat prick under her arms at his serious look. She tried to joke about it. "And how many girls do you know?"

"I've met a few. None are like you."

She turned to walk on and they strolled side by side along the gallery of paintings. "Well, I've never met anyone like you either. You seem so much older than your age."

"I'll miss you when I go home."

Maeve didn't want to think of it. "We better enjoy the time we have then, hadn't we?"

———————

August was at an end. It was one of the last nights of their stay. Tea was long finished, and Maeve's Mam and Elizabeth were deep in conversation. The boys played checkers and Maeve's father had fallen asleep in his easy chair with the newspaper across his chest.

Daniel leaned in close to Maeve. "I read in the paper that we can expect a sky full of shooting stars tonight. It's dark enough now. Shall we go out in the garden to watch them?"

"Oh, yes. Let's."

They stood and Mam looked up. "Where are you two going?"

Maeve waved her hand towards the garden. "Just outside to see the shooting stars. Would you two like to come?"

"Perhaps in a bit."

Maeve led the way into the garden and they strolled to the farthest end so that the light pouring out of the windows didn't distract from the view.

They stood side by side gazing up. Daniel pointed. "There! Did you see that?"

"No. Darn. Where are you looking?"

He put his arm around her shoulders and pulled her close, his temple touching hers. "There towards the plough."

A star flared across the sky.

Maeve gasped. "Oh! How lovely." She felt Daniel shift and then she was looking up at him rather than the sky. She couldn't see his eyes in the darkness but imagined them gazing down at her. She shivered as he placed both his hands on her face, drawing her towards him. His lips touched hers and she felt every fibre in her body respond. She pressed closer to him and pulled him in, her arms circling his body. They kissed again, and she felt as though she might melt against him.

They parted, her breath racing. In the silence she heard the door open and the sound of her mother's voice calling her. "Maeve? Where are you?"

They moved apart, and she tried to calm her voice. "Down here, Mammy. You can see the stars better here, away from the house."

Maeve took a step along the path to meet her mother, leaving Daniel. She heard his breath rasping as he tried to steady himself.

Maeve, Daniel and the two mothers stood for a few moments, admiring the stars as they put on their magical display.

When they said goodnight without Maeve having another chance to be alone with Daniel, it seemed to her that she almost dreamt those moments in the garden. She wrote in her diary: *my first kiss. I think I'm in love. Surely it wouldn't have been so amazing, had I not been in love?*

It was time for Elizabeth and Daniel to leave. There had been some talk of staying on, but it would mean Daniel missing his last year at school, so even Elizabeth had to concede that it wasn't a good plan.

There had been no other chance for Maeve to be alone in private with Daniel. It felt as though her mother had conspired to ensure that wouldn't happen. Maeve knew that her mother had noticed the time she and Daniel spent together. Once her mother gave her a piercing look when she noticed the two of them laughing together. Maeve had automatically reached out to grasp Daniel's arm as she emphasized her point of the argument. Maeve saw the look her mother gave and released his arm as though it were on fire.

Now, as Elizabeth and Daniel waited for a taxi to take them to the train station, Maeve sensed that Daniel would reach out, perhaps to kiss her cheek. She longed for it but knew her parents would find it inappropriate. The taxi rolled up. Maeve held out her hand to shake his.

A shadow of a frown passed across his face and then he placed his hand in hers. "Goodbye, Maeve. Thank you for being such a friendly hostess. I've enjoyed our conversations." He gave a small bow and then turned to shake the hands of the boys and Maeve's parents.

He turned for one last look to Maeve who nodded, her eyes holding his for a second too long. He smiled. She felt the warmth in her cheeks.

He helped his mother into the car and then, in a puff of diesel, the auto was gone, and the Ryan family turned to go back into the house.

Maeve felt a lump in her throat. *Don't be silly. He's just a schoolboy.* She knew he wasn't just a schoolboy though, despite what she tried to tell herself. He was so mature. And he had captured her heart.

She climbed the steps to her room, but not before she heard her mother say to her father, "I think it's a good thing they've gone."

Da laughed. "Had enough of house guests, have you?"

"It's good that *one* of these house guests is out from under our roof, anyway."

Maeve didn't hear anything further. She went into her room, picked up the book she was currently reading and sat with it in her lap, unopened until she was called to come down for tea. Instead of words on the pages of her book, she kept seeing hazel eyes with chocolate brown flecks.

They would write to each other, they agreed. It was the best they could do.

32

Dublin, May 1942

Maeve loved attending University College Dublin. She thrived in the atmosphere of learning and discussion. She joined the Folklore Society and the College Debating Union, the same debating society her father had belonged to when he was at school. She came home in the evenings full of chat about the people and ideas she encountered.

Robert, two years behind Maeve, complained of the daily discussions. "Ah, no. Please not more about politics. Can't we have a conversation about football at the dinner table for a change?"

Malachy waved his fork at his brother. "Robert had a brilliant goal today."

Mammy smiled. "Did you, love?"

Robert shrugged. "I don't know if it was brilliant."

Malachy nodded. "It was. You should have seen it."

Her father frowned. "And was this before or after you did your homework?"

Robert sighed. "Yeh, I know. I have to get good grades to get into college. Maybe I don't want to get into college like Maeve. Maybe we're all sick to death of hearing how great college is."

Maeve wrinkled her forehead. "Well, I'm sorry if I've been monopolizing the conversation. Please go ahead. Tell us something of interest."

Robert pushed his plate away. "May I be excused?"

Mam picked up the plate. "Don't you want a bit of tart?"

Robert shook his head. "What's the point when there's hardly any sugar in it anyway? With the rationing, we might as well be eating sawdust."

Her father frowned. "What's gotten into you today?"

"Nothing at all."

Her mother nodded. "Go on, then."

Maeve watched her brother disappear. They finished their meal quickly and after Maeve and Malachy helped their mother with the dishes, Maeve went up to speak to her brother.

She tapped on his bedroom door. "Robert, can I come in?"

He opened the door for her and then flung himself back on his bed.

"What's wrong? I know I go on a bit about school, but I didn't know it bothered you so much."

He pushed himself up to lean against the wall at the head of the bed, with his arms folded. "Sometimes I just feel like Da is living in the past. He's always going on about the history and now that you're at his old school and even in the debating society, it's like you and him are in a club of your own. Malachy and me, we don't seem to matter."

She sat on the edge of his bed and rested a hand on his leg. "It's not like that. I just have similar interests I guess, and although you have different interests, it doesn't mean you're any less important to Da, or to me."

He closed his eyes and tipped his head back for a moment. When he opened them again and rested them on Maeve, his grey eyes were shiny with tears. "I'll never be as good a student as you and I couldn't care less about all his old stories. In fact, I hate it when he goes on and on about those things. He's a big hero. We all know that. I'll never live up to what he is." He took a deep breath. "I want to quit school, Maeve."

Maeve stared. "Oh, Robert."

He went on. "If I don't quit, I suspect the Brothers will recommend it anyway."

"Are you doing so poorly?"

He shrugged again.

"Could I help you to do better?"

226

He sat up straight. "I'm just not interested. I'd rather be an apprentice somewhere. I've seen a card in the window of.."

"Of?"

"The baker down at Doyle's Corner."

"The baker? Good Lord."

He flushed. "You think I'm foolish, don't you?"

"No, no. I don't think that. It's just a surprise. I always assumed you'd go to college as well."

"Now you know. I want to be a baker. Even with the rationing I bet I could do better than what Mam makes."

Again Maeve was at a loss for words. "Oh, my."

Now Robert held his chin up. "What should I do?"

"You've got to talk to Mam and Da, obviously. I would say though, just to keep your options open, like, you should try your best to finish your year with a passing grade. Meanwhile, talk to the baker and see if it seems like a possibility for you. Why not? Having a baker in the family would be a grand thing, Robert."

He smiled shyly. "Do you really think so?"

"I do, of course. Robert, I'm sure Da never meant to make you feel small with all his stories. It's just who he is. I always loved them, but that's just me. You need to let him know who you are without being angry or disrespectful. I'll go with you if you want when you talk to them."

He bit his lip. "No, I better do it on my own. Thanks, though."

———

Maeve quickened her step, so she wouldn't be late for the debate. She wasn't speaking, but Patrick was, and she wanted to be there early enough that she could say hello before he took the podium. To divert herself with the long walk along the length of Earlsfort Terrace through the cold wind, she held her collar tight and thought about when she had first met Patrick Dermody. Her mind went back to the beginning of the school year when she joined the debate team with such enthusiasm. She remembered feeling so alive. She knew so many nuances of the political arguments, having been schooled at the knee of her father.

After the first time she went to the podium to argue a point, a young man from the opposing position, Patrick, approached her as she walked down the steps outside on the way to catch the tram. "You're quite a speaker. You have great passion."

Maeve felt the flush rise in her face. This man had made a complete fool of her. "It seemed like you thought I was an idiot."

He widened his eyes. "Not at all. I thought you held your own."

Maeve wanted to turn away from him, and yet she was drawn to him. "That's not how it felt. With every point I made, you destroyed me."

He laughed. "I have more experience than you. You'll get there. I liked some of the things you said. Especially when you talked about the unfinished work in our nation."

She felt herself relaxing. "I believe strongly in a united Ireland."

He smiled. "Me too."

Maeve felt a shiver rise the hairs on the back of her neck. His dark curls held streaks of copper in the sunlight. He had the wild, somewhat dangerous looks of the people her mother called tinkers. He had a dark shadowed chin as though he hadn't shaved in a couple of days. There was something magnetic about Patrick's intensity.

He held out a hand to take her book bag. "Let's go for a cup of tea."

Maeve handed over her bag, falling into step with him without thought to her family waiting at home for her to join them for tea. She'd say she'd gone out with her friend Brigid. The two girls were in psychology class together and her family had met her when she came to the house to work on a project. Brigid wasn't political but she was fun to be with and Mammy liked her. They'd forgive Maeve.

———

After the third debating club meeting and thus the third time they were going out for a drink, they walked along the river to The Dropping Well. They squeezed into a corner and he went to fetch her a shandy.

He set the drink down in front of her. "Are you all right here? You look rather flushed."

228

She nodded and then shrugged. "I'm not used to going to a pub."

He frowned. "You never go out?"

"I've been with my parents, but I can't say even that has been very often. It's usually tea for me."

He studied her from across the table. "Would you be more comfortable if we left?"

She took a sip of her drink. "No, no. Not at all."

Once they began talking, Maeve relaxed. On that occasion, she made sure that her parents knew she was going out. After that first time when there had been holy hell to pay for not coming home when expected, she was more careful.

Mam had almost been in tears when she hadn't returned until after they had finished tea.

"Do you know how worried we were?"

Daddy had kept everyone calm. He had put his arm around Maeve's shoulder. "Now Mam, our girl is growing up. We knew she'd meet new friends once she went to school. Maeve won't scare us like that again though, will you? Just let us know your plans, sweetheart. That's all we ask."

Maeve had felt wretched about the worry she'd caused and vowed to avoid it in future.

So that night, her family knew she was out with friends, and they were having their tea without her.

Inevitably the conversation came around to politics.

The beer loosened Maeve's tongue. "My father was there in the beginning. He and his best pal Liam, both."

"In '16?"

"Yes." Maeve knew her voice held the pride she felt.

"Mine too. I would have like to be there." His eyes lit up. "Wouldn't it be fantastic to be a part of something so important? The forming of a nation?"

She nodded and smiled. "We were born a little too late."

"Not necessarily."

She frowned and tilted her head, but he changed the subject. "Where was your father?"

"He was part of the Fingal Volunteers."

"Really?" Patrick drew the word out: *reeely*

"You've heard of them?"

"This pal of your Da's. Liam, did you say?"

"What about him?"

"What's his last name, then?"

Now Maeve was cagey. "Why do you ask?"

Patrick looked quickly over one shoulder and then the other. "I know a fella named Liam who was with the Fingals in '16. Liam Kelly's his name."

Maeve took another drink from her shandy, stalling for time. "It's a pretty common name."

Patrick leaned back. "It is. The man I know wouldn't appreciate us talking about him."

Maeve nodded, but the glance between them revealed more than words. *He knows Uncle Liam. Patrick must be involved somehow.*

———

Maeve arrived at the hall and went inside, thankful to be out of the cutting wind. She ran her fingers through her curls in an effort to tame her hair and then went into the auditorium, greeting her friends as she made her way close to the front. She was too late, and Patrick was already on the stage, but he saw her and smiled, sending a wave scalding through her. She slipped off her coat and laid it on the chair next to her. She didn't want anyone sitting next to her. She liked to sit alone and focus on the debate. On Patrick's words.

After the debate, she and Patrick, along with a few others, made their way to Hartigan's Pub for drinks. She and Patrick sat alone at a small booth with their drinks, while the others pushed two round tables together and crowded around there, still discussing the merits of the debate points.

Maeve relaxed in the relative quiet of the booth. "You don't want to sit with the others?"

"No, I wanted a quiet word with you."

Maeve felt her heart beat faster. His dark looks, and intensity had drawn Maeve to Patrick, but they had never taken their friendship any further than talking and drinks.

Her breath came faster. "Oh?"

He took her hand and she felt the heat of his skin on hers. "We've become good friends these last few months."

She nodded and swallowed.

"So, I didn't want you to hear this from someone else."

He's engaged. Oh God. "Very mysterious, altogether."

He smiled, still clasping her hand between his. "Not really. It's just that I'll be leaving college when the year is over in a couple of weeks."

Her mouth fell open. "Oh. But you have another two years to go, don't you?"

He loosened her hand. "I've decided I can better use my time elsewhere."

She frowned. "Have you got a job somewhere?"

"You could say that."

"Where? What is it?" Her mind flitted to her brother Robert who was to be an apprentice.

He lowered his voice and she leaned in to hear him above the noise of the pub. "I'm going North."

She frowned. "North?"

"Yes. North."

Suddenly she understood. The Cause. He was leaving school to fight. She licked her lips, at a loss for what to say.

He must have seen the change on her face. He nodded. "You understand?"

"Yes, I think so."

He drained his glass, relaxed now. "Can I get you another?"

She nodded. "Please."

As he fought his way through the crowded room to the bar, she had time to think. *I'll never see him again. How come the fellows I like go away?* She felt queasy and didn't really want another drink. And then she had an idea.

He came back with their drinks.

"Thank you." She leaned in, her voice as quiet as his had been earlier. "If I wanted to help out as well, how would I do that? I don't mean that I'd leave school or do anything big, but surely there must be something I could do as well. You know how I feel about Ireland."

He looked at her over the rim of his glass. He shook his head. "I don't think it would be a good idea for you."

She clenched her jaw and sat back. "Why not? What's wrong with me?"

"Nothing. It's just that you have no experience and it just isn't for everyone."

"And how does one get experience if not from participating in some kind of action?"

He set his drink down and lifted his hands in defence. "Fair enough. Who am I to turn anyone away? I'll tell you what. Once I see what the lay of the land is, I'll send word to your Uncle Liam if I think there's any way for you to help. Is that fair?"

She nodded. "All right."

He clinked his glass against hers. "I've enjoyed our friendship, Maeve. If things were different" He shrugged. "But they aren't different. So there it is. I'll miss you, though."

She blinked back tears. "And I, you."

They went on to talk about the latest war news and Maeve pushed away the thought that soon she'd have to say goodbye to him.

33

Dublin, August 1942

Maeve and her youngest brother had spent the day with their Nana and Granpa Mallon, she ostensibly helping in the garden, although half an hour of pruning roses had concluded with hours sitting in the garden chatting and drinking lemonade. Malachy had learned to play chess and was delighted to go home with a set for himself.

When they arrived home, it was obvious that they had company. Maeve paused in the foyer. "Who do you think it is, Malachy?"

They listened and then Malachy grinned. "It's Uncle Liam."

"Ah, yes. I believe you're right."

Malachy swung open the parlour door. "Hi Uncle Liam. Do you play chess?"

Maeve followed, her heart quickening. *Is he here to see me? Did Patrick send word?* She stepped to his side and bent down to kiss his cheek. "Hello Uncle Liam."

Liam stood up balancing his cup and saucer. "I'm afraid I've never learned the game Malachy, but I think your father plays." He turned to Maeve. "You're lovelier every time I see you, Maeve."

Maeve felt the heat rise to her face and shook her head but was saved from having to respond by her brother setting the chessboard down on the small round table.

"I can teach you, Uncle Liam."

Maeve's mother admonished Malachy. "Let the poor man drink his tea. Take your game away for now, Malachy. After tea perhaps, you can convince your Da into a game."

Mam turned to Maeve. "Did you have a nice afternoon with Gran?"

"I did, of course. We had a great old chat. Her garden is so pretty. It makes me think that we could do more with ours. In fact, I'm going out to look at the garden while it's in my mind."

Liam stood up. "I'll go out with you and have a wee smoke."

Mam shook her head. "You're developing a Belfast accent, Liam."

He smiled. "I spend a lot of time in the North these days, but my heart belongs to Dublin."

Mam stood to gather the cups and saucers. "I should hope so."

Liam followed Maeve outside and, after lighting a home-rolled cigarette, he paced beside her as they walked the length of the garden.

They stopped at the back gate and Maeve looked up at him. "Do you have any news for me?"

He took a deep draw on his cigarette before exhaling a cloud of smoke up into the air above Maeve's head. "Are you still interested in any news I might have?"

"Very much so."

He faced her, his back to the house. "This isn't to be taken lightly."

"I know that."

He finished his cigarette, grinding it out under his foot. He sighed. "I'm taking a drive on Sunday night. It will be late, after most law-abiding citizens are in their beds."

She bit her lip, her heart beating hard. "And you're inviting me along?"

"It can be useful to have a woman along on trips like this."

"And will we be back on the same night? I'm not sure how I could stay away overnight."

"We'll be back the same night."

"Count me in."

"You should think about it. It should be straightforward, but there's always risk."

"I don't need to think about it. Let's walk on."

They continued to stroll down the other side of the garden, Maeve stopping to point out an area as if they were discussing the flower beds. "Where do I meet you?"

He shook his head. "Your parents will skin me alive if they find out."

"They won't. And I'm the one making this choice. Not you."

"Fair enough. Meet me in front of St. Peter's at eleven o'clock. Can you get away then?"

"I'll be there."

They went back into the house and despite her mind spinning with the thought of what might come in just four days' time, she talked to her mother about roses and Welsh poppies for the garden. She was glad that her brothers carried the conversation at tea, with Robert full of baking news and Malachy pestering her father about chess.

———

The night of the thirtieth of August was black and sultry. The rain spit down and Maeve had a headache. *It's so feckin' hot.* A trickle of sweat slid down between her shoulder blades. The darkness cloaked her, and she was glad for it. She didn't feel quite so conspicuous standing alone in front of the old church as she might have if it were a bright, clear evening.

Uncle Liam was suddenly beside her. She smelt the musky odour of him, knowing it was him, before she turned.

He rested his hand on her shoulder briefly. "Are you sure you want to come along?"

She tried to pierce the darkness to look into his eyes. "You won't go back on your promise, sure you won't?"

"I won't. I'm just telling you there'd be no shame in changing your mind."

Maeve shook her head. "No chance."

Liam took his cap off and ran his hand through his thinning hair. "Your Da will kill me if he thinks I've coerced you into this."

She laid her hand on his sleeve. "If he finds out, and why should he? But if he does, I'll make sure he knows it was entirely my idea and decision."

Liam nodded. "Right, then. Let's go. I need someone like you to go with me, so if you're sure, that's good enough for me."

He led her around the corner to where he had a lorry parked. They climbed in, and Maeve settled onto the hard seat. Maeve wore a simple working dress, in keeping with the story that she was Liam's niece and they were delivering a load of lumber. She reminded herself of the details. *My Da, Liam's brother, took ill and decided he wasn't able to drive the lorry. That's why we're so late. Da kept thinking he'd manage, but finally decided he can't.*

Liam concentrated on driving through the drizzle, so they didn't speak as he navigated them through the dark Dublin streets. The rattle and drone of the lorry made conversation difficult anyway. Maeve felt queasy at the thought of all the munitions hidden in the back of the lorry. *What if we're stopped?*

She looked at Liam. His face was a grey shape in the darkness. "How long is it to Newry again?"

"Couple of hours." He threw her a quick look. "Not having second thoughts?"

"No, no."

She saw him nod. His voice was quiet, and she could hardly make him out over the noise of the engine. "I should never have let Paddy and yourself talk me into this."

"Uncle Liam. If Patrick thinks I can be of use, then I'm glad to be here. If nothing else, I can at least help with the unloading. An extra set of hands can't be a bad thing."

He sniffed. "Patrick. A fine college man. At least he should be. Now that he's left college to go north, who knows what his future holds?"

She bit her lip. "I happen to agree with you, Uncle Liam. I think he should have stayed in school as well. He's so clever."

They fell into silence again. With the blackouts, everything was pitch dark. They drove through the night towards Newry where they would cross the border to unload weapons for the IRA to continue the fight for Irish unity. It crossed Maeve's mind that she may be doing this just to see Patrick. She expected he would be there to receive the munitions. *No. It's not that. Patrick is lovely, but he's not looking for a girl. His love is all spent on the Cause.*

Maeve dozed but awoke in the sudden quiet of the lorry being turned off. "Where are we?"

Liam cranked the handbrake on. "Coming in to Dundalk. We'll take a few minutes to stretch."

Maeve climbed out. The rain had stopped. They were pulled over on the side of the road. There were bushes along the side of the road and Maeve fought her way through them to a secluded spot. *I shouldn't have had that second cup of tea at supper.*

She made her way back to the side of the lorry.

Liam was smoking a cigarette. The tip glowed in the dark. "Do you smoke these days?"

"No."

"No bad habits, then?"

"Not that one, anyway."

Liam chuckled. "I wonder what your Da would have said if I had asked him to come along on this trip instead of you."

Maeve bit her lip. "He probably would have jumped at the chance."

"You think so?"

"Yes. Whenever he's talked about his actions you should hear his voice. He's very proud of the work he's done."

Liam nodded and took another drag. "Yes, I know he is. No question but he's a grand man for telling the story."

Maeve felt herself tense. "He spent time in prison. He has a right to be proud of his participation. You make it sound like he's full of hot air."

"Ah now, no need to get defensive. I know better than anyone what your Da does for the Cause. There are bits that I suspect he left out, though."

"Like what?"

Liam chortled. "He never had the stomach for getting dirty. I don't suppose he ever mentioned how many times he gave up his lunch when things got hot."

"He can't stand blood." Maeve conceded the point. "He's not a coward, though."

"No, I'm not saying that he is. I just think that he wouldn't be as enthusiastic about this sort of thing as you are."

"How did you stay friends all these years if you're so different?"

The tip of the cigarette glowed as Liam took a deep draw. "Maybe it's because we're different. We both want the same thing, but we have different ways of getting there. The Cause needs both of us."

A snippet of poetry occurred to Maeve. "Crying *Whát I dó is me: for that I came.*"

"What's that when it's at home?"

"It's from a poem by Gerard Manley Hopkins. It talks about how we each have our own gifts to bring. You know, everyone is unique and what you do is different than what my Da does, but you bring your own talents to a thing."

There was a silence as Liam finished his cigarette and ground it out. "It seems to me that your talents lie in the way of education, like your Da."

Maeve shrugged. "I promise not to throw up." She changed the subject. "Tell me again what you want me to do when we get to the border."

"You're to say nothing. We shouldn't even see anyone on the road I'm taking. If we do get questioned by anyone, let me do the talking."

"And when we get to the drop-off?"

"You'll be the lookout. You've sharp eyes and you'll need them in the back of your head to make sure no one comes upon us. With the new aerodrome at Kilkeel, the area's crawling with soldiers."

Maeve nodded. "I won't let you down."

Liam reached for the door handle. "I know you won't. You're Emmet's daughter, aren't you? Ready to go?"

Maeve felt a glow of pride. She jumped back into the lorry with a renewed excitement.

The clouds were scudding across the sky when they approached the border. The rain had stopped completely, and the light of the waning moon cast grey shadows on the landscape.

"Damn." Liam cursed.

Maeve saw the faint light of a torch ahead. "Guards?"

"Soldiers. Quiet, now." Liam slowed the lorry to stop at the temporary barrier erected at the border. Each of the two guards took positions on either side of the lorry. Liam rolled down his window and as Maeve looked out her window the guard made a motion for her to open it as well.

Liam adopted a cheerful, casual tone. "Wet, ould night for standing around in the dark, Corporal."

The soldiers each shone their torches into the truck cab and for an instant Maeve was blinded.

The one on the driver's side called over to his colleague. "Search the back, Lynn." He then asked Liam for identification and questions about where they were going.

Maeve rested her elbows on the open window and looked out at the soldier on her side before he stepped away. "My name's Maeve. What's yours?"

She felt him hesitate. "Private Henry Lynn."

"As in Vera Lynn?"

He sighed. "Yes."

"Are you related?"

"I wish. It would be nice to have some of *her* money."

She sang the opening lines from *The White Cliffs of Dover* softly. "Come on, sing it with me."

She heard him chuckling as he moved along the length of the lorry, flashing the light under the carriage. "You wouldn't want to hear me sing."

She continued to tease him as he reached the back of the vehicle. "People always say that, but I'll bet you have a fine singing voice."

She heard the canvas flap pulled back and when she stretched to peer out, she saw the flash of the torch as he waved it around the back in a quick search. He didn't climb inside, and he was back at Maeve's side in a moment.

He pointed the torch at the ground, so she wouldn't be blinded again. "I think the Irish and the Welsh got all the singing talent and left none for the English."

"Except for Vera Lynn."

He laughed. "Yes, except for her."

The Corporal called out. "Anything?"

"No, Corporal. All clear."

He nodded to Liam. "Have a good evening."

Liam touched the brim of his cap. "Cheers. Good luck, now."

The soldiers moved the barrier and Liam drove on.

When they were well away from the checkpoint, Liam expelled a breath as if he had been holding it for a while. "Jaysus. I didn't expect that."

"I know. I thought I'd be sick."

He glanced at her. "You were extraordinary. You sounded as cool as a cucumber. I could hardly listen to what 'yer man was asking me, for listening to you chatter away. You had him completely bewitched, I think."

She smiled in the darkness. "When I started, I was afraid he'd just tell me to shut up."

"Every man likes a sweet girl chatting him up. You made his evening."

"Why were they there? Were they tipped off?"

"No. They're looking for Germans. There's been a report of a plane going down, so they've got patrols everywhere. Just what we need."

"Ah. So now we need to watch for British patrols, German parachutists and the Royal Ulster Constabulary. Very good."

She heard the smile in Liam's voice. "I would say you're up to the challenge."

They drove on without further conversation. Maeve felt drained after the adrenalin rush. She kept expecting to hear shots or shouts, but all she heard was the continued grind of the engine labouring its way along the old, pot-holed road.

It wasn't long before they pulled into a dirt track. *How did he even see where to turn?*

Maeve strained to see through the Guinness-dark night but all she could make out were dark shapes on both sides of the track. Shrubs, trees, a broken stone wall. Liam drove slowly along the track. Maeve's spine was jarred in the awful bumping and she clung to the armrest for support. They pulled alongside a rocky outcrop and then the vehicle stopped. Liam switched off the engine and the sudden silence closed in on her. The hot engine ticked as it cooled.

They sat for a minute in the dark stillness as Maeve became adjusted to the night sounds. Just as she took a breath to ask, 'now what?' Liam whispered. "There."

Maeve followed his pointing finger and saw what he had seen. A flash of light. A torch on and then off again.

Liam's breath sounded ragged, as if he had been holding it. "It's safe."

Liam climbed out, closing the lorry door behind him with a soft *snick*.

Maeve was careful as well when she climbed out. She pushed the door gently, so it barely clicked closed. The sound of a slamming door would carry far on such a night.

Her eyes adjusted, and Maeve was surprised at how much she could see in the intermittent milky light of the sliver of moon. Shapes that she had taken for rocks began to move. From the shadows one shape became Patrick. Her heart raced to see him again.

He went first to shake Liam's hand. "No trouble?"

Liam shook his head. "Nothing we couldn't handle. A plane's gone down somewhere so there are British patrols out. We need to be as quick as we can. You'll have to take the lumber that's back there as well in case we run into the same patrol on the way back. They'll wonder why we didn't unload."

He came then to Maeve. "You came, then."

She swallowed. "I did. It's good to see you."

"And you. Brave girl. I knew you were one of us."

And then he sprang into action. He gave orders to the three men with him. "Ta, get the lorry. Back it in here." Patrick waved to the others. "You two start unloading. We're exposed here and need to get this done as quick as we can."

Liam jumped into the back of the lorry to start handing wooden crates down.

Maeve touched Patrick's arm. "Where shall I go?"

Patrick nodded back along the track. "Down along there fifty feet to the bend in the track. Keep a watch. If you see anything at all suspicious, let us know. Can you whistle?"

Maeve shook her head. "I can sing."

Patrick chuckled. "I remember those songs in the pub. You sing like an angel, but that's not what's wanted now." He handed the torch to her. "Flash it at us if you see anything. Off you go now."

Maeve ran back along the track and then crouched down beside a heap of rocks. She was shivering despite the sultry heat of the night. She clenched her teeth to keep them from chattering. *Please God don't let anyone come.*

She felt her legs cramping but didn't dare move. She heard a lorry start up behind her. *Are they done?*

Maeve almost yelped when Patrick put his hand on her shoulder. "You frightened the shite out of me. I guess I'm not such a great watcher."

He pulled her to her feet. "Sorry about that. I've had plenty of practice at moving quietly. We're finished."

When she stood, he pulled her to him and put his arms around her. She smelled sweat and oil on him and felt intoxicated. He leaned in and kissed her. His lips were soft, but the stubble of several days beard growth rubbed her harshly. His tongue pried its way into her mouth, and she whimpered with longing. Then he released her.

Maeve was dizzy. "Patrick."

He put a finger to her lips. "It's time to go."

He held her hand as he led her back to where the men waited, and then in the darkness she felt his hand slip away from hers.

She heard one of Patrick's men mutter. "Come on. Let's get the feck out of here."

Patrick shook Liam's hand again. "We'll be in touch."

Liam climbed into the lorry while Patrick turned to Maeve. He steered her towards her door with a hand on her back. She turned and gave him a quick hug and then he was opening the door and handing her up. She rolled down the window and touched the rasp of his cheek as Liam started up the engine. "Stay safe." Her words were lost as Liam began backing the lorry to a place he could turn around and she never knew if Patrick heard her.

The drive back was uneventful. Maeve was exhausted, and she sensed that even Liam was tired. The adrenalin that had taken them to Newry was gone now and Maeve just wanted to get home. When they got to the border, the temporary barrier was gone and there was no sign of the soldiers.

The sun was rising when they reached the outskirts of Dublin. Her eyes were gritty and sore.

Liam took the lorry back to its owner who had a delivery service. Maeve stood on the curb while Liam and the man had a short conversation. She felt exposed in the morning light. *I need a bath.*

Liam joined her. "Do you fancy some breakfast? I know a place that opens early."

Maeve shook her head. "Honestly, I just want to get home. With any luck I'll get in before anyone else is up and about."

Liam nodded. "Right. That's probably a good idea. You did well tonight."

Her heart swelled with pride. "I'm not sure I did much."

"You showed your mettle."

She smiled. "Thank you, Uncle Liam."

His voice was quiet. "I won't give you a hug, but I'm proud of ye. Now, go on. Get home."

When Maeve made her way to the kitchen door, it appeared that the house was still asleep. She didn't see any lights burning and didn't smell the tell-tale sign of cooking breakfast. She took her shoes off outside and carried them in. She crept up the stairs to her room, pulled off her clothes and crept in under the covers of her bed.

Her first foray for the Cause had been a perfect success, and she couldn't wait for another opportunity.

34

Dublin, September 1942

Maeve looked up from her breakfast to see her mother watching her. "What's wrong?"

Bridie sat beside her daughter. "Are you all right?"

"Yes, fit as a fiddle. Why? Do I not look all right?"

Bridie tilted her head. "I'm not sure. You slept most of the day yesterday, so something must be wrong."

Maeve patted her mother's hand before continuing with her porridge. "Mammy, I'm fine. The day of rest cured whatever it was that ailed me."

"School starts next week. I wondered if you were worried about that."

"Not at all. I'm looking forward to going back."

Bridie stood, seeming to be satisfied. "Will you join the debating team again?"

Maeve nodded. "Probably. I'll see." *How can I tell her that it seems so tame now?*

Maeve finished her breakfast. "Do you need me, Mammy? I might take my book and walk down to St. Stephen's Green for a bit."

Bridie waved her away. "You go on. I want to write a letter to Elizabeth anyway."

Maeve paused on her way to the steps. "How are they?"

Bridie shrugged. "Elizabeth worries over Daniel, of course."

Maeve frowned. "Has something happened?"

"Aside from the fact that he's off fighting in this hateful war?" Maeve sat back down. "You didn't tell me that. He joined the army?"

"I thought the two of you were pen friends?"

Maeve swallowed. "We haven't written each other for...I can't remember now...a long time."

Bridie saw her mother bite her bottom lip. "I thought I mentioned it."

Maeve shook her head. "No, I would have remembered that. Daniel's a British soldier now?"

"You sound like your father. Don't say it like that. It's not like Daniel's here occupying Ireland."

"I know. It's just a shock. Poor Elizabeth. Of course, she's worried. Does she know anything about him and where he is?"

"When she wrote this letter, he was just starting training."

Maeve had a sudden thought. "He's not gone as a medic, has he?"

"No, unfortunately not." Bridie went to the writing desk and rummaged for a letter. "Here it is. He joined the infantry. 59th Staffordshire Division."

"That's so awful. I hope nothing happens to him."

"Yes, we'll say a prayer for him."

Maeve nodded and rose to retrieve her book and shawl. "I'll be back later."

She walked to her favourite bench overlooking the water, but instead of opening her book, she sat lost in thought.

Daniel. I thought you were studying to be a doctor. I'm sorry I stopped writing. Could I have changed your mind? Probably not. A British soldier. I guess that's the end of us, then. She recalled his gentle manner, and unbidden, she thought of Patrick. She compared Patrick's rugged looks and strong decisive character with Daniel. She closed her eyes in the warm autumn sun and remembered Daniel kissing her and compared his gentleness with Patrick's rugged insistence and then her eyes flew open. She glanced around to see if anyone had watched her as she imagined kissing a young man. No one. She sighed. Patrick was exciting, but as she thought of them, it was Daniel that she could imagine walking with, side by side, here in this park. Daniel, whom she could talk to about anything and everything. Daniel, whom she had spent weeks thinking about after he and his mother left last year. *Why did I stop writing letters?* Maeve felt a lump form in her throat. *I was so wrapped up in school, the debating team and Patrick.* She resolved to write him again. *I'll put a letter in with Mammy's. It can be forwarded.*

She opened her book and was soon lost in the poems of W.B. Yeats.

———

Maeve got home to find the house empty. She went up to her room to begin writing the letter to Daniel but was distracted when she heard her brothers arrive home. *I'll finish this later.*

She came to the parlour where Robert was waggling a finger at his brother. "What are you two arguing over now?"

Malachy waved the newspaper folded open to a sports page in front of her. "The League of Ireland finals."

Maeve had no interest in sports, but she glanced down at the paper. "Malachy! What are you doing bringing the *Independent* into the house? Daddy'll go mad."

As if conjured by magic, their father walked into the front door. "What's all the ruckus about?"

Malachy laid the newspaper in his lap and folded his hands over it. "Just sports, Da. Nothing serious."

Emmet gave Maeve a kiss on the cheek. "Where's your Mam?"

Maeve slipped her hand through his arm. "Not sure, Daddy. I've been out enjoying the fine weather and she was gone when I got back. I'll go and check with Róisín."

It was a luxury to have a girl to help with the housework these days. Maeve knew that Róisín's father had been killed in a factory accident, and suspected that her father had convinced her Mam to hire the girl more to help Róisín's family out than because Bridie needed help.

Emmet smiled. "Check when lunch will be served as well, will you? I have to get back for a meeting."

As Maeve stepped out of the room, she heard her father's voice. "What's that you have there then, Malachy?"

Maeve reached the kitchen where the girl was busy making lunch. "Róisín, do you know where Mammy is?"

"She went out to post a letter. I'm sure she'll be back any minute now."

There goes my plan to add a letter for Daniel.

"Right, thank you. Daddy was wondering how soon he could have his lunch as he's in a bit of a hurry."

The sound of raised voices reached them in the kitchen. Róisín eyes widened. "I'll be as quick as I can."

Maeve patted the young girl on the shoulder. "He's not angry with you. I have a feeling it's something Malachy did."

Maeve wasn't surprised to see her father with the newspaper in his hand. Her father's face was flushed.

Maeve took the paper from his hand. "Daddy. It's not worth getting so worked up."

Malachy sat with his arms crossed, looking sullen, while Robert had shrunk down into the easy chair in the corner.

Emmet's eyebrows were pulled into a deep frown. "That rag is not welcome in this house. The traitors that put that so-called news out, should be in jail."

Maeve made her voice as gentle and calming as she could. "I know, Daddy. I agree with you, but Malachy's only a boy. He didn't mean any harm."

Malachy muttered. "I only wanted to see the sports results."

Maeve frowned at her brother.

Emmet took a deep breath but before he could say anything further, Bridie came in, unpinning her hat.

Maeve smiled at her mother. "Mammy, Róisín is just getting lunch organized and will be ready shortly. Daddy has to eat early."

Maeve left them to discuss lunch as she slipped away to throw out the offending newspaper. *What was Malachy thinking bringing that paper in the house?* Everyone knew her father had a bitter disgust for the paper that always represented the Treaty side of the argument.

Maeve went out to the back garden to throw the paper into the bin, but in the midst of rolling it up, she stopped. She felt the blood drain from her face and thought she would faint. She stumbled to the wrought iron stool and crumpled on to it. The words blurred in the burn of her tears as she read the article buried on the back page.

She hadn't taken the time to read their own newspaper this morning, so the story was a shock.

Maeve read about the load of munitions which had been captured in Hannahstown, County Antrim. The authorities knew now that the weapons had been delivered by persons unknown two nights previously but they had only been discovered as they were moved to a hiding place at McCafferty's farm outside Hannahstown.

Maeve skimmed over the details.

There was a gun battle.

One RUC member was wounded, and Patrick was...Maeve could hardly take it in. *Patrick is dead.*

The newspaper lay open on the small garden table when her father came outside. Maeve looked up at him and saw the scowl on his face turn to a look of puzzlement and then concern. She stood. "Oh, Daddy."

He patted her back as she cried against his shoulder. "There, there."

When her sobs quietened, he gently pushed her away from him to look in her face. "What is it, Maeve? What's happened?"

She turned and pointed at the newspaper. "I knew him."

Emmet picked up the paper and read through the story. "This Dermody man? You knew him?"

Maeve nodded.

"How could you know him? This was up north. It was probably just someone with the same name."

He crumpled the paper and went to the bin. He closed the lid and came back to Maeve to lead her inside. "Run in and wash your face, dear. You don't want Mammy to worry. I'm quite sure you'll find it's just someone with the same name and not your friend at all."

Maeve wanted to hold him there and tell her father everything. He would understand. After all, he had inspired her to be involved. Then the moment was gone, and Maeve watched the door close behind his retreating back.

She followed slowly. She went up to her room and poured cool water into her basin. She bathed her eyes and wiped her face, inspecting herself afterwards. The freckles across her nose stood out against her pale skin. Her eyes still swam so it was hard for Maeve to be objective.

Robert shouted up the stairs. "Come down, Maeve. We're all waiting on you."

I'll have to go down for lunch, but I'll be sick if I eat anything. Maeve took a deep breath. "I'm coming now."

She took her place at the table and her mother said grace. She took the smallest amount she felt she could get away with, but still her mother noticed.

"Are you feeling all right, Maeve? You just don't seem yourself."

"I'm fine, Mammy." Maeve tried a smile.

Her father snorted. "It's all the upset of having the traitor's paper in the house."

Maeve saw Malachy flush. "It's nothing. Please, let's just eat lunch."

By the end of the meal Maeve was in control of her feelings. *I must be strong to carry on. That's what Patrick would expect.*

It wouldn't be easy, but she would do her part.

35

Dublin, Christmas 1942

The Emergency, as the war was called in Ireland, continued to cause rationing, but aside from that, life was quite stable compared to other countries. Robert thrived working in the bakery and at first he brought home misshapen loaves that represented his early attempts, but these offerings became less frequent as his skill rose.

Maeve went back to school although she was heartsick after reading of Patrick's death. Soon after learning the news, Liam had come to the house. He and Maeve had a few moments alone in the parlour.

It was a relief to shed a few tears over Patrick, but then she dried her eyes with her embroidered handkerchief and asked Liam what she could do to be involved.

He took her hand. "You need to focus on school. The country needs different work now. Work that you're suited for."

Maeve squeezed his hand. "I *am* focused on my studies, Uncle Liam. That doesn't mean that I have to give up the other."

He shook his head. "I'd never forgive myself if something happened to you."

"I do this of my own free will. Anything worth having is worth fighting for. Didn't you and Daddy teach me that?"

Liam folded his arms across his chest. "There are different ways of fighting. You said so yourself, and your Da taught me that when we were in America."

Maeve frowned. "He doesn't talk much about his time in America."

"That's because he doesn't take the pride that he should in his work there. The speeches he wrote, and articles he published were very inspiring to thousands of people."

"I guess he feels it wasn't the same as taking action, getting his hands dirty, as you call it."

Liam sighed. "He thinks that's what other people feel."

Maeve shrugged. "Tell me what's next. What can I do to help?"

Liam shook his head. "I'm leaving for a while. I'll be out of touch."

Maeve clenched her teeth. "You're deliberately leaving to prevent me from helping."

Liam shrugged. "Things are quietening down right now. The war has changed the priorities."

"I don't believe you."

"The time will come when you'll be called upon. Meanwhile just study and think about how you could change things in a different way." His voice dropped. "Without guns."

"This coming from you. You believe that's possible?"

"I think anything is possible."

Maeve knew he wouldn't help her any further. "Fine. Then leave. I'll find my own way."

"Don't be cross. You're like a daughter to me."

Maeve sighed. "I'm not cross, Uncle Liam. I just feel lost somehow."

———

Maeve did focus on her studies. She faded away from the debating society. She didn't officially resign, but she didn't go often. She didn't have the heart.

When she read the war news in the paper, she found herself thinking of Daniel again.

"Mammy, did you hear anything more from Daniel's mother about where he is or what he's doing?"

Her mother shook her head. "No, I've had no response to my last letter."

Maeve bit her lip. "I thought I might write to him, but I don't know how to get a letter to him."

Her father who was at his desk working on an article at the time raised his eyebrows. "The same Daniel that's now a British soldier?"

Maeve bit her lip. "Uncle Liam was once a British soldier too."

Da nodded. "That's true, but for entirely different reasons. He was in it for the money and it helped support his family when times were very tough. This fella's in it for his country."

Maeve jutted her chin. "So I suppose he's doing what he thinks is right, going over to fight for the Allies."

Mammy interrupted. "I'm sure he would appreciate hearing from you. We can put it inside an envelope to Elizabeth and she will know how to send it on. I'll write a quick note to Elizabeth as well if you're doing a letter."

"All right, I will."

Dear Daniel,

I'm sorry I haven't written for a long time. I do think about you, though and wonder how you're managing. We hear such awful news and, as usual, the Irish are torn about the war. Some say that England's problems are good for Ireland, but others say that there are so many terrible things going on that Ireland should stand with the Allies. I don't know what the answer is. None of it seems to have anything to do with a United Ireland, so I just wish it was over. When I think of you somewhere in France or wherever, trying to live through appalling circumstances, risking your life every day, I worry.

I had a friend who died recently. He was at school with me, and just seemed far too young and alive to suddenly be gone. I hate to imagine that you risk that every day. I might seem very bold to you, but I must say that I would like to see you hale and hearty, here in Dublin again one day. I did so enjoy our walks and talks, and star-gazing. Let's make a promise to enjoy those things again. All right?

Write back when you can. Meanwhile, be well.

Your friend,

Maeve K. Ryan

She sent her letter just before Christmas, imagining what Daniel's holiday might be like. *Will he even have a holiday? War doesn't stop just because it's Christmas.*

She didn't hear back from him and as the weeks passed with no word from him, she wondered if she was too late.

36

Belfast, April 1943

Maeve decided she wouldn't be put off simply because Liam wasn't there to help her. She started by tracking down a man that she had met with Patrick a year previously. He went to her college, and while he was a year ahead of her, everyone came to the library eventually. She spent as much time in the reading room as possible, hoping to see him eventually. When she did, she reintroduced herself.

He seemed startled when she approached him. He sat at the long library table with his books open, blinking rapidly at her. He was thin with straight, floppy, dust-coloured hair and his round, steel-rimmed glasses gave him an owlish look.

"I don't know if you remember me. My name is Maeve Ryan. I was a friend of Patrick Dermody's."

He nodded. "I remember."

"I'm sorry, I've forgotten your name."

Even that seemed like more information that he was willing to give. He licked his lips. "Eamon Connolly."

"May I sit down, Eamon?"

He shrugged and then stood to pull out a chair for her.

She sat and then leaned in close. "I miss Patrick."

"We all do."

"I'd like to continue to help, but not sure how."

He studied her. "Patrick trusted you."

She nodded. "He did."

Eamon tore a piece of paper from his notebook and wrote down an address. "We have a discussion group you might like to join. Tuesday evening at seven."

"Thank you. I'll be there."

Maeve left him to his studies and moved to a quiet table in another corner. She saw her friend, Brigid coming to join her.

Brigid stacked her books neatly and then sat across from Maeve. "Who's that you were talking to?"

"No one really."

Brigid frowned. "You were sitting with him. I saw you when I came in. He must be someone."

Maeve glanced over and saw Eamon watching them. She turned back to Brigid. "He was a friend of Patrick's."

"Oh. The boy from your debating team?"

"Yes."

"Right. The one who died up north?"

"That's him."

Brigid touched Maeve's arm. "Stay away from him then, Maeve. You have no idea what those people are up to or are capable of."

"What do you mean?"

"My father said those IRA ones are all murderers."

Maeve pursed her lips. "I think that's rather an overstatement. Anyway, don't worry. I just saw him sitting there, so thought I'd say hello. Nothing more."

Brigid nodded and opened one of her books. "Let's get started on this paper."

———

The address that Eamon had given her was close to school. She easily found the shop on Stable Lane near Leeson Street Lower. She tried the door of the shop but it was locked. As she stood there peering in to the darkened bicycle repair business, she heard steps approaching and moved away from the window. Two girls, a little older than her, looked at Maeve curiously.

"The shop closes at five every day." One of the women offered.

Maeve nodded. "I wasn't actually looking for the shop itself."

The two looked at each other, and then the other woman spoke. "Why are you here, so?"

"I was given the address by someone who thought I might be interested in a discussion group."

"Come with us, then."

She followed the two around the side of the building where there were doors leading up to the flats above the shops. The flat was a small bed-sit with half a dozen chairs in a circle grouped around a round low table. A single bed in the corner looked rumpled and a young man with tight red curls and the shadow of a red beard lay stretched on it, balancing an ashtray on his stomach. On the floor beside him was a glass of red wine. Aside from him, Eamon and another young man sat at the low table, also drinking wine and smoking. The boy on the bed waved the girls and Maeve in.

"I see we have a new recruit this evening. Welcome. I'm Des."

"Maeve."

Eamon nodded to her. "This is Mickey."

"Hi Mickey."

The girls hung their hats and coats on the hooks on the back of the door and then introduced themselves.

The taller of the two, wore her fair hair in an elaborate set of waves high on her head. She looked like a professional working woman who had come directly from an office somewhere. "I'm Aislin, and this is Irene."

Irene wore her chestnut hair in waves on her shoulders, similar to the way Maeve wore hers, which made Maeve instinctively turn towards her for conversation. "I'm Maeve. I'm at UCD."

"Ah, with Eamon?"

"Eamon's ahead of me, but yes. That's how I came to be here."

Irene took Maeve's hand. "You're very welcome."

Des got up from the bed and came over to the circle. "Let's get started. I don't think anyone else is coming tonight. We've got a lot to cover, including the details for the Belfast trip."

Maeve's heart quickened as she listened. As the evening wore on, she knew she had come to the right place. And when she was asked if she was interested, she was quick with the answer. "Yes. Count me in."

———

Maeve recalled all of this as she sat on the train heading north. They were each travelling separately and would meet at a house close to the Broadway Cinema in Belfast. The window was streaked with spring rain. The sound of the wheels clicking was hypnotic, but she wasn't sleepy. She stared out the window to avoid talking to the woman across from her. Maeve didn't want to talk. She wanted to think. Unlike her last trip to the north where she had Uncle Liam, now she was alone.

Should I have talked to Daddy? She closed her eyes and rested her forehead against the cold glass. Her parents knew she was on a train going north. It was Easter weekend and she was supposedly going along with a school friend to spend the holiday with relatives of her friend.

Her mother's words still sounded in her head. "But we'll miss you for Easter dinner. And what about mass? Where will you go for Easter mass?"

Her father had put his arm around her mother. "Let her go, Bridie. She's not a child anymore. It's natural that she spends time away from her family once in a while."

He's so understanding. So why did I not tell him the truth? Maeve couldn't answer the question, other than to admit that she wanted to avoid arguments.

Mammy was so reluctant. "Will you look up the Carsons? They're back at their own home in Belfast again."

Her Da spoke on her behalf. "Ah, Bridie. She'll be with friends. She can't go off and visit with the old school friend of your mother. Surely you see that?"

Maeve had gotten up to give her mother a hug. "Write out their address Mammy, and if the chance comes up, I'll go by, but I'm making no promises, right?"

She had given them each a tight hug before leaving.

Her brother Robert had laughed. "Sure, you're not going to Alaska. We'll see you on Monday."

Malachy had flinched away from her hug with a grimace. He was at that age.

Maeve opened her book and attempted to read, staring at the same page for minutes on end, time and time again.

The Great Victoria Street Station in Belfast was chaotic. People dashed past, dragging children and suitcases in the hustle to get home for Easter. Maeve pressed against a wall and pulled out the hand-drawn map that Eamon had given her, directing her to the house where they were all meeting. She fell into the stream of people moving towards an exit, and once outside, looked around. She stood under the grand portico and tried to get her bearings.

This is hopeless. I'll be lost in no time. I'll take a taxi.

She waited her turn in a taxi queue and then gave an address a few houses down from her actual destination. Again, she kept her face turned towards the window, to keep from talking to the driver.

The taxi pulled over. "Are you sure this is where you want to go?"

The number she had arbitrarily given belonged to a rather rundown looking red brick terrace house, like all of them along the street, except this one had a broken pram, discarded tools and other debris in the front garden.

She handed the money for the fare to him. "Yes, this is fine, thank you."

The taxi driver shrugged and took her money. "Right, then. Happy Easter, Miss."

Her stomach fluttered, and her words came out more like a cough than the 'thank you' she attempted.

Maeve waited until the taxi was gone and then walked up to the address she had been given. The curtain twitched. There was a watcher tracking her progress.

Before she could knock, the door was opened, and Eamon greeted her. "You made it then."

She straightened her shoulders. Clearly, he had expected her to back out. "Yes, as you see."

"No problems?"

"None at all."

He nodded and turned into the front room, dismissing her. Eamon was not here to look after her. She was on her own. Maeve looked in and then turned her attention down the hall to where the sound of women chattering made a welcome noise.

The front room was already crowded so she chose to go down the hall. There were two women she didn't know, and her friend Irene from Dublin, in the kitchen making sandwiches. Maeve shrugged off her coat and laid it over the back of a chair. "Can I help?"

"Aye. Another pair of hands to help feed the masses would be great." The oldest woman handed her a butter knife and pushed over a stack of sliced bread. "I'm Kitty, and this" she gestured to the younger woman "is my sister Maureen."

"I'm Maeve."

"You're welcome."

Irene smiled at her. "I'm glad you came."

Maeve nodded. "Me too."

Maeve and Kitty continued to butter, Irene slapped on ham or cheese, and cut the bread and Maureen took the platters around.

Someone opened a back door and a black Labrador retriever galloped into the kitchen, nose twitching at the table with sandwich ingredients.

Kitty yelled, "Who let that dog in?"

Maeve knew Irene was mad about dogs and smiled when she saw her friend slip a piece of ham to it.

Irene smiled down at the dog. "Don't kick her out. She just wants to be a part of things. What's her name?"

Kitty frowned and turned away to get another pack of butter. "Blackie."

Maeve and Irene looked at each other, stifling giggles at the no-nonsense name of the dog. Maeve bit her bottom lip as she felt laughter bubbling inside. She knew it was nerves.

Maeve raised her eyebrows as Maureen brought back the empty platter in minutes. "I couldn't eat a thing."

Kitty raised her head from the fresh loaf she was slicing. "Nervous stomach?"

Maeve nodded.

"Don't worry, lass. This is just a commemoration. Nothing will happen. You'll be fine."

Maeve gave a small smile and focused on the sandwiches. *So if it's a peaceful demonstration, why do we need so many armed men?*

37

Dublin, April 1943

Bridie pulled the ham out of the oven to baste it. The fat was browning nicely. Róisín was off to celebrate Easter with her own family, but Bridie didn't mind. She enjoyed cooking and baking and was glad to have the kitchen to herself. She looked up at the knock on the front door. She waited to see if Emmet would go and then called out to him where he sat in the parlour: "Emmet. Someone's at the door. Can you get it, please?"

She continued, brushing the pan drippings across the top of the already crackling skin. She breathed in the aroma of the onions, pork and seasoning. *There's nothing like the smell of a roasting ham to give a place a homey feel. Thank God Emmet's parents have a farm so we haven't suffered from shortages like so many have.*

She put the ham back in, took her apron off, hanging it on the hook near the cooker, and went to the parlour to see who was there. She heard his voice and smiled. *Liam. How nice. It's been ages since we saw him. He's come for Easter dinner.*

She walked in with her arms raised to give him a hug but dropped them at the look on Emmet's face.

Her heart beat faster. "What's wrong?"

Neither man answered. Liam was flushed in contrast to Emmet, whose very life-blood seemed to have drained from his face, except for the redness of his ears. For a moment Bridie paused, puzzled. It looked as though Emmet was furious with

Liam. He had such a scowl on his face and then it changed, and he looked frightened, eyes wide open, nostrils quivering as he sucked in his breath.

Bridie quickened her step to cross the room. She perched on the arm of Emmet's chair. "Emmet. What is it? Your brother? Your parents? Tell me what's happened."

Emmet took her hand. He licked his lips. "Bridie." He gulped and looked at Liam.

Bridie patted her husband's hand, trying to give him comfort from whatever shock he'd received. "Tell me, love."

Emmet's voice was choked. "Liam's come to tell us something."

Bridie frowned at the way he'd said, 'us' instead of 'me.' "Go on."

Liam suddenly spoke up. "Bridie. I should have said something sooner. Told you. She asked me not to though, and I had to respect that. Didn't I, Emmet?"

Emmet scowled again, his jaw clenched.

Bridie shook her head. "I haven't a clue what you're on about."

Liam looked at Emmet who gave a small nod. "It's about Maeve."

Bridie blinked quickly. "Maeve? What about Maeve?" She stood and faced her husband. "Emmet Ryan. You speak to me. Has something happened to Maeve?"

He rose. "No, no love. Nothing's happened."

Bridie took a deep breath. *Thank you, dear God.* "What is it then? Is it a scandal? I won't believe it, whatever it is." A fleeting memory crossed her mind of a story she had recently heard about a girl who had gotten into trouble. *Not our Maeve. She's a good girl.*

Emmet led her to the couch, so they could sit side by side. "Sit down now and I'll tell you."

Bridie bit her lip and let herself be pulled down beside Emmet. "Right, so. Here it is. It seems our Maeve has joined the IRA."

Now that the worst was out, Liam seemed anxious to talk. "Not the really rough stuff. No shooting or bombs. Nothing like that."

Bridie put her hand to her throat. "What, then? What else is there?"

Liam shifted on his chair. "Just a support role, if you like."

Bridie felt the blood pounding in her head. "If I like? Is that what you're saying to me?"

Liam flushed. "I didn't mean that. I meant, she goes along just to make up the numbers, or act as a lookout. That sort of thing." He hesitated and then blurted: "I thought if I left town she would lose interest without me around. I didn't want to influence her. But it didn't stop her."

Bridie took several deep breaths through her nose to steady herself. "Liam Kelly. You did this. You led her into this. You recruited her."

Now that Bridie was angry, Emmet seemed to want to defend his friend. He patted her knee. "Ah, now Bridie. That's not a fair thing to say to Liam. She's a grown girl and has a mind of her own."

She flinched, twisting her knee away from under his hand. "You're right. It's not his fault. It's yours. Completely and utterly, yours. All those stories you fed her with her childhood porridge."

Bridie stood and felt her heart pounding. She glared down at Emmet and wanted to slap him. "When that girl gets home from her holiday, you are going to talk to her. Explain to her, it's all done and over. Tell her she can't be a part of such a thing. You'll tell her...I don't care what you tell her, but it's over. That's the result of it."

The two men glanced at each other and Bridie knew there was more. Something they hadn't yet told her. "Liam, why have you come today to tell us this? Why now? You said she made you promise not to tell, so why now?"

Liam took a deep breath. "She hasn't gone on a holiday."

Bridie widened her eyes, staring at Liam. She smelled the ham and felt her gorge rise. "Where is she?"

"She's gone to Belfast all right, but she's gone to join some others. There's a quiet commemoration of 1916 planned."

Bridie frowned. "A demonstration? A meeting? What? What sort of a commemoration?"

"They're going to take over a cinema."

"Dear God."

Emmet stood in front of Bridie and put his two hands on her shoulders. "It's nothing to get too anxious about now, love. It's all going to be very peaceful. From what Liam's said, there'll be some speeches. Nothing more."

She pulled away from him. "It's Belfast. We don't know what might be peaceful or what might erupt." She turned to Liam and pointed her finger at him. "You don't know, and you're worried. That's why you came here. You think there will be trouble."

Liam held up his hands as if to shield himself from her anger. "I don't expect any trouble. Honestly, I don't. I just thought it was about time I told you. I owe you both that."

Liar. Bridie couldn't look at Liam. She clenched her fists and glared at Emmet. "What do we do now? Should we go after her?"

Emmet turned to Liam. "What do you think? Should we?"

Liam shrugged. "I would just leave it and then have a chat with her when she gets home. Let her know I've betrayed her. I can live with it. There are better options for her these days. I tried to tell her that myself, but coming from you, it will have more weight. If anyone can convince her that there are other choices for her, it's you, Emmet."

Bridie felt the lump in her throat. "So, just do nothing."

Emmet nodded. "I think Liam's right. If we go bolting off up north, what could we do? Drag her back forcefully? She'd never forgive us. Besides, what about the boys? They'll be looking for their Easter dinner in a couple of hours."

Liam ran his hand through his hair. "I probably should have waited until she was safe and sound back at home and then had this talk. I didn't know what to do when I heard she'd gone along."

Emmet shook his head. "You did the right thing coming to us, although I wish you had done that before she went off. Better late than never." He took a deep breath. "Damn you, Liam. Why, of all people, did you have to recruit my daughter?" He turned to his wife. "It's better we know though, isn't it Bridie?"

She gave a small nod. "It's better to know, even if it means I'll be in knots until she's home."

Bridie had an idea and felt a surge of hope. "I'll ring the Carsons."

Emmet frowned. "And say what exactly?"

"Just that Maeve is up there, and, well maybe they can go past this cinema and they'll see her and take her in hand." Even as Bridie said it, she knew it was a mad idea.

Emmet tilted his head, his lips pressed into a thin line.

Bridie sighed. "All right. I won't." A tear rolled down her cheek and she brushed it away. "I feel that I should do something."

Emmet walked back to her and put his arm around her waist. "The best thing you can do is to carry on making the Easter dinner. Maybe put the kettle on to start with." He turned back to Liam. "You'll stay for supper?"

Liam looked at Bridie.

Bridie nodded. "You're welcome to stay and share our dinner. I wouldn't turn you away, but..." she left it at that.

Liam nodded, understanding her anger. "I will, so. Thank you."

Bridie's shoulders slumped. She rubbed her hand across her head to relieve the pounding as she made her way back to the kitchen to carry on as if her mind wasn't 87 miles north, in the city of Belfast. She had to carry on as if everything was normal, but she knew that life had suddenly changed forever.

38

Belfast, April 1943

The sandwiches had all been eaten. The Irish whiskey had made the rounds. Maeve felt warmed inside after Kitty convinced her to take a small one to "settle the nerves". She did feel steadier. Not relaxed, but not so shaky. The clock ticked on.

Maeve followed Kitty and Irene when shouts called everyone to gather in the front room. Maeve looked at the man who stood in front of the gathered fifteen men and women. *He looks a bit like Daddy. The same ears and kinky hair.*

She leaned in to Kitty. "That's Harry White, isn't it?"

"Aye. He's the O.C. of Northern Command."

Maeve nodded. The Officer Commanding the group. *This could be Daddy if Mammy hadn't made him give up the fight. I'm here now, Daddy, to carry on.* She straightened her shoulders and felt his blood pumping in her heart.

She focused on what the leader was saying.

"Remember, we only have a short window of time for everyone to take their places. The projectionist will be out for a smoke between films. He'll be sure the door is open for us. You've each been told about where you'll go, but if you're unsure, ask now. We don't want to stand around having a chat once we're on the ground."

White's pale eyes surveyed the room. "McAteer and Steele. You're ready?"

Hugh McAteer held up a roll of paper and waved it as affirmation.

Jimmy Steele patted his pocket and nodded.

White pulled out a revolver, checked it and tucked it back in his belt under his jacket. "I don't expect trouble, but, like those who have gone before, we need to be ready for anything."

Maeve felt her breath catch in her throat at the sight of the gun. All around her, men followed White's lead, checking that their guns were loaded and ready before tucking them away again.

White checked his watch. He took a deep breath and then spoke. "Irish men and Irish women. We're here today to preserve the spirit of the movement. Let history write that we, here now, were ready to stand up for the freedom of our brothers and sisters still living under the oppressor's thumb, made even worse by the addition of American troops, here without the permission of the Irish government or people."

He went on to remind those gathered of the historical parallels of today's commemoration to 1916. "By going to the Broadway Cinema, today we will honour where the Willow Bank Huts once stood. Where the Belfast Volunteers mobilized in 1916. Just like then, we continue to be engaged in our own war, in the midst of another World War. All around us we see the evidence of British forces. Today we will turn the focus of our people back to *our* cause instead of foreign wars."

Maeve joined in with the *hurrahs* that rumbled around the room.

White gave a thin smile. "The film today is *Don Bosco,* an inspirational film, I understand. Enjoy it."

With that, he made his way to the kitchen door and gave each person a word or pat on the shoulder as they slipped out, singly and in twos, into the garden and through the back gate.

Maeve left with a young volunteer named Richard O'Meara. She took his arm, feeling the scratch of his wool jacket under her hand. He was tall and wore a bow tie. He had a thick head of hair combed straight back. In another circumstance she'd find him handsome, but now Maeve couldn't even speak, let alone enjoy his company. She trembled as they passed an armoured car surrounded by uniformed Royal Ulster Constabulary brandishing rifles.

Richard put his hand over hers. "No need to shake so."

His voice was low, and with his thick Belfast accent, Maeve had to concentrate to understand him. She tilted her head towards him to hear.

He patted her arm and then let his right hand fall to his side again. "Those boyos are everywhere today. They've got the Falls Road looking like an armed camp."

Maeve licked her lips. "I'm fine."

He grinned. "Good. We need to look like we're having fun. Give us a smile."

She looked up at him and smiled.

"That's great. That smile might even take me to Dublin some day."

Maeve forced herself to broaden her grin as they passed a group of patrolling British soldiers. "You'd be very welcome."

She took deep breaths to control her shaking. *Why are there so many soldiers around here? Do they know something?*

And then they were passing under the marquee where the word Broadway proclaimed the cinema's name in large letters.

Maeve had a sudden urge to relieve herself. Her stomach cramped but she knew it was only nerves. Now was not a time to visit the toilet.

She took her seat beside Richard at the aisle end of the row near the back of the room. The dusky light of the cinema fell and when it was dark as night the film began. Maeve couldn't focus on the story of the warrior priest.

With every spoken word and gesture, with every passing moment, the time crept closer when armed men would take over the cinema, and all hell would break loose. Hell, in which she had a part to play.

In the dark, she felt Richard nudge her. Wordlessly, she followed him as he made his way to the back of the room. She made her way to a door at the side of the cinema that led to the lobby. Her eyes had now adjusted to the light and she saw one of the other volunteers join Richard at the main entrance. They would prevent people leaving and more importantly, from entering.

The flickering images on the screen came to an end. Maeve sensed people begin to shift, pulling on shawls and straightening hats as they waited for the house lights to come on.

Some people rose and moved towards the exits despite the dark, and then Maeve heard McAteer's voice ring out. "Everyone keep your places."

Maeve could hear muttering, but people sat back down.

A gasp went around the room. Instead of the lights, a slide flashed on the screen. Voices murmured the words as some people read the statement aloud:

This cinema has been commandeered by the Irish Republican Army for the purpose of holding the Easter Commemoration for the dead who died for Ireland.

The house lights rose, and Maeve saw McAteer and Steele on stage. She swallowed. It was all happening to plan. Two volunteers stood nearby, each holding a man captive. *The manager and the projectionist.*

Maeve glanced around the room. All eyes were glued to the stage. She felt the constriction around her chest ease. *So far, so good.*

Maeve was swept up in the words as Jimmy Steele, in full dress uniform, read out the original 1916 proclamation. He began with the words that always made her heart beat faster.

'Irishmen and Irishwomen. In the name of God and of the dead generations from which she receives her old tradition of nationhood, Ireland, through us, summons her children to her flag and strikes for her freedom.'

Like everyone else in the cinema, she was mesmerized so didn't see the child slip out of a door halfway along the side wall. That wasn't her door to guard. She didn't see him put a pebble in to keep the door from locking behind him. She knew that each entrance was being monitored by the volunteers. She didn't know that, like her, many were fascinated by what was happening on the stage and distracted from their responsibilities.

Steele took his time and read with passion. He read the last words, slowing to enunciate each one.

'..by the readiness of its children to sacrifice themselves for the common good, prove itself worthy of the august destiny to which it is called.'

There was a momentary silence and then a smattering of applause.

Hugh McAteer stepped up and read out a statement from the IRA Army Council focusing on the presence of American soldiers, invited into Northern Ireland by Britain. As he came to an end, Maeve had time to think that they had pulled it off. *A peaceful commemoration. Da, I wish you were here to see it.*

McAteer called for two minutes' silence to remember those who had died for Ireland. The silence in the room made the sound of the side door crashing open, seem like an explosion.

Richard had locked the front door during the reading of the proclamation, so he and the other Volunteer began to move towards the side door where soldiers were pouring through. They would try to stop the flood coming in to allow the others to escape.

The screaming tore through Maeve's mind. *Escape.* The instructions were that everyone should escape as best they could, if the worst should happen, and now the worst was happening. Her eyes searched around the room and saw the stage already empty except for the manager and projectionist who stood with their hands tied, looking bewildered.

She looked over her shoulder. Richard was close behind her. His revolver was lifted. He was going to fire at the oncoming soldiers, but she was in the way. She was frozen, her mind blank.

Richard shouted, "Maeve! Out, out! Open the front door and get out!"

People rushed along the centre aisle now, trying to get to the main entrance. She could mingle with them. *Escape, escape.* Her feet didn't move.

Maeve's mind clicked back in. She turned once more to see where the soldiers were. No shots had been fired so far and now the audience poured out through both side doors, stopping any more soldiers from coming in.

A glance before whirling to leave. *Is there time to run? Can I make it?* A soldier had his rifle lifted. He had seen Richard and was ready to fire.

The eyes. Maeve knew those eyes. Even below the beret of an English uniform, she knew those eyes.

Richard was beside her now, his gun hand lifted, his other hand trying to shove Maeve away.

She sucked in her breath and stepped in front of Richard, hearing him curse behind her. She held her hands before her to stave off the bullet. "Daniel! No, Daniel! Don't shoot!"

Her cry was a split second too late.

She was aware of a flash of light, and the sharp, sweet tang of cordite filled the air. She felt a *push* of air as the concussion struck her and then a blaze of pain in her chest that stopped her breath. She felt herself fall back against Richard. Did she hear him say 'damn you'? Perhaps. Just before the silence engulfed her and the cinema went dark.

39

Dublin, April 1943

Emmet paced the sitting room. There were no newspapers published in Dublin on Easter Monday. He stood staring out the window, hands behind his back. *How can I find out what happened?*

He turned to Bridie, who was knitting furiously. "I may go into the office and see if there's any news come in on the wire."

The clicking stopped as she looked up at him. "Can you do that?"

Her hopeful expression convinced him. "I can, of course."

She set aside her knitting and walked over to him, resting her left hand on his shoulder while cupping his cheek with her right. "Go, then. Go now while the boys are out at the hurling match, otherwise they'll think it strange."

He took her hand from his cheek and kissed the palm. "I'm sure she's fine and on her way home."

Bridie nodded, then turned to get his hat.

Emmet heard her cry 'oh' as a knock thumped the door. He was a step behind his wife as she pulled open the door.

A boy stood there. "Telephone call for you at the call box, Missus."

Emmet pulled a tuppence from his pocket and handed it to the boy. "Thank you, son."

Not for the first time, Emmet had the passing thought he should have a telephone installed in the house instead of using the public call box down the road like everyone else on the street.

Bridie didn't even wait to remove her apron. She lifted her skirt and trotted the half block to the public telephone box at the corner of the street.

Emmet wanted to run ahead of her. He wanted to snatch up the receiver and shield his wife from whatever news was waiting at the other end of the line. They knew very few people with telephones. They never received telephone calls, but the one family who did have a telephone in their home was the Carson family in Belfast.

Emmet was winded when he crowded in the call box behind his wife. She already had the receiver pressed against her ear and was shouting into the mouthpiece. "Hello? Hello?"

Emmet strained to listen to the voice leaking through the receiver, but only heard his wife's voice.

"Yes, yes. This is Bridie and Emmet is here with me." Bridie nodded towards Emmet as if the listener might see her movement.

"Yes, Mr. Carson. All right, I'll give Emmet the telephone then."

Emmet stared at her, raising his eyebrows. She was pale, and the soft faded copper colour of her hair looked stark against her white face.

She shrugged and then shook her head, mouthing the words. "He won't talk to me. Only you."

They squeezed past each other in the cramped space so that Emmet could take the handset from her. Now it was his turn to press the receiver against his ear. "Mr. Carson. Good of you to telephone. How is Mrs. Carson?"

He listened to the tinny-sounding voice of Mr. Carson. "She's well. We're all getting older and have the aches and pains that go along with that."

"Yes, of course." Emmet struggled to keep his voice calm and polite as he spoke to the older man.

"Listen, Ryan. The reason I'm calling."

There was a silence. *Dear God.*

It seemed that Mr. Carson had to catch his breath, but now he continued. "There was an incident here yesterday. Perhaps you heard about it on the wireless?"

Emmet swallowed. "I haven't heard anything. We don't have a wireless in the house."

"Ah. Right. My wife thought perhaps you didn't."

Bridie was pulling on Emmet's sleeve. "What's he saying?"

Emmet shook his head. "*Shh.*"

The quavering voice continued. "Some of those fellows took over the Broadway Cinema. Some sort of commemoration, apparently."

"Those fellows?"

"You know. The IRA."

"Right. What happened?"

"It almost went off peacefully, apparently."

"Almost?" Bridie was pulling on him again. "Mr. Carson, just let me catch Bridie up with what you've told me before she has me pulled to pieces."

Emmet repeated what he knew so far.

Bridie pulled at his hand holding the receiver. "Let me listen with you."

Emmet gave in and held the receiver at an angle. "Go ahead, Mr. Carson. You were saying that the commemoration almost went off peacefully."

"Aye. Then it all went awry when a boy slipped out and tipped off a passing troop of British soldiers. They were on high alert, expecting some sort of trouble, so they didn't waste time getting into the cinema."

Emmet waited. They could hear Mr. Carson's wheezy breath as if he was steeling himself to go on.

Bridie was clinging to Emmet's wrist, pulling the receiver towards her own ear.

"There was a general rush for the doors apparently. A real melee."

Silence again.

Emmet closed his eyes, picturing the chaos. His heart thumping, he prompted Mr. Carson. "Was anyone hurt?"

In a rush then, as if in a hurry to get to the finish, Mr. Carson's voice was stronger. "I'm afraid so. There was a shooting. We didn't find out until much later you understand, or I would have called sooner. I would have called yesterday, but by the time we were contacted and got the full picture, well, this is the soonest I could call you."

Emmet was confused. "Why were you contacted at all? I'm sorry. I don't understand how you came to be contacted. I thought you just heard something on the wireless."

Mr. Carson's voice wavered with emotion. "Because our Daniel was involved. It was our Daniel who was one of the first through the door."

Emmet and Bridie stared at each other. "Daniel. Good God. I thought he was in France or Belgium. I had no idea he was in Ireland. I'm so sorry." *It's all right. He's calling to tell us about Daniel because he's Elizabeth's son and Bridie would want to know.*

Emmet closed his eyes briefly for a wordless prayer of thanks. Even still, he had to ask. "But what about our Maeve? Did you hear anything about our Maeve?"

Emmet had to drop the receiver to catch Bridie as she fainted. After hearing 'yes', the rest of the words were lost as Emmet clung to his wife, who slipped through his arms to the wet, winter-grimed pavement.

40

Belfast, April 1943

The darkness receded. Maeve swam to the surface and heard, not the screams of the crowd, but the rubber squeak of soft shoes on linoleum.

She forced her gluey eyes open and immediately closed them again in the white light. She heard a man's voice calling for help. "Sister, Nursing Sister. I think she's awake."

She smelled antiseptic and perspiration as someone bent over her she felt a cool hand on her forehead.

She opened her eyes again to focus on the red cross-encased bosom hovering above her.

A nurse smiled down. "Hello Maeve. We're glad to see you. I'm going to call Doctor. Can you try to stay awake for me?"

Maeve tried to speak, but there were tubes in her mouth and throat. She gave a tiny nod.

"Good girl."

The nurse squeaked away, and Maeve closed her eyes again. She felt the edge of the bed compress as someone leaned on it. She heard his breathing. She knew it was a man. He wore an unfamiliar aftershave. *Not Daddy.*

Maeve took an inventory of how she felt. Fuzzy headed. Pain. Big pain in her chest. She wiggled her toes and fingers. All in working order.

She risked opening her eyes again and looked straight into the hazel eyes she had last seen staring from under a soldier's beret.

Daniel sighed, puffing peppermint and tea into her face. "Thank God. Thank God. Maeve, I..I..." He fumbled and stopped as the white-coated doctor hustled in.

The nurse rested her hand on Daniel's shoulder. "Please wait outside."

Maeve watched Daniel stand, his dark grey civilian business suit showing a muscled outline, before the beige curtains enclosed her with the doctor and nurse.

The doctor pulled back the starched white sheet and thin green blanket. "Now then, Miss Ryan." He peered at her over the top of heavy black glasses. "I'm just going to check you over. Don't be afraid."

He listened to her heart. With a practiced hand, he loosened the ties behind her neck and slid the gown down to her waist.

Maeve shivered and closed her eyes, feeling herself flush in the chill of her exposure.

The nurse began a soft, stream of words. "Doctor is just going to lift the dressing to check the incision. He had to pull a bullet out of you. It's a sad day when a wee lass like you is caught up in such things, but you'll be right as rain again. Don't you worry."

The doctor pulled away the medical dressing, the sticky tape peeling off her skin with a faint tearing sound. He pressed and smelled and studied. "Right Sister, you can change this dressing if you please."

He laid the dressing back down and pulled the sheet back up to her chin. "Sister is quite right. You were lucky. An inch over and we wouldn't be having this conversation. As it is, I expect you'll make a full recovery."

Maeve nodded, already feeling better now that she was covered up again.

The doctor instructed the nurse. "She's breathing fine, so let's get the tube out of her right away."

"Yes, Doctor."

The doctor stepped out of the curtain circle, continuing to give the nurse directions about diet and medications.

Maeve felt the throbbing become more localized. The pain that had been her whole chest now became centered above her right breast. *I'm going to be all right.* The relief was followed by a scurry of other thoughts. *Am I charged? Will I go to jail? Why is Daniel here? I wish Mammy and Da were here. Do they know?*

The nurse and a younger girl, in the crisp white pinafore of a trainee's uniform, came back in. The older nurse was soothing. "This will be uncomfortable, but once that tube is out, you'll feel much better. Try not to fight it. Just relax now. Just relax."

Maeve gagged as the tube was pulled out, clenching the sheets in her hands, knowing that she was moaning and trying not to.

"Good, you're doing fine. Nearly done now."

Her throat was raw and sweat dripped from her forehead. Maeve tried to relax her muscles. The young aide took the metal basin containing the tube and mess of retch and spit away.

Maeve breathed deeply, trying not to flinch as the nurse pulled back the sheet and blanket again. Her voice was a whisper. "Sister, do my parents know I'm here?"

"*Shh.* Try not to talk now. I'll find out, but I believe I heard that someone telephoned them."

Maeve digested this. *Will Daddy be angry or proud? Mammy will be angry.*

Sister finished changing the dressing and retied the gown. "The young man that was here earlier is out in the hall. Do you want me to let him in, or are you ready to sleep again?"

Maeve swallowed. "Sleep."

"Right you are. I'll check on you in a wee while." Sister whisked the curtains open on her way out.

Maeve closed her eyes. *Why is Daniel here? What can I say to him?*

She heard Sister's quiet voice. "You'll have to let her rest now. Sleep is the best thing for her."

Daniel's voice was deeper than she remembered it. "Couldn't I just sit by her bedside? I won't make a sound."

Maeve peeked out from under her eyelashes and saw Daniel's back. He was definitely a man now. *How did I even recognize him?*

She watched as the nurse put her hand on the small of his back, propelling him away from her room. The voices faded, and Maeve was glad to close her eyes to sleep. She thought the pain would keep her awake, but she was fuzzy again. *They've given me something.* She drifted off imagining Daniel and her father talking.

The image was clear. Her father with his hand on Daniel's shoulder. Gripping it? Ready to punch him? Or kindly? *What are you talking about?*

She slept.

41

Dublin, April 1943

Bridie came back to consciousness after her faint and with the help of a neighbour, Emmet got her back to the house and onto the settee in the parlour.

The neighbour, Joe Mulhall, lingered. "Bad news, then?"

Emmet saw the frown on Bridie's face. "Nothing to worry about. Just a bit of a shock combined with not having any breakfast today."

Mr. Mulhall nodded. "You should have an egg every morning, Missus Ryan."

Bridie licked her dry lips and tried to speak in a normal voice. "Thank you, Mr. Mulhall. I'll take that under advisement."

Emmet walked to the door and opened it for his neighbour. "Thank you again for your help, Joe."

Emmet closed the door before the man could continue to probe him for information.

Bridie was standing by the time he came back into the parlour. "Emmet, we need to get to Belfast."

Emmet nodded. "Yes, of course. I'll have Robert cycle over to your parents to give us the lend of their motor. I hope he's got some petrol coupons he can spare."

Emmet pointed to the writing desk. "Why don't you write a quick note for your Da while I go and find Robert."

She was at the desk pulling paper and an envelope out before Emmet left the room.

Emmet climbed the stairs. *What do I tell the boys? Because of me and my stories, your sister has been shot? Is that what I say?*

At the top of the steps, Emmet called out. "Robert, Malachy. Are you about? Come here please."

Both boys emerged from their rooms. Robert came quickly when he saw his father's face. "Da. What is it? Is Mammy all right?"

Emmet put his arms around the shoulders of each of his sons and gave a quick squeeze. "Your mother's fine. Don't worry about her."

The boys pulled back, facing their father. Malachy glanced back over his shoulder to his room. "What is it then, Da? I'm working on a paper for school."

Emmet took a deep breath. "It's your sister. Maeve's been hurt and is in hospital in Belfast."

Robert stood silently, waiting for more.

Malachy put his hand to his head and pushed his fingers through his hair. "What happened? Is she all right?"

Emmet rested his hand on his youngest son's shoulder. "We're not sure how serious it is yet, so we need to get to Belfast as quick as we can."

Malachy pulled away. "She had an accident?"

Emmet hesitated. Robert stuffed his hands in his pockets. "She's been in some IRA thing, hasn't she?"

Emmet tilted his head. "Why do you say that?"

Robert shrugged. "Has she?"

Emmet nodded. "She was at a peaceful commemoration when the damned British soldiers came storming in. She was shot."

Malachy's eyes welled with tears. "Will she be all right?"

Emmet touched Malachy's head. "Mr. Carson told us she's had an operation but she's alive and resting. We're all going to say our prayers to make sure she is."

Malachy's Adam's apple bobbed as the boy swallowed several times. "Can I go see her?"

"You boys will stay here with Nana and Grandpa Mallon for a few days while your Mammy and I go to fetch Maeve home." *Please God.*

Emmet turned to Robert. "Your Mammy is writing a letter right now to your Grandpa to give us the lend of his motor. Robert, can you please jump on your bicycle and deliver that as quick as you can? You can come back with him and then you'll pack a few things and together the three of you can take a taxi back to their house."

Robert whirled to run to his room to fetch his jacket and cap.

Malachy stood in the hall. "What can I do? I want to help."

"You pack up your things now like a good lad. Don't forget to take your school books. You'll have to finish your paper once you get to Nana's house."

Malachy bit his lip, then flung himself against his father for a hug. "I didn't want her to hug me when she left."

"Son, she knows very well that you love her, that we all love her. Don't you worry, and you'll give her that hug when she's home, right?"

"I'll say a rosary, and Nana and I can go to church to light a candle."

"Good man. That's the way of it."

Emmet gave Malachy a gentle push towards his room before turning to go back downstairs. Robert had gone down ahead of him and was already standing at the front door.

Emmet stopped halfway down the steps. "You have the letter from Mammy?"

Robert waved it before tucking it in his inside pocket. "I do."

"Be careful. We don't need anything to happen to you as well in your mad dash across the city."

Robert closed the door behind him without responding.

He blames me.

Emmet went to the kitchen to talk to Róisín. "Did you hear what's happened?"

She bobbed her head. "I have sir, and I'm that sorry to hear. Missus came in to tell me and to get the kettle going."

Emmet nodded. "As always, she's two steps ahead of me."

Róisín went back to setting cups on the tea tray and Emmet walked down the passage to the parlour.

Bridie sat at the desk writing notes.

Emmet stood beside her looking over her shoulder. "What are you doing, love?"

Bridie kept writing. "I'm just organizing what we are to do. I need to take some clothes for Maeve. I need to cancel the butcher's order. I must send a note to Father O'Donnell to let him know I can't help with the flowers this week."

Emmet knelt in front of her. "Róisín can do some of those things. Why don't you come and sit for a moment? Róisín will be in with the tea and we'll talk it through. I can help with some things."

Bridie narrowed her eyes. "I think you've done enough."

Emmet felt the heat rise in his face. He stood and walked to the window to stare out the window. *I love my country. Has that been so wrong?*

He turned back to her. "I've put my family first since the day I got married."

"What about the pension?"

Emmet clenched his teeth. "That again. That damned pension. It wasn't a fortune I turned down. It wouldn't have bought a new pair of shoes for one child. Surely to God, a man has a right to stand up for his principles, once in a while. As you well know, that pension was offered by the Pro-Treaty government as a bribe to us. Do you really believe that if I had allowed myself to be bought off by the government who betrayed our country, this would never have happened? That Maeve would be here and safe?" He knew he was shouting and he stopped to take a deep breath.

Bridie stared at him.

Emmet pounded his chest with his fist. "I believe we would still be in this same place, except that Maeve would be ashamed of her father. That would be the only difference."

He slumped down on the sofa, shaking.

Bridie came to him and took his hand, enclosing it in both of hers. "I'm sorry, Emmet. I've become accustomed to being angry about the pension. She squeezed his hand. And don't fool yourself into thinking it wouldn't have been useful."

Emmet sighed.

Bridie stroked the back of his hand. "But. But, it's not the pension. You're right. That wouldn't have made a blind bit of difference. It's because Maeve always listened to your stories in a way the boys never did. She caught on fire. She got that from you."

She lifted his hand to her mouth now and kissed the freckled skin. "I've always loved the passion in you, Emmet. You know that."

"But?"

"But the country didn't always need you as much as your family has." She patted his hand before releasing it. "Never mind all that now. As you said, Maeve is her own woman now and made up her own mind about this, and I wouldn't change the strong woman she's become, for all the world."

Emmet blinked, feeling the burning behind his eyes. "Ahh, Bridie. I would change it if I could. I would have her here safe."

She nodded. They sat in silence for a moment, engulfed in their own thoughts. Emmet bowed his head and offered up a silent prayer.

Dear God, I've made mistakes and I'll try to be a better man, but please don't ask me for my child. Take me instead.

He raised his head as Róisín came in with the tea tray. Emmet suspected she had waited for the quiet before intruding.

He smiled at her. "Thank you, Róisín."

"Will I pour?"

Bridie shook her head. "I'll do it."

Róisín left the room, pulling the door closed behind her again.

Emmet tried to wash down the lump in his throat with the tea. "I don't know how my parents have gone on after losing Kevin." His voice cracked. "I couldn't bear to lose her, Bridie."

Bridie finished her tea in a few big sips. "We aren't going to lose her. I'm going up to pack so we'll be ready to go as soon as Daddy gets here with the motor."

Emmet topped up his tea. "I'll talk to Róisín about the butcher's order."

He sipped slowly. *This may be the last peaceful moment of my life. If she's permanently injured, I'll never forgive myself.*

42

Belfast, April 1943

Emmet had to stop three times to ask directions before he found his way to the Royal Victoria Hospital. Bridie sat frozen in the passenger seat, gripping the edges of her seat. He navigated around the double-decker trolley bus and pulled in to the car park.

The engine clicked to a stop and Emmet released a quiet groan. "Dear God. That was desperate."

Bridie stretched her fingers, as if to unlock them from their cramped grip.

Emmet turned to her and took her right hand in his left. "Now Bridie, you mustn't get too emotional here. Whatever the situation, we'll all face it together, right?"

Bridie nodded. "She's going to be fine. Mr. Carson would have told us otherwise."

Emmet smiled a thin smile. "Right you are. Let's go up, so."

They clung to each other, feeling dwarfed by the massive dark red brick entryway. Emmet kept up a stream of words. "Look at all the Nursing Sisters. This is a grand place and Maeve will have been getting the best of care here."

They stopped at a reception desk. Emmet had to repeat Maeve's name twice before the porter heard him. Emmet swallowed, his throat felt dry and scratchy.

The porter stood and leaned across the desk to point out the passageway they should take. "Down that hall, turn right at the second passage. Take the steps up to the third floor. Follow that hall to the end and then ask the duty Sister which room your daughter is in."

Emmet nodded. "Right. Thank you."

They set off and immediately Emmet was in a muddle. "Is this right? Is this the way he said?"

Bridie tugged on his arm. "This way then we turn right."

"Here? Do we turn here?"

"No, the second turn he said."

Bridie led the way up the steps to the third floor.

They emerged in the middle of a long hall. Emmet looked right and then left. "Which way?"

Bridie bit her lip. "I'm not sure. I don't think he said."

Emmet stood looking right and then left again. *Just pick one, man.*

A nurse stopped. "Are you lost?"

Bridie's voice was choked. "Our daughter, Maeve Ryan is here somewhere, but we haven't a clue where."

The nurse looked at her clipboard and then pointed to Emmet's left. "All the way to the end and turn left. Room 323."

Emmet found his voice. "Thank you, Sister. You've been a great help."

She smiled and nodded.

Emmet took Bridie's hand and slipped it through his arm. He felt stronger having the weight of her hand resting on him.

Sounds swirled around them. Moans of pain, the clink of rolling carts and instruments, a burst of laughter quickly extinguished and hushed conversations.

Emmet leaned close to Bridie. "Jaysus, I hate the smell of these places."

Bridie steamed forward, ignoring his effort to talk.

At last they arrived at her room. Through the open door Emmet saw the curtain drawn between the beds.

Bridie pulled her arm free. "Let me go in first in case she's having some treatment."

Emmet gulped, a vision of his daughter covered in blood, swimming before his eyes.

He nodded and watched his wife disappear around the curtain. She stepped back again and held her hand silently out to him, gesturing him to come.

Emmet's heart pounded in his temples. When he joined his wife on the other side of the curtain, he exhaled.

His daughter lay sleeping, a little paler than usual but otherwise looking fine. The deep copper curls, so reminiscent of her mother's, lay fanned out against the white pillow. The freckles across her nose stood out against her pasty skin.

Emmet squeezed his wife's hand. "She looks all right."

"*Shh.*"

They stood, holding hands, watching their daughter sleep. Emmet felt he could watch her forever.

They stood for several moments and then a doctor and nurse came in. The sound of their arrival woke Maeve and she opened her eyes. Her head was turned to the nurse and she smiled at the Sister, blinking sleepily.

The nurse pointed to Emmet and Bridie. "Hello Miss Ryan. There are people here to see you."

Maeve turned her head and started. "Mammy! Daddy!" Her arm came from under the blanket and reached out to them.

Emmet nudged his wife forward and Bridie perched on the edge of the bed, leaning down to gather Maeve up in her arms.

Maeve rubbed her mother's back. "I'm fine, Mammy. I'm fine."

Emmet stumbled to the bedside chair, collapsing in an awkward crouch-sit. He stroked his daughter's hair. "Are you all right, Maeve? Are you truly?"

Maeve left off rubbing her mother's back to clutch at Emmet's hand. "I am, Daddy. I am."

Her mother sat up and fished out a handkerchief from her bag. She blew her nose and then crossed herself. "Thanks be to God."

Emmet nodded. "We didn't know what to expect. That damned Carson was so vague about it all. He said you had an operation and were resting, but I thought he was just trying to gloss over it."

Maeve lay her hand back down. "The Carsons have been so good. They came in and sat with me." She touched her mother's arm. "Elizabeth is coming over."

Bridie dabbed at her eyes. "Elizabeth? I'll be so pleased to see her, but why on earth is she coming?"

Maeve pulled the blanket back up to her chin, hiding her arm under the covers. "You don't know?"

Bridie looked at Emmet.

Emmet frowned. "Carson said something about Daniel, but for the life of me I don't know what it was now. Once we heard you were shot, everything else went out of my mind."

Bridie laid her hand on Maeve's leg. "Daniel was never shot, was he?"

Maeve closed her eyes. "No Mammy." She took a deep breath. "It was Daniel who shot me."

Emmet clenched his fists. "By God, I'll kill him."

"No, Daddy. If it hadn't been Daniel, I would probably be dead now."

Bridie put her hand to her mouth. "God Almighty."

Emmet felt the blood pound in his temples. "What do you mean?"

"I mean that he realized it was me just as he was pulling the trigger and he wavered, throwing his aim off. If it had been anyone else, I would have been shot dead."

Bridie was silently weeping.

Emmet leaned it to Maeve. "Can you tell us about it? From the beginning?"

Maeve shook her head. "I'm tired now. When you come back next time."

He rose. "Of course. We'll leave you now to get some sleep"

Emmet kissed Maeve's forehead and then watched as Bridie stroked the girl's face before kissing her first on one cheek and then the other.

Maeve's face was ashen, her freckles and hair like stains on a white sheet.

Emmet and Bridie sat in the motor. He tapped his hands on the steering wheel. "What do we do now?"

"The Carsons are expecting us."

"I can't face Daniel."

"No. But sure, he'll be at his barracks, won't he?"

Emmet nodded. "I suppose so."

Still they sat. Bridie turned to look at Emmet. "Maeve seems to have forgiven the boy. In fact, she seems to credit him with saving her life."

"He's a British soldier. What the hell is he doing here shooting innocent Irish civilians?"

"Perhaps we should make our way to the Carsons and if things don't go well, we'll leave again and say we want to stay nearer the hospital."

Emmet nodded. "You're the wise one in the family, Bridie. What would have become of me if I hadn't met you?"

She patted his hand. "Luckily, we'll never know. Now, do you know where you are going?"

"I think so." He pulled out a street map from his inside pocket and unfolded it.

He traced the route to show Bridie. "Your eyes are sharper than mine. Help guide me through this bollocks of a place."

They drove slowly through the streets of Belfast until they found their way up the Antrim Road, to the stately home on Cliftonville Road.

Emmet parked the vehicle in front of the house, climbed out and walked around to open the door for Bridie. "I'll give you a look if I want to leave, right?"

Bridie looked at Emmet's deep frown and smiled. "If you look like that, they'll ask *us* to leave."

Emmet managed a wry smile. "All right. I'll try to be a little subtler."

The door of the end house opened before they had a chance to knock. Emmet recalled the strong, vibrant woman who had come to Dublin for their wedding. This small, thin silver-haired woman who held out trembling arms to pull Bridie into a hug looked nothing like that woman. Bridie broke down in tears and held Mrs. Carson close.

Mr. Carson appeared in the doorway. "Let them in, for goodness sake."

Mrs. Carson released Bridie and nudged her towards the door. She turned to squeeze Emmet's arm. "Come in now while James gets you a brandy."

Emmet followed them in, feeling his defences crumble.

Inside, Mrs. Carson seemed stronger, as she gave directions to her servant. "Betty, take their coats and then get the kettle going for Mrs. Ryan and me."

Emmet shrugged out of his coat and handed it to the girl. Mr. Carson touched his arm. "Come with me to the library and we'll leave the ladies to their tea."

Emmet sank into the leather chair beside the fire, resting his head against the high back.

Mr. Carson handed him a brandy. "Get this into you."

"Thank you, Mr. Carson. It's been a tough old day."

"Please... call me James. The lass seems well, though. I saw her yesterday and it looks like she's on the mend."

Emmet felt the warmth of the brandy seeping into him. He was tired and was glad to be here. "You're very kind to have us here."

Mr. Carson waved his hand. "Nonsense. I was afraid you wouldn't come because of Daniel."

Emmet licked his lips, tasting the sweetness of the brandy. "I'll admit I didn't know if I could face you, but sure, you couldn't control what happens with Daniel any more than I can control Maeve. In fact, I should have had more control over her."

"No. We've hardly seen the lad since he's been here. I admit we were shocked to find him here in Belfast. When we heard he'd joined up, we imagined him shipping out to France."

Emmet downed the rest in one burning swallow and Mr. Carson stood up to top up the glass. Emmet nodded his thanks. "I hadn't thought of it, but it must have been a shock all around, for you to hear that your nephew had joined the British army."

"My wife's nephew."

Emmet smiled. "So, have you spoken with the boy, James? Will there be an investigation, or will they just pin a medal on him?"

Mr. Carson sank into the chair on the other side of the fire. "I've spoken to him. He's destroyed by what's happened. I don't think there'll be any investigation. As far as the authorities are concerned it was rightful, whatever any of the rest of us may think. Daniel, on the other hand is crippled with guilt. If he could get out of the army today, he'd do it."

Emmet sighed. "It's a mess."

They sipped their brandies in silence, watching the low flames.

Emmet sighed. "He seemed like a good lad when we had him down in Dublin."

Mr. Carson nodded. "He still is good. He tells me that he's putting in the papers to transfer to the medical corps."

"Sounds like more of a fit."

"Can you forgive him?"

Emmet held the glass up to study the colour of the liquid against the fire. Held at a certain angle, it was a deep blood-red. He looked up at Carson. "I don't know. At this moment, I hate him." He sighed. "But who am I to forgive or not forgive? According to my wife, it's all my fault that Maeve was here to get shot, and maybe she's not wrong."

"How's that?"

"When she was young I talked about it all. The Cause of Ireland's freedom was in my blood and I suppose I couldn't help myself. It was all so new and powerful." He bowed his head as he recalled all the times he told his stories, embellishing to make them more exciting for a youngster. He looked up again. "She was my first-born. I wanted her to understand and not take it for granted."

Carson nodded for him to go on.

"When Collins signed the treaty, he knew he was signing his own death warrant. It was a betrayal of the Cause. We were all so angry about it. Ireland is one country and I, along with so many others couldn't let it be."

Carson frowned. "I'm sure I shouldn't ask, but you aren't in the IRA, though?"

Emmet shook his head. "You shouldn't ask, but no. That doesn't mean I haven't believed in the Cause, though. I'm loyal."

Carson shrugged. "Being loyal to an ideal isn't a bad thing."

"That's how I've always felt."

They were silent again and Carson loaded the fire with more turf.

Emmet's voice was low. "Can a person be *too* loyal? Bridie thinks so. She thinks Maeve is lying in a hospital bed because I chose loyalty for my country over loyalty to my family."

Carson shook his head. "You've always supported your family, Emmet. Anything I've ever heard and seen of you has shown me that you are a good husband and father."

Emmet nodded. "That's true. I have always supported them. They're sponges, though, aren't they? They soak up all those things we don't even realize we're saying or doing. Their attitudes and view of the world are shaped by what we say and do." He felt his eyes burning when he looked at Carson. "I wanted to shape her ideas, but I-I didn't expect to be so successful."

Tap-tap-tap. Emmet jumped at the sound. Mrs. Carson opened the door. "Tea's laid. Come and have something to eat, won't you?"

Mr. Carson rose. "We'll come now."

Emmet drained his drink and rose. He laid his hand on Mr. Carson's arm before following Mrs. Carson to the dining room. "Thank you for listening, James."

Carson nodded. "Maeve's a strong-willed girl, Emmet. Don't shoulder all the blame for what's happened. She strikes me as someone who forms her own opinions."

43

Belfast, April 1943

Maeve woke and looked straight into Daniel's eyes. "Hello."

Daniel wiped his hands on his uniform trousers. "Hello yourself."

"How long have you been sitting there?"

"A few minutes only. I didn't want to wake you. I would have left in a few moments."

Maeve licked her dry lips. "Can you pour me some water?"

Daniel poured water from the jug on her side table and then held the glass to her lips to help her drink. "Probably shouldn't take too much."

She lay back against the pillow. "Daniel..."

He held up a hand. "Please. Let me speak."

She nodded.

He leaned in, his voice quiet. "Maeve, I didn't want to shoot. At all. And then," he closed his eyes briefly before continuing. "And then, when I suddenly knew it was you and it was too late to stop. My God. I dropped my rifle. My corporal had to pick it up and he was roaring at me the whole time, but I couldn't understand a word he was saying. I ran to you as quick as I could."

"I can imagine."

He shook his head. "It was like one of those nightmares where you're running through quicksand. The seats of the theatre were a maze. I couldn't get to you. I saw you fall. The stain of blood spreading across your chest. I was crying as I was trying to get to you. Not very soldierly."

A phrase came to Maeve's mind and she murmured:

But alas, she was going much too slow
For already on the brilliant white blouse
A purple patch of death was spreading across the middle of
the back.

Daniel stared at her. "Yes. That's how it was, only I was the one who went too slow. What's that from?"

She thought for a moment. The drugs made her fuzzy. "It's from O'Casey's play, *The Plough and the Stars.*"

"You Irish have a way with words. You're poetic."

She gave a small smile. "You once recited poetry for us. You're partly Irish too."

Daniel leaned back in the chair. "I think that's the problem. I never wanted to come here, Maeve. I like being near my aunt and uncle, but the looks people give me in my uniform. It's been terrible. I want to say 'Don't look at me like that. I'm one of you.' I feel like that now. I didn't used to, but now I do feel partly Irish. But I can't say any of that because I'm a British soldier. They hate me."

She studied him. "I don't hate you."

He leaned back in towards her and took her hand. "Can you ever forgive me, Maeve?"

She bit her lip. "You were doing your job. I understand that. What I can't understand though, is how you can do that job, feeling as you do."

"That's just it. I can't do this anymore. This is not what I signed up for. I thought I'd be going to France, but instead my unit was sent here. It was a shock. I feel more Irish here than when I'm at home, and yet I'm supposed to be on patrol, prepared to fire against Irish men."

"And women."

"Dear God. Yes. And women."

"So, what will you do?"

"I have to wait to see what happens from all of this. I think they want it all to blow over as quickly as possible. They're trying to say the shooting was rightful or some say accidental, but in any event, I don't think there will be charges against me."

"So it'll be business as usual?"

"No, Maeve. I told you. I can't be here at war with my own blood. I've requested a transfer to the medical corps and if that's granted I'll be shipped out. I think the unit wants rid of me as much as I want rid of them."

"You can't just get out, I suppose?"

"No. After the war is over, but not before."

"I hate to think of you over there fighting."

"Better than here fighting."

"Yes, that's true."

Daniel still held her hand. "Maeve. I've thought of you so often. In fact, I was intending to try to get down to see you when I got some leave. When I suddenly saw you through my rifle sights, it was like a hallucination. I had pictured you so many times, for a split second I imagined you weren't real."

Maeve nodded. Her hand was comfortably warm in his. "I've thought of you as well. I wrote to you. Did you get my letter?"

He shook his head. "No, and now maybe it will never find me. What was in it? Maeve, can we still be friends?"

Maeve smiled. "In my letter I told you how much I enjoyed looking at the stars with you."

He flushed and smiled, clearly remembering the kiss as well as she did.

Maeve squeezed his hand. "I believe our friendship will survive this."

He nodded and heaved a great sigh. "I imagine my transfer will be granted, and then I'll probably be going to North Africa. I can't make any plans beyond that right now, but it would give me something to think about if I could write to you."

"I'll write back. I promise I will. I'm sorry I stopped before."

"I'd like that."

They were quiet for a moment and Daniel released her hand. He licked his lip. "I'll have to see your parents."

Maeve nodded. "My Da may not be too friendly."

"Of course, he won't be. I have to see them though. To apologize."

"If he's awful, don't let it get you down. He'll come around."

"He doesn't strike me as a man who relinquishes an idea easily. He'll blame me for shooting you and may do until the day he dies."

"I have some power over him."

Daniel smiled. "Yes, I can believe that. We'll see how it goes and if I need your magic touch, I'll let you know."

He stood. He took her hand again and kissed the back of it before laying it gently back on the white sheet.

44

Belfast, April 1943

Emmet and Bridie had been with the Carsons for four days before they saw Daniel. Elizabeth had also arrived. Bridie and Elizabeth spent long hours together talking about neutral topics such as shopping and gardening. They didn't talk about Elizabeth's son, even though Emmet and Bridie both knew that she had seen him.

Daniel arrived one evening after supper.

Emmet heard the young man's voice in the hall and looked at Bridie. His wife made a small 'oh' with her mouth and Emmet saw the worry in her eyes.

Elizabeth rose to meet Daniel at the door of the parlour. "Daniel, my boy. How are you?"

Daniel looked past his mother's shoulder to Emmet. "I'm fine, Mother, thank you."

He kissed her on the cheek and then stepped around her to stand before Emmet. Emmet rose, and they stood facing each other. Daniel's face was flushed. His mouth worked as though he were trying to say something, but the words wouldn't come.

Bridie rose also and slipped her arm through Emmet's left arm, clinging to him. Emmet felt the warning weight of her hand on his arm.

Daniel held out his hand to shake Emmet's. "I am profoundly sorry for what happened. There's nothing you can say that will make me feel worse than I already do, and despite that, I want to ask if I have your permission to be friends with Maeve. We would like to write to each other."

Emmet's heart pounded, and his fists were balled as he stared at this British soldier whose hand now trembled, waiting for Emmet to shake it. In his mind's ear, he heard Bridie's voice. *Your family or your cause. Where does your loyalty lie?* Emmet knew how his daughter felt about this boy and knew what the price would be if he turned away in anger. For a moment, the face of his own father-in-law came to him, denying him a blessing on his hopes with Bridie.

He felt a pressure on his arm from his wife and then he reached out and grasped Daniel's hand.

"I know it wasn't your fault, Daniel."

Daniel's hazel eyes filled with tears. "Thank you, sir." His hand clasped Emmet's like a drowning man's. "I didn't want to be there. I didn't want to shoot. My Corporal was right behind me shouting. 'Take the shot, take the shot.' I thought someone was about to shoot at us."

Emmet nodded, leaving his hand clutched in Daniel's.

Daniel's voice was thick. "My finger was already squeezing. I was aiming at the fellow behind, not even seeing her. But then. Oh God. But then, she stepped in front."

Emmet felt Bridie squeezing his arm. He closed his eyes and saw it. The momentum of the pull on the trigger already in motion and then Maeve appearing in his sights.

Daniel dropped Emmet's hand as though suddenly aware he was still clinging to it. "I jerked, but it wasn't enough."

Emmet put his arm around his wife as she dabbed at her eyes with her handkerchief. "We heard Maeve's version, but appreciate hearing yours as well."

Daniel turned to drop into a chair. He leaned forward with his elbows on his knees. Emmet and Bridie sat together on the sofa while Elizabeth perched on the arm of her son's chair. Mr. Carson had left the room but returned with glasses of whiskey for each of them.

Bridie shook her head, but Emmet lifted a glass from the tray and handed it to her. "Drink it. We all need it."

Bridie took it, coughing as the fiery liquid went down.

Daniel took a glass and tossed the whiskey back in one gulp. "Mother, I've come tonight to let you know that my request for transfer to the medical corps has been approved. Apparently, they're in desperate need for replacements in North Africa."

Elizabeth covered her mouth with her hand.

Daniel took her other hand in his. "I'm shipping out tomorrow."

Tears slid down Elizabeth's face. "I knew the day would come. I was grateful when you were sent here for training with the Americans, but I knew that one way or another, it was only temporary."

Daniel nodded. "At least now I'll be helping people. I should never have been in the infantry."

They talked quietly for an hour before Daniel stood to go back to his barracks. Once again, he shook Emmet's hand. "I hope one day to make it up to you and your family."

Emmet shook his head. "Just look after yourself. Keep your head down."

Daniel took Bridie's hand in his. "I intend to write to your daughter. Is that acceptable to you, Mrs. Ryan?"

Bridie pressed his hand. "I'm sure we would all like to hear that you are keeping well, Daniel."

Elizabeth walked her son to the door. Bridie closed the parlour door to let them have their few minutes of leave-taking in private.

Emmet and Bridie went up to their room a few moments later. In bed, Bridie reached for Emmet's hand. "Thank you for your kindness to Daniel."

In the darkness Emmet held her hand. "I didn't know myself how I'd react when I saw him, but it's obvious he's very upset by the whole business."

"Maeve will be glad to hear that you shook his hand. She's very fond of Daniel."

Emmet snorted. "How did you and Daddy meet, Mammy? Oh, he shot me." That'll be a fine story to tell children."

Bridie exhaled a long sigh. "It may not come to that, what with one thing and another."

Emmet felt a pang when he remembered that Daniel was heading off to war. "No, perhaps not."

———

Two days later Maeve was released from hospital. She was loaded into the back seat of the motor and tucked into one of the Carson's down-filled duvets. She was still on medication, so they were barely on the road when Emmet saw in the mirror, her eyes droop and head nod.

He glanced at his wife and mouthed the words: "She's asleep."

Bridie nodded and smiled.

Emmet spoke quietly as they drove. "Your Da will be glad to get his motor back."

"I'm sure he will be. They'll all be home when we get there so he can drive it home himself. I think he'll be even happier to get his granddaughter back in once piece."

Emmet nodded. "The boys, too."

They stopped in Dundalk to eat.

Maeve had a bowl of beef-barley soup. "It's grand to have something with flavour again."

Bridie smiled. "You'll get no end of fattening up when we get home. Your Nana Ryan wants to bring a couple of chickens for roasting. I'm told they're far better than anything we can buy at the butcher. Your Nana and Papa Ryan will be down at the weekend to see how you're doing."

Maeve smiled. "I know I don't deserve this pampering." Her face over the table was suddenly serious. "Mammy, Daddy. I know we really haven't talked about it, but I am sorry to have put you through all this."

Bridie shook her head. "Hush, now. You've said that already. There's no need to be sorry. We'll discuss it all through when you're feeling better."

Emmet brushed a tendril of hair from his daughter's forehead. "I'm hoping we can come to some plan for your future that doesn't involve guns."

Maeve smiled and nodded. "I agree."

Emmet paid the bill. "Shall we go, ladies?"

Maeve took his arm. "Yes, please. I'm aching to get home."

45

Dublin, June 1943

Maeve made up her school work so that she finished the year with her classmates. She didn't talk much about what happened, other than to say that she had been in the theatre with a friend when the shooting happened.

Eamon approached her in the library one day. "You're up and about again, then."

She smiled at his way of stating the obvious. "I am."

"I'm sorry I didn't come to the hospital."

She shook her head. "It was best that you didn't. Irene came, and we just told the police that we were simply there to see the show and got caught up in the fray. No one really questioned us too much about it."

He stood there, seeming at a loss for words. "I'm graduating and then I'll be going to Derry for work."

She nodded. "I think it's best that I give up the discussion group. Irene and I are friends, but I think we both have had enough of the other for the time being."

"Right. Well, take care of yourself."

"Yes, you too."

One mild June evening Emmet took Maeve for a walk. She didn't have the strength to go far, but they enjoyed short strolls together.

They walked along arm in arm.

Maeve waited until a train of three double-decker buses passed before continuing. "Did I tell you I had a letter from Uncle Liam?"

He looked at her as they strolled/meandered along. "You didn't. Is he still happy to be in America?"

She smiled. "He seems to be. He's working at the dockyards in New York City.

Maeve was quiet for a moment and then she shook her head. "He belongs to something called the United Irish Counties Association. He seems to think that they can do great things for Ireland over there."

Emmet shrugged. "They're very passionate in America and they seem to have loads of money, so if Liam thinks he can do some good there, I believe it."

She nodded. "He tells me that they've begun a big campaign called the 'anti-partition campaign' to highlight the division of the Republic and Northern Ireland."

"I've heard of it all right."

She smiled. "He told me there'd be lots for me to do if I went over there. He even suggested I could make some extra money singing. There's a club called 'The Four P's' where he drinks and they're in need of my voice to sing the old songs."

Emmet tilted his head. "You're not thinking of going, are you?"

Maeve laughed. "Daddy, I'm just trying to poke the bear. Is it working?"

Instead of admitting she had made his heart race, Emmet snugged her hand against his side. "I'm very proud of you. You'll do great things right here at home, using your brain."

She grinned. "Don't worry. I'm not intending to get involved in anything that isn't brain work in the future. I am thinking of politics, though."

He pressed her hand against his side again. "Am I walking beside a future president of Ireland?"

She laughed. "Oh, Daddy. I think not."

"Why not? Anything's possible. Women in Ireland have always helped to lead us."

She was quiet for a moment and then she nodded. "Anything *is* possible. I do believe that." She stopped and turned to him. "Yes, you're right. Why not? A woman president in Ireland is highly likely."

"How did you get to be such a clever girl?"

"I had a very fine teacher. A man who taught me that being passionate about a cause is not a bad thing. I learned from an early age to believe in something and to stand up for my beliefs."

He looked down at her. "There was a time I thought that my beliefs had torn us apart as a family. I was afraid of what I had taught you."

Maeve was still as she stood facing her father. She pulled her hand free of his arm, so she could cup his face. "Daddy, I couldn't have wanted for a better teacher. I am who I am because of you."

He felt his throat close. "And Mammy. I may have lost perspective at times. It's Mammy who taught you to apply common sense."

She smiled. "Yes, and Mammy."

Emmet kissed her forehead. "You're the best of both of us. Passion and perspective."

She fished her hand back through his arm and stood for a moment. They both tilted back their heads to look up at the rising moon, as they had done so many times before when she was a young girl. They stood in silence gazing at the night sky sparkling above and then she nudged him forward to walk on through the beautiful evening.

The End

Acknowledgements

This book is the result that comes from over forty years of listening to Irish ballads and stories. I have lived in Ireland and walked the streets and hills where these events took place. I've stood by monuments and gravesides of those who took a stand in the fight for freedom and heard their spirits whisper to me. These were my inspirations.

To help me realize the inspiration, I am indebted to, in part, the following people:

Barbara Kyle for the initial manuscript review and coaching (https://www.barbarakyle.com), the Writers' Community of Durham Region (WCDR) who provide such fantastic support and awarded me the Len Cullen Writing Grant to help fund my learning journey, Paul O'Brien for some research assistance, (http://www.paulobrienauthor.ie/), Jimmy Carton for authenticity reviews, Ruth Walker for her insightful editing. (https://writescape.ca/) Sharron Elkouby for yet another perceptive job (I've lost count how many projects this is now!) with editing and proofing, Shane Joseph (https://shanejoseph.com/) for steering me to my cover artist, Robert Scozzari for an amazing cover (https://www.inspiringdesign.ca/) and my family for always believing in me.

As much as possible I have followed the actual details of historic events, except for the 1943 Commemoration of the Rising at the Broadway Cinema. There were no injuries reported during the actual event.

Select Resources

Coogan, T.P. *Michael Collins Part 1.* Arrow Books, 1991
Coogan, T.P. *Michael Collins Part 2.* Arrow Books, 1991
Dwyer, T.R. Eamon de Valera. Poolbeg Press Ltd., 1991
O'Donnell, Dr. R. *America and the 1916 Rising.* An Phoblacht, 2016
http://www.militaryarchives.ie/collections/online-collections/bureau-of-military-history-1913-1921/reels/bmh/BMH.WS1399.pdf#page=15
http://www.1916rising.com/pic_battleashbourne.html
http://www.theirishstory.com/2012/05/23/today-in-irish-history-the-burning-of-the-customs-house-may-25-1921/#.XbmkhXdFyBZ
https://en.wikipedia.org/wiki/Gormanston_Camp
https://www.historyireland.com/20th-century-contemporary-history/moral-neutrality-censorship-in-emergency-ireland/
http://www.theirishstory.com/2017/04/16/preserving-the-spirit-of-the-movement-the-ira-the-broadway-cinema-and-the-1943-easter-rising-commemoration/#.XbnHCXdFyBY

https://jeffreykwalker.com/a-terrible-beauty/
https://www.ria.ie/library/about/services

Song Credits
Foggy Dew. Traditional
Mother Machree. Ball, E and Johnson-Young, R.

Poem Credits
Ingram, J.K. *"The Memory of the Dead"*
https://www.bartleby.com/246/214.html
MacNeice, L. *"Rugby Football Excursion".* Wikipedia.org,
https://en.wikipedia.org/wiki/Rugby_Football_Excursion
Hopkins, G.M. *"As Kingfishers Catch Fire".* Poetry Foundation,
https://www.poetryfoundation.org/poems/44389/as-kingfishers-catch-fire
O'Casey, S. *"Drums Under the Window"* Ireland Between History and Memory,
http://archives.evergreen.edu/webpages/curricular/2009-2010/ireland0910/miscellaneous/poetry/drums-under-the-window/index.html

Printed in Great Britain
by Amazon

17092923R00178